SERPEN

LIMERICK CITY LIBRARY

The Gra
Mich

Tom Morton is a broadcaster, author and award-winning journalist. He has hosted a weekday afternoon show on BBC Radio Scotland since 2002 and is the author of various books, including the acclaimed novels *Guttered*, *Red Guitars in Heaven* and *The Further North You Go*, while his whisky travelogue, *Spirit of Adventure*, was made into a successful television series.

From the Murkiest Corners
of Britain's Secret War Comes . . .

SERPENTINE

TOM MORTON

MAINSTREAM
PUBLISHING

EDINBURGH AND LONDON

First published in Great Britain in 2009 by
MAINSTREAM PUBLISHING COMPANY
(EDINBURGH) LTD
7 Albany Street
Edinburgh EH1 3UG

ISBN 9781845964986

This novel is a work of fiction. Names and characters are the product
of the author's imagination and any resemblance to actual persons,
living or dead, is entirely coincidental

A catalogue record for this book is available
from the British Library

Typeset in Garamond and Headline

Printed in Great Britain by
CPI Mackays of Chatham Ltd, Chatham, ME5 8TD

I was never caught. Only betrayed.

Walter Norval

One hears it said, 'I call that inhuman', the reference being
to the fact that there is no dining car on the train. 'It's degrading for
the poor man', one hears with reference to an employee
who is being given the unpleasant jobs. 'It's absolute torture to me',
and what the speaker means is having to sit
through a boring lecture or sermon. There is a lesson to
be learned here on the potential danger of hyperbole.

*Sir Gerald Fitzmaurice, from his minority judgement
in the European Court of Human Rights ruling on the
case 'Ireland v. United Kingdom', 18 January 1978*

MR AMBROSE'S PREDICAMENT

Murricane was bored, but tense.

In this kind of situation, boredom was bad, tension good. One blunted your senses, blinded you to the fine detail of your surroundings; the other pumped the blood with adrenalin, prepared you for fight, flight or a final goodnight. Tension. He needed more tension. He tried to think of worrying things, tried to upset himself. Strutting through his mind came salmon farmers in blue boiler suits, clanging along the gangways of industrial sea cages, cackling with laughter as they shot innocent seals. Upsetting, yes. Angering, even. But wholly inappropriate. He was in the Gaza Strip, for fuck's sake. Being kidnapped.

Well, sort of. His hands were behind him, cuffed with that cheap but effective piece of terrorist hardware, a plastic cable tie. He had flexed his wrists fiercely as his captors pinioned his arms, leaving him a tiny bit of leeway when he relaxed them. On the whole, though, he wasn't relaxed. He was bored because he had been through this sort of thing before, he knew exactly the level of fanaticism and stupidity he was facing and he was truly fed up with it. He was sick of Muslim extremists, ticked off with Jewish fundamentalists and had grown seriously fucked off with the Christian variety decades previously, during a Scripture Union mission at his school that had ended badly. For the Christians. And for him.

But he was tense, too. Just not tense enough. Salmon farmers. They were almost as bad as al-Ghurabaa or those muscle-bound pricks at Premillennial Security, who only recruited Southern Baptists. Big bastard Baptists with heavy steroid abuse problems. Then there were the atheist fundamentalist ranters,

7

like that dickhead Dawkins: I don't believe and you can't either, you moron. Whatever happened to live and let live?

This wouldn't do. He was becoming distracted: aquaculture and theology did that to him. And several other things, too, had that personal potency. Too many things. He blinked behind his blindfold. Lack of concentration, his teachers had agreed. Prone to wandering. Focus, boy, focus. He tried to do just that.

They had him walking slowly along what sounded like a bare concrete corridor, a cheap Syrian copy of an AK47 jabbing painfully into his back. He knew it was that particular variety of ersatz weapon, not because of the barrel's feel, but because that was what these guys, this particular band of thieves and murderers, were known to use. He had seen the research. He had handled that kind of gun, often, in many forms and national variations. Fired, field-stripped, re-assembled. He literally could do it blindfold, if necessary. But it probably wouldn't come to that.

There was the noise of a door being unlocked. A chain, padlock, two deadbolts. Sounded like something really solid, possibly reinforced with steel. Then he was pushed into the room, the door slamming behind him. He heard it being locked again. But he could also hear breathing. Laboured, nasal breathing. There was a terrible smell – shit, sweat and dirt. Pop festival toilets at the end of a hot July weekend. T in the Park in the old days. Only with a hint of cinnamon and garlic. Rock the fucking Casbah.

'Who . . . who's that?' The voice was hoarse, gritty with lack of use. English, upmarket. Just short of public school. Grammar with knobs just about still on.

'Mr Ambrose? You're blindfolded?'

'English . . . oh, thank God.' Murricane caught the gulping whimper. 'Thank God, thank God.'

'I'm sure God appreciates your gratitude, Mr Ambrose. You can leave Him a tip later. Or Her. Once you've decided whose God to reward properly. If you're in a position to do any thanking, that is.' Bored. He was already bored with Ambrose. 'Can you see?'

'No, no I can't . . . yes, blindfolded. Don't know, maybe I've forgotten how to see. Haven't had this off for . . . how long? I don't know. Who are you? It's so good to hear an English voice . . .'

'You can call me Mark. And this is not an English voice.'

'Christ, I'm so sorry.' Desperate to please, apologetic. Ambrose probably sneered at Jocks, Jockos, Seeyoujimmies, when he was in his cups, Boris Johnsoning his way along Kensington High Street. 'Scots . . . Scotch. I'm so sorry.'

'No, not Scottish. But close.' Murricane stopped himself saying more, clamped down on the distraction. Concentrate, *focus*. He crouched down, cautiously. If he knelt, his bound hands could just reach the millimetre edge of the razor blade carefully inserted into the crêpe rubber heel of his left desert boot. Cable ties are very strong, but they can be cut remarkably quickly. Within a few minutes, his hands were free.

Murricane massaged his wrists, then removed his blindfold, blinking slowly in the fading light of the evening. There was a small, barred window high up on one unrendered, breeze-block wall. The dipping sun laid a shadow grid on the floor, which was rough concrete. A plastic bucket sat in one corner. It was the source of that rock festival latrine aroma. The spicy perfumes coming from outside mocked the cell's squalor.

'Close your eyes, Mr Ambrose. I'm going to take off your blindfold. Don't screw them shut. Just keep them lightly closed, then open them when I tell you.'

Ambrose's voice was firming up, some desperate grasp for lost authority creeping in.

'Who are you? Mark, you say? They'll kill me. They said they would. If the money didn't come. We should sit tight, wait for the money to come. My company will pay. They always do. They said they always did. They said . . .'

'Open your eyes, Mr Ambrose.' He was getting really pissed off now. Dangerous. Short attention span. It had always been his curse when other people were around. Alone, he could sit for hours, prone, sometimes for days. Had done, had entered a trance-like state of complete contentment. Watching. It was dealing with people that threw him. Life in the normal sense of the word. He remembered that line from *Repo Man*, Harry Dean Stanton to Emilio Estevez, out of their brains on speed: 'Ordinary fucking people – I hate 'em!' And he did. He really did. Salmon farmers, especially. Though who could say if they were really ordinary? Why, remember . . .

Concentrate.

Ambrose was dressed in a thin orange boiler suit, a cheap parody of the ones used by the Americans at Guantanamo Bay. His feet were bare, his

9

face, that of someone in his late 50s, was filthy and fatigued. Unshaven for all of the six weeks he'd been in here, or elsewhere in the Strip. He had probably been well-groomed, once, the thinning hair cut to his best advantage. Murricane knew he was 47 years old. His hands were cable-tied, too, but loosely. There was a bloodstained bandage around all that remained of his left little finger.

'Money,' muttered Ambrose feverishly, his eyes, inflamed and watering badly, fixed on the face of his unexpected companion. 'We should wait for the money.'

'I am the money,' said Murricane.

The job was dangerous, complicated and, in the more inflamed corners of the Middle East, fairly commonplace: kidnapped company executive, extreme Islamic group nobody had ever heard of, ransom demanded, often with a cornucopia of more or less irrelevant political stuff attached (prisoners to be released, American president to stand trial for war crimes/be castrated, that sort of thing). In almost every case, the people responsible were simply bandits, extortionists taking advantage of local conditions. Capitalising. It was, Murricane always thought, capitalism in a very pure sense: you see a market, you move in, acquire your product, market it. He himself was simply responding to demand. He'd often thought that he'd be better doing the kidnapping himself, rather than being faced with retrieving the kidnappee. It would be a kind of wholesaling. He could offer discounts.

Ambrose was in telecommunications. Cellular telephones were essential to every variety of official and illegal activity in the Gaza Strip, and Ambrose worked for a service provider called Fontokk. He and two colleagues had been finalising an agreement with the Hamas administration in Gaza on installing an extended and much more reliable mobile phone system, an officially sanctioned role which should have given them both adequate protection and immunity from any kidnap attempts. But the bodyguards provided by Hamas had been bought or threatened, or there had been collusion at a higher level. Anyway, backs had been turned and all three Fontokk executives had been lifted at gunpoint from a supposedly safe hotel lobby. No shots fired. A statement from the Populist Front for Islamic Direct Action took 24 hours to reach a local Reuters stringer by email, demanding the release of 20 Palestinians held in Israel. Outraged Hamas officials had applied pressure and two of the men were almost instantly, and suspiciously, released unharmed. For Ambrose, the price went down to ten prisoners.

'They'll go off the record, ask for ten mill, drop it to five, making threatening noises the whole time,' Murricane had told Fontokk's Middle East VP, a dumpy Virginian in his 40s with buzz-cut hair and knife-edge creases in his short-sleeved, cotton shirt. 'They may cut something off just to show they mean business. Hopefully, nothing essential. An ear lobe, or a finger, maybe.' They were in Fontokk's regional office, in Dubai. The air conditioning would have solidified nitrogen.

'Fuck,' said the Virginian, whose name was, allegedly, Smith. His over-muscled jaws worked all the time on what smelled like Juicy Fruit gum, even, Murricane imagined, when eating meals or drinking coffee. 'Gentleman Bobby fucking Ambrose knew what he was getting into when he went out to the Palestine boondocks. Marginal exposure area supplement, insurance, bonus on safe return. But it'll play fucking hell with hiring personnel if we don't get him back. I mean, I'm comfortable with them chopping chunks outta his unnecessaries, man, but I draw the line at dick. How would I explain that to his wife? Think five's a bit hefty for us in current cash flow circs, though. Hey, we got the others back gratis. Hamas were, like, totally embarrassed. I oughta be grateful, listen, I am grateful, they signed the deal, sorta shamed into it.' The rhythm of those masticating jaws never faltered. How many strips of Juicy Fruit were in there? Four? Five? Did he spit or swallow? Someone had once told him that if you swallowed chewing gum, it could block your appendix. Even kill you. Wrigley syndrome, it was called. Supposedly.

Marginal exposure area supplement. Hell's teeth. How much? Probably more than he was getting from Fontokk. Or rather, how much M&P Consulting were getting. Not that it made much difference. The P in M&P, Dennis Peterson, was dead, had been dead for over a year. Murricane supposed he could change the name to Murricane Consulting, but somehow it felt wrong. Everyone he worked for knew it was just him, a one-room office in Nicosia and the lovely but intensely sullen Alexandria, secretary, sometime lover and fluent curser of tardy payers. In five languages.

'Tell you what,' he said, looking around the luxurious office on the 21st floor of the unquestionably penis-shaped Akhbar Building. He could have sworn there was frost settling on the desktop . . . a cold front over by the drinks cabinet, threatening snow. 'Make it a bottom line of two mill in dollars and we'll work it out with them. I think they'll settle for that. Though it could still get a bit messy.' Two mill. These jokers could afford that for an extended lunch.

'Messy?' Smith laughed, an odd glutinous squelching noise coming briefly from his mouth, the smell of Juicy Fruit strong in the air. 'Hey, for two mill, I can live with messy. Deal done. Let's call it overheads.' He leaned forward, offering one stubby, scarred hand.

Two days later, a fingertip arrived in Dubai by UPS, via its Gaza affiliate. Courier services have to function, one way or another. Everywhere.

That left Murricane some leeway. They probably had a few more fingers, toes, ears in mind before killing the poor bastard. And assuming Ambrose had the full assortment of physical attributes, there was time to make arrangements. He couldn't do this kind of thing alone and, in this particular situation, that meant hiring a couple of old, occasionally trusted, friends.

Their names were Moshe and David. He liked them, or thought he did. Didn't always trust them, but sometimes affection was better. And they had clout, they had form, official form that extended to the wearing of genuine uniforms when necessary. He'd paid them. Would pay them again. But one thing was for sure. He wasn't paying the bastarding Populist Front for Islamic Direct Action. It was a point of principle. And it was business. He was sure clients like Fontokk knew what really happened to the so-called ransoms. They weren't stupid. Maybe they even approved. They believed in private enterprise, which was what all of this was: the 'terrorists', himself, Moshe and David, Fontokk and their ilk. All were cash-fuelled.

'You're the money?' Ambrose was staring at him, his eyes lidded with sweat and dirt. A lot of the foul smell in the room was coming directly from him, Murricane noticed. 'What, have you got a traveller's cheque tattooed on your bum? Diamonds up your arsehole? What the fuck do you mean, you're the money? That some Scotch thing? What's that fucking accent about, anyway?' He was talking smart, now, to hear himself, thought Murricane. After all that enforced silence.

'Never heard that expression? It was big in Hollywood a few years ago.' Murricane reached for the softpack of Marlboro Lite he'd carried in his breast pocket until five years ago and hadn't ever got used to not having. 'It's money, babe. You're money. Means that something's solid, sorted out. And it's not a Scottish accent. Scotch is a drink, by the way. A term only ever applied to whisky. The word is Scottish. And I'm not, precisely, that. Shetland. Shetlandic. Halfway to Norway. It's an island group. Viking heritage. I mean, look at me.' It was a joke. He was dark and wiry. Pictish genes, if anything. He inhaled an imaginary cloud of carcinogens. 'So, anyway, what I'm saying is, it's cool. Kosher, in a manner of speaking. And to be completely literal, I am not just money, but THE money. Or I was until I handed your Populist Front of Fucksville friends a briefcase fifteen minutes ago.'

'Jesus.' Ambrose let out a long sigh of relief. 'They did pay up. But how come . . . how much, anyway?'

'Three mill. Dollars. If we'd held out for one and a half, we could probably have got you out OK, maybe minus another finger and/or ear. But your pal Smith crumbled.' Untrue, but Murricane thought he ought to try and ease Ambrose into the realities of his situation. He warmed to the fiction. 'They seemed set on five at first. Not as hard as he likes to think, old Smithy, or whatever his name is. He seemed perfectly willing to let them cut your dick off at first. First two joints of your pinky was enough, though. I thought he was going to faint.' As if.

'Yeah well.' Tears welled in Ambrose's eyes. 'Pair of wire cutters. Pricks. Disinfected it with iodine, though. That's when I . . . I thought that was hopeful.' His voice cracked. He began to sob. Murricane took off the boot with the hidden razor blade and began sawing with the heel at the plastic holding the man's hands. Terrorism without cable ties: unthinkable.

'Thing is, Mr Ambrose, there is one little . . . well, problem with the money. Or some of it. It depends on just how observant and aware the members of this so-called Populist Front really are.' Ambrose's hands came free. Murricane did not put the desert boot back on his foot. He held it in his right hand, loosely.

'What do you mean?'

'Well, in actual fact it's not real money. Not all of it.' There was a silence. Ambrose seemed to have forgotten how to sob. Or breathe. 'When I say your Mr Smith crumbled, he was only prepared to crumble so far. To two mill, to be precise. Time being of the essence, I took an executive decision to pad out the two mill with some . . . padding. Put it this way, it's printed in colour. Well, photocopied. On both sides. And there's two million in real 100-dollar notes, right enough. So there's bulk. It's initially impressive. But they could, they just might, smell a rat.'

'But . . . then they'll come back here.'

Murricane smiled for the first time. It was a very powerful, brilliant smile, displaying the dental work he'd had done in Poland, part of a favour he'd been owed. By a man who had returned to dentistry, eventually, after a colourful career in inflicting more extreme forms of pain than the merely oral. But Murricane's grin was not reassuring. It was full of amusement and it was full of charm. And it was, once you got to know him, a very worrying sign indeed.

'I certainly hope they do come back here. I'm rather depending on it. Otherwise, we're going to have a lot of trouble actually getting out of that door.' There was the sound of shouting and running feet. At first faint, then coming closer. 'Looks like they do have someone perceptive on their staff when it comes to colour photocopying. I knew we should have used thicker paper.' Without changing his tone, he spoke, absurdly, into the boot he still held in his hand. 'About 30 seconds, Moshe.' Wonderful thing, footwear, he thought. Adaptable. He made sure his smelt bad, too, which always discomfited prospective searchers. He moved to the hinge edge of the door. There was a faint rattling from the other side. The shouting, high-pitched, in a peculiarly guttural form of Arabic, grew louder. 'Move over beside me, but leave me some room.' Ambrose threw himself into a squatting position near Murricane's feet. Carefully, he put his desert boot back on. No socks. Murricane wondered what Ambrose would have said if he'd known the truth: that there had only been a quarter of a million in real notes. And that only the first layer of padding had been photocopied at all. The rest was newspaper. And the *Jerusalem Post*, at that. It had been a question of provoking a reaction. Time. Timing.

The door flew open. Murricane caught it as two thin, white-clad arms, holding an AK47 in a very agitated way, came through the gap. Then he threw his entire weight against the door, closing it on the disembodied arms. There was a cracking noise, quickly drowned by a desperate scream of agony. The gun fell to the floor. It did not go off.

'Safety catch,' muttered Murricane to himself. 'Dickhead.' He dropped to the floor, rolled and picked up the Kalashnikov in a single movement, remaining tightly crouched in the gap between door and wall. Then several varieties of hell began breaking loose.

First, the door was blown back open by a burst of firing from whoever still had a pair of functioning arms. Screaming continued from someone who didn't. Murricane glimpsed three men, all dressed similarly in suit trousers and white shirts, long sleeves carefully buttoned at the wrist. One had a checked shemagh wrapped around his head. He was the one lying on the floor writhing and trying to prevent his smashed arms from coming in contact with the ground. Injured seagull: the thought flickered through Murricane's mind. A scorie, he would have said. Focus. He flicked off the safety catch on the man's weapon, firing two short raking bursts up into the chests of his companions. At such close range, the result was, Murricane noted with a kind of interested indifference, extreme. Soft-nosed bullets, he thought, his mind seeming to turn the facts over slowly, almost lazily, as flesh and bone erupted around him. Illegal. International treaty. But when it comes to guns and bullets how can you say . . . and at that point the world exploded. The heady aroma of cordite filled the air and he felt that adrenalin zing of erupting blood pressure thrust through his skin. Fight or flight. Do or die. Better do, on the whole.

Claymores, he guessed. Good old Moshe. He was the supplies man. Moshe obtained the fuzzbox and David knew how to use it. What would Greater Israel do without them?

A thick fog of dust filled the room and corridor. It tasted of dried mud and death. Beyond the ringing in his ears, Murricane could hear coughing and a keening, moaning noise which had to be Ambrose. The use of the word 'fuuuuuuuuck' was a giveaway. Gentleman Bobby Ambrose. Some minor public school, or geographically privileged grammar. Fuuuuuck.

'Come on,' he shouted, or tried to. Nothing came out at first but a dry splutter. 'Come on, Mr Ambrose. Time to go.'

AK47 in one hand, Ambrose's arm in the other, he clambered over the bloodied mess in the corridor, pulling the groaning Englishman behind him. The man with the shattered arms was moaning weakly. They were a few feet past him, when Ambrose clutched at his shoulder.

'What about him? Are you just going to leave him?'

'Want to take him home as a souvenir?'

'No.' Ambrose's face was a mask of dirt, snot and tears. 'I want you to kill him. Bastard. Fucking bastard.' So much for a civilised education.

Murricane dragged Ambrose away.

'I don't think the people responsible for that rather large explosion would be too pleased, Mr Ambrose. They'll be hoping for someone they can politely ask a few questions about who the Populist Front for the Return of Fucking Baywatch really is.' Moshe and David may have been operating at Murricane's request, or rather $100,000 of Fontokk's cash, but the beauty of this kind of activity for them was that their superior Israeli Special Forces officers rather liked having the chance to find out the whos and whys of Gaza kidnappings. They liked to make connections, to find out things like why bodyguards suddenly failed to guard bodies. Truth to tell, Dave and Moshe were supposed to do this kind of thing for nothing. Murricane just liked them to be happy in their work.

'Who was right?' The voice was pure Brooklyn and it came out of the dust. 'Last chance: who was right?'

'Sal Paradise!' yelled Murricane. 'Sal Paradise was right.' A figure emerged. It was small, wiry, a white T-shirt and jeans wrapped in combat webbing and carrying an Uzi.

'Little slow, Murricane. Thought you knew all those Hold Steady songs off by heart? Thought Craig Finn was your man, man?'

'*Boys and Girls in America* . . . that's the album,' said Murricane. '*Stay Positive* is shit, man.' He briefly touched closed fists with David. 'Moshe outside?'

'Ten four, babe. Wait till you see his wheels. He's got an old Land Rover, armoured. British Army surplus, straight out of fucking Derry. You'll feel quite at home, Murricane! Mind your feet. There's some dead meat at the bottom of the stairway.'

'Got a live one back along there. His arms are in a bit of a state, but he might be worth stroking nicely.'

'Cool. I'll listen for the screams. Take it easy. Hey, you shouldn't have any trouble.'

They didn't. Outside, in the cooling evening, Moshe, big and bulky where David was small and thin, was sitting at the wheel of a long wheelbase Land Rover, still in its Belfast green. It was as camouflaged in this environment as a Dayglo stretch limo. Blocking each end of the street were two Israeli Army Hummers. Beside both of them crouched two soldiers, Uzis at the ready, covering the doorway Ambrose and Murricane had emerged from.

'Came mob-handed, I see.' Murricane opened the Landie's passenger door, shoved Ambrose inside, then climbed in after him. Less than a minute later, David was in the armoured back loading bay with his prisoner, who had been dragged screaming, but with surprising ease, by the wiry Israeli. Seconds after that, the three vehicles were roaring away.

'Mob-handed. I like that,' Moshe laughed. His teeth were immaculate. 'We are the angry mob. Oh yeah!'

'Kaiser Chiefs. Named after a South African football team. But you knew that.' The glitter of those beautiful teeth once more. Murricane suspected some serious investment in Moshe's dentition. Tel Aviv was jumping with cosmetic dentists. Dental tourism was a growth industry. He was developing a bit of a thing about teeth, he realised. Just something else to distract him.

'Would we ever let you down?' Moshe was pretending to be mortified. 'Have we ever let you down? We are a peacekeeping force, committed to international good relations, you know that! Do you like my new vehicle? A symbol! It is a symbol of good international relations. And profitable relationships.'

Murricane breathed in the instantly familiar aroma of hot Land Rover. Despite the heat, the dust, the lack of rain and the absence of coal smoke from a thousand parlour fires, it took him right back. To a place he really didn't want to go. He shut his eyes and, suddenly, there she was: Millie.

The tension was flooding away and the boredom was allowing his mind to drift. A bad sign. This job was over, bar the haggling. He would need to find something else to do, and quickly. Or perhaps it would find him.

PRECOGNITION

PRECOGNITION

LONDON REVIEW OF BOOKS, JANUARY 2009, INTERNET EDITION.
WEEKLY UPDATE, SUBSCRIBERS ONLY. RSS AND ATOM ENABLED.
MARLOWE'S DIARY

Splendid to see my old friend Fergus Mellors in such good form at Soho House the other night. Of course, this is not an establishment I frequent out of choice. Merely, dear reader, out of duty. And since this fine organ has once again assumed its rightful position on the High Street news-stands, thanks to our esteemed new owner, Lord Morgan of Wapping, I have the expense account to deal with such exigencies!

At any rate, Mellors (a fine literary name for a PR flack, or public relations consultant, if you must) is verily in the pink, following rather a lean spell since he set up on his own. Many of his former clients fell by the wayside, or pitched themselves bodily onto said wayside after that sad little episode on Hampstead Heath. And one thought we lived in liberal times! At any rate, over a frosted glass of very nearly acceptable Cava, Mellors informed me, cheerily, that things were looking up and that he was now advising 'a very sexy little client indeed', someone with a timely tome to flog and 'governments to bring down, careers to ruin, all the good and jolly stuff'. Someone he could not, alas, name.

'Something from the dark side, old chap,' he told me. 'Coming in from the cold, if you know what I mean.' Then he swore me to secrecy and told me all, as folks are wont to do! Well, he told me something, and, with joy, I hereby relay it. Such is my role in life.

It may all seem like ancient history, but Mellors assures me that the '70s in Ireland were interesting times indeed. What could have been happening there? I'm much too young to know. 'It's going to be the Serpentine in my crown,' he said, tapping his nose with his index finger in what I suppose was meant to be a meaningful way. 'Little Johnny Serpentine, that's my man.' I understand this to be a reference to a song by an obscure beat combo known as The Television. I have never knowingly heard any of their so-called music. I am more of a Radio, ahem, head. And so, so 'down' with the ah, kids! Perhaps that Cava had gone to his head a little. At any rate, he implored me to say nothing, which I took to be in reality a plea to reveal all. Inasmuch as I know anything. Which I, of course, dear ones, am happy to do! More when I get it! Toodle pip!

LONDON REVIEW OF BOOKS, MARCH 2009. INTERNET EDITION. WEEKLY UPDATE, SUBSCRIBERS ONLY. RSS AND ATOM ENABLED.
MARLOWE'S DIARY

Desperately sad news about the demise of old Mellors – no time to go into detail, as I am positively rushing, my dears, towards an electronic deadline down here in Deptford; but I am sure his many friends and colleagues in publishing will be raising a glass in his memory. A full obituary will of course follow. But to fall from the platform at Tottenham Court Road, after all these years, seems more than careless. And with such high hopes for the future, too!

We shall all miss him. Toodle pip, dear old chap!

A GOOD WALK IS RATHER SPOILED

The Turnberry Hotel – or the Westin Turnberry Spa and Resort, as its management were schooled to call it – glittered on the Ayrshire skyline like a particularly elongated beach chalet. It sprawled, low and white with a red tiled roof, along the ancient raised beach that reared out of the surrounding linksland. Below the hotel, meticulously cultivated grass, gorse and pockmarked bunkers of yellow sand stretched to the shoreline, where a storybook lighthouse soared, guiding a ruffled, ice-blue sea to the horizon. There, a dome-shaped island glowered greyly back at the Scottish mainland.

It was 6.30 a.m. on a spring Monday and there were a few hardy souls braving the buffeting wind for their expensive shot at the legendary Ailsa course, one of the venues for the Open Championship and scene of triumphs by some of the greatest of golfing heroes. The hotel guests who had enrolled in the Colin Montgomerie Golf Academy's special pre-Easter course were still hung-over and cosseted in their expensive linen sheets and so the other two, less desirable, courses, the Kintyre and the Girvan, were deserted. Except for the spry figure who could be seen striding away from the large, well-camouflaged complex of sheds and agricultural buildings next to the A77, the main road from Ayr to Stranraer.

He was carrying his own club-crammed Ping bag without apparent effort, but as he was now in the rough at the edge of the Girvan course, he had clearly gone well astray from the tee on the nearest hole, the long fourth. He was desultorily scything the grass and heather with what might have been a seven-iron, apparently looking, none too keenly, for his lost ball.

No one had asked him for green fees, or for a hotel pass, an hour earlier, when he had emerged from an innocuous rented Ford Mondeo in the Colin Montgomerie Golf Academy car park, dressed in Mizuno finery and ready, it appeared, to practise religiously what the master had taught him the day before. They came, after all, from across the world to learn at Monty's feet and worship on the altar of Turnberry turf. An early rise was a small additional price to pay.

There were no staff around. Up at the hotel, only the breakfast crews were preparing for the morning appetites. His few practice swings on the first tee looked competent. He used an old-fashioned, linked-finger grip, which would have had the most successful golfer never to win a major wincing, but his tee shot was true and long. Considering he was playing ultra-cautiously with a seven-iron, its face tightly closed, for length. He drove like someone who knew what he was doing. His age was difficult to discern, but he was no longer young. White hair peeked from beneath his woolly Nike hat. The huge, packed Ping golf bag seemed something of an affectation. Surely it wasn't strictly necessary?

His fairway shot on the fourth had sliced towards the maintenance buildings, which were empty at this time of day. The greenkeepers didn't start work until 7.00 a.m., unless there was a championship looming. He seemed a little confused then, sweeping the thick grass and heather with . . . surely not still a seven . . . the heavy bag still on his shoulder. For about half an hour, he disappeared completely from view, as if he'd actually entered one of the buildings. It was not beyond the bounds of possibility that his ball had snuggled into the lee of a greenkeeper's bothy or a mower workshop, but there were no windows to break and it was unlikely that his brand new Titleist was anywhere but in a clump of gorse or plugged in sand or mud.

Nevertheless, a close observer might have noticed the tall, elderly man emerging from a steel-clad building, his Ping bag visibly lighter and less bulky. He appeared to lock the door behind him with some kind of key.

He played a new ball from the fairway, an open-faced seven-iron, to within three feet of the pin. After sinking the putt, he appeared to lose interest in playing further, striding towards his car, his studs crackling on the tarmac as he placed the Ping bag in the boot.

Only someone actually looking over his shoulder would have noticed that there now seemed to be only two clubs in the bag, a modern carbon-and-composite seven-iron and a wood-shafted putter.

As he drove away towards Ayr, no one noticed him go, except an eleven-handicapper from Surrey, making the most of his Turnberry package with an early round on the Ailsa course. He blamed the blue Mondeo's revving engine for his missed putt at the first green. It would put him 21 over par, at the end of a frustrating round. He was not best pleased.

Golf courses when the paraphernalia of TV-covered championships is absent – no cherry-pickers, grandstands, tented villages or irascible security guards high on self-importance and high-handicap resentment – are deserted and easily accessible during the hours of darkness. Golf cannot be played under floodlights, despite attempts to make such blasphemy possible in city-centre driving ranges.

And no tall fences on traditional Scottish links courses, either. Just dry-stone dykes, traditional walls much coveted by the designers of imitation courses in America. There, they tend to be topped with brutally barbed, high-voltage electrical cables.

Not at Turnberry. Technically, access to the beach has to be open to the public at all times. Which meant the tall old man had no difficulty, having parked his car on the prom at Girvan, in walking along the high tide line and then up and over the dunes onto the Ailsa course.

Burdened only by a small rucksack, he was no longer dressed in golfing Gore-tex, but in what looked like lightweight black military fatigues and a ski hat with no brand name. The head torch was a military-issue, shaded Petzl. Once more, he disappeared into the clump of maintenance buildings next to the road, emerging with five short-shafted, apparently gripless golf clubs, all irons. They gave off a distinctive clanking rattle as he carried them in one large hand. In the other, he held a wooden mallet he had found during his quick search of the greenkeeper's shed that morning. He had known something like it would be there. Hoped, really, having forgotten to bring one with him. But then, tents were a part of every golfing competition: tents for starters, finishers, guests and gophers. And where there was a tent, there were tent pegs needing to be hammered into the ground.

Tent pegs, he mused, had always been associated with death, ever since Ashkelon was killed with one in the Old Testament.

That ancient, murderous implement would also have required a hammer.

On the deserted 18th green of the Ailsa course, scene of so much final-round drama over the years, he knew that despite the darkness he had to move quickly. Lights blazed above him from the hotel, its origins as a destination for Victorian railway travellers now usurped by a grandiloquent American vision of what a 'golf spa' ought to be. The modern clubhouse and golfing academy buildings were in darkness.

The threaded, identical heads of the golf clubs were unscrewed; choosing patches of rough grass and heather bordering the outer edge of the green, he used the mallet to sink each shortened steel shaft into the sandy, stoneless ground, circling the putting surface, covering the top of each with finger-fumbled sand and spittle. When he was done, there was no sign, under torchlight, that anything had been hammered into the putting surface's outer lip. And this particular green's dimensions had never been altered in the past six decades of competition, so there was no risk that they would be discovered. He used a small trowel he'd brought with him to excavate a hole three feet from the last shaft, in some short rough. There, he buried a small metal cylinder. A copper wire sheathed in black plastic led from a hole in the box, which he had sealed with silicone. He threaded it through the bottom stalks of heather, pushed it lightly down so it was just above the sandy ground.

He was a careful man. He put the club heads – genuine, from an old set of Wilsons – in his rucksack. He made his way back to the maintenance sheds and replaced the mallet where he had found it, next to a well-maintained Ransome's 30-inch mower, locked the door behind him with the skeleton key set he had owned for the best part of 40 years, and then, silently, carefully, jogged back across the links to the beach. The adrenalin release made him run along the hard-packed sand to Girvan. By the time he was unlocking the Mondeo, stripping off his surgical gloves and preparing for the long drive north, his heart rate had returned to normal. He was, after all, still a very fit man indeed. For his age.

LAST SUMMER I WENT SWIMMING

Cable ties. They were available everywhere and in so many different styles. Colours, too. There were even re-usable, releasable ones. She knew they were available at Highland Industrial Supplies, out on the Longman estate. She'd once considered using them in some kind of art project, a statement about imprisonment, impotence, frustration. And boredom.

The ones on her wrists were not the reusable kind. Once ratcheted tight they could only be cut off. And her captors had been carelessly brutal, so her hands, she knew, were now bloated and purple behind her back. Her ankles were trussed together too. She was a package, an animal readied for slaughter. Hog-tied, she thought. Sow-tied, that was it. Pigmeat, trussed for killing. That they planned to kill her was obvious.

Her hands had been sore and now they were numb. Her feet had lost sensation almost immediately. They had hit her and gagged her. Once she realised she was not going to choke to death, she gradually calmed down. Now, she felt the same clarity she remembered from the last time something like this had happened. But that had been different. That had been training. This was very evidently real. From the attack until now, feeling the van moving over increasingly rough ground, had maybe been ten minutes. She needed to make a move. Fast. Not enough practice, she told herself. Slack. Too slack. She thought of Freya. Oh Christ. Oh sweet Jesus Christ Almighty.

They hadn't attempted to rape her. Neither of them had shown any interest in her as a woman. Maybe that was significant. They had been casual, efficient, as if they had done this kind of thing many times before. Neither had said a word. The small one had stepped out onto the towpath from behind a

24

rhododendron bush, she had swerved, fallen off her lovely little folding bike. Bromptons. She'd always had one, even Over the Water. Over the Water. Those wee wheels. 'Inherently unstable,' Mark had said. 'And difficult to control. Like me. Like you.' She felt herself smiling at his terrible, terribly untrue joke. Even now, even so far away, so long ago, he could make her laugh. All those jokes. All those tricks. She should have paid more attention. Her head spun. But she had, she remembered fuzzily. She had done that one thing, kept doing it, a kind of penance, a remembrance. Stupid.

The big one had picked her up, held her while his companion secured her wrists, then her feet. Not before she had caught the larger man's instep with a ferocious downward stamp. He had breathed in sharply, that was all. That was when the smaller one had hit her.

She had tried to shout, managed a brief scream before a strangely soft hand had cut it short. That part of the canal, between the permanent clutter of berthed boats at Dores and the beginnings of urban Inverness, cut through woodland so heavy that the waterway almost became a tunnel. Too late for any yachts or cruisers to be motoring through. Too late, really, to be taking the route on her own. Even in the balmy midnight twilight of a Highland summer.

Risky. She'd been warned it was risky, to be on the towpath so late, a wee woman like her. Even in her lovely, adopted Inverness, so gorgeous, so secure, it was something Freya had told her not to do, but she'd shrugged it off. On a bike she could ride like the wind, she boasted. No one could catch her. She was free, she'd laugh, flipping the Brompton into the tiny package it became when she wanted to carry it, wheel under wheel, a mechanical wonder. Safer than running, faster, and there was room for shopping, too. She'd been picking up a Chinese from that non-MSG place they both liked. Her and Freya. Ah, fuck. Mark . . .

The hitting, the gagging, the trussing. So fast, so unexpected, and she cursed herself for her poor response. One kick she'd managed, one bite, maybe, and then the stunning blow to the back of the neck that had left her temporarily paralysed. She'd been dragged through undergrowth, along a rough path to a van, nondescript, not white, or maybe it was white . . . impossible to know the colour in the dim sodium streetlight. One of the alleyways that backed onto the great rash of new housing in Kinmylies. Searched, roughly – they took her purse and her keys. Thrown into the back, the bike, badly half-folded, chucked in beside her, a pedal catching her already battered head. And then they'd driven away, were driving. Now they were bumping along, off the road, somewhere stony and rough. Then the engine was switched off. When the reek of diesel and exhaust cleared, she could hear moving water and smell the harbour, the tainted freshness of the River Ness meeting the salt firth. There was a mustiness, a hint of rotting vegetation, chemicals, sewage. The outfall of the city. Nothing moved. Her captors were still in the cab. She could hear the quiet murmur of someone talking on the phone. She would need to be quick. Pain surged through her. She managed to kneel, reached her cable-tied hands towards her heel. Oh yes, one of Mark's little tricks. She hoped it worked. She'd never had to try it out since those stupid macho manoeuvres in Cumbria. Force of habit had kept her doing it with every single new pair of shoes or boots she bought.

The two men were relaxed, unhurried, certain of what they were about to do and sure of their victim's helplessness. The one called MacDougall got out of the Mercedes Vito's passenger seat, closed the door carefully, and stood listening. The liquid rustle of the river overwhelmed everything else. Gradually, his ears detected the rumble and hum of distant traffic. Then there was the high whine of midges gathering, one of the perils of these Highland nights, especially near water. They were on a cleared site next to an old timber pier, a jumble of broken concrete and, by the yellow warning tapes they'd pushed aside earlier in the day to ensure access, asbestos. Hume thought what they were about to do was probably unnecessary, if not insane, but Billy Boy had assured him and MacDougall that they were hard bitches, nasty fucking perverted old cunts, and that leverage would be necessary. Leverage, that was the word he'd used. MacDougall had laughed. Hume wondered what he'd got himself into.

'Well, if we're to have some leverage, we'd better have a lever,' MacDougall had said, with that Gaelic lilt of his.

Now Hume was standing beside him, smaller, more compact compared to the Hebridean's hulking frame. They were both wearing latex gloves. MacDougall reached into one of his parka's many pockets, checked the knife was there. His lever. The Randall he'd had smuggled in from America via Dublin. His pride and joy. In another pocket was a digital camera, a Sony Cybershot. He liked Sony stuff. It felt like it had some kinda history behind it. Heritage. Samurais and that.

'Sure about this?' Hume's voice was soft, curiously high. 'We're going to get bitten to fuck if we stand out here for long.' But he made no attempt to sweep the cloud of midges away from his face.

'All right.' MacDougall crunched over the uneven ground to the larger of the van's two back doors and turned the handle.

There was a razor blade hidden in the heel of her trainer. In every right shoe she owned. A simple job. The tiniest edge protruding. She'd had to warn Freya not touch her shoes. They'd laughed about that. A fetish, Freya had said, how exciting. Cable ties didn't stand a chance. Now her hands were agonisingly free. She flexed and rubbed them, but there was no time to do it properly. She hooked her fingers around the d-rings in the floor meant for securing bungee cords or cargo straps, then braced her bent legs against the right side of the three-quarter door, where the lock was. The pain was beginning to overwhelm her (*Hurry up, you pricks*) when she heard the handle turn. All the pent-up pressure in her diminutive body erupted outwards as the latch released and she straightened her fingers just in time to avoid breaking them on the d-rings.

Every nerve, every sinew was tuned to survival pitch. She had very little chance of getting away from two pros. She could only hope they had allowed themselves to be lulled into a false sense of security, just as she had been. But it had been much longer for her, before the attack on the bike path. It had been years. In just a few minutes, she'd had to reboot a long-unused operating system.

The edge of the door took MacDougall in the face, breaking his nose and cheekbone. He went down like a felled tree. She catapulted out of the van, landing like a crab, her feet on the ground, her hands behind her, fury and fear fuelling her as Hume, reacting very quickly, raised a clenched fist and began to bring it viciously towards her. But she was already rolling away, feeling the sharpness of broken concrete on her body. Her hands scrabbled for grip as Hume sprang, looming close above her just as she found a loose lump of broken breeze-block, lifted it and threw it without thinking. It caught his eye, hard enough to stun and briefly blind. He swung an arm, missed and stumbled. Kicking out, she caught his ankle and he fell, grabbing at her squirming legs. She could feel her heart drumming, could hear it, and somewhere, moving water. The river. Up, she had to get up. She managed two strides, then something told her she was at a drop, an edge. Momentarily, she hesitated, then jumped into the deep stillness of the Ness. The cold was brutal, instantly more agonising than anything she'd experienced that night. She felt a slow current take her, pull her, tumble her into icy darkness. She made no effort to fight it.

ROAMING IN THE GLOAMING

Another fine summer's day had faded into a warm Highland gloaming when Liam Gunn launched his fibreglass punt out into the apparently still waters of Inverness Harbour. Midges, the dreaded biting *Culicoides impunctatus*, swarmed around his leathery head. He ignored them. They were attracted by the carbon dioxide in his breath, but Gunn had for many years been impervious to their voracious appetite for blood. Some of the Ferry kids whispered it was because he'd been sucked dry of the red stuff decades ago.

Now in his early 70s, Gunn was still fit enough to drag his rowing boat out of its tumbledown shed and down to the water's edge. On fine nights like this he liked to row a little way out and drop a spinner over the side, slowly reeling it in on his ancient Shakespeare rod. He had a Ness licence for salmon and trout, cheap for a local pensioner, but that didn't cover the two small nets he had weighted down at favourite spots, deep eddies where the wharves ended and the eroded banks of the firth began. Liam was a poacher, had been for the best part of 60 years. It was in his blood. His father had slashed it into him with the broken end of a cane fishing pole.

And he fished for other things, too. All kinds of stuff came out of the Ness, or in from the sea, and much of it could be sold. Wood, sometimes big lumps of tree trunk from forestry work on the Black Isle or beyond. It was his civic duty, he thought, to haul the timber into the bank, and hide it in the scrub along the undeveloped part of the Longman shore. He knew a man with a chainsaw who paid him a fiver or so for a decent-sized one. Shopping trolleys, they were worth nothing, but bicycles were forever being chucked off the slipways and bridges. Clean them up, down the car boot at the old

Clach ground, that was another few quid. Once, he'd found a fridge, floating, completely airtight. Opened it up, there were still half a dozen eggs and some Carlsberg Special. Both had tasted all right to him.

Floaters, too, occasionally, if they'd thrown themselves off the Kessock Bridge in the right tidal conditions. The river was treacherous, full of black holes, strange currents, shifting levels. Bodies could find their way back up the river from the firth, snagging like sacks of rotting fruit on sandbanks and gabions. Or they could sweep out to sea and never be found. He could feel it in the boat sometimes, that pull, taking him to hell or Findhorn. Which was why he was careful when he went out on the water. What was it the Good Book said: unstable as water.

No firth tonight, though. Just the river and a few casts with the old rod. A couple of hours, tops, a wee check at the standing nets. This was recreation, call it that if you want, or habit. What passed for peace in his life was out here. An absence of thought, or a diminishing of pain.

It was late by the time he came out of his dwam and realised he'd failed to land a single fish, found nothing but a few small sticks swirling on the tide. Still, he felt rested, even satisfied. Now it was time to check the nets, just in case. Back to the shed for a nip of rum, maybe. He could feel the chill creeping into his heart.

The old Maglite he used had seen better days and better batteries. Mounted with rubber washing machine drive-belts at the bow, it gave off a yellow glimmer of light, but it was enough. He knew every inch of the river. Still, he watched the liquid glimmer of torchlight as he approached the first net, anchored at the upstream outfall to a pool, in the lee of an old jetty on the northern shore. The land beyond had been cleared for construction. He remembered the wood yard, the great trees over from the west, down from Sutherland, before the pulp mills and the chipboard factories. Now even they were gone or going.

They were planning to build flats, even more godless modern flats for the bloody young and the bloody rich, or the worthless creditworthy. He despised those young people, artificially fit and bronzed from their expensive health clubs. Good health was wasted on the young. He could feel the pain growing in his own body, a dull ache where there had been nothing before. He knew what that was. But he would fight it, then let it take him; suffer it, thole it, accept it. Fuck the damn quacks, it was getting time to go. Age was a bastard. But this was it. No dress rehearsal.

He felt the boat rock and swung round, startled to see a small hand shine wetly in the torch's limp glow, then a face, twisted in effort, swollen, he thought, but definitely female. He recognised it.

The small body collapsed in the bottom of the boat, gasping, fluttering like a caught fish.

'Hallo, Liam.' The voice was weak, but strangely unafraid. 'Any chance of a lift?'

THE BLUE POLKA

Hume and MacDougall were in a Vauxhall Vectra that had seen many and better days, Jimmy Shand on the stereo, Hume's choice; they were watching a fire, waiting for it to become more satisfying.

The white Vito had not exploded. It was a diesel and it had taken MacDougall three attempts with a fuel-soaked towel stuffed into the tank before he'd managed to get it alight. He was handicapped by the double vision and killing headache he'd suffered ever since regaining consciousness. His face was tight, swollen and, he guessed, blackening badly. All the teeth on one side were loose and wedges of bloody paper tissue protruded from both nostrils. That bitch. Middle-aged, soft, Billy Boy had said. But Jesus, she was still hard at heart. They had underestimated her. That was bloody obvious.

'Never was much of a starter, that Vito,' said Hume, who had shown him no sympathy and whose left eye looked like a hard-boiled egg left too long in the fridge. 'We'd better get back to Billy Boy.'

'He's not going to be happy.' MacDougall's Hebridean brogue was more pronounced. He whistled slightly when he talked, like a burst accordion, thought Hume, or bad bagpipes.

'When was he ever happy? We'll find her. She may have drowned.' MacDougall laughed, the noise oddly like a shunting steam train.

'Drowned? It would take more than water to drown that cunt. Put her in a vat of nitric fucking acid and she'd use it as bath salts.'

Hume gave a snort of mirthless laughter.

'Don't overrate yourself, Mac. She's not that good. We were both careless and she was lucky. We forgot. We forgot who she is, where she comes from.'

'Well, I won't do it again.' MacDougall instinctively felt for the Randall in his pocket. 'And I won't waste any time, either. I'll cut her throat and smile nicely afterwards.'

'Fine,' said Hume. 'But try to control yourself if we meet her in Marks and Spencer's.'

'I don't shop in Markies.' MacDougall stared straight ahead as Hume started the car. 'I have problems with their fair-trade policy.'

Hume laughed. But there was nothing from MacDougall but a pained wheezing. Maybe he wasn't joking.

By the time the van was sedately alight, a pungent smell of roasted plastic filling the air, Shand was on his classic 'Bluebell Polka', the rattling martial snare drum and accordion buzzing from the Vectra's ruined speakers. They were in one of the least gentrified parts of the Ferry, the housing scheme named after the old ferry between Inverness and the Black Isle. The Ferry was undergoing something of a transformation, though parts of it were resisting. Inverness was being touted as a kind of Boulder, Colorado with midges, all computer whizzes with mountain bikes and eco houses. There was even a sort of university, manufactured using the Internet and several technical colleges. There had been private and public investment, huge developments of commuterland family homes in blond brick and half-arsed concrete or pseudo-Scandinavian timber, renovation after renovation after renovation, amen. But there were pockets of intransigent decay, like fungus resistant to eradication. Mainly in a labyrinth of streets named after Liberal politicians who had been big in the '70s. Inverness, after all, had once been a Liberal stronghold with a capital 'L'. So there was a Thorpe Street, a MacLennan Court, an Ashdown Drive, a clumsily hyphenated Russell-Johnston Crescent. And there was Kennedy Avenue.

In this maze named for the wilfully middle-of-the-road, most of the flats had been emptied and boarded up, their inhabitants decanted to God knew where, possibly purgatory, while the council wrangled with a private developer over how many apartments could be sold, how many rented privately, how many provided for council tenants. For what promised to be more than a brief interlude, this part of the Ferry had become a strange little lawless enclave, studded with squats, one or two early and brave bourgeois pioneers who brought their IKEA furniture in a bit too early and the stunted kids who made such places their playground.

33

As the Vauxhall's tyres crunched over broken glass, small, dark figures began to appear, then vanish as if they'd been summoned by the fire from the ground itself. It was just like a jungle, thought Hume, except here the fire drew the animals in, instead of keeping them away. They passed a sign which said: *Ness-side Village: Renewal and Regeneration.*

'That's a fine sentiment,' he murmured.

'Aye, right,' said MacDougall, who stank of blood and diesel. Hume had told him to stuff their surgical gloves into the van's tank, make sure they were destroyed. 'Do we need Jimmy fucking Shand on?'

'Mama's got a squeezebox,' said Hume. 'I'm not a fan, mate. It was in the stereo when I lifted the car in Glasgow. I'm more a Belle and Sebastian man myself.'

'Fuck,' said MacDougall glottally. 'I just remembered. I left two Runrig CDs in that Vito.'

'Runrig.' Hume shook his head, then wished he hadn't. His eye hurt badly. 'Corries for the middle class. Best place for them.' He turned to MacDougall. 'What about the bitch's bike?'

'Shit. Och, it'll melt down to nothing. Nobody'll bother about it.'

'I hope you're right. I left her bag in the front seat. There was nothing in there. No driving licence, no documents. Nothing. Just some cash.'

'Which you kept.'

'First rule of searching the dead or the nearly dead: always keep the cash. Fifty quid is fifty quid.'

'Come on,' MacDougall coughed blood onto his hand, wiped it on the seat cushion. 'Billy Boy's waiting. It's not far. Better face the music.'

CYPRESS AVENUE

CYPRESS AVENUE

Murricane got off the Air Cyprus 737 at Nicosia feeling, on the whole, that he'd done a good job. Good enough, at any rate, for Fontokk to pay up without a quibble, despite Ambrose's hysterical complaints that his life had been needlessly put at risk.

Smith had looked quizzically at him when Ambrose started gabbling about the fake cash, but in the end, the Fontokk boss had said nothing more, just kept chewing that gum of his. Juicy Fruit. Made to make your mouth fucking water. Once Murricane had settled up with Moshe and David and whatever other branches of the Israeli armed forces they'd felt like sharing some largesse with, he'd cleared 300 grand. That was his fee, plus the share of the ransom cash he'd split with Moshe and David. It was in Switzerland now, or at least somewhere in the electronic ether on its way to Banque Suisse de Capital Montagne, SA. Money nowadays was handled on laptops and PDAs, hustled to and fro across the globe using cyber cafes and secure websites.

He deserved a holiday. Somewhere soothing. South Africa was quiet these days, if you didn't actively flirt with trouble. Which meant with the poor and the black, not necessarily the same thing any more. He could get in and out without problems, if he went to Botswana first. Maybe a bit of elephant tracking in one of the game parks that did it on foot. Tension and relaxation, that would do the job. Momentarily, his thoughts turned to home, to the damp coolness of a Northern Isles summer, the endless days, the twilit nights. But there was no going back there. Not any more. Not ever. Not with all those fucking salmon farmers about.

A WINDOW OF OPPORTUNITY

A WINDOW OF OPPORTUNITY

Billy Boy was, indeed, unhappy. Hume felt nervous in his presence at the best of times, but in the overheated flat, with the woman tied to the chair, twitching and groaning occasionally, it was hard to resist the temptation to bolt. Yet he was curious to see how it would turn out. And, he had to admit, he felt both revolted and excited. It put his own pain in context, seeing what had been done to the woman.

'Well?' Billy Boy's accent of the moment was clear in that one word, stretched and burred at the edges. The tearing tones of Belfast contrasted with MacDougall's quiet island lilt. 'She got away, did she? A wee woman manages to outsmart and outfight the two o' youse. You unmitigated bastard fucks.' He sighed, reached for the woman's face – virtually the only part unbeaten, unruined – and gently stroked her closed eyes and pursed mouth. As if, thought Hume, he was trying to cure her of blindness and dumbness. Which in a way he was.

'Darling, darling. Freya, Freya. Oh, Freya, I want you to open your eyes and your mouth and speak to me and see what's going on.' The accent moved now, to Radio Four continuity, received pronunciation. And back to the Short Strand. 'Your little friend has apparently managed to evade my colleagues, which is a pity. I was hoping the photographs they were going to take of her . . . fate – not to mention her face! – would encourage you, if such encouragements proved necessary. Which of course, it turns out that they are. Or would have been, would have been. Alas, the opportunity has been denied us. You're being . . . how can I put it? Recalcitrant. Of course, maybe I've underestimated you, as my useless associates underestimated her. Mistakes, misjudgements. Anyway, we'll find her. Maybe she knows more than we thought. Maybe you shared with her more than just bodily fluids and fucking fingers, eh, darling? For the moment, you're my only girl, my own sweet girl. Recalcitrance rarely lasts, as you well know. What a lovely word that is. Re-cal-ci-trance . . .'

He began to sing. He had a pleasant tenor voice. '*If you were the only girl in the world and I was the only boy* . . . I wonder if that little bitch is alive? And if she is, will she turn up here, try and rescue her tongue 'n' groove companion, eh?' He turned to MacDougall and Hume.

'That occur to you boys, I wonder? Did you lock that door behind youse?'

'She's probably dead.' MacDougall pulled out the Sig Sauer 920 he carried in a shoulder holster, began screwing on a suppressor. 'Anyway, this time I won't take any chances. And yes, the door is locked.'

'Maybe she'll have a key,' said Billy Boy. 'She does live here. *Oh, you, you possess, I guess, the key to my heart, the key to me* . . .' His singing was interrupted by the sound of grunting, a liquid scraping and rattling, from the woman. The man was all concern. 'What's that love? Can't quite make out what you're saying . . . Och, is it your poor ould mouth? Shall we give it a wee wipe, God love you . . .' Roughly, he prised open her lips. He was wearing the same variety of surgical rubber gloves Hume and MacDougall had used. They had put on fresh sets before entering the flat. The woman moaned softly. 'Ach, you can so speak. I was wondering maybe if you'd bitten off your tongue. Or the cat had got it. Not that you have a cat. Which I'm a wee bit surprised at. Don't all lesboes have cats? All you fine followers of Sappho? Got something to tell me, ye desiccated ould dyke?' His voice veered in and out of broad Ulster, used for effect. 'Come on, you're not hurt that badly. You remember how it works, don't you? You remember me, of course you do. You remember ould Billy Boy?' Again, he burst into song. '*Hallo, hallo, we are the Billy Boys* . . .' Theatrically, he cocked one hand over an ear and leant closer to her face. The words were barely decipherable.

'No,' she said. 'Not . . . no.'

'She's still alive, for the moment,' said Billy Boy, his voice velvety. 'Of course, I could lie and tell you we'll leave her be, let her live, if you tell me, if you give me what I need. I could say, oh, darling, you can save her. But you know that's not true. We'll kill the bitch anyway. But we might not cause her quite so much pain. Just tell me. Just tell me where she is.' Eyes flicked open, were suddenly steady and wide. China blue, thought Hume, you rarely see that. That really deep blue. The colour of summer twilight. And then her voice, clearer now, West Country overlaid with something else, something posh. Audible, though her breathing, through the grinding of broken ribs, was hard won.

'Billy Boy . . . you were always a . . . liar. If she's not dead, she will be soon.' A pause. 'You'll . . . rot in hell for this, Billy Boy. But before that . . . before that . . . you'll be screaming . . . screaming for mercy. You have no . . . fucking idea . . .'

Billy Boy caught the look of surprise, even shock, that threatened to engulf his face, held it, turned it into a sardonic grin.

'And is that – to quote Mister Who Wants to Be a Fucking Millionaire? – your final answer?' There was no reply, only two laboured, crackling breaths. 'Suit yourself.' And with both hands he grabbed her greying hair and violently twisted her neck. There was a splintering, fleshy crack. The ragged breathing stopped.

Billy Boy stretched himself, stood to his full height. His mottled, shaved head and heavy jowls went well with the smart camel coat, thought Hume. Christ, he was big. He looked like something the Kray Twins had dragged in. But he was undoubtedly Manderson Manderley, former chief superintendent with the Royal Ulster Constabulary's Special Branch, known to one and all as Billy Boy because, and this was a typical Ulster joke, thought Hume, he had been born into a Catholic family from Derry. Not that it had made him in any way sympathetic to the Republicans that came through his hands. Quite the reverse.

'I'm not a religious man,' he had said to Hume, back when they had first met up for this job, drinking with MacDougall in the anonymous Edinburgh tourist bar which had been their rendezvous. MacDougall and Billy Boy had known each other from before, from Over the Water. Hume had been there, had known them both by reputation. And was consequently uneasy. Billy Boy had waxed loquacious, all beautifully enunciated English basso profundo and screeching street Belfast: 'I was the token Tim in a Proddie police force, but that's what worked to my advantage. Stick with me and you'll see what advantage means. Taking it. Even now. Even these days.' Hume had heard the stories. In that murky world Over the Water, nobody had ever been better at taking advantage than Billy Boy Manderley.

'Right, pixel-boy,' said Manderley, nodding to MacDougall. 'Have a look at the computer.'

MacDougall pulled various bits of electronic gubbins from some of the many pockets of his parka. A flash card, Hume thought it was called. Flash bastard. And the bigger box, the thing like a bulked-out iPod, that would be a hard drive. Thought he was the dog's technological bollocks, MacDougall did. Well, every unit needed a techie. Thing was, MacDougall was cruel, big and gifted in the sparky department. Bastard. Twisted bastard, too.

'Piece of crap,' the younger man said, looking at the woman's PC, which stood on a plain pine IKEA table next to the window. 'Still, anything worth having on it's already mine.'

'Take the rest of the place apart, Hume,' said Billy Boy. 'I'll help you in a minute.' And then he began, systematically, to turn the dead woman's face to a pulp. Unhurriedly. Seemingly without anger. But Hume knew he was raging. She had got to him, somehow. Maybe even frightened him. And that was something Hume had never seen before.

'Has it occurred to you,' said Hume, eventually, 'that if, heaven forfend, Miss Millicent Fairweather is still alive, she may simply call the police?'

Billy Boy smiled that politician's grin, except he didn't have a politician's teeth. His incisors were big and yellow, like those of a horse, crossed with a crocodile.

'We don't have to worry about the police, I don't think, Mr Hume. We have a window of opportunity, a period of grace. The night, so to speak, is ours, or so I have been given to understand. Subject to the maintenance of contact. It is a question,' – and he nodded to himself – 'of taking advantage of contacts.'

'Advantage,' said Hume. 'Yes.'

CALL ME

She had shivered her way to something approaching warmth in Liam Gunn's shed, in front of his two-bar electric fire, sipping bad instant coffee and good dark rum, Watson's Navy, trying to slow her mind down. Those Meindl trainers, expensive, but they dried quickly. So did the Rohan summer gear she habitually wore when cycling. The razor blade in the right trainer was still there, but blunter now. She'd need another one. She needed to plan.

Planning. It was time to plumb the depths of her past for the ruthlessness that had once taken her through the really bad times, some of them with Mark, and had led her in the end to the comfort and love and solidity she had found with Freya.

'I don't suppose you have a mobile, Liam?' She had first met the old man during one of her solitary bike rides along the riverbank. He had helped her fix a puncture, tried to fondle her in a mild and fumbling kind of way, and ended up with a staved thumb as a result. His apologies had been profuse. He had then waited for her on a daily basis to offer ever-increasing sorrow. Until she told him, in no uncertain terms, to leave her alone. Now he was hovering like a nervous auntie.

'What? Like a telephone, you mean?' She grinned wanly. Stupid to think he might have. To her surprise he pulled out from his grimy, waxed jacket a primitive Motorola in a leather pouch. 'Only telephone I have, or need,' he said. 'Some wee lass threw it away, left it in the Bught Park a couple of years ago. I just kept it. There's a stall in the Market sorts them out for you . . . kind of cleans them, puts your name in them, or something. I give them money every month and it works. You can use it, dearie, of course you can. Would you like more coffee?'

'No thanks, Liam.' She took the phone and began dialling the number.

In the flat, an electronic trilling brought the three men to a sudden and complete stillness. Billy Boy grinned.

'Now then. Who do you think this could possibly be?' The telephone was an old-fashioned '60s Trimphone, its coiled lead a tangle of knots. Billy Boy picked up the angular handset, saying nothing.

She heard the breathing on the end of the line, recognised it as male. As not being Freya's. An overwhelming sadness swept over her, but the hardness at her core, the hardness that had anchored her to Freya, and had brought and lost her Mark, broke the wave of emotion, stood firm.

'Could I speak to Freya, please?'

'And who shall I say is calling?' An Ulster voice. Male, a wheedling edge of . . . what? Contempt? She had once been familiar with voices like this one.

'It's just a friend, tell her.' She could feel a dryness in her mouth spreading through her lungs, her whole body.

'Do you know, I think I recognise that lovely, lovely tone. You'll probably realise we've been doing a wee bit of eavesdropping over the past few weeks, darling. Millie, isn't it? Those were very nice vibrators in your bedside cabinet, by the way. Lovely. I'm a bit of a connoisseur, myself. Do you know who this is?' Billy Boy spoke softly. Listening to his voice, which had been modified by the years of interrogation and command into something flexible, slippy, but still identifiably and sometimes crudely Northern Irish, was like being slowly flayed. 'We've never met, but I know all about you, Miss, or should that be Ms, Fairweather. Fair weather friend, aren't you, to your cunt-buddy? Failed to protect. Failure, that's you all over, Millie, isn't it? Always has been, always will be. Oh, she's in a bit of pain now, still alive but suffering. I think she'd like to see you, Millie.'

'Can I speak to Freya, please?'

'Well, let's see . . . Freya? Freya! Your fuck is on the phone!' His voice returned to its interrogative, velvety, corrupted intimacy. 'D'you know, darling, I think she's indisposed. But why don't you come on over . . .' The line went dead. 'Shiters. We'll have to check with the buggers, but she wouldn't be stupid enough to use her own mobile.' He laid the receiver down in its base. 'She's a wee bit clever, you know. How're you getting on, boys?'

'I've copied the hard drive,' said MacDougall. 'I'm ready to go. But . . . there may be a problem.' His battered face was turning a mottled blue and purple.

One hand was shaking slightly. Manderley hoped he had done a proper job.

'What problem?'

'Security erasure. It's possible there was a program ready to remove everything as soon as I . . . as soon as someone tried to get at the files.'

'Christ.'

'We'll have to see.'

'Aye, and go to fucking sea to see what we can fucking see, no doubt. Any joy, Hume?'

Hume was systematically searching the small flat, replacing everything as he went. There were two approaches to searching on the hoof: search and trash, disguise what you'd been up to, what you were looking for. Or tidy up as you went. Hume couldn't really help himself. He was a neat person. He hated loose ends.

'I could do with some help,' Hume said. 'How much time do we have?'

Manderson 'Billy Boy' Manderley said nothing, but pulled out his mobile and found a number he had stored in its memory. 'Sure, I could be using darling Freya's landline,' he muttered, 'but I don't want to be running up a bill for the poor old girl, now do I?' The call connected. 'Hallo, it's meself. We'll need at least two hours. Can you make sure nothing disturbs us, no matter what mad stories are being bandied about? Good.' He listened. 'No. We're one down, one to go. You might put out something low-level and innocent. You know, missing person, missing mental patient, suicide risk, that kind of thing. You have the description. The younger one. That's right. Just observe and report, kind of thing. That's very British of you. And a very good night to you, too.'

An hour and a half later, they had failed to find what Billy Boy wanted. An indication. An identification. An address. An individual's spoor. There were one or two keys, some of which they couldn't match with anything in the flat or the old Volkswagen Polo that was parked outside, in blatant defiance of the predatory local kids. It was an anonymous car, dull and the worse for wear. The kind nobody could be bothered stealing. Hume had risked a check of its interior, boot and engine bay without raising local curiosity, finding only a neat bundle of receipts he was now in the process of going through.

'Receipts, eh?' Billy Boy drummed the mobile, a cheap Nokia, against his thigh. 'That's careless. All your movements, right there, darling Freya.'

'Well, there's not much movement to report,' said Hume, wiping agonising tears from his rheumy, inflamed eye. 'They're mostly receipts from the Hilton Service Station for petrol; not much, not often. They were mainly staying put.' Suddenly, he stopped flicking through the small sheaf of paper and unfolded a larger sheet. 'Wait a minute, though. How do you fancy personal storage?'

'Should've thought of that,' said MacDougall, his words slurring as the bruising on his face tightened.

'Yes, well, thank you very much, Mr Fucking Sexton Blake.' Manderley's voice was low and savage. 'Personal storage where?'

'Longman.' Hume was already preparing to move. 'KeepGuard.'

'Gloves still on? Then let's switch off the lights and go. Check you've left nothing.' As he moved to the door, Billy Boy blew a kiss at the shattered remains of Freya Enderby, nicknamed (never to her face, but sniggeringly known as such to one and all) 'Randy', his former colleague and fellow servant of Her Majesty's Government. 'Randy Freya,' he muttered. 'We can't keep meeting like this.'

Hume had her keys and used them to lock the door. It was heavy, steel and had four deadlocks, good ones. Just as well they hadn't had to break their way in, he thought. But then, Billy Boy was kind of official. Very official, in an unofficial, deniable kind of way. And the woman had opened the door to them without a qualm. She'd known him. Perhaps she knew it was all over and was hoping to protect her girlfriend. But he and MacDougall had left to lift the Fairweather bitch after it had been made plain what would happen if they did not get the co-operation they were looking for. Billy Boy was looking for. Which he hadn't got. The whole thing was falling into several large lumps of shite, he reflected. Still, he was used to that. Used to coming out smelling of . . . not roses. But not shite either. Not entirely.

There was loud music coming from the bottom flat, but they met no one. Hume thought the ground-floor tenant might be out of hospital in a couple of days. Or maybe not.

AT THE BOTTOM OF THE GARDEN

AT THE BOTTOM OF THE GARDEN

She and Freya had grown slack, had let their guard down. Had grown older, soft, despite knowing what they knew, despite their various abilities. Their past skills. Lost? Not entirely. It was just a question of remembering. Remembering hard.

Millie took the sim card out of Liam's phone and snapped it in two as the old man watched with puzzlement, adoration and fear in his eyes.

'Liam. Sorry about that. The guys in the market will give you a new one. I'll need a lift. Then I'll get out of your life.' The crispness in her voice was new. Or old. Liam nodded meekly.

His pristine Toyota HiLux pick-up was a surprise. It smelled of new plastic and was obviously the old man's pride and joy.

'Aye, right enough.' *Raaaiiit Enaaff*, that Invernessian twang. 'It's no' a bad motor. Present from my son. He's in that place, what is it, Kazakhstan? Drilling for oil. Doesnae know what do with his cash.'

They stopped outside the KeepGuard personal storage units, housed in an anonymous, grey building in the Longman. Despite the time, there were several cars and vans in the car park.

'Wait over with the other cars, Liam. I'll be back in a minute.'

She waved at the CCTV camera above the entrance door, then punched a series of numbers into the keypad above the lock. A buzz and metallic click gave her entry and she waved again at the reinforced glass window to her right, where the night security guard, Gussie Macdonald, was dozing drunkenly in front of a portable television. He flipped his hand at her, never taking his eyes off what was probably some quiz show. Sudoku for nitwits.

Then she was past the giant lift, clanging up the metal stairs to the first floor, a metal honeycomb of compartments inserted into the vast space of what had originally been some kind of warehouse. It was modern, smelt of rubber and shaved metal, and as far as the eye could see there were doors, numbered and locked. There was nobody else in sight. Kafkaesque, Freya had always called it. 'The Shining,' Millie had always replied. 'Lookout Hotel, only spookier. You'd need a tricycle to get around this place. All work and no play makes Jack a dull boy.'

She found the door she was looking for, spun the combination on the brass padlock, and was inside a space roughly two metres by two. It was uncluttered, containing only two office-sized filing cabinets and an old-fashioned office safe, dull green in colour. Freya had been delighted to find it for sale as part of a displenishing roup at a Dingwall engineering works. It had taken four men and one of those tiny, hand-operated forklifts to get it in here.

'Gone are the days,' Freya said. Used to say. Millie shook the shards of sadness away. There was no time, no spare energy for it. 'Gone are the days of station lockers or security vaults. This is as close as we get. It's not perfect, but it'll have to do. Here's where our get-out-of-jail-free card stays.'

Millie opened the safe. All these combinations . . . well, two. She'd always had that thing with numbers. Telephone numbers, codes . . . she'd been good at codes. Inside there was no card, just a small nylon daypack. Heavy, though, with memories of the day they'd put it in here. She shivered, then locked up and got out of there.

Liam was where she had left him, humming along to a John Denver CD. 'Rocky mountain high,' he sang softly and tunelessly. 'La la la . . . mmmmm.'

'Let's go, Liam. Now, just one more favour. I know it's a lot to ask . . .' She laid a hand on his shoulder. The old man jumped, then smiled shyly. 'Can you drop me off at the cathedral? I need to say my prayers.' The smile froze on his face.

'I never had you down as a religious woman.' He shook his head. 'Religious women have been nothing but damnation to me, all my life. My mother, my wife . . . she's dead now, but Robert couldn't wait to get away from her. Buggered off to the rigs and then abroad first chance he got. Now she's in heaven, though she probably thinks she's in hell. Nothing will be up to her standards.'

45

She was momentarily stunned by this soft outburst. Then she motioned towards the ignition key.

'I know some religious women, Liam, and they don't believe in heaven or hell. Sort of religious. An order of . . . sisters. I'll settle for what they've got, at least for just now. For a while.'

He started the diesel engine. The turbo whined.

'If they don't believe in heaven or hell,' he said. 'What do they believe in?' And she began to laugh. She tried to stop herself, but couldn't. Tears flooded her eyes as Liam pulled out onto Longman Drive, heading into the city centre. She was breathless and light-headed, and desperately, desperately sad.

'Fairies,' she said, eventually, her breathing coming in whoops. 'They believe in fairies. At the bottom of their garden.'

IN THE DEPARTMENT OF LOST CAUSES

There are killings and killings, deaths and deaths. In the high Highland summer, some stink more than others.

Doing a job like this, eventually you encounter almost every variety of demise, even in this small country's smallest city. I've seen adult corpses, not all of them female, battered into hamburger. Poisonings, burnings, shootings and cuttings. Children of all ages, their lives ended by every conceivable method. From a callous or brainless lack of care to the kind of savage sadism that puts a baby in a microwave. Inverness, Queen of the Highlands, can be a vicious, psychotic old bitch.

It would be glib to say this was different. They're all different. All human beings, extinguished, by accident or design. As soon as you forget that, you're fucked.

You stop noticing the stink of death after a while. Early in my career an elderly Scenes of Crime officer plucked away the handkerchief I was holding to my face and told me, kindly enough, to breathe in the foul, two-month-old aroma of closed-window summer death until I stopped retching.

'Sailors don't get seasick,' he muttered. But that isn't true. I know fishing skippers who vomit every time they go to sea.

I'd seen the results of torture often enough. Small time stuff, usually, various combinations of drugs and drink, sex, revenge, punishment, the extraction of information. Most of the deaths accidental, a process pushed too far, an indulgence of someone else's desire, passion, perversion. Some other bits and pieces, more professional, calculated acts. But this? This was systematic, thorough, extreme. The act of an angered man in full control and yet heedless of the consequences.

'Run of the mill stuff,' said Freeman. 'Leave it with you, if that's all right. It's your kind of thing, isn't it?' I glanced at that preoccupied, moisturised face, younger than mine. Everybody was younger than me. 'Your remit, these days?' he added.

'Well,' I said. 'Department of Lost Causes, that's me. But this, surely this is something a bit unusual, sir. This woman's been tortured to death.'

'Mustn't jump to conclusions, Sergeant. Besides, these kids, nowadays, out of their heads on drugs, I would think. Don't you agree?'

'Yes, sir. They are well and truly out of their heads on dope and speed, sir.'

'Good.' He nodded. Either he wasn't listening or he thought it was a good thing for kids to be out of their heads on dope and speed. I couldn't tell. He looked at his watch. A lower-caste, dateless Omega. Aspirational, but a long way to go. Herr Breitling and Monsieur Cartier were calling from afar. 'There are one or two specific . . . irregularities with this case. It's why you . . . anyway, I need absolute traceability on this investigation, line of command from me to you. I need to know what you know, nothing going astray. You have, um, pathology and you have electronics cover, the Scenes of Crime people are Team A. No talking out of turn, out of school, do you understand?' I detected (and after all, I was a detective) something feverish there, something really, deeply nervous. 'I have to get on, Sergeant. There's a constable at the front of the building, we're letting residents to the other flats in and out, and you'll want to speak to them. SOCOs will get here when they can, but it's not a priority. Obviously, or . . .' Or it wouldn't be handed over to me. 'Anyway, keep me posted. It'll be . . . ah . . . relatively straightforward, my guess. But please be thorough and report everything you find to me. And only to me. Everything, d'you understand? Line of command. Trace . . . trace . . .'

'Traceability, sir. I understand.' He had Vicks ointment in two little streaks below his nostrils, a nosegay, a greasy moustache. Its pungent, medicinal odour there to counteract the death reek: a mixture of shit, blood, meat, piss, vomit, household dust, filth, food. Matured into an instantly recognisable perfume of murder.

The door – unexpectedly heavy, steel-reinforced, bristling with serious locks – slammed as Freeman left. I wondered what was really going on. He sounded pissed off. Angry that someone as busy and important as he was should be bothered with some morning body down the Ferry. Kennedy Avenue at that. Mooted for the long scrabble up the ladder towards gentrification, but faltering on the first rung. He was afraid of something, too. And he had brought me in, old hands, safe hands. Maybe slightly dirty hands. A wee bit shaky, but not much. Just a controllable tremor. There had to be a reason.

The chief inspector had a sergeant waiting in the Range Rover downstairs to drive him. Freeman had places to go. His sergeant, Robinson, as well groomed as his boss, would remind him to wipe away that Vicks ointment for his next appointment. It was unlikely that he'd be facing two corpses in a row.

I, on the other hand, saw them quite a lot, these days. Well, a couple a month. Of late I'd been specialising in the old and dead, the elderly murdered. I'd seek out those cases, trying to reconstruct forgotten lives. Maybe because my mum and dad had both passed away the previous year, unmurdered other than by the companies that manufactured their joint obsession: Embassy Regal cigarettes.

There were lots of old people in Inverness. Lots of them dying. Lots of them alone and unnoticed, until the smell permeated the double-glazing or the insulated floors. I made myself the master of forgotten corpses. I had my own department, after all. If I wanted to specialise, I could. And I had. I'd overheard two of the new breed of management-speak coppers, the ones rejoicing in the looming end of the Northern Constabulary and the creation of the National Scottish Police Force, or NSPF. They were talking about me. Inspectors, but then nearly everyone's an inspector these days. Of one kind or another. They were enjoying a joint piss, I was having a shite in a cubicle, glancing through an early edition of the *Courier*.

'Odd having a department under a sergeant.'

'It's not a department. It's just a filing cabinet. A box-file, really.'

'Shuffling him off until retirement? He's not that old, surely?'

'No. Acts it, sometimes. But he's got a history. Done stuff you don't ask about. Not here. You know, elsewhere. He knows stuff. They need that knowledge. Or they're afraid some of it might leak out elsewhere. There's some things you don't want privatised. And it's the attitude, really, isn't it? It won't wash in this day and age, that sort of thing. Team players are what we need. Goes on courses and upsets the tutors, sits and gives off this air of fuck-you-laddie. And then there was that . . . you know, that business in the Black Isle.'

'Aye, that.'

'Card marked for good. Personally, I can't see that what's in his head is that valuable. Best if he just gets out, takes the pension, does security somewhere.

Consultancy work. Writes his fucking memoirs if the politicians don't block it. I mean, he's a sanctimonious old cunt, basically. A dinosaur.'

'Aye. With a violent streak. I can see him watching monitors in a car-park office somewhere, probably getting ready to kick the shit out of trespassers.'

'No room for that sort of thing in the modern service.'

'Nah.'

That was when I opened the cubicle door, tripped and . . . sort of fell into the inspector who'd made that last observation. He hadn't quite finished doing up his flies and his dick somehow got caught between his zip and the ceramic lip of the pisser. There was a surprising amount of blood. I've always favoured button flies myself. Buttons would still be sore in that situation, but you wouldn't get the tearing effect.

'Sorry,' I said, as he was being helped away by his colleague. 'I'm not so steady on my feet these days. Tendency to shuffle.' The look he gave me was that weird mixture you sometimes get of contempt and fear. I think the two are quite closely related. I wondered if I'd hear any more about it. Maybe some sort of demand for a medical assessment on the basis of dangerous clumsiness. But there had been nothing.

There is no Department of Lost Causes, nor one of Apparently Unimportant Deaths. But that is what I do. It's what I choose to do. I could probably announce that I was specialising in Playstation Abuse, if I was interested, and they'd let me get on with it. Generally, they leave me alone, until someone like Freeman comes calling, demanding, insisting I do his will. It's a police force, I suppose. I mean, some of them even wear uniforms.

I have a small office, a box-room, or box, if you prefer, unconnected with the teeming open plan, hot desk homes of Serious Crime, Vice, Fraud, Murder, Grimacing in Public and Very Bad Shoplifting. It's just me, a table, a computer and a telephone. I get calls. People ask me things. And I've been specialising, as I say. In lots of ways, it suits me fine. In some way, I do care about these dried up, liquefying, stinking bodies that were once people. I want, like a good undertaker, to give them a decent burial. And I have time, too. Time to think about things. The past. Too much time. Though I have my wee hobbies, things to calm the mind, stave off the memories.

While I waited for the SOCOs to arrive, I began to search the flat, looking for the other person, the probable murderer, the woman whose spoor was everywhere: the lover. There were two record collections, two vibrators (different sizes), two sets of clothes. Stuff missing. Papers. Documents. A systematic untidiness. There was a little light lesbian porn, some of the classic texts. Two lots of stuff, compatible tastes in flesh. The other woman was smaller, probably younger. No mention of that from Freeman, though he must have noticed. But then again . . .

The call, according to Freeman, had come in anonymously, on the sneak-line, the free number advertised widely and mostly used by embittered neighbours or ex-lovers informing on drunk drivers. Everything looked as if it had happened overnight, but there was no obvious trail, no bloodied footprints, and there were signs of wiping, of careful track-covering. Except in that mad beating, that horrendous destruction of a person.

The smell was shuttered slaughterhouse; the warmth had brought about a sourness, a brutal reek. It was a beautiful summer morning outside and, even in the northern clime of Inverness, too warm for heating. Forensics would be able to get something, surely. It was too soon for flies to be swarming, but the maggots would be there already.

It was a renovated, ex-council flat in the Ferry, Inverness's former dumping ground for the poor, now in the slow process of gentrification. *Ness-side Village, Renewal and Regeneration.* There were signs. It had to be true. Kennedy Avenue, named for wee Charlie Boy, Lord Kennedy these days, former Liberal, then Lib Dem Hero brought down by allegations, the admissions of drink, now shunted off to the House of Lords. We were just around the corner from Grimond Way.

It was a corner close, with just one two-bedroom flat on each landing. It offered privacy. The Highland capital is one of the most gloriously sited cities on Earth and the Ferry, potentially a wonderful place to live. In, say, about 50 years, once the poor, the violent and the unpleasant, the drunk and the addicted have been killed, cleared out or allowed to die from some new unstoppable virus, it'll be lovely. Might be worth investing now. Just ignore that old wino snuggled into a close-mouth next door. It's easy. If you practise.

There you could be, sitting on your balcony with a glass of chilled Cava, gazing across the Kessock Narrows to the Black Isle, which isn't, of course, an island at all, just a peninsula with pretensions. No need for a ferry now, with the Kessock Bridge, a kind of truncated, grey version of the Golden Gate, having turned the Black Isle into an expensive Invernessian commuterland.

And above all, above everything, the hulking mass of Ben Wyvis, flat-topped to the extent that Munro-baggers are never sure where its 3,000-foot summit really is. A massif, rather than a mountain, and deceptively dangerous. Like much else in the romanticised landmass known as the Highlands.

Maybe that's what Mrs Smith, Mrs W. Smith, as indicated by the name on the security entry system and the small stack of letters and bills on the hall table, had been doing. Along with her, so-far, anonymous companion. Because the flat, once you got past inevitable deathliness, bore all the signs of a right-to-buy sell-on, owner-occupied and with considerable pride of ownership at that. It was in the preferred position, looking directly over the firth, towards North Kessock. People walked their dogs, injected drugs and fucked on the grass, the half-built promenade, directly across from the close, between the road and the water. There had been a lot of stuff shipped from the nearest IKEA, which was in Glasgow. But there was old and carefully chosen furniture there, too, some of it probably inherited. There were two tastes, mostly in harmony, but not entirely: a Warhol-style print of Pete Doherty from that Babyshambles band; Klip-framed, casual. And a set of Victorian landscapes, mezzotints from a book, professionally framed with precision and at considerable expense. The place gave every impression of having been turned over, quickly, hurriedly and professionally. Things had been removed. What was left looked as if it had been . . . fingered.

I eyed a cracked Chinese screen with some interest: a bit of fixing up and it could be worth something. There was a lost, strange beauty there. But there was nothing beautiful about what was left of Mrs . . . Smith.

Music and technology were always good indicators of age. The computer was a desktop PC, no broadband, no apparent Internet connection. Odd. There was an ancient-tech cassette answering machine, its indicator light off. I had on a pair of disposable rubber gloves, as dictated by regulations, and punched the power button. The hard disk wheezed and hummed, and a green light began to flash. The computer screen came up a flat blue. No operating system, nothing. I powered up the answering machine and checked for messages. Everything had been erased. Then I began to check the things that Mrs Smith and her companion had left behind. And that the searcher or searchers had missed or considered unimportant.

The missing woman was called Millicent Jones according to a bill I found underneath the newspaper lining an empty bureau drawer. It was from Villiers Watch Repairs in Academy Street. A total of £100 for servicing and cleaning a Rolex Ladies Submariner. Not a pauper, then. And someone with a serious taste in watches. But there were no personal documents, no handbags, no purses. No passports, folders, household accounts or birth certificates. It was more than odd. Smith and Jones. Smith and Jones. And a watch. I checked Mrs Smith's wrist: broken in two places, it looked like. But the watch was still there. It was a Cartier Tank, the real thing. And that was really strange. That it was still there. And that it was real. Twenty grand's worth of watch.

Curious. It was all curious. There was some food, some good food. Plenty of signs of people who cooked, and cooked carefully: the fridge freezer was full, some leftover goulash or something cling-filmed and ready for reheating, a lot of decent wine, no corked bottles. Loads of empties, hoarded for recycling. Which was always the sign of a drinker, I thought. Personal experience. Papers, bills, receipts . . . innocuous stuff. And things missing, maybe. Somebody else had been here first.

I stopped and drew breath, sat down on a cheap pine dining chair, leaned an arm on the old oak table and took in my surroundings properly, for the first time. Shut my eyes and then opened them again. The mix of solid old and cheap new furniture. The pictures on the walls. Scottish Colourists, I noticed. Was that a Peploe? A print, surely. Some daft rock star pictures, photos of people like KT Tunstall, Paolo Nutini. But that little James Kay pastel was definitely the real deal. What was this place? Who was Mrs . . . I glanced at the pile of mail I'd picked up from behind the door . . . W. Smith, Flat Three, 125 Kennedy Avenue? There were books, too. A respectably well-read set of books, and not just the dyke stuff. I got up to look at the gappy bookcases, one elderly, one veneered chipboard. There was a small selection on Ireland, I noticed with a lurch in my gut, on the Troubles: Dillon and Lehane, *Stakeknife*, that Mark Urban book about the SAS. And more. An amateur interest? Christ.

The stereo was interesting. Big old walnut finish speakers, a vast tuner amp, a receiver as they used to call it. A decent, first-generation CD player. No tape machine, no tapes. No turntable, so no vinyl. But two of those CD towers. One had some jazz, mostly bebop, Miles, Bird . . . the rest '70s student rock and California folk, the kind you'd expect in . . . a flat like mine. Late 40s, early 50s kind of age range. Zeppelin, Tull, Heep, Wishbone

Ash, Browne, Ronstadt, Nyro, everything ever recorded by Joni Mitchell and nearly everything it was possible to get by Van Morrison. I flicked through some of the Belfast cowboy's past glories: *Veedon Fleece*, the wonderful live double *It's Too Late to Stop Now*, *Astral Weeks*. God, how long was it since I'd listened to Van the Man spinning his psychedelic tales of Madame George and the like? Suddenly I felt old, remembering the first time I heard the album, a cheap German vinyl pressing, played on my bedroom Dansette. My surgical gloves left temporary prints on the CD cases: John Martyn, Nick Drake . . . it was basically a vinyl collection repurchased on CD. Not young enough – or maybe gadgety and male enough – to go down the iPod route. Enough of a serious music fan to want to listen in quality. Enough of a nostalgist to want to wallow, it seemed, in the early '70s to the exclusion of almost everything else. Damien Rice. There was that Damien Rice CD, but then every ageing hippy bought that. At least there was no Katie Melua. There was a 14-inch telly with a built-in DVD player, notably nickable. A few DVDs, mostly French classics: *À bout de souffle*, *Diva*, *Betty Blue*, *Le Cop*. Pretentious? *Moi?*

The other CD tower fitted in with the breezy indiepop pictures on the wall, but again, no sign of an iPod charger or USB cable to the computer. So maybe not that young. I was jumping ahead of myself. It was time to call in the League of the White Wellies. Or forensics, if you insist. And their associated technophiles.

I pulled out my mobile and dialled.

'Jimbo? Unmourned and unwanteds here. Listen, can you get down to the Ferry? I've got some electrical goods I need you to look at. And tell Scenes of Crime I'm ready for them.'

Jim Smeaton was a member of the electronic evidence team. I had a bad feeling about that computer.

And a worse one about the remains of Mrs Smith herself. I stood over her and looked at the ravaged face, checking the neatly-cut, dyed-brown bob, such a weird and sickening contrast to her ruined features. I leant in close. She was – had been – wearing a small, art nouveau pendant on a tarnished silver chain. Her dress was linen, a khaki green, severely, but fashionably, cut. Not Inverness, I thought. Boden maybe. The shoes. That was interesting. Not slippers. Converse All Stars, low-tops, black. Classic rock 'n' roll shoes. Good for running short distances, absolute hell if you had to walk far. Unless you were light, and she was. Small breasts. Noticing such things was important, I told myself.

I checked the wardrobes, two of them. Two women, after all, and one with a taste for clothes. Same as the music, there was nostalgia there, a mothballed but still pungently goaty Afghan coat, old Biba dresses, some boots so high and laced up it made you think of strange, joyous '70s sex, before AIDS, before death. And newer things, Next, H&M. A lot of smart stuff. And the other woman, Millie, Rolex-girl, was all fleeces and Gore-tex, a couple of smart Ted Baker frocks, but mostly practical. Gap shirts, M&S. Somebody fit. But capable of causing the kind of damage that had eventually killed her companion? I wasn't so sure. There was no sign of restraints, no ropes. I checked her ankles and wrists again, touching nothing. All were broken. It had taken strength, to hold her down and do that. Strength and bulk.

No photographs. Where were they? Who had taken them? Had there been photos here in the first place?

Fifty-five, at a guess, maybe sixty. Maybe 45. And Millicent I was putting at around 40. But why had all the documentation disappeared? Where was the guddle of identity? I looked through the pile of mail. Bills, cards from would-be meter readers, circulars without a name. And the rest just to Mrs or Ms and occasionally Miss W. Smith.

I was alone, dumped here at the behest of Freeman, in what was increasingly feeling like something very nasty and very dodgy. It had 'spook' written all over it. And that was another reason they had dragged me into it, wasn't it? Because I had a bit of skulduggery on my CV. More than was actually on the official record. But all of it, all of that nefarious experience gained in one place, the place that this flat suddenly stank of: Northern Ireland.

Did I need this? Could I cope with it? No, and no. But I was here now and there was no way out, not really. Fuck, it was a police force. You did what you were told, went where you were pointed. That was how it had been in Ireland, during my brief sojourn. And that was how it was here. Kind of.

I crouched in front of her, of W., W. Smith, Mrs Smith, and looked into what would have been her eyes. They were hidden in blackened and torn flesh. I tried for a few seconds to do that *Red Dragon* thing, that deep, soulful policeman profiler act where you connect with the dead person, engage emotionally, spiritually even. She was in her 50s, maybe, pretty much the same as me, give or take. Maybe fanciable, in another time, another world where such tawdry, ridiculous terms meant something. I'd never fancied a Smith, to my knowledge. Maybe I should promise to . . . what? Honour her death in some way? Not allow what – undoubtedly in my mind – a murderer had wanted: that she slip away in anonymity, swept up in the overworked, over-administered shambles that was policing in the Highlands? Or the shadowy, secretive obfuscation of the dark side, the spooks I could feel haunting this flat and who would doubtless come soon enough, to gather and clean and deny. All I could say to her and myself was that I'd do what I could. Despite the fact that I was here, I was pretty certain, as window dressing.

The SOCOs arrived, two of them, noisy, bored, with the clank of roughly-handled equipment, togged up already in their white paper ghost overalls. Jim Smeaton just behind them, quintessentially geekish in his combat parka and trailing, wide-bottom jeans. He was desultorily struggling into a boiler suit on the outside landing.

'All right?' Fergus Grant, one of the Scenes of Crime officers, looked at me with a degree of nervousness. 'Looks fairly nasty. Called the diggers and baggers yet?'

'Still got the doctor to come. He's been due for over an hour.'

'*She*,' said Grant. 'It's yon Sheila Dartington that's on. She'll be up at that bairn thing in Scorguie. That's where Freeman is too. And that cunt, Robinson. Reporters, telly, the lot, all skirmishing about. Three weans, all poisoned to death, the mother claiming it was leakage from the canal into the water supply or something. It's gonnae go national, that one. Nothing much for us, though. Munchausen's Syndrome by Fucking Proxy, except it isn't because the fucking courts say it doesn't exist any more.'

'Christ, Baron Freeman'll love that,' I muttered. 'And Dartington'll take forever to get down here. Wrong side of the fucking tracks.' Or to be precise, wrong side of the water, the river and the canal both. The Ferry was caught on a sliver of land between the two of them.

'Ach well,' said Grant, as his so far silent colleague unzipped a rust-coloured nylon bag. Practical shade, I thought. 'Read this like a book. What is she, maybe 50? Slips and falls, pulls herself into the chair, hits herself several times with a hammer which she then swallows. Dies alone, probably of natural causes, heart attack, stroke, whatever. At least there's no Marie Provost dog yapping around, bloated on mistress flesh. Saw that once, in Wick.' He looked suddenly nostalgic. 'Ah, Caithness. You should see the size of the maggots in

Caithness. Fuck, I hate the Ferry.' He leaned in close to that ruined face, just as I had. 'Tell you one thing for certain.'

'What is it, Fergie?' The other SOCO was young, with a high voice. I didn't think I'd seen him before, though it was hard to tell because he was wearing a biological protection mask. Fat lot of good that would do him. The whole idea was to smell things. To sniff it all in and come to some bloody conclusions, possibly useful ones.

'She's deid.'

We all laughed. SOCOs and coppers specialise in that kind of thing. Black humour. I used to do it pretty well myself, coming on like a sort of comedian, laugh a minute. Just like we were in some kind of movie. Until one black afternoon, on the Black Isle. The punchline that day had wiped away everyone's smiles, sent the sun into the sea early, left me talking nothing but shite, unfunny shite. Oh, there was plenty of banter, loads of jokes, but the punchline, that was a bastard, something from a different act altogether. Laugh? I nearly died. Others weren't so lucky.

My mobile phone bleeped. Text message. There was no indication who it was from. It read: *Smith Jones Enderby Fairweather Freya Millicent/Millie.*

Names. Someone who didn't want to reveal his own, or her own, was taking an interest. Which was nice.

I COULD DRINK A CASE OF YOU

Millie shouldered the rucksack as Liam drove away into the Inverness night. The cathedral was on the river, shadowed on the opposite bank by the so-called Inverness Castle, a crenellated Victorian monstrosity, which housed the city's courts. The massive front doors were locked against vandals and other demonic forces. Not that she was expecting sanctuary. It was just a landmark, a dropping-off point. And somewhere neutral for Liam to tell his inevitable interrogators about. From the cathedral she could have gone anywhere. To the bus or rail station, a taxi to the airport. Hitching into Fort William along the A82. But what she actually did was duck in behind the massive lump of imitation gothic perpendicular, skirt around its rump and then cut through the Eden Court Theatre car park, and down to the riverbank.

This was one of her favourite parts of Inverness. She was on the eastern bank of the river, which broadened and split at this point, forming the wooded enclaves called the Ness Islands. They were linked to the east and west banks in various places by cast-iron suspension bridges, spans that bounced in a rhythmic and childishly appealing way if you kept your pace steady while crossing them. Soldiers marching in formation were meant to break step on bridges, she remembered. They could set up a destructive wave of energy that could cause weak structures to collapse.

It was warm, soft, still and summery and there would probably be the odd lost soul flitting among the trees, she thought, even this late – she looked at the old Rolex that had somehow survived the night with her. Mark had given it to her, given her the watch and the razor blade trick that had saved her.

Given her time. That blunt blade was still in her shoe. A talisman. 'Keep the watch on, all the time,' he'd said. 'It's self-winding. Movement keeps it going. When you die, it dies.' That was so like a man, she thought. She looked at the dial, seeing the time now instead of her memories.

Three a.m. Late August. The eerie perpetual twilight of midsummer – Mark's beloved and lost Shetland simmer dim – had gone, but it would still be light soon enough. She had to move.

Lost souls. Lost souls like her. Homeless, down and outs, maybe some lonely gay man looking for mutual solace with another of his kind. She grinned without any real amusement. Of her kind, really. But for her, it wasn't the same thing at all.

There was a glade she knew, across one of the bridges, then down to the river's edge through thick rhododendron. It was scattered with old, tiny gravestones, mostly broken and stained green with fungus. The first time, she and Freya had stumbled upon it, looking for a suitable location for some of the alfresco sex Freya occasionally favoured – she had scraped the mould off one or two of the stones: *Affectionately remembered, Bouncy*, one had read. Another said *Yum Yum – loved and loving*. It was the remains of Inverness's pet cemetery.

Crouched among the memorials to lost dogs, cats and, for all she knew, guinea pigs and goldfish, she shrugged the rucksack from her back. From the front pocket she took a halogen head torch, slipping it over her forehead and switching it on. Then she opened the main compartment.

First, there was a light bivvi bag in Gore-tex. Wrapped inside was one of those hiking towels, ultra absorbent and packing very small, a vintage Fairbairn-Sykes commando knife, double-edged, completely illegal, some flint and lint. In a neoprene case, there was a MacBook Air laptop and, in a sealed plastic bag, a Nokia, with spare battery and mains charger. In other small sealed bags, there were tampons, dried fruit and chocolate. A steel double-dram whisky flask. And at the bottom of the bag, in first plastic and then a towel fragrant with oil, a Glock 720, loaded with 14 cross head soft tip bullets, specified and checked by Freya. A spare clip was wrapped separately. An iPod and a GPS.

She ate some apricots and some Green and Black chocolate, then switched the Nokia on, picking up a strong signal. She dialled a number – yet another combination of digits she knew off by heart – and left a terse message on the machine that picked up. Then she went through the phone's menus until she found another number, one she had never bothered to memorise properly, though she could probably have dredged it up. This was easier than trying to remember. She was getting tired. Cold, too, despite the mild night. There was shivering starting deep in her body.

A woman's voice, clipped and fully awake, despite the time. The American accent roughened and etched by age.

'Hallo?'

'I could drink a case of Bunnahabhain.'

'I do beg your pardon? Were you looking for Mrs Carole King?'

'And still be on my feet. No, but if Miss Nyro is in, I would like to speak to her.'

'This is Miss Nyro. How can I help you?'

Freya's code, all based on female singer-songwriters Millie had barely, or in two cases never, heard of.

'I'm afraid I have bad news and I wondered if we might share it face to face. If that were convenient.' Some strange formality was taking her over. Her voice sounded thick and her lips felt rubbery.

'And when would be convenient for you?'

'Soon.'

'Very well.' There was a pause, as if a hand had been placed over the mouthpiece and someone else was being consulted. Was there someone else there? 'Do you have liquidity?'

'I have liquidity.'

'Forty-five minutes, then. Please leave the door unlocked.' And the phone went dead.

Millie ran through the codes they'd exchanged, wondering if she had everything correct. She switched the phone off, replaced everything quickly in the rucksack, put it on and, after pushing her way through the slippery leaves of the bushes, began to run, looking for all the world like some pre-dawn jogger. There was a faint blue streak in the eastern sky, but she was running west. Where it was darkest. Where the land turned to liquid.

Millie jogged the canal towpath, feeling the damage she'd suffered earlier in the kidnapping attempt with every jarring step. But the discipline of long ago, heavily laden night runs came back to her, the self-hypnosis techniques they'd all been taught: *calm, confidence, control.* As the rucksack straps burned into her shoulders and her ankles ached, she took herself off to her special place of absolute relaxation. It was a tiny beach on the North Antrim coast, the place Freya had taken her. Seduced her, she supposed. But that wasn't how she thought of it. She thought of sunlight on dappled water, the tang of ozone, salt on her skin. Their skins.

She reached the Dochgarroch lock within 40 minutes. Slow. But soon enough. A line of sleeping yachts had been tied up on the Inverness side all night. Nothing stirred. Clara must have been watching through binoculars from the vegetation on the north shore of the loch, because no sooner had she forced her way down to the pebble beach west of the main channel out of the lock than she heard the rasping purr of a four-stroke outboard. It was halfway between darkness and dawn, that opaque blue Highland twilight, and it was difficult to tell where the noise was coming from until she caught the phosphorescence of a bow wake just as the engine died and the Zodiac glided in towards her.

The bow of the inflatable crunched ashore; Millie grabbed and held it, then began to push it back into the loch. As the hull came free, she waded with it into about three feet of icy water, awkwardly straddling one of the gunwales just as Clara lowered the engine back into its vertical position and started it. By the time they were heading west, Millie was slumped, breathless, in the bottom of the boat, trying to keep the rucksack clear of the water she'd brought in with her on her sodden shoes and trousers.

'Going to be a lovely day,' said Clara, not looking at her. Millie said nothing. 'You look as if you've been back in the wars, honey.' The accent was American, southern, exaggerated because she was having to shout over the noise of the outboard. Millie looked up at the woman steering the boat, hand on the throttle-cum-tiller of a 25-horsepower Mercury.

'Back in the wars. Yeah, you could say that. Only problem is, I don't know which war, or who the enemy is.' She could feel her throat closing. The effort of making herself heard over the motor was too great. But Clara continued.

'Did Freya know?'

'Don't know. I'm hoping I've got some stuff here that'll tell us.'

'Tell *you*, babe. You. Not us. We're strictly neutral in this . . . I'm strictly neutral. Aid and succour to a friend, non-intervention, that kinda thing. Happy to help. But hey, I wanna keep these hands clean.'

'Always the American way, Clara. Neutral until it starts to put the price of petrol up.'

A smile crossed Clara's lips. She was older, older than Freya. Freya had once been Clara's Millie, she had long guessed. But they had been introduced only as friends, with Freya telling her, once they were alone, that Clara should always be regarded as first fallback option in an emergency. Millie had puzzled over the ambiguity of that statement, wondering if Freya was making some kind of oblique sexual point. But in the end, when push came to shove, in the darkness of this dreadful night, she realised that Freya had been more than hinting, that she had laid a trail of mentions, occasional visits, an insistence that Millie keep that telephone number in her phone's memory. So that Clara was the first point of call. The fallback option. The Sisters.

'Self-interest. Yeah. But I'm real sorry about Freya. I wouldn't like to think she suffered.'

'Protecting me.' Millie's throat dried. She tried to swallow. Said nothing more.

Past the giant metal shed that was the base station of the Foyers pump-storage power generator, past the house that had once belonged to both Jimmy Page of Led Zeppelin and Aleister Crowley, so-called wickedest man in the world, the trees cluttered the waterline and the loch grew silvery and viscous as light began to flood in from the eastern sky. The boathouse was like something from *Swallows and Amazons*, a pitched, wooden structure you would miss among the oak and birch remnants of the ancient Caledonian forest, if you weren't looking for it. You couldn't see the infra-red CCTV cameras among the trees, but Millie knew they were there.

The house was wooden, long, low, built in a U-shape. It had been imported from Estonia, she knew, as a kit, and designed in committee by the three women who lived there. The Sisters, Freya had called them. Mark had called them the Witches. Millie had always thought of them as the Nuns, a sisterhood of secrecy. They each had a self-contained suite. These days, they spent most of their time in the place they had named Valhalla, a godless heaven for warriors. Originally, they had pooled their resources to build it as a retreat. Sometimes, they made a little cash by renting to relatives and trusted friends. They were Clara, Nigella and Veronica. Two had served in the British Army, notably in Northern Ireland. One had been CIA liaison with the US embassy in Dublin, chasing Noraid contacts and arms shipments. That was Clara. These days, all three lived, retired, on the shores of Loch Ness, more or less full-time. They were comfortable with each other and each other's secrets. In some cases they were the same secrets, commonly held.

Nigella had worked in information analysis, dealing mostly with transcripts from phone taps and bugs. She rarely talked about anything she had seen or done across the water, though Millie had been at a few briefings by her during her stint with 14th Intelligence Company, the legendary Det. For her, Valhalla was a place of refuge. Veronica had been hands-on in the early years of the Troubles, one of the first female undercover operators, given a truly hellish time at selection school, so it was said, though she had never complained. Command had belatedly realised that undercover observation without some kind of female presence was hugely limited, especially as PIRA (much more than the Protestant paramilitaries) had women right up their command structure and were completely used to seeing them live and die in the front line. Matriarchal Catholicism and Marxist terrorist organisation, Freya used to say. Killer combination.

Clara was pure-bred Agency, working the collection-can trail, passing on names when she could, or when her political masters thought it beneficial to their interests, keeping lines of communication open. They had bonded, the three of them, holidayed together, discovered a shared love of the Scottish Highlands, though none had family connections there, and hatched the idea for Valhalla when a derelict property on the lochside came up for sale in the early '90s. Despite Mark's bitter assertions of some kind of weird sisterhood involving black magic, only Veronica dabbled in crystals and other New Age paraphernalia. He had met them all, knew them through work, and it had been Veronica, in fact, who offered him and his lover, Millie, a fortnight in Valhalla as a romantic break. For £300 a week, which they had barely been able to afford.

Obviously, that had been before Freya. But not long before. Because she had turned up, as if by accident, on the last weekend of their stay with Clara.

'Who's at home?' They were trudging up the path from the boathouse. Millie could feel the dawn sunshine beginning to break through the forest canopy, surprisingly warm for so early in the day. The musty smell of summer pine was everywhere. An aching weariness was beginning to consume her body.

'Just me. Nigella's in Mallorca visiting the grandchildren.'

'Grandchildren?'

Clara gave her a wintry smile. 'Grandchildren. She was once married to someone who is now a lord, you will be delighted to know. You're not the only one around who swings both ways, little Lady Fondle Roy. Veronica's doing some charity work, I believe it's called. In Eritrea.'

'Charity work?'

'Well, aid work. The best kind. Well paid. Paid for by charities. Just topping up the retirement funds.'

Millie said nothing. She was beyond sarcasm.

In Clara's guest bedroom, Millie first of all stripped off her clothes, feeling a kind of overall tremor in her body as at last she stood naked before the full length mirror in the bathroom. She was bruised and cut in various places on her legs and arms. She examined herself dispassionately: compact, at five foot four, and still reasonably fit for someone on the edge of middle age, though the hard muscle of combat training and the resilience of youth were fading. One or two scars she didn't care to think about. Short hair, dyed blonde, and the face, Mark had once told her, of a dissolute elf. 'Female elf,' he'd laughed, as she'd play-punched him, carelessly drawing blood from his lip. 'Elfy elf.' It was the full lips and sharp nose, an odd combination. She'd grown used to the way she looked. For 45, she was OK.

A bath in the soft, peaty water that came from Valhalla's own spring and, wrapped in one of Clara's fluffy dressing gowns, Millie sat cross-legged on the raw pine floor and opened the rucksack, carefully laying out its contents.

There was the MacBook Air, beautiful and silvery. Much better looking, Freya had insisted, than the smaller, much cheaper Asus Eee PC they'd also considered. In the end Freya had insisted. 'Beauty fucks practicality' she had said, too loudly, in the Aberdeen John Lewis store, stubborn and somewhat pissed after a long lunch in Bistro Verde. They had occasionally caught the train through to the silver city for a treat, a trip, some shopping. 'There's nowhere like Aberdeen for fish,' Freya used to say. 'And there's precious little else but fish and oil. And money.'

She had been at university there, a lifetime or two ago. Sometimes, if she was drunk, she'd talk wistfully of its highly traditional ways, the ancient cobbled university village known as Old Aberdeen, gowns compulsory, carefree races along the endless beach. But she'd been recruited and it had all come to a sudden and solemn end. After that, life for Freya had become darker, more serious. Her trips to Aberdeen with Millie were ventures into a past that was lightsome and lost.

There was the whisky flask, Millie's choice. Freya was a wine drinker, a winebibber she'd described herself as, a toper. Millie liked the sudden burn of neat malt, preferably something from Islay. It was something Mark had taught her. They'd even had a trip together to that glorious island, where the very air could get you drunk. And it was in the gift shop at Laphroaig he'd bought her the flask. It was full of a rare 1973 Ardbeg, the last of it. She unscrewed the cap, raised the flat metal container to her lips, filled her mouth. It was like a vicious, stolen kiss. The warmth flushed through her. Mark.

The iPod, the classic model in a crystalline plastic case. It had a massive 160GB hard disk and while there was a little music, something for both of them, a range taking in Prokofiev and Sufjan Stevens, it served as extra storage for the computer. Everything was backed up there, including the files from the home PC. The Mac ran a version of Windows and could read them. The PC should have erased itself as soon as it had been turned on by whoever had killed Freya. An abstruse set of keys had to be held down with the power switch to prevent that happening. The same security measures had been programmed into the Mac.

The phone, a simple one. A basic Garmin hand-held GPS. A small bag containing water purification tablets, a collapsible plastic cup, waterproof matches and the Fairbairn-Sykes killing knife, designed in the Highlands during World War Two by a pair of the Special Operations Executive's dodgy gentlemen killers, Mr Fairbairn and Mr Sykes. That was it. She put everything back except for the Mac and its power lead, which she connected and plugged into a wall socket. As the laptop began charging, she put on a worn and too-big tracksuit Clara had left for her and made her way to the kitchen, keeping the mobile handy. She was, she realised, absolutely starving.

Clara fed her a delicious nettle soup, some home-made bread and goat's cheese. There was a half-decent Malbec, product of Clara's days as a military attaché in Argentina. 'Yeah, during your little adventure,' she smiled, thin-lipped.

'Not me. I was just a baby,' said Millie, on her second glass.

'Still are, sweetie.' Millie looked for some sign of attempted seduction, but there was none. There was a glimmer of tears in Clara's eyes. 'Do you have any idea who was responsible? Any names? Identifying features?'

'The two who lifted me were pros, but slow. Not used to dealing with women, maybe a bit reluctant. One was big; one was bigger. No talking. Military, I'd say. Special Forces, maybe. Superannuated. Not very good. After all, if I was able to get out of their clutches . . .'

'Anything else? What about Freya?'

'They must have been watching for a while. Waited until I was out for the shopping, got to Freya then. I still can't work out why she . . . she must have let them in. That door was solid.'

'Maybe she knew them. Or at least one of them.'

'It's possible. One of them spoke to me, when I phoned. Actually spoke to me. I half thought I recognised the voice. It was Ulster, that almost crooning, singing Ulster you get when some patronising bastard is treating you to his little woman schtick. I'm sure I . . . I'm almost sure . . .' She shook her head. 'Christ, I shouldn't have had that wine.'

'Well, don't have any coffee. Drink some water and have a rest. We can talk again in the morning.'

'You were in Ireland with Freya. Does it ring any bells, that voice? More Irish than he really was, if you know what I mean?'

Clara shook her head.

'Come on, sweetheart, get to bed. I'll do the dishes. We can talk in the morning.' Millie smiled gratefully and lurched to her feet, just slightly unsteady. 'Good night, Clara. And thanks. I know you and . . .'

But Clara swatted away any further words. 'See you in the morning, honey. Sleep tight.'

Back in her room, Millie drank a glass of water and splashed some more on her face. Any trace of tipsiness had disappeared the moment the door shut. She took the fully charged Mac into the bathroom and spent the next two hours sifting through what, for the most part, were housekeeping files, domestic records of her and Freya's life together. And then there was the folder tagged 'Serp'. Locked, even to her.

She hooked up the iPod and began to check the files there – they were mostly duplicates and again there was the Serp folder, secure and inaccessible. Mocking. She sighed, put the Mac to sleep and went back into the bedroom. She lay down on the bed with the iPod, fished out the earbuds, connected them, pushed them carefully into her ears and flicked to iTunes. Some Joni, maybe.

She scrolled through the artists, feeling that nauseated boredom with music that sometimes attacked her, the notion that there was nothing worth listening to, nothing which would please her. And then she noticed the files near the end of the list of artists, between Tom Waits and Neil Young: Freya sings. She pressed 'Play'.

And Freya was drunk, of course. Millie remembered her asking about the iTalk microphone attachment, how it worked. She'd shown her how simple it was, how it automatically created an iTunes file, how you simply talked into it.

My name is Freya Jane Enderby and I love Millie. Millie, this is for you. Of course it is. There are no witnesses. Always better that way. Always best, we would say, just to get a confession.

A chink of glass, a swallowing sound.

I've been in Inverness for about three weeks. Like they said, it's a pleasant enough town. It wasn't exactly an order, but I'm still on the reserve list, so I'm supposed to do what I'm told. Official Secrets, that sort of thing. Of course, I had my own, unofficial, little secret. Have. Have and hold, have and hold.

It's stalked my life ever since it happened. We're embroiled. Both of us. Must be a better word. Can't think of it, though. I think they know, actually, maybe they always knew, that I was lying to them. No longer on their side. We've been trying to get the whole thing into the public domain. We thought we were being careful. But not careful enough, it seems. Millie, they're onto me. My old friends in the trade.

A bitter laugh. God, she could put it away.

Nothing certain, just a feeling. There's so much at stake. Or maybe we're OK, my darling. That's all that matters to me. The two of us, secure in our bed at night. Except there's three. I sometimes wonder, were you just for protection, Millie? Like back in Belfast, after Valhalla. I got you as personal protection for my sweet self. Now, sweetest Millie, I'm personally protecting you, even though you don't know it. You didn't know about Serpentine. But you'll know now. Oh yes, I expect you will. Anyway, fuck you – as I have done, my dear. Let's talk about me. I want to tell it, have it recorded for my own benefit, not like all those statements they have, secret, not for public consumption. That's a laugh. Public consumption. Not for anyone outside that little coterie. God, what a mess, my love. In the end, it's all down to love. It's love brings us here, screws us up. You have to deal with what it brings. Serp . . . one, two, three o'Leary. Four, five, six . . .

Sleep fled. Millie listened for a lot longer. A lot. She dozed off, woke with a start in the shaded sunlight of a forested afternoon. She went back to the MacBook, to the Serp file. *One, two three. An 'O' and an 'L'. Four, five, six.* It opened. After a while she looked at her watch, took the phone off charge, checked for reception – always good; there were masts all along the loch – and punched in the number she had always remembered effortlessly. Couldn't forget.

She and Clara ate dinner in almost complete silence. The older woman had an office – she called it a den – but Millie had never been in it, had never been invited in. Until now. After they'd loaded the dishwasher with plates bearing little sign of what they'd eaten – hot smoked salmon, some cold venison, rowan jelly, scalloped potatoes, no wine, just water – Clara stood up and beckoned her to follow.

The den was masculine, there was no other word for it. Clubby. Leather settees. Bookshelves. A Morocco-topped table, with both a desktop and laptop. An old-fashioned, very scarred, filing cabinet. Some souvenirs. A rug from Argentina. A Murphy's Stout advertising placard. Something that looked very like, and Millie very much hoped was not, a shrunken head. Possibly from Guatemala. Clara had been in Guatemala. Millie sat on one of the sofas, perched, really. Clara lolled in a heavy office chair and looked at her in silence for a while before she started to speak. 'Billy Boy. You remember Billy Boy? Not the generic term. A proper name.'

Millie started to shake her head, then stopped. Clara was fiddling with the laptop. A picture appeared on it of a heavy man, bald, or shaven headed, in a Crombie coat. Snapped unknowingly, a surveillance picture. Cold, black tie. Maybe a funeral. An old picture. He had that prematurely middle-aged look cops got, too much authority too young. And then it was coming back to her.

'Manderley? Like in Rebecca? Some kind of policeman?' She was remembering a figure on the fringes of her life Over the Water, someone who was always with other people, never introduced, seen flitting in and out of buildings she was flitting into and out of. Some kind of reputation. One you didn't want to know about. One it was better not to know about.

Clara gave a kind of grim snort. 'Almost. Manderson Manderley. Yeah, some kind of policeman. Rose through the ranks, token Catholic, played upon it. Made a joke of it. Had an image thing going: tougher than tough, rougher than rough, more bigoted than the bigots. Special Branch. Interrogation specialist. Resigned from the RUC just before the European Court of Human Rights stuff really hit home. After Stalker got fucked over. Vanished from the face of the earth.' Clara put on a pair of half-moon spectacles, peered over them at Millie. 'I'm not telling you this, my dear. You do realise that? You're not hearing any of this.' Millie nodded slowly. Clara took a deep breath, exhaled, checked something on the laptop. 'We . . . had cause to . . . refer to him. As in the United States of Amerikay-yay. Occasionally. He set himself up as a consultant. You know how we love private enterprise. Consultancies. There's always a budget for consultancies.' She scrolled through some pages on the screen. 'He did some, let's call it training work for us. More recently, he's been a bit more hands-on. Not just for us. This extraordinary rendition thing, flying of suspects all around the place. Experienced interrogators are hard to come by.'

'Jesus Christ, Clara.' Millie exploded, her face pinched with rage. 'What the fuck are you saying? Are you telling me the Americans got this Billy Boy to come to Inverness to interrogate Freya?'

There was a brief silence.

'Calm down. I said he did consultancy work. For anyone within his terms of reference. You think the Brits were innocent in all that lifting and questioning stuff? It wasn't just 9/11, you know. There were the London bombings, 7/7, 21/7, all kinds of things. Jesus, 21/7. Talk about a lack of PR advice! If they'd waited three days it would have been 24/7. Nobody would have forgotten that.' She shook her head. 'You needed the information as much as us.'

'I was out of all that. Never really in it. I was just doing close protection and observation at the tail end of the Irish stuff. We were living a quiet life.'

'Yes, I know. In Cornwall. Escape to River Cottage or whatever you want to call it. The girlie idyll. Hens. Bit like Valhalla without the frustrated, overachieving old bags, who can't leave well alone. Ever wonder why you moved to some godless ex-council flat in Inverness?'

'Freya said she missed the Highlands.'

'She thought you might be safer here, both of you. But there was another reason.' Clara looked straight at Millie. 'You know, don't you? If she didn't tell you, she must have left something for you, in case of my demise, that sort of thing.'

It was the word 'demise' that did it. Suddenly Clara was weeping, great gasping sobs shuddering through her frail body. Millie felt a wave of grief rising in her and reached for the older woman's hand. She gripped it, felt the brittle fingers. Gripped harder, felt them begin to crack. Clara's crying stopped. She fell silent. Millie squeezed harder.

'You knew, didn't you?'

'Knew . . . what?'

'Knew this was coming. You didn't warn her. Did fuck-all.'

Clara took two shuddering breaths, then spoke through gritted teeth.

'You stupid little bitch. You were her lover, you were her protector, you were supposed to look out for her. And where the fuck were you? You were out shopping. On your stupid little bicycle. You let yourself become her fucking lapdog, didn't you? I could have . . .'

Millie stood up, let go her hand. 'Yes, you could, couldn't you? But you didn't tell her. You didn't warn her.'

Clara began to laugh softly. 'I did. That's the thing. I did tell her. I told her Billy Boy had been contracted, along with some hired help, to find her, and to find Serpentine. Informally, of course. Billy Boy had his own agenda. That's what they were counting on. Serpentine's the big deal. But you know about Serpentine, don't you? Serpentine's what this is all about. Serpentine's what nobody wants to mention. A clean-up job. A crap British one, far too late in the day. Far too many tainted people.'

'Have you told anyone I'm here, Clara? Now you've got me in your lair, are you just going to turn me in to Manderley? Revenge for me taking Freya from you?'

Clara's mocking laughter had an edge of hysteria. 'You never took Freya from anyone. Or anywhere. Freya took you. That's what Freya did, always. She was a taker. Take, take, take. Loved for it, but not always liked. Was she still drinking as much? Stupid, I know she was. All that Chilean Cab Sauv she used to get through when she was out here. I turned her on to that, you know. Special sources. She came to visit when you were away, on your little trips. What was it, shopping? That's what you said. Not down to Glasgow to see your beloved Mark on his trips back from those little contracts of his? Oh, no, nothing like that, you unfaithful little cunt. She knew all about it.'

Millie didn't react, but she had to work at it. Those meetings with Mark, the chaste kisses, that one night in his Clydebank bolthole. She'd always come back, though. Freya had owned her, body and soul. Flattered her with her need.

'A mother thing, wasn't it? You and Freya? Your mother died, didn't she, when you were . . .'

Suddenly Millie had had enough. She flattened her hand back at right angles to her wrist and moved forward in a crouch, accelerating all the way. Using a fraction of the power in her right side, she hit Clara neatly on the jaw with the base of her palm. Her hostess cannoned backwards, her head narrowly missing a jutting bookshelf, colliding instead with the hefty spine of a handsome, leather-bound edition of Sir Walter Scott's *Tales of a Grandfather*.

Millie was on her in a flash, pulling her upright, slapping her hard on the cheeks, one-two, back and forth. 'I don't want to hurt you. And you've been trained to withstand worse than me. Worse than Manderley. Maybe he gave you the benefit of whatever evil shit he acquired along the way, I don't know. I just want to know how long I've got.'

Clara's gaze was unflinching, her eyes completely static. For a moment Millie thought she'd killed her. Christ, she was out of control. Then the woman spoke, her voice bleak.

'It's a hierarchy, like all intelligence systems. There are those at the top you never see, maybe they don't even exist. There are those further down the ladder telling somebody to use some black-bag account to fund Billy Boy and his gophers. Further down, there's a fail-safe, an official line of enquiry. Some hapless foot soldier who's only trying to do his job. Doesn't realise it all feeds back upwards in the end. Chain of command. Chain of knowledge, Millie. Anyway, there might be some cover there, at the bottom, with the foot soldier. He's a policeman. Detective Sergeant Zander Flaws. He knows about you, he's going to be looking for you. I left a message for . . . that would get to him.'

Millie used the simplest method of securing Clara – she pulled the hand-knitted Shetland jumper the older woman was wearing over her head, pulled her arms out of the sleeves and used them to knot her hands together behind her neck. It was crude, effective and probably ruinous to the jersey. Mark used to joke about knitwear like this, she remembered. Gansies, he called them. The islander in him, never buried too deep. Finally, she dealt with the older woman's feet. Clara was wearing an old pair of Reeboks, which she tied together using their own laces.

Millie looked at her watch, then skipped back to her room, where the packed rucksack waited. Her clothes were drying in the kitchen, over the bar of a lovely black oil Aga. She dressed, thanking the gods of Rohan again for the quick drying qualities of their fabric. The Meindls were damp but serviceable. Within five minutes she was heading up the narrow path that led into the old Caledonian forest, climbing steadily from the Loch. Access to Valhalla was not just by boat. There was a gravel track coming up from the power station access road and she was guessing the police, or Billy Boy, or whoever, would come that way. Clara was a liar, a very experienced one. She had no idea how much of what she'd told her was true. Or what the real agenda was. But Millie had to assume she had no time; she had to be prepared for pursuit, imminently. She couldn't think far ahead. For the moment, she knew where she was going. She knew about the other way in. She hoped he'd be there. She knew he would.

Murricane unlocked the third double-throw on the reinforced door to his flat, checked the hairs he'd left spittled in place over the hinges, found them undisturbed and pushed it open. The place was cool, oddly musty. The air conditioning was on a timer, but he suspected it had become polluted by some Cypriot bug. The cool dryness of the place had an overtone of soggy old Shetland knitwear in winter schoolrooms. Or perhaps that was just his imagination. He had a bundle of mail in his hand from the box in the lobby. He sorted through it quickly. Nothing of interest, except a postcard from Iraq. A friend working for Blackwater in the Baghdad Green Zone, doubtless doing close protection on senior American soldiers who didn't trust their own forces. Having a lovely time, wish you were here, it said. Very funny.

The answering-machine light was blinking. He pressed 'Play' and heard the electronic voice – female; in moments of drunken loneliness, he would sometimes talk to it, to her – he called it Rosetta. 'You have four messages.' Two were from Alexandra, bored, sounding annoyed, which was par for the course. At the moment, they were not lovers. Alexandra got jealous during their occasional periods of mutually assured lust, most of which coincided with her having split up with one of her much more suitable Cypriot boyfriends. There was work to be had, was the message behind the brief instructions to call as soon as he returned from what she called 'your holy day'.

One call wasn't a call, just a replaced receiver. And the other was from the deep, dark, best-left-unremembered past, the past he could barely help dredging through on a daily basis.

'Mark? Millie. We've had a bit of black on red. At my sister's, up by. If you can make it, be good to meet up. Soon.'

The message had been at 4 a.m., local time. After the fourth listening to that bitten-back voice, he switched on the PC in his study and checked out flights to Scotland. He checked his watch, heard the Rolex winder whirr as he moved his arm. What was it he'd told Millie? Like a heartbeat, or some such tosh. Kind of watch that lives while you live. Christ Almighty. It was 9.00 p.m. There was an Airtours charter to Prestwick with several spare seats leaving at 4.00 a.m.

Oh Jesus, Millie. Black was a fatality, red was pursuit. After everything that had happened, she expected him to come. What else?

A POLICEMAN'S LOT IS NOT A HAPPY ONE

A POLICEMAN'S LOT IS NOT A HAPPY

'Well, that was a fucking waste of time,' said Jim Smeaton. Technicians had proliferated like gerbils in the new model Highland offshoot of the of-course-much-more-important police forces in Strathclyde and Lothian. But Jimbo was a reasonably useful gerbil, for computer semi-illiterates like me.

'How's that, Jimbo?' I was on reasonable terms with Jim, having bought an old (which is to say, one year old at the time) laptop from him and subsequently having to pay him to sort it on three occasions. He had one of those vending machine business cards. It read 'Smeaton PC Consultancy'. Working for the safety and good of mankind and the greater forces of justice obviously didn't pay enough. But I already knew that.

'Fucking computer's completely zonked. Nothing on the hard disk at all, wiped clean as a whistle. No operating system, no files, nada. Kind of thing you get when a company needs to junk its computer stock, replace them with new stuff. They just run a wee program – there's dozens of them. *Scrubber*, *Wiper*, *Eradicator* – and then, *bada bing*, not a shred of memory left.' He grinned, a ghastly, sleepless games-addict's grin. Jimbo had tried to engage me, during one of his repair visits, in the glories and wonders of all-night interactive *Guild Wars*, *Total Warfare* or *Bioshock*, or whatever these online geeks did instead of sex, eating and drinking. I'd just looked at him as if he was some kind of alien life form. Which in a sense he was.

'Like a magnetic pulse, kind of thing?' I was floundering. 'Like why the Russians used to have valves in their MIG aircraft electronics, because nuclear pulses wouldn't knock them out?'

Jim fixed me with a pitying stare.

'No. It can be applied externally, or kinda self-inflicted. Lurks in the background, doing nothing as long as the correct start-up sequence is keyed in. Get that wrong, try to mess about, and it's goodnight Irene. Or someone could have just removed all the files. You need a portable hard drive, big enough to handle what's on the computer. Not that big in this case. Start up the program, it transfers the entire contents of the computer to your own hard disk, then wipes the original memory. You unplug and off you go, ready to zap through it at your leisure. Anything stored on CD or flash card wouldn't be affected, of course. But there's nothing here, is there?'

Jesus. You ask for a simple explanation and you get *War and Fucking Peace*, the Bill Gates translation.

'No, looks as if it's just music. No data as far as I can see.' I felt my use of the word 'data' made me sound quite the technophile. 'All right, Jimbo, thanks. Do you want to bag up the PC and take it away to see if there's anything more you can do?'

Jim stood up, shook himself. A small cloud of dandruff flickered into the shafts of late summer sunlight coming in the window. He didn't seem bothered by the presence of what I was now calling Freya Enderby, or the sour smell of death, which was dissipating slightly since the SOCOs had opened the windows wide. They'd dusted for fingerprints and looked, rather desultorily, I thought, for any other forensic evidence. I knew from long experience that there was no point in arguing with them. Now the whole place was filled with dust, blown by the breeze. The doctor wasn't going to be happy. Where the fuck was she, anyway?

'No, Sergeant, there's no point. The data's gone. One way or another, somebody's spirited it away. There ain't no ghost in this here machine. It's been exorcised.'

A North Sea wind billowed through the open windows. The angry slap of rough terrain trainers on concrete echoed through the open front door from the stairwell, a probable indication that we would momentarily have the pleasure of Dr Sheila Dartington's company and medical advice. I prepared myself for trouble.

'You fuckers,' were her first words. 'You careless fuckers. This is a sudden death, and you've got fucking *El Niño* blowing every shred of evidence around the place.'

'Calm down, Sheila,' said Grant. 'We're up to speed here, got all we need.

Taken the snaps, too, now that digital cameras have rendered photographers obsolete. Or crime scene smudgers anyway.' He waved what looked like a domestic compact camera in Sheila's face. 'Smile, darling. One for the fans.' There was a flash. I thought Sheila was going to hit him. 'Just thought we'd freshen things up a bit for you. You being such a sensitive soul and all.' He smirked, then glanced at me and looked pointedly out of the window. 'Maybe there's dodgy doings afoot,' he said, ruminatively, like something from a Victorian murder-mystery, 'but it's not going to be affected by a bit of a breeze. Maigret here might actually have to do some detective work for a change, instead of moping over his homeless old folks, the mummified mummies. Yeah, you'd find that a bit of challenge, Sarge, wouldn't you? Stop complaining and start finding things out?' Our eyes met. There was a bitterness there. I'd forgotten that he'd been friends with Salveson. Both into model trains or some such. The Black Isle business, back to haunt me like a bad Brigadoon.

'Freshen things up?' Sheila Dartington was in her 40s, not so much slim as desiccated through decades of dedicated Benson & Hedges consumption. She'd given up, melodramatically and with due public acclaim, a year before. Quite clearly, she was still missing them, despite the Nicorette gum she chewed incessantly. 'What's the fucking point of a pathologist if the aim in life of Scenes of Crimes officers is to blow away the cobwebs, add a little pleasant perfume to the average crime scene, make it a little more bearable for sweet wee Sheila? You pricks get on my fucking tits.' I'd never worked out if the Dartington schtick was a defence mechanism against the horrors she dealt with as a pathologist, day in, day out, or if she'd been like that all her life, a foul-mouthed bitch from hell. Foul-mouthed bitch from hell from birth seemed more likely.

'Sergeant? I expect better from you.'

'Cut it out, Sheila.' I nodded towards the body, towards . . . Freya. Freya. Freya, Freya, Freya. It was harder and harder to think of it as a person, as her. I looked out of the window. Ben Wyvis reared like Table Mountain, constant background to this part of the low Highlands. The firth was being rippled by a small, warm wind. That was the Black Isle over there, all green, fertile. Here in the Ferry, dust blew around the houses. In the flat, the smell had faded to a background garbage dump hum, a hot day at the landfill site. 'She's dead. And tortured and beaten. The exact nature of the wounds may give us a clue to known techniques and the deployers thereof.'

She snorted. '*Deployers thereof*? Is that some fucking rock band?'

'Just do your fucking job, Sheila,' I said wearily, 'and tell us what we already know, then fuck off. And then tell us something we don't know.'

Dr Dartington gave me a thin smile, exposing large teeth which had never been anything but smoker's yellow. And never would be anything but. She had the teeth of a wolf, in a large mouth, which always made me nervous, as if she was going to eat me up and swallow me whole.

'Charm still as devastating as ever, I see. Well, if that's how you feel about it, why don't you fuck right off, all of you, and leave me to my business. And shut those bloody windows, Grant, you bastard. That fresh air is playing havoc with my sinuses.'

'We were just leaving, matron,' said Grant. 'Lovely to converse with you once again about the finer things in death.'

'I'll speak to you back at the ranch,' I told Jim. 'I'll need some more detail for the report. Fergus – anything you can be bothered passing on to me, I will be, as usual, grateful. Nice to meet you, Watson. Or is it Crick?' The pimply assistant SOCO stared at me over his facemask. 'Dr Dartington, a pleasure, as ever.' She nodded grimly as I headed for the door. I'd need to watch the repartee. Sometimes that stuff just came out without me thinking about it. Watson and Crick, indeed. Wasn't Watson some kind of racist these days? Maybe he'd always been that. Too much exposure to DNA was morally risky, maybe. But not as morally dodgy as sex with Dr Sheila Dartington was, at least for me.

The thing was, I could never get that wolf image out of my mind. Sex with Sheila was wild, often scratchy and sore, and sometimes it felt like a sort of desperate struggle against opposing forces, an affirmation of life. Maybe both of us felt like that, not just me. I sometimes thought I was the great Satan in the relationship and all her struggle was against what I represented. That she resented, sometimes hated me. And given some of the things that had happened, maybe that's what I was. I had, briefly, got so near to death, I had almost become it. Possibly it excited her. You know that bit-of-rough thing you find with some highly intelligent, educated, bourgeois women? What form might it take with someone whose life was filled with the clinical analysis of the dead, with the reasons behind bodily decay? I suppose you either went for toy boy vigour in an attempt to regenerate yourself, or deeply and perversely into the dark side. I was grateful Sheila had taken the second option. Flattered, even.

Or maybe I was just complicating things. It was, admittedly, complicated sex. What had brought Sheila and me together in the first place was a common interest in – you could say, love for – motorcycles. I had messed around on two wheels ever since my teenage years, progressing through Honda 50s to insane Yamaha 250 two-strokes and settling down in my 30s and 40s to BMWs, as befits an elderly biker. Sheila was a latecomer, half-seduced in middle age, I think, by the leather and the chrome. She had a cut-down Japanese Harley clone, a Yamaha Dragstar 1100, having done a residential course and passed her test from scratch in a fortnight. I had asked if she'd ever seen Marianne Faithfull in *Girl on a Motorcycle*. She denied it. I bought the DVD and we spent an evening fucking to it in various bits of motorcycle leather, on her ox-skin sofa. It was squeaky and sweaty. Ever since, sex and leather had been, if you will, hand in glove for us. It was daft, immature. Surprisingly, it didn't seem to pall, though I knew it would in the end. Sex always does.

It was 24 hours after our verbal jousting match over the body of Freya Enderby. We were all calling her that by now. Information received, I would mutter darkly. Anyway, it came to pass that Sheila and I met up for copulatory purposes at her flat. Our 'arrangement' was usually as brutal as that, at least on the surface. I think we liked each other, enjoyed the cut and, well, thrust of conversation. We were clever, we were old, we were damaged. Enough in common to be going on with. And that's without even mentioning the job.

The job. The Enderby case was coming up stinking, absolutely reeking of Very Bad Important People. Enquiries into her past had drawn a series of very official-looking blanks, one or two of which Sheila had filled in. The torturer, presumably the same person who had killed her, was big, strong, right-handed and had probably done this sort of thing before. Forensics had shown that there had been more than one person in the flat, possibly as many as three. A witness had been found, an alcoholic dog-walker, who claimed to have seen someone, a man in the Volkswagen Polo that was registered under the name Smith at the Kennedy Avenue address. No one could find anything at all about Millicent. All I had in her case was that receipt. Freeman had insisted I drop everything else, all my forgotten and too-easily-forgettable old ladies and gentlemen, and concentrate on the case.

There had been a tense meeting in his office, which was an attempt at sumptuous that didn't come off. B&Q wasn't very good at sumptuous.

'Two women, two lesbians, and they seem to have arrived out of nowhere, left hardly any traces.' He drummed his fingers on the plastic-topped desk. 'I need to know where this Millicent person is now. I'm not so concerned as to backgrounds.'

'With respect, sir, backgrounds are crucial in finding anyone. I mean, why were they in the Ferry anyway? They could've been in bloody Madeira. Or Dingwall.'

'Listen, Flaws, don't patronise me. I'm under pressure here.'

'From whom, sir? To be frank, this thing smells all the way to fucking Wick, if you'll pardon my Caithnessian. It's got "spook" written all over it. We're blanked on these women's names, which I take to be a sign that my information is accurate: they are, in fact, Enderby and Fairweather. Passport office is coming up with "refer to HMG". You're being cagey. I've signed the Act, I've been to Belfast and back, you know that. Tell me.'

He swallowed hard. There was sweat on his pale, suspiciously plucked-looking brow.

'No, I can't tell you. There are reasons for that.'

'Well, why me, then? Aren't there younger, more vibrant, better dressed people who could be handling this?'

'You were asked for, Flaws, by name. Requested. More than that. I was told. Just you. Hinterland, somebody said, I can't remember who. You have the right hinterland. You know what that means?' There was a silence. I looked at his Mapplethorpe prints. Amazing what B&Q did these days. Over the Water, I thought. Over the Fucking Water. That's what the fucker's talking about. He wasn't talking about the Black Isle. He was talking about Ireland. He was talking about The Taint.

The naked-under-armoured-leather approach to sexual congress can present various hazards. And I was always nervous about fucking in Sheila's garage, actually on the specially lowered, quilted leather seat of her Dragstar 1100. True, she was slim, light, and she'd had the bike modified with a heavy-duty centre stand. But the risk of the Yamaha falling over and trapping one or both of us, half-undressed in Belstaff's finest, was never far from my mind. Distracting. Still, there had been no accidents so far.

Sheila liked music while she fucked, never too loud, but loudly enough, I suspected, to drown out any of her passionate yelps. It was just an ordinary garage, a walk-through from the kitchen in her detached villa. Her Hilton neighbours, in identical houses, were nice folk with kids and late model hatchbacks. It seemed unfair to disturb them.

That night it was beardie American Ray LaMontagne on the iPod, growling through a set of powered speakers; his second album, a near-classic among seduction records. Not quite in the Al Green class, but getting there.

It was difficult to take this kind of sex entirely seriously. But woe betide the Dartington lover who laughed. For her it was anything but humorous. And I was, if not happy, content to indulge her. We didn't speak. Half-naked, half-processed animal skin, slightly too cold, we coupled with a not entirely false ferocity. Soon enough, it was over.

And you'd have to be stupid not to see the connections, wouldn't you: it's bloody obvious, the sex-and-death thing, *la petite mort*? Jesus, it's like *Crash* or *The Atrocity Exhibition*, that Ballard stuff when he was mourning his wife and the world and writing about wounds, probing the biggest wounds of all. There we were, the two of us, half-naked beneath the slick, silicone-treated blackness of animal skin, draped across an instrument of injury and death, because that's what a motorcycle is, feverishly trying to create a union without necessarily creating babies, both of us beyond that, probably. A couple of damaged creatures in a frenzied search for pleasure, a grasping at life, the machine ticking away beneath us, the metal contracting as it cooled, because it wasn't right, it wasn't going to work, if she hadn't been out for a ride on the bike first, or at least had sat on it while revving it up in the garage: strap your hands across my engines, baby, that kind of stuff.

Sheila popped some Nicorette and shrugged herself loosely into an oversized leather jacket.

'You'll see the report tomorrow, once I get it properly word processed.' I wondered about the kind of woman who liked, post-coitally, to talk business. To talk death in appalling detail. 'Major trauma inflicted before and after death to the head and face. Probably died from cervical spine fracture. Fractures to both ankles and wrists. All fingers badly damaged by crushing. Christ, I could murder a fag.'

'Really?' Once upon a time I would have been unable to resist rising to something like that, unable to stop myself saying something like, 'Hey, I didn't know you were a homophobe,' or 'Surely murder's a bit strong? Slicing their goolies off would suffice.' But I'm cutting down on that wisecracking cop routine. I reckon police go for black humour because they've read books where cops behave that way. But the truth is, most of us haven't the wit for wittiness. We're plodding plodders. Plods. That's what makes us good at what we do. We take things slowly, we collect and examine the evidence, we come to conclusions, we fuck the pathologist. It's life and death, for fuck's sake. No place for prima donnas.

Carefully and partially zipped, I headed into the kitchen from the garage and from there to the downstairs bathroom. There was an en suite as well, of course. These days, there's always an en suite. When I came back, dressed in post-coital civvies, jeans, trainers, sweatshirt, all dark, Sheila was at the kitchen table, still leathered up, pouring herself a Lagavulin. Settling in for a night of drink, Nicorette and possibly more sex. Depending on my stamina. And my availability. And possibly the availability of the little blue pills Sheila kept for emergencies.

'I have to go out,' I said.

'No.' She swallowed a neat shot of cask-strength Islay malt. The peaty aroma of seashores and rotting feet spread through the garage. 'No. You have to go. Not go out. Just go. Get.'

'Fine.' I had my bike leathers in an Adidas bag. I hadn't felt like taking out the BMW tonight. Besides, I'd known I'd need the car. 'Look forward to the full report tomorrow, Dr Dartington.'

'If you're lucky, Sergeant. If you're a good boy.' She appraised me, coolly. I looked at that cigarette-lined face, that whiplash body, honed in gyms and her beloved Tae Kwon Do. Don't mess with this pathologist, boy. There had been a husband, once, I had learned, though not from her. Dead in some freak microlight accident, back in her native Fife. It figured.

'See you later, then.'

It was 10.30 p.m. I checked underneath the Escort, which was stupid, unnecessary and pathological behaviour. I'd learned to live with it. No bombs, which was always good. A bomb could really ruin your evening. Then I leaned over and felt cautiously under the front passenger seat. The sawn-off Mossberg side-by-side 20-gauge was there, Velcro taped to the seat frame, slick with gun oil and loaded. I assumed it was still loaded. I'd certainly loaded it before putting it there and it had been loaded a week ago when I'd last checked it.

Hand-packed cartridges, non-lethal, rock salt and coarse sand. Jo'burg load, one of my old RUC mates had called it. 'Good if you want to blind someone.' Carrying that Mossberg in the car was another bad habit I'd never rid myself of, something to do with a psychopathology I didn't care to examine. I'd never use it. Obviously. It was just good, necessary, for it to be there.

CALL DOCTOR SHOTGUN : : :

CALL DOCTOR SHOTGUN

The first time I fired a shotgun, I blew a hole through the nearside door of my father's Series 2 Land Rover.

Not that blowing a hole through any Land Rover door is particularly difficult. Unless we're talking about Discoveries and Range Rovers, upgraded for the use of Hollywood brats, plutocrats, aristocrats or, for that matter, plain old paranoid twats with too much money or covering government power. Diplomats, for example. Autocrats, acrobats, fatcats, proletariats . . . well, in the last case, only if there's a dictatorship involved.

It's true that an average 12-gauge, birdshot-loaded gun might not make much of a hole in bodywork belonging to one of the newer Discoveries and Range Rovers, the ones that meet the less demanding European safety regulations, possess heaters and luxuries such as airbags. And seats.

Old Land Rovers, the square, ugly, boxy ones, have flappy aluminium bodies bolted and pop-rivetted onto huge steel beams. Even the latest Defenders are built to the same basic '40s design and are so crude they don't, can't, have airbags. A colleague once joked that if you had a Land Rover, you didn't need airbags; you had other cars. He said it when the two of us were attending a grisly pile-up on the A82 near Fort Augustus, along with an elderly local doctor who'd spent far too much time dealing with the remains of drunk crofters pulled from rolled'n'wrecked Landies.

'Aye,' said the doctor thoughtfully. 'Actually, when a Land Rover crashes, you do have something instead of airbags.' He took a suck at his unlit, hand-rolled Gauloise; a stink of spilt fuel filled the Loch Ness-side air. 'Your frontal lobes.'

Our old Land Rover was Dad's pride and joy and he wasn't best pleased at having a fist-sized gap in the passenger door. I had been holding the gun at the time, a Laurona over-under-under 12-gauge, across my knees, pointing away from him. Single trigger, firing first the bottom, unchoked barrel, then the second, upper, choked one. Click-click. Easy to make a mistake, really, easy to press-release-press, reflex action. Especially for a child. But pointing away from Dad, towards the aforementioned crappy aluminium door. Which was really just as well for all concerned, especially Dad. It was loaded, the safety had never worked properly, there was a bump in the track leading down to the sea. And my eight-year-old fingers had crept under the trigger guard, as eight-year-old fingers will. I was John Wayne in *Stagecoach*, Napoleon Solo in *The Man from U.N.C.L.E.* Except all my uncles were seamen or crofters, with the exception of Uncle Larry, who was in Australia. Last heard of in prison for selling antifreeze to aborigines. In a territory with no frost. Click-click. Reflex action. Press-release-press.

The noise was extraordinary. Contained within the Land Rover's all-metal cabin (even the seats were sheets of riveted aluminium), it was like the end of the world. Twice. Both barrels, two holes, one bigger, one slightly smaller. Choke – the dispersal of the shot – makes little difference at really close range. Especially to Land Rover doors. The recoil staved my index fingers, scraped both my bare legs and thumped the heavy Spanish oak stock bruisingly into Dad's thigh. In the circumstances, it was a miracle the consequent swerve and thump into a handy ditch didn't perform frontal lobotomies on both of us. Seat belts? Be serious. The thing had plain metal benches to sit on, padded with raw fleeces stinking of lanolin. It was like something out of *Mad Max II*.

We swerved, thudded, stalled, stopped. Dad's ears must have been ringing as much as mine. I was too shocked to cry, just sat there, numb with horror at what had happened. Gently, he prised my sore fingers away from the gun and lifted it from my knees.

'Now then,' he said, thoughtfully, his voice, as ever, lilting and quiet. Quieter than normal, in fact, as I was half deaf from the noise. 'Let me see your hand, Zander.'

There were no recriminations. There was a visit to Maisie MacPherson, the district nurse, to have my staved and swollen fingers strapped. Afterwards, my father, his voice barely audible above the rattle of the ancient diesel, suggested that my mother might be happier knowing that I had fallen awkwardly chasing one of the ewes in the field above the shore. I had nodded, happy to be bound to him in a small conspiracy.

How did he explain the hole in the Land Rover door? I have no idea. Perhaps Mum didn't notice. Or maybe he smiled his slow smile at her and blamed a stray seagull, or a particularly frisky ram. At which she would have snorted with laughter, then turned back to her knitting, her Norman MacLean records, her Bible and her whisky. Maybe Maisie told her, later. But she never said anything to me about it. Nothing at all.

The first time I had a shotgun fired at me, a load of number three rabbit shot ripped through my uniform and tore a substantial chunk of skin and fat from my upper arm. The understandably nervous and, indeed, guiltily considerate bank robber wielding the weapon (a sawn-off Mossberg 20-gauge pump) had actually tried to scare me by pointing the thing to my left, but I had spoiled things by leaping sideways at him. Brave and stupid. Brave or stupid. Or just stupid. The previous night's whisky (cask-strength Ardbeg '73, the Gordon & Macphail bottling; funny how those things stick with you) probably hadn't helped. Gaelic courage. And it makes you bleed more. Thins the blood. I was much more of a drinker in those days. Much more of everything. Funnier, sharper, cleverer, thinner. Younger.

As I lay groaning, bleeding copiously all over Inverness High Street, the distraught robber, a hopelessly sentimental drunk from Wick called Sydney Obadiah Mouat, ripped off his stocking-mask, threw away his shotgun and, weeping, attempted to give me the kiss of life. Either that, or he had been overtaken by lust. I preferred to think it was the former. I still remember the reek of Trawler Rum through his stocking-mask. Trawler Rum, not Stewarts, not Morgan's. I knew that smell, that taste. I used to have a cultivated palate. And it didn't go well with the Ardbeg, either. You should never mix your drinks. At any rate, he was still holding me like he was Gable and I was Leigh when some of my esteemed colleagues arrived and arrested him. He was done for armed robbery, attempted murder commuted to assault with a deadly weapon and a separate charge of assault. Though that was dropped in a plea bargain, as the procurator fiscal later told me. 'It was an Inverness kiss, no' a Glasgow one. Nae tongues.' Lawyers. They're hilarious.

Eventually, someone remembered to call an ambulance and thus my arm, not to mention my life, was saved. I received a Commendation, nearly got the George Cross (but not quite) and within the year had my application approved for a move to CID. Where I reside, uneasily, to this day. Sydney was still in Porterfield Prison, happy, I think. Ever since, he has sent me a Christmas card with the word 'sorry' scrawled in infantile letters across it. I do not reciprocate. The three kisses at the end, after his name, always bring back the taste of rum and make me feel queasy.

The second time someone fired a shotgun at me, everything changed. It happened on the Black Isle. But maybe you guessed that.

I was a sergeant, still relatively sharp, on the up and up. All was well in the pre-National Scottish Police Force days in our beloved old Northern Constabulary. I was heading for inspectorhood. I thought I was fucking Dashiell Hammett. Well, not actually fucking him. I had ambitions to be him, or one of his whip-sharp characters with their cynical verbals. I was a cop who'd write the crime book to end all crime books. Or be in it. I'd out-Chandler Chandler, because I really had walked those mean streets of . . . Inverness. And Dingwall. The man firing at me was, according to information received, or half-absorbed, called Ernest MacIsaac. He was a depressed Black Isle farmer. As such he was certainly not alone – most Highland farmers have periods when they are less than cheerful, normally when Brussels sheep subsidies are late coming through and they can't make the payments on their Toyota Land Cruisers. Personally, as the son of a crofter, I'm not particularly enamoured of farmers. Ah, you may ask, what is the difference between a crofter and a farmer? Well may you ask. It's about land tenure. Crofters are smallholders with extra historical chips on their shoulders. Farmers are bastards, obviously.

Anyway, there are precious few crofters in the Black Isle, which, as I've already said, isn't an island at all, but a large lump of very fertile, very valuable land separated from the rest of the Highlands by two small firths – the Beauly to the south and the Cromarty to the north, both offshoots of the much bigger and bouncier Moray. It's good soil for trees, oats, barley and grass, both edible and smokeable. And for housing. The flat, thudding bang of the shotgun being fired (this was a big beast, a 10-gauge, as it turned out, with the cartridges loaded for deer) was followed by the weird, whooshing whine of the shot passing over my head. Only just over my head. I had dipped below the dry-stone dyke that marked the southern garden boundary of MacIsaac's farmhouse seconds previously, having shouted through an electric loudhailer the immortal words: 'Now, Mr MacIsaac, I'm Zander,' which is what they teach you in hostage negotiations skill module three at Tulliallan Police College: 'Establish personal intimacy at the first opportunity. Show respect for the suspect, address him formally, but offer him yourself.' The instructor, a civilian psychologist, had seemed nonplussed at the ribald laughter that had broken out when she read out this statement. A large, gel-spiked DC from Strathclyde somewhere (probably the industrial boondocks by the look of his cheap Slater suit) had said, loudly: 'What, d'ye mean shag them, oral or jist phone sex?' It had not been the most illuminating of courses, but then, most of us were drunk or hungover the entire time. Help! Murder! Polis! Michty, gie's a drink! As they no longer say in Auchenshoogle.

'Fuck,' said Detective Constable Batley, my then right-hand woman and occasionally obtainable fantasy figure. It was a black tights thing. 'He must know you.'

'No, I don't think so,' I said. 'Mind you, Zander's quite a common name in Sutherland. Short for Alexander. And being a Black Isle Ross-shire loon, he could have an anti-northlander streak. Celt versus Viking thing.'

'Or maybe he bewares Greeks bearing loudhailers.'

'Whit's this? A classical education? Help ma boab!'

'Or maybe some Sutherland Zander shagged his favourite sheep one time and he's been jealous ever since.'

'Dairy farmer.' I looked at the crushed sheaf of paper in my hand, now mud-spattered. 'Mid 50s, wife's been shacked up with a feed salesman in Dingwall for the past three weeks. Cows, that is. Animal and human.'

Fiona regarded me balefully. She hadn't noticed the streak of mud that now adhered to the left of her two prominent cheekbones. She must have hit the deck as hard as I had when McIsaac fired. 'It was me,' she said, 'that gathered that information from the local sub-postmistress. I know he's a dairy farmer. I knew that FIRST . . . sir! And frankly, referring to women as cows is pretty lame stuff in this day and age. Sir. Sergeant, sir.'

'DC Batley, I thank you. I take back the cows. And pray keep your urban Invernessian humour to yourself. We rural types are sensitive when it comes to sheep. Some of them are very dear to us.' Add sex to the mix and I was ready to talk like Al Pacino in a very bad gangster movie. Say goodnight to the bad guy, as Tony Montana would have it. There was another bang and the sound of shot, this time rattling off the wall. 'Alone in there, you think, Fiona? No bairns, neighbours, hostages of any sort? Wife safely tucked up in the feed salesman's love barn?' She nodded and shrugged at the same time.

'Far as I know, we're clear of bystanders and potential victims. No reports of anyone else. There's an old drunk helps with the cows but he's slumped in the snug at the Crown Hotel in Rosemarkie, or was half an hour ago. Nuke him if you want, sir. Call in an air strike with a clear conscience.'

I sighed. Sometimes Fiona was a little hard to take. But I had to admit, this was a somewhat tense situation. And anyway, so was I. Somewhat tense, that is. I was conscious of a desire for a cigarette. And I had never smoked, back then. Well, not much. And then only drugs. But that's the problem with smoking joints, really: the tobacco. Hyper-addictive, legal and very expensive, plus it kills you. But not quickly. High turnover over a long period of consumption. The perfect capitalist drug. Later, of course, I took up smoking B&H with a vengeance and then struggled to give them up, all in the space of six months. It was a kind of penance.

'Where the fuck is fucking Firearms?'

'You mean the Mobile Armed Response Unit?' Fiona shifted slightly. 'I believe its arrival may be imminent.'

There was a thunder of heavy breathing and then a thump behind me as a large body threw itself down into the grass. I turned to look at what appeared for all the world to be Robocop's slightly slimmer cousin, a bandoliered and body-armoured figure in an unbadged forage cap, clutching a Heckler & Koch semi-auto.

'Zander, you bastard,' came a breathless voice. 'Have you been shagging his sheep? Or his wife? Again?'

'*Sergeant*, have you been shagging his sheep or his wife,' admonished Fiona. 'Where's your sense of rank, Inspector, sir?'

I regarded Inspector Philip MacCalman, firearms officer, sternly.

'Is this it, Phil, sir? Firearms Unit usually implies more than just one run-to-seed copper with a burp gun and a flak jacket? I'd have been better calling up the Inverness Archery Club. They wouldn't have made as much noise. Or maybe the Phoenix Bar Darts Team. Sir.'

'The whole point of firearms officers is to make noise, Zander.' Phil wiped spatterings of Black Isle mud from his face with the back of his hand. 'We make noise, we shout, we fire our guns in the air, we scare the living shit out of shotgun-wielding farmers, they surrender and everyone goes home happy. Except the farmer, who goes to jail or psycholand.'

'Or else you shoot the farmer dead,' muttered Fiona.

'Or else we shoot the farmer dead and everyone gets suspended on full pay for months while there's an inquiry, which isn't too bad. And you lose the right to ever play with machine guns again, which is bad. Because, as you know, Sergeant, most of us hair-trigger boys are stunted adolescent gadget freaks who get our sexual kicks from polishing our barrels. So to speak.'

'Right enaaaafff, sir,' said Fiona in her version of an extreme Invernessian drawl, allegedly the result of interbreeding of local Highland women with Cornish soldiers in Cromwell's invading army. Not by Fiona personally, but oh, a number of years ago. I poked the loudhailer cautiously above the dyke and spoke into the microphone.

'Mr MacIsaac, this is Zander Flaws of the Northern Constabulary, Chief Inspector Zander Flaws. I'm here to help you.' There was silence. Or what passes for silence in the vicinity of a farm. Cows mooed, hens cackled, the wind sifted barley and grass, and Phil MacCalman noisily chewed gum. Juicy Fruit, by the smell. Memory and aroma are profoundly connected they say. Even now, every time I catch a whiff of Juicy Fruit, I think of Phil. 'I wonder if we can have a wee conversation, Mr MacIsaac, just the two of us?'

There was another shotgun blast, this time, muffled and clearly coming from inside the house. Phil and I were both instantly up and running, silent, apart from Phil's emphysemic puffing and despite his recent explanation of the essential noisiness of 'T-Hs', or Trigger-Happies, as we gunless cops called our armed colleagues.

The house was a '60s monster, poured concrete, ugly and shabby, but large. Like a child's drawing of a house, two windows up, two down, big front door in the middle. We were being foolish, I knew. Everyone said the essential thing in a siege was to wait, wait, wait. But that last gun blast had reduced our options considerably. Any unknown hostage could be bleeding to death. Reason had gone out the window. I have to say, I liked that feeling. That adrenalin rush, that heedless, hunter-killer, gatherer-rescuer, entirely male set of reactions. That would be why Fiona hadn't come with Phil and me: she was a woman. She had brains that actually controlled what she did or didn't do.

Reason, to be precise, had gone, not so much out of the window as through the door, which was slightly ajar. I cannoned into a hallway piled with tattered oilskins and old boots, muddy, unkempt. I could smell blood, shit and cordite. That abattoir aroma.

'Back, Zander, let me through,' ordered Phil. I let him do his Tom Cruise (only taller – but then, isn't everyone?) impersonation as he Mission Impossibled his way onto the floor and then through the doorway on our left, knocking the door wide with the H&K and then squirming through, astonishingly quickly for such an unfit lump of a man. It's amazing what watching all those movies can do. I remained flattened against the left-hand wall. Waiting for what seemed like minutes for Phil to say something, for more gunfire, for . . .

'Clear, Zander. Call in Fiona and the cleaners. It's a mess in here, but pretty much as you'd expect.' My radio crackled.

'Sir, are you all right? Do you need support? Armed Support backup team on its way.' Hell's teeth, they'd be blasting in here with live rounds and twitchy digits any second. Thank God for Fiona. Calm, confident, controlled. Most of the time.

I flicked the radio to multi-channel, noticed my fingers were trembling, and began bellowing in a calm, confident and completely out-of-control way.

'All secure, Fiona. Stand down firearms. Repeat, stand down all armed support. Suspect down, repeat suspect down. Paramedics at the double. All officers fine. Unharmed, repeat unharmed.' Then I went into the room, the stench of burnt powder and blood getting weaker as my sense of smell accustomed itself to it. Amazing thing, the nose. Juicy Fruit, Cordite, burnt bone, seared flesh. Rot, decay, shit. All the memories locked in.

MacIsaac – at least, I assumed it was he – had done a Hemingway on himself, sticking the shotgun (a rather nice Holland and Holland, I couldn't help noticing; but a 12-gauge, which was weird. I could have sworn the load whizzing over my head had been bigger) into his mouth, holding the barrel securely with both hands, and pulling the trigger with his . . . both shoes were on. That was odd. I was sure it had sounded like a bigger gun.

'So . . . suicide, then?' But there was something wrong. I was thinking about Hemingway, about the fact that he'd had bare feet, or a bare foot, because to pull the trigger you needed . . .

'Stating the bloody obvious, aye,' said Phil, who had picked himself up from the floor and was looking decidedly grim. 'See it all the time. Same old same. They mean it if they use a shotgun. Nae cry for help that, eh?'

'They mean it if they know what they're doing with guns,' I said. 'Shotgun'll kick right up, give you a frontal lobotomy or just a serious haircut. You've got to hold it in place.' It looked as if MacIsaac had known what he was doing all right. And meant it. The upper part of his head was a bloody, bony splatter on the wall. The blast had blown the kitchen chair he'd sat himself in over backwards, leaving his essentially headless torso sprawled clumsily on the chequered linoleum. The smell. I knew it would stay with me. It always did. That and the absolute lack of dignity. And the feeling that . . .

There was a shuffle from the stairs, then a blinding flash and the thunderclap smash of a shotgun. Big gauge. Phil spun backwards, a gout of blood coming from his unprotected neck. A small woman came into the room, squat in a faded Barbour jacket, short grey hair in a Presbyterian bun. She was raising the barrel of that mammoth 10-gauge, which had been shortened, I noticed, presumably so she could cope with the weight.

'Aye, nice balance,' said what I could only presume to be Mrs MacIsaac, reading my mind. Or maybe I'd been shouting. My ears were ringing. I could barely make out what she was saying. 'Ernie did it himself so I could take off the pigs. Didn't think he'd end up being taken off himself, but then what a pig he made of himself. What a swine, truffling and snuffling away wi' yon slut from the Tribulation Croft. I wouldnae hae been so vexed, but to be so brazen.' Abstractedly, I thought, she fired the gun again. There was a scream from behind me and to my left. Jesus Christ.

'Fiona? Fiona, don't . . .' But there was only a bubbling moaning sound. And nothing from Phil at all.

'No, she wasnae Fiona. She was one o' they white settlers, wi' a posh name, Gwendoline or some such. Fiona's a fine name.' I dived for the gun. Two shots, she hadn't reloaded. But it was a pump action, an illegal five-shot. As I made my move I heard that incredibly scary racking rattle. Dear God. Time slowed down as I grabbed, stupidly, for the barrel, missed and we fell together in an orgiastic jumble of limbs. The shotgun roared, deafening me. But no pain. The squirming little body beneath me went limp.

The end result was this: two dead, one severely injured, retired on medical grounds. Phil bled to death, half his neck torn away. Fiona had part of her left arm blown off and injuries to her lung, but survived. She's living in

Dumfries now, on the compensation. Or Dundee. I forget. Mrs MacIsaac, deceased, with her head smashed on a stair tread, untouched by that final blast of cordite and buckshot. And me? Uninjured, a pariah in the police force for the rest of my life. Bad luck, bad vibes and, the inquiry found, bad policeman. Never mind any small past glories, the stuff Over the Water, not getting shot. Stuck at sergeant. Mouthing off about this, that and the other, depressed, depressing to be around finally, sectioned off in the department, the cupboard of lost causes. Because I was one.

None of which has anything to do with me keeping a sawn-off shotgun in the car. Or not much.

THE FURTHER NORTH YOU GO

Prestwick was a down-at-heel remnant of transatlantic travel's lost past, with a statue of Elvis Presley and a café named the Graceland Grill. It was here, in 1959, he learned, that Elvis's feet made their only contact with British soil, while he was in transit back to the USA from his army service in Germany. One for the money, thought Murricane, two for the show.

The flight, from Larnaca, had been packed with blotchily-burnt package tourists, fair Celtic skins ravaged by Mediterranean ultraviolet. Skin cancer a certainty for some, he thought. He'd already had two moles removed, neither malignant, thank God. An Australian SAS major he'd met in Kabul had laughed at his concern. 'Save your own skin, mate! Back home, malignant melanoma's like the fucking flu, man. Maggie Mel, they call it. You live in the sunshine, you pay the price.'

It wasn't sunny in Ayrshire. A fierce Atlantic wind blew in over the golf course – Prestwick, or was it Royal Troon – as he waited on the platform for the Glasgow train. This coastline was one big golf course, he remembered, all the way down to Turnberry. He had a small rucksack he'd taken onboard the ageing Airbus as hand luggage and his thin Rohan jacket wasn't coping well with the weather. He shivered; he needed to get to Clydebank.

It would have been easier if he'd managed to get a flight into Glasgow Airport proper, what they used to call Abbotsinch, just outside Paisley. Instead, he had to get a train from Prestwick to Paisley, which wasn't too much of a problem, and then a taxi over the Erskine Bridge.

The garage flat in the garden of the big detached house off Dumbarton Road hadn't been broken into or vandalised, thanks to the security cameras and sensors which protected the main property, a photography studio. The garage and flat were rented at a very reasonable rate from a man only ever called Eggy. Egmond. Funny how some people got nicknames and some didn't. He was ex-regiment, now into photographic portraiture. Nothing dodgy, Eggy had assured him. 'Art, mate. Fuckin' art.' The beautifully-framed stills that adorned the building were impressive, but straightforward commercial fare. He could remember some of the furtive snaps Eggy had taken during their tour together in Iraq-the-Second. The infamous Abu Ghraib torture pictures had nothing on what Eggy had captured.

'This kind of stuff, mate,' Eggy had said. 'It's boys cuttin' the legs off baby crocs just for fun.'

'It's because they're afraid.' Murricane hadn't taken photographs, didn't want to remember. 'Who was in this sector anyway?' He, Eggy and a corporal called McGlynn had been on their way back to commmand with some lead-sealed boxes they'd been told not on any account to open. Or lose.

'Don't know. Don't want to know,' said Eggy. 'Otherwise, I'd have to kill them.'

It was a joke, Murricane was almost sure.

There was time. His instincts were to head north, but he had a timetable of sorts and rushing might leave him dangerously exposed, thrashing about waiting for contact. He had learned to rest when he could, eat when he could. To take all opportunities. Preparation was sometimes doing nothing. Acclimatising.

There was no landline in the flat and, while the two Nokias he kept there were charging, he walked to the local Indian takeaway and ordered the full Glaswegian Bangladeshi gut-buster – pakora, spiced onions, nan bread, mutton vindaloo and fried rice – and picked up a couple of bottles of Staropramen to go with it. Then he sat in his attic, gazing out of the window at the jets landing and taking off over the river, feeling the familiar burning sensations, the prickle of cold Czech lager. His mind slowly emptied in the rise and fall of the landing lights, the afterburner's faint roar, the settling of the heavy, spicy food. Afterwards, he dialled a number both phones had etched into their simcards. There was the faint chatter and whine of electronic screening, and then someone breathing. Whoever was there said nothing.

'Is Old Fettercairn there? I'm calling on behalf of the Bunnahabhain Memorial fund.'

There was the sound of a throat being cleared, and then a male voice, neutral.

'We only support the Lagavulin and Bowmore charities. Hallo. You are now domestic. Please remember that. Domestic.'

Mark coughed. 'Any . . .'

But the connection was cut. Murricane sat and looked at the aeroplanes, the phone in one hand.

There was still no sign of Eggy next morning when Murricane left Clydebank. The photographer had a flat in the west end of Glasgow, a boat at Helensburgh, a private aeroplane at Cumbernauld Airport and, the last time they had talked, four steady girlfriends in west-central Scotland alone. Success, thought Murricane. It was early, before the rush hour traffic into Glasgow, and anyway, he was heading out of the great Clydeside conurbation. A raid on a 24-hour hypermarket, just one of the massive retail developments that had replaced almost all the redundant heavy industry of this old shipyard town, and he was ready to go, the old Volvo 240 estate – it had started first time – rumbling like the Swedish thoroughbred it was. He felt secure in the car, despite its age. The back was better than a tent, though he had a bivvi bag packed into his North Face rucksack, along with clothes, sleeping bag and the one or two other pieces of equipment he thought he would need. Tools. He kept a small selection of tools locked in a steel-lined cupboard underneath the garage apartment's stairs. Tooled up, then, that's what he was. He remembered that Scots law had been changed so that there was an automatic five-year prison sentence for anyone caught in possession of a firearm. And something like two years for a knife with a blade more than three inches long. As he drove north-west towards Loch Lomond into a morning that was lush, golden and heather-purple and blue in a way that couldn't help but lift the spirits, he laughed. Scotland. It had its own parliament these days. Maybe it could legislate the weather. Maybe it could save Millie from whatever was pursuing her, if she was alive. But he rather thought the Scottish Government, as the nationalists liked to call it, might find that a little beyond its remit.

Or maybe she was already dead. He wasn't thinking of that, though. He was acting, moving, doing. But as he drove, the bastard thoughts kept crowding in.

Ireland had been his thing, the tail-end, really, but it was where he'd made his bones, cut his teeth, killed his first terrorist. Or civilian, if you listened to the Provoganda. It had been a place to learn, mentored by the old hands who had been there in the '70s and '80s, the ones who had seen it all, seen too much, done too much. A place to be frightened, really frightened. Not like in the drills, the exercises. The real deal, terrified in some fucking housing scheme, just like home, but not quite.

By the time he had made it into the regiment – second attempt, his first training exercise scuppered by an ankle injury he couldn't shake – the smell of peace was in the air. But there had still been a lot of work to do, maybe not as dirty as it had once been, but some nasty bits and pieces, nevertheless. Tedium, of course, the endless, sweaty hours and days cooped up in the forward bases, Crossmaglen, Coalisland, wherever. And then the throat-paralysing terror of plain clothes patrols undercover in cars and worse, out of them, sauntering down through the badlands, among the women with their prams and the children and the bad bastards you couldn't recognise, not always, sometimes never. Browning or Glock sticking down your arse most of the time, wired up for sound, hoping it didn't give you away with a squawk of static or howl of feedback. He remembered that time it happened to Freddy and how three women in Armagh got hold of him, a big Scouser, nails and teeth and heels, and he didn't pull his gun. They got a car in and pulled them off, but not before he'd lost an eye. And there had been a Woolworths and a Ladbrokes just down the road. It was fucking homeland stuff.

Some good things had happened, too. Despite the shite, the sheer un-remitting brutality of it, that overbearing burden of history, he had liked Ireland, liked many of the people he'd met. Loved Millie. Respected . . . disliked Freya, and then hated her, of course, the bitch. Now she was dead and he wasn't sorry. It had to be her who was dead. He knew it was. Otherwise Freya would have taken charge, kept him right out of the picture, no question.

He was in it now, though. Whatever it was. Millie's message. The meeting place was interesting. Somewhere only the two of them knew. 'Up by.' She had given him time, too. There was no point in rushing headlong. He needed to get there. But he needed to get back in touch with this landscape, which was nearly home. Nearly, but not quite.

The 240 was a Torslanda model, modified by Volvo for Arctic conditions and he'd tried to keep its various cold weather accessories, all of them ageing, working. The heated seats were a joy for someone easing his way back into the frigidity of a Scottish summer after the brutal heat of Gaza and the Mediterranean bakehouse that was Cyprus at this time of year. He wallowed in the womb of Swedish motorised protection as Ben Lomond loomed to his right, across the Loch. At Tyndrum he felt the familiar thrill of recognition, the tug of the far north as the true ferocity of the Highland landscape began to kick in: Rannoch Moor, a great tundra, a steppe, a desert of bog. Then, the overwhelming, doom-laden power of Glencoe.

The two-litre engine, 200,000 miles up, showed no sign of its age, as the Volvo corkscrewed past Kingshouse and across the Ballachulish narrows. He stopped in Fort William, eating mush heavily and deliberately at the Nevisport café, adding a few accessories at the absurdly well-stocked outdoor shop underneath: a better, full-colour GPS navigator, some instant packet food he hoped he wouldn't need, methylated spirits for the Trangia stove. Chocolate. You could never have enough chocolate.

He took the Inverness road, entering the massive geological fault called the Great Glen, the 100-mile rift connecting the west coast with the east, a spillage, between mountains, of long, thin lochs connected by Telford's Caledonian Canal. He branched off the main road towards the Commando Memorial at Spean Bridge, stopping to pay a few moments' quiet tribute before the rather too chunky statue. Then he drove back to the Aonach Mor turn-off and parked the car among several hundred others, many of them sporting empty bike racks. The cable car here carried skiers to the diminishing snowfields in winter and, in summer, mountain bikers raced each other towards broken necks and spines on one of the most dangerous downhill tracks in Europe. Climbers and walkers, too, used the car park, which was patrolled regularly by staff whose job it was to check for vehicles left too long without explanation. To allay any suspicions and stop anyone getting excited, Murricane followed climbing tradition and left a note on the windscreen, stating that he was wild-camping overnight and giving a fictitious mobile phone number. He left one mobile in the car, switched off, and took the other. He repacked the rucksack, including the GPS and the meths, and locked the secure compartment below the spare wheel after removing the small collapsible Austrian crossbow. William Tell, eat your fucking heart out. He laced up his Raichle boots and set off, feeling the prickling rub of the straps on his shoulders, the pleasure of moving off into the wilderness alone, balanced by concern for Millie. How long did he have now? He glanced at his watch. Make it ten hours.

The deer came, as he'd known it would, driven away by the younger stags, gouged and bleeding. Defeated, old and seeking shelter. He could smell it, the rank odour of a male red, coupled with something else, something darker, deeper.

He'd excavated a shallow pit among the roots of serried sitka spruce, dug himself in. Now he was invisible in the sterile dimness of the commercial woodland. The ground beneath the tightly packed trees was brown and bare, except for pine needles and the occasional hardy weed. The acidity of this kind of desperate, cynical forestry killed everything else off. Now he was wearing dirt-camo face paint and very light, German surplus, Gore-tex waterproofs. But he'd carefully brushed loose dirt and pine needles over himself as he settled in for what turned out to be just five hours. He'd smeared himself with the fresh urine of the does he'd disturbed earlier, watched the old stag fight its last desultory skirmishes, and then prepared a welcome.

Murricane could tell that the animal was a curiosity, a character. He'd bet the local gamekeepers had a pet name for him. Archie or Hamish or Prince Charlie. Not Bonnie though. The other one. His ears stuck out and he was mangy, going bald. He stifled a laugh. Not that any of the royals would ever stalk on this estate, this hard-managed, Arab-owned stretch of several thousand acres. This was a mix of ever-expanding commercial forestry and some occasional bouts of erratic, inebriated shooting by the sinning sheikhs and their guests. All secondary to the sex and drinking in the restored, hardly-used lodge. He didn't know if the other stuff still went on. The things that had brought him here originally, all those years ago. Probably not. Probably they'd found somewhere else, by now. Somewhere more suitable for the 21st century. He had come to reacquaint himself with the earth, the trees, the place that was Scotland. Shrug off the desert sand and submerge himself in peat bog and pine.

In his fantasy life, he considered himself strictly a 1900s sort of guy. Favourite decade, probably the '20s, just as long as he wasn't poor. Ever since reading *The 39 Steps*, *Greenmantle* and *The Three Hostages*, he'd wanted to be Richard Hannay, a rough diamond from the colonies . . . made good, cleaned up and at ease in every level of society. Heroic, tough, sensitive. Capable of surviving anywhere, an outdoorsman. Rich, adaptable, a pillar of society. A gentleman. For a wee boy from the Shetland Isles – clever, a bit wild, short attention span, good with his hands – it was an ambition that could only have half a chance of being fulfilled in the army. So he'd joined up.

Anyway, he didn't turn into Richard Hannay, rough diamond aristocrat, general and finally lord. Those were the days. You could say it wasn't real, that it was fiction, but Hannay's creator, John Buchan, was his own model. Son of a Presbyterian minister who ended up as Governor General of Canada, Lord Tweedsmuir. But such glories were not for Murricane. Instead, society had trained him to be a useful cog. In all kinds of unpleasant and dangerous machinery. And he'd grown accustomed to being useful. Used. Depended upon. Needed.

The stag was coming now. Cautiously, wearily. Driven by the need to follow that flicker of desire, the program to procreate, some genetic impulse. Even though it had been bested by the younger beasts, hurt, was probably arthritic and sore. He saw its great, stooped head emerge from behind one of the bare sitka trunks. And there it was, the cruel joke humanity had played on its pride, the final insult.

There had once been a little museum over in Torridon, painstakingly put together by a legendary old stalker. And he'd seen things, there, sets of antlers of immense grandeur and poise, and sick jokes like the one he saw before him now.

Young stags were curious beasts, attracted by shiny, highly coloured objects. And so, half-grown antlers were thrust through tins, broken bottles, bits of abandoned Tupperware, fertiliser bags, rolls of fencing wire, even. Sometimes, they got stuck and as the antlers grew, became permanently attached, the compressed solidified hair of the horn becoming entwined, almost merged with it. Until, as in this old beast's case, the dull white decay of old aluminium had almost become one with the horn and the head, like some kind of cyborg. Like a sort of royalty. A corroded, dying king. Monarch of the polluted glen.

It was something from a crashed aeroplane, he guessed. There were several scattered along the slopes of these hills, remnants of the erratic piloting skills of youngsters flying World War Two missions from the numerous airfields strung along the east coast. The Great Glen was still a favourite with jet jockeys from Lossiemouth or Kinloss, who would scream their Eurofighters between the hills, flicking them beneath the level of the roadway, leaving drivers staring into their flaming afterburners. Or it could be a bit of roofing, a slice of chucked fridge. Could be anything, he thought, as the stag drew nearer, and he raised the crossbow from its covering of dusty wood waste and pine needles and cones.

The animal still hadn't noticed him. He had set the Proctor sights for 10 metres or less and he was more or less at that distance when he pulled the trigger, 200 pounds of tension releasing the unbarbed bolt. Ted Nugent, eat your heart out. Eat your fucking heart out, you fake rock 'n' roll poseur, you. And yet he found himself humming in his head: what was that song on the first album? 'Motor City Madness'? Richard Hannay would have been ashamed.

Inappropriate, he thought. Absolutely and totally inappropriate. He watched the big old deer stop, falter down on its knees, the bolt embedded in its eye. A good shot, he registered the fact . . . and then he was up and running towards it, shaking the cramp from his legs and arms, drawing his Fairbairn-Sykes knife from its oiled leather sheath. Seconds later, he was behind the stag's head, pulling it backwards, the animal stunned and near death already, punching the double-edged blade deeply into its throat, Feeling the hot blood pulse over his hand. Then he was out of the way as the thrashing began and the blood sprayed around like some Peckinpah clip, only faster, much faster, flicking onto the dull greyish brown of the too-close tree trunks, the deer making strange, hoarse, gasping, snuffling noises.

Eventually, the rearing and shivering was over. The old wild spirit of the moors had fled and all that was left was flesh, bone, hair, and that battered, broken and waste-defaced crowning glory of antlers. Really, he should have gathered some of the blood, caught it in his hands. If he'd been serious, having to survive, he would have husbanded it, stored it for the days and nights ahead. That's what the instructors had taught him to do, on the XTS course that had first brought him here. Extreme Survival. They had been hard men, insistent on not revealing their names, older, some retired Falklands veterans. Years later he'd spotted one of them on television, some reality show that involved living on a tropical island. He was calling himself Old Joppa and looked as though he despised himself as much as the hapless celebrity wannabes he was supposedly training.

When he was teaching Murricane the lore of living off the land, he had drunk half a pint of fresh stag's blood, smacking his lips afterwards. And a fat lot of good it had done him.

Gralloching, the locals called it: the careful gutting and hanging of a deer. Murricane had no time or inclination for that. He tore the stag's chest open, cut out the liver and split it, checking for disease. Then he carefully wrapped it in the cling film he was carrying. It was useful for all kinds of things, including human waste disposal. The deer was too old for the traditional cuts of meat to be palatable without extensive marinating and that was something he didn't have time for. He left the rest for the ravens and golden eagles. With some difficulty, he retrieved the crossbow bolt, the charger. It was unbarbed aluminium with a carefully weighted point. They were hand-made and too easy to identify, though there were other things he could use. Had used. Sometimes you had to adapt.

He went back to where he'd left his rucksack, dug it out from its camouflage of broken branches. He felt a creaking stiffness in his bones as he dismantled the crossbow and prepared to leave, but a sense of connection, too. Of being in this place, this land. Moshe, David and the feverish, gritty brutality of Gaza seemed far away. The carcase would be pecked and gnawed for its sustenance over the coming weeks. A bit of pungent natural reality in this artificial forest. It had been a ritual, a preparation, and he felt stronger, better for it, despite the gnawing sense of age and decay in his own body. Drinking the blood, Old Joppa – who'd called himself Fred back then – he'd said it was something that American Indians did, absorbing the spirit of the kill. Maybe he should have knocked back a mouthful, just for the hell of it. But what he really wanted now was a whisky. Something like an Ardbeg, the '73 Gordon & Macphail bottling. Or perhaps, if push came to shove, simple old Powers Gold Label. Best blended whisky in the world. Biggest bargain. And so many bad memories. Blood and whisky, the cocktail of the gods. Back when he was a god, walking with gods, delivering life and death, that's what they'd drink back at base, locked in behind the wire, caged up until the choppers howked them up and away, or they howled their unmarked cars out at high speed, driving like maniacs.

He was back at the Volvo by dusk and, as the summer half-darkness fell, he was on the back road out of Fort Augustus, heading east along the southern shore of Loch Ness. He pulled into an unmarked forestry track, drove down it for a mile until he came to a grassy clearing with a ruined stone croft house on its western edge. When he switched the engine off, the silence was thick, like syrup, until he began to pick out the ticking of the cooling car, the scuffle and chirrup of a pine marten, the cooing of pigeons.

He built a small, virtually smokeless fire and let it burn down. He was roasting the stag's liver, wrapped in nettles, in the ashes, when Millie found him.

KATRINA AND THE WAVES

MacDougall finished flicking his fingers across the laptop's keyboard and, with a discreet whine, the portable hard drive connected to it ceased spinning.

'Nothing,' he said. 'Nothing but a pile of letters to Scottish Gas, some to whichever ruthless scumbag was renting them the flat, complaints to the Scottish Parliament for existing, some recipe downloads, some bits and pieces off the Internet. But the thing is they're all old. At least a year old. Must've used a time-sensitive erasure program. As I thought.'

Billy Boy was drinking, as daintily as his bulk allowed, a glass of red wine. 'So what does that tell us, darling boy? Has some cyber-bomb wiped all the juicy gobbets of information we desire from Freya's lovely computer? At Freya's behest?' He sounded slightly slurred, but this was his first and only glass of organic, fairly-traded South African Pinotage, an experimental purchase from the local shop, and a mistake. It was his way of relaxing, to let his speech disconnect from his brain. A conscious thing.

'Yes. Could be. A creeper, a program triggered by anyone not using the correct combination of keystrokes. But no, not necessarily.' MacDougall's soft lilt was more pronounced than usual. 'I mean, there could be something left, somewhere. Or even everything. Because this is . . . this could be a red herring. It's possible there's another computer. Almost definite, I think. I mean, how could they live in this day and age? Bad enough there was no broadband in the flat. Nothing, no wireless hub, no sockets on the walls. But then again, maybe they used an Internet cafe and kept everything on web servers thousands of miles away. Easy enough to do that. Just set up a Google Docs account and Rupert Murdoch's your uncle.'

'Oh, that's just dandy.' Billy Boy took another delicate sip at his wine. 'That's just hunky-dory. No news of Miss Millicent, nothing on the computer for which I, personally, had such hopes. And, of course, Miss Millicent was able to access her . . . what's the correct term? Storage facility. Bolthole. Stash.' He shook his head, a momentary flash of anger crossing his face.

They had reached the Keepguard secure storage units only to find them deserted, apart from Gussie Macdonald, the janitor, pished as usual. A split-second decision by Billy Boy had meant that money, not violence was traded for access to the locker used by Millie and Freya, but there had been no time to open the safe inside. Nor, for that matter, the requisite explosives. A description, by a suspicious drunk, only partly assuaged by cash, of the departing pick-up had been slurred and vague. They'd driven around for an hour or so and seen no sign of the fugitive truck.

'I place such faith in you, Seamus.'

MacDougall flushed. 'Sam, if you don't mind, or MacDougall. I can't be arsed with all that Gaelic shit.'

Billy Boy was on him in a second. 'Ah, ashamed of your proud heritage, dear boy? Tut, and, if you will, tut. I've read your file so many times I could recite it like the Lord's Prayer.' He sipped. 'And to my certain recollection you were once very active in the movement for a Greater Gaedhealtacht here in the Highlands of Caledonia. Sang in a Gaelic choir, appeared at the National Mod. Won a medal. Churchy, it says. Very Free-churchy.'

'That was before.'

'Before your service of Her Majesty? What dreadful effect did that have on you, that cost you your past? Sure, and many's the proud Hebridean boy who has marched off to war, muttering prayers in Gaelic or thinking of his darling.'

'Before I . . . sinned.'

'Sinned? Do you sin especially, in some particularly sinful sinning sort of way? I only ask as a boy from a broader church, one that offers forgiveness. Though I surmise that the Free Kirk also had that tool at its disposal. Couldn't be worse than the fucking Jesuits.'

'I sinned, and discovered I was uncalled, not one of the elect. One of the unelect.' MacDougall spoke soberly and factually, as if they were talking about the weather or the condition of local pavements. 'And after that, it seemed to me that I should put away those childish things and concentrate on the future. My future.'

'Which of course took you into my orbit, dear lad. And very useful you proved to be. Could still be. Your abilities on computers are matched by your trustworthy abilities in the infliction of pain. I always felt you modelled yourself on a greater master, namely myself, but perhaps there was an earlier model?'

MacDougall's steady expression didn't change.

'No, it was in me. That was the sin that I found in myself, that ability to hurt. The willingness to do it. The desire to do it. And grace could not touch me. There was no forgiveness.' His voice took on a sonorous quality, the sing-song rhythm of the psalms.

'Ah yes, I remember now.' Billy Boy took another swig of the wine. 'You know, this South African organic fairly-traded muck I'm drinking is . . . shite. So, you fucked the choirmaster's wife.'

'Precentor. Yes. He was comparatively young for such a post. She felt abandoned. Resented the place the psalmody had in his life.'

'What age was she?'

'Fifty. I was 16. When it all came to light, I was told in no uncertain times that I belonged to the Devil, that there was no place for me in the forgiven body of Christ. They forgave her, of course. He forgave her. He was a good precentor. A fine baritone. He had memorised three tunes for every psalm. I was really nothing more than a competent light tenor.'

'And so you left to join the army.'

'I did.'

'We should have talked before. All these years and we've never discussed your faith and its sad loss. The association with Gaelic was too strong for the language to survive in your heart with the religion, I take it?'

'That's correct.'

'And do you believe in predestination, then, Sam? That we, for example, were predestined to come back together after you left the army?'

'I do.'

Billy Boy smiled. 'And I do too. I mean, what's a little fire? You were nowhere near Stornoway when it happened, were you? Your poor paramour and her husband, incinerated in their home while abed and, one presumes, asleep.'

'Nowhere near.'

'Indeed. And let's keep it that way, shall we?'

'What had they to fear, anyway? They were forgiven. I had no forgiveness. Nothing but hell to look forward to.'

SERPENTINE

Billy Boy held up a single finger, waggled it from side to side. 'Lad, lad. Let's tiptoe out of these moral and theological minefields together, shall we? I merely muse on these things to let you know I care. And, more to the point, know and remember things that bind you to me. Loyalty. I am a loyalist, with a small "l". I repay loyalty. And I need to be sure of what we're looking for. So check that fucking hard disk again and then we're going to have to investigate your theory of the Mysterious Missing Computer. If you're sure it exists.'

'It exists,' said MacDougall. 'As sure as sin exists in this world.'

'Fine. But if you don't mind, make a few more checks.' There was a complicated knock at the cottage door, which led straight into the kitchen, a facsimile farmhouse affair in stripped pine. Sometimes it seemed as if IKEA owned the entire world, he thought. 'That'll be the victuals.' But he took a small modern Walther pistol from his trouser pocket before shouting 'Come in, the water's lovely.'

Hume's muffled voice came in reply: 'Aye, it's cold and clear.' Which meant he was alone and unpursued, and they could look forward to some very average Cantonese food for their evening meal.

They were renting a cottage in Findhorn village, the old seaside settlement which had spawned, like a spiritual rash, the Findhorn Community, a massive, New Age holiday camp that dealt in everything from witchcraft to water divining. It ran courses all year round for visiting seekers and dabblers. The current, month-long affair was called 'Men in Search of a Mighty Manhood'. There were little knots of males in all shapes, sizes and ages to be seen in the evenings, often bonding over spirits a great deal more tangible than the ones they were being taught to embrace during the day. But it meant that Billy Boy, MacDougall and Hume were almost invisible.

They had been there for three days, as MacDougall had fought with what he said initially was a surprisingly tough form of security coding. Now he was admitting what he had known for the past 24 hours: he had been able to take nothing meaningful from this computer. Either it was somewhere else, or it had been erased.

While he worked, Hume had taken a number of long walks on the seemingly endless beach, part of which was, he reported, reserved for naturists. Billy Boy had disappeared for most of the previous two days, reappearing at night. He made no calls on his mobile, as far as Hume could see, but he was probably talking to whoever he needed to when he was out and about.

106

Hume munched glumly on some bean shoots and pondered his attachment to the other two men. MacDougall and Billy Boy had met back in Belfast. They had struck up a partnership based on their common abilities in extracting information and inflicting agony. The two were not unconnected. Hume was simply a soldier of misfortune, a competent squaddie fallen on bad times. Or at least that's how he saw himself. Ireland, for him, had been a closed world, secret patrols, surveillance and endless hours in mud and grime. With the occasional terrifying outbreak of furious violence. He had tried to stay away from the MacDougalls and the Billy Boys. And look where it had got him. Obeying orders. That's what he'd learned to do. He had been a sergeant, full of pride and piss, until retirement. Too young, at 45. The move from security into mercenary work had been quick, easy and lucrative. Like most of the clean-hands guys involved, he did occasional favours for the spooks, passed a word here and there. And that was how this had happened. One of the Whitehall wankers had contacted him, asked if he would babysit – babysit, that was the word he'd used – 'a couple of freelances on a bit of a jaunt in Fiveland'. Which was worrying. The money on offer had been exorbitant, though, and it was semi-official, if deniable. Stuff for Six always was. The problem was the word 'Fiveland'. He was being asked to get involved in some kind of arm's-and-leg's-length operation within the UK, where Five, not Six, had responsibility.

'It's house-cleaning, old chap. All sanctions.' Christ, they still talked like that. And then it turned out to be Billy Boy and his boy, on a torture and killing cruise. Not that he was too bothered by that aspect. That was presumably why he'd been chosen. He was reporting back to the faceless men with the posh accents, Billy Boy was talking to someone else; and MacDougall, that psycho Seamus, was talking to God. He heard the muttering late at night. The big, posh God, who was dreadfully sorry, but couldn't save him because it wasn't allowed under the theological rules. Old Chap.

Hume was gathering up the fouled dishes while MacDougall sipped a Coke and Billy Boy stared unseeingly into the remnants of his lemon chicken.

'I have to go out,' the big man said, rising from the table with the fluidity of movement that always surprised Hume. Billy Boy was in his 50s, overweight, but carrying muscle where others had fat. He had the agility of a boxer. A boxer who had hit, and never been hit in return.

Hume locked the door behind him and returned to the table. MacDougall was still drinking the Coke in small, regular sips, swirling the sugary liquid around his mouth, squelching it through his teeth as if it were vintage claret. He never touched alcohol.

'Well then,' said Hume. 'How was it with the computer stuff?'

'Nothing,' said MacDougall. 'He wants me to check but there's no point. There's nothing. And I don't believe those two women kept everything in their heads. Nobody does nowadays. Not even people who grew up without computers. Either we missed something, or the young one had a laptop. Has a laptop. And they must have had some fucking Internet access.' The swearing slipped in and out of MacDougall's conversation in waves. Sometimes he sounded pious as a new convert; minutes later he could be cursing like . . . well, a trooper.

Hume continued to clear up. MacDougall made no move to help him. After a while, the door was rapped in a rhythm, which Billy Boy had insisted was from the opening bars of Katrina and the Waves' hit single 'Walking on Sunshine'.

'Leskovich,' said Hume.

'Bisexual,' came Billy Boy's voice. Hume let him in.

'Right, it's eight o'clock,' said Billy Boy, suddenly bustling and cheery. 'We'll give it four hours and then I think we'll take another look at Kennedy Avenue. A final clean-up, so to speak. I believe we have a wee weather window. Everything should have assumed a degree of clarity by then. The key, I am led to believe, will be under the mat. In a sense.'

'Fine,' said Hume. 'So we won't be disturbed.'

'No,' said Billy Boy. 'And we'll take all night, if we have to. We should be able to relax, in a way, by then. Assuming, of course, that the darling believer-boy here is correct and there's nothing in the lump of digital turgidity he has allegedly examined. So far, to no avail.'

'I'll have another look,' said MacDougall, 'but there's nothing there.'

'Well, assumptions are always worth challenging and checking.' The big man grinned. 'Assiduous, that's what I'd like you to be. Assiduousness, it's next to godliness.'

'After cleanliness,' said Hume.

'No, assiduousness. Cleanliness is overrated. You'll excuse me, boys, I must go and wash my hands.'

———◆———

KATRINA AND THE WAVES

They hugged for what seemed like a long time, felt each other's coldness, said nothing. Millie kissed the roughness of his neck, smelling those old familiar aromas – dirt, sweat – then cleared her throat. 'We should go. Now. Clara's been chattering to the wrong people.'

'I have the car. The Swede.'

'Jesus, you've still got that pile of shit?'

'Still goes. Where do you want to go?'

'We need to go north, even further north.'

'Not Shetland. Don't say . . .'

'Don't worry. Not quite that far. Too many fucking salmon farmers.' They both laughed. 'But first, I have an errand to run. In Inverness. There's somebody I need to speak to. Somebody I forgot.'

The sudden, brief Highland night had descended completely by the time they reached the Volvo. But Murricane could feel something stirring in the trees. The summer beginning to grow restless for fall. The limpid heat about to give way to something much more savage and elemental.

ZED'S DEAD, BABY

I parked the Escort two streets away from Kennedy Avenue, just the right side of the vandalism line, and crunched through the light showering of broken glass, used condoms and fag ends, to Mrs Enderby's close. The yellow chevrons of the incident tape fluttered in the cool breeze coming in from the firth. I could see the red and green flicker of riding lights from boats waiting to enter the Clachnaharry sea locks, the entrance to the Caledonian Canal. Seagulls wheeled and screeched, searching for sewage and carrion to feast on. Flying rats. I remembered as a young policeman stationed in Mallaig being called, one freezing November day, to a fish factory. Me and a humourless animal welfare officer from the council, a fat vegan called Simpson. Someone had complained about exploding herring gulls. It turned out the gutters had been amusing themselves by inserting lighted fireworks, the bangers you can't get any more, into gutted mackerel and throwing them in the air. The gulls were catching them and swallowing the stuffed fish whole. Then exploding.

After something of a confrontation, I managed to prevent the gutters and filleters, some of whom were very dodgy creatures from Glasgow, working tax free under false names, from eviscerating Simpson, and promised the shaken cruelty man I'd sort things out, that it might be better if he left me to it. And then I got the lads to demonstrate exactly what they were amusing themselves with.

It wasn't as spectacular as you might imagine. Not with one banger. If you placed a bundle of four in a fish, and a particularly hungry bird managed to gulp it down, then you could face a bloody shower of guts, fish and feathers and have to run for cover. They stopped when they ran out of fireworks. I never liked herring gulls, verminous seaside infestation that they are.

There was the dull thump of bad techno from the ground-floor flat, that 160 beats per minute vibration, the kind you get from Chavmobiles, cut 'n' shut Vauxhall Novas – always with the name badges removed – at any set of traffic lights on a Friday night. I leant on the security entry buzzer for about five minutes, until a tinnily slurred voice, the digital bass drum now reduced to a telephonic crackle, said, 'Fuck is it?'

'Selling?' I put on my broadest Invernessian twang. Syeeeling.

'Wheet're ye waanting?'

'Whit ye got?' My answer was the buzz of the front door lock being released. I had the keys in my pocket, but the torn pieces of Rizla on the pavement had let me guess right: the dealer was in. I was in the mood for a conversation.

He was scrawny, runtish and stooped, in uniform: trainers, tracksuit bottoms, hoodie, baseball cap. Eyes wide, pupils staring. There had been no name on the wee security button thing, the voter's roll and rates register had come up with no one in that flat, but I knew the little shit by sight. Roddy 'Wanker' Winton.

'Wanker,' I said, grabbing a firm hold of one shoulder. 'Nice to see you again.' I was shouting against that crap car sound system beat.

'Fuck sake.' His face changed. From blank, displaced anticipation of what he was used to: flogging shit hash – shit shit, as well as heroin cut with talcum powder or speed laced with Ajax, to a kind of woozy, wandering search for escape. Deep inside that drugged calm, panic was breaking loose. 'Flaws. Bastard. Got a warrant? I dinnae need to speak to you.'

'Aye, ye do,' I said, propelling him backwards into the flat, which smelt overwhelmingly of cat pee. That would be the speed. 'You just invited me in, remember?' There was a two-generations old eMac desktop computer sitting on a Formica topped table, a screensaver dancing multi-coloured balloons in some headachy holding pattern. The music was coming from a TV surround sound system. On the screen was MTV Dance. I reached for a mains plug, yanked it out of the wall. 'And it's not about drugs. Far as I'm concerned, you can flog ecstasy to the chief constable. In fact, he would probably benefit from it.'

His face shrank in on itself. It was as if he was collecting his thoughts from four different corners of the universe.

'There's nae chief constable nae mair . . . cannae fool me. It's all run fae

Glasgow now. It's jist a name, Northern Constabyoolery. And no' even that for much longer. You, you're just a fuckin' foot soldier.' He stared at me for a minute. 'An' naebody likes you.'

'That's right.' I released his shoulder and straight-fingered him in the solar plexus. 'And you ken what foot soldiers like to do. Like in Afghanistan or Iraq. Fuck what they like, no questions asked. You kill Mrs Enderby, Roddy? Mrs Smith, to you?'

Doubled up in pain, he sank slowly into a badly stained sofa. It was cut moquette and probably would have been worth something to a collector, if it hadn't been in urgent need of burning on sanitary grounds.

'I telt yon uniforms earlier. I never even seen her. Well, just to say hallo to, pass the time o' day. Telt them that. I was oot that night. In the hospital. Some bastard fuckin' lamped me on the way back frae the pub. Woke up in fuckin' Raigmore.'

I already knew this. But it was always worth hearing from the horse's mouth. 'Who was it did that to you, then? Some girlfriend? A pissed-off customer?'

'Nae idea, man. Motive-fuckin-less. Someone just wanting to get some kicks, man, know what I mean? There are some sick fucks out there.'

'She never buy any gear off you then?'

'Who?'

'Mrs Enderby. That was her real name. Mrs Smith.'

'Dinnae be stupid. She was straight, man. Her and her pal. Well, no' straight that way, ken, they were bent as fuckin hairpins that way. Live an' let live, I say. Well, she said she wisnae intae substances. Nicely, like. I even offered her a wee bit o' blow as a kinda neighbour thing, ken, welcome to the hood, a' that. She wisnae intae it. Right enaaff, she wis old, but no' as auld as some I've selt tae. She liked her auld, druggy music, though. Could hear it all hours. Kept me awake. Felt like complaining. Couldnae hear masel think.'

The thought of Wanker complaining to a neighbour because the music was too loud was irresistibly funny. I grinned. 'No visitors, then? Family?'

'Ah telt they black and whites a' this. She and her squeeze moved in maybe, dunno, six months since.'

'What was her name, the girlfriend? Millie, wasn't it?'

A hesitation. Some flicker of guardedness.

'Aye. Maybe. I think so. Millie. No Willie, onyway. Ken whit ah mean? Nudge nudge.'

'Yeah, very funny. What did they bring their stuff in? A van? Pals with a hired Transit? Where'd it come from?'

Wanker's turgid synapses struggled to keep up.

'Removal lorry, something big, ken. Pickfords . . . fuck knows. More and more o' they boorjoyzee moving in, squeezing out the old residents, the fucking natives, man. Aw, come on, give us a wee break. Ah'm knackered. Got stuff cooking, too.' Some semblance of insight flitted across those slack-jawed features. 'Aw, Christ. It'll be fucking ruined.' He started getting up. I could smell the acrid smell of burning kitchen appliance above the acidic aroma of cat's piss and wondered, for a minute, if he was being stupid enough to try and turn cocaine hydrochloride into crack using a microwave. The chances of causing an explosion with that technique are very high.

But in the kitchen, a toxic cavern of grime and grease, the smoke billowing from the old electric oven was soon revealed as a Domino's pizza on fire. Or to be precise, a Domino's pizza box on fire. the pizza inside looked . . . black. Maybe it was liquorice.

'Never good,' I said, 'to put cardboard in the oven, Wanker.'

'Dinnae call me that.' He gave up trying to lift the blackened box from the oven and closed the door with a groan. 'Tell you what, yon women up the stair, you dinnae want to be going there, man. Best leave well alone, ken whit ah'm saying?' His face creased with something that was meant to look like cunning.

'What do you mean, Roddy?'

'They were, like, protected, man. I mean, I didnae mind doing a favour for them, for the auld yin, like. Millie was . . . anyway. I wasnae happy. But she said it'd be OK.'

'What favour?'

'Och, it wasnae a favour really. She was doing me a favour. Gave me a wee present.'

'A present? Did you tell the uniforms about this?'

'Fuck no. I didnae want them taking away the fuckin heart of my business, man.' His face closed up. 'Actually, forget aboot it. All I mean is she gave me some moolah to run some errands. That's aw.'

'No it's not, Roddy. Come on, we've got this far. You can tell me.'

He said nothing, but he couldn't control his eyes. They flitted momentarily towards the eMac. I felt a jolt of recognition, almost physical, at the insight that I'd stumbled onto something crucial. I moved towards the computer. Wanker crumpled, as if I'd hit him again.

'Ach, no, man, no, I promised. Fuck. Fuck, fuck, fuck!'

The eMac is a one-piece computer, like the original iMac, with all the processing gubbins built into the screen. I knew I'd be out of my depth as soon as I started stabbing keys or messing about with the mouse. This was a job for Jim Smeaton. He'd only be doing something like playing *Guild Wars* anyway.

I thumbed his number out of my mobile's memory. He was on one of those wireless hands-free affairs. I could hear the echoing room and the sounds of gaming. Cries and explosions.

'Zed?'

'Zed's dead, baby. Zed's dead.'

'Fuck off, Zander. I'm not on duty. Is this you got a problem with a virus on your Dell at home? I told you to upgrade your protection.'

'Got something for you, Jimbo, urgent. Please. You'll like it. Remember that crime scene in Kennedy Avenue? Same close as fast as you can, only the ground floor. Just you.' No APB. Just Jimbo. It suddenly struck me that I needed to keep this one as restricted as possible.

'What is it, anyway? Have you found a router or something?'

'A what? No, it's a Mac.' I could hear the groan. For Jimbo, Macs were toys, not real computers. 'What do you mean, a router?'

'Struck me it was odd that these folk didn't have broadband. No wi-fi card in that old computer, no router, no base station, not even any sign of broadband in the house. Then I thought, maybe they're using someone else's. Got a wee Bluetooth arrangement with someone in the block. Simple security measure.' The gaming noises had disappeared.

'And you never thought to mention it?'

'Only occurred to me in the midst of Clan negotiations on the game, man. Old PC, new Bluetooth cord. Shoulda said. Anyway, have a look for something with flashing lights and maybe two stubby wee aerials. I'll be right there.'

I found it in a cupboard with louvre doors next to the fireplace. It wasn't hard to follow the cable that ran from the Mac, under the horrible carpet. A substantial box with aerials, just as Jimbo had said, flashing green and red lights. Another small black box next to it. Clever. Simple and clever.

'How much were they giving you, Wanker?'

'What's it matter? Nice wee bit o' business online. Gave me the computer, unlimited interspace, ken? Email orders're the way to go, man. Fuckin' beezer. They boxes in the cupboard. That old lady, Mrs Smith . . . Enderby, she knew her stuff. Put it all in. Millie, she was, like, just standing around. As if she was some kind of lookout or something. Ah dinnae ken what she was doing the likes o' here. Thought she was too good for us, onyway.'

'Ever go up to their flat?'

'Ach, a few times. They wouldnae let me in. Neither one. But they were always doon here, ferreting aboot. Thinking because she gave me money, it was hers. Theirs. I went up, wee can o' something, just bein' friendly. Wouldnae let anybody in. See that door up there? Ye'd think they were the ones dealing. Not that I do much, ken. Just for friends. You want some?'

I shook my head. 'No, Roddy, I'm trying to give it up.' I looked at his swivelling eyes, at the filth in the kitchen, and sighed. 'Who else is in the building?'

'Just me. Top floor is Greg, he's on remand in Porterfield. A wee difference of opinion wi' a traffic warden.'

My mobile buzzed. Jimbo, I thought, but it was Freeman.

'Flaws? There's been a sighting. The young woman.' His voice sounded high, edgy. He spoke quickly, gabbling. 'Out past Loch Ness. She must have had a boat. There's a house, a kind of timeshare, out past Foyers. Can you . . .'

'I'm actually following up a lead, sir.'

'What kind of lead? This is urgent, Flaws.' What was wrong with the man? His voice was high-pitched, screechy.

I sighed. Jimbo would be here soon. 'All right sir. I'm on my way.'

'It's called Valhalla,' Freeman said. 'Texting you the co-ordinates. You've got GPS on that car of yours? Right. It's a bit isolated. Uniforms are on their way, but they have instructions to wait for you. I have the armed response squad attending. They'll be under your orders, Sergeant, despite your junior status. You have experience in that regard.' Jesus Christ. I felt my throat go dry. His voice seemed to have steadied.

Jimbo arrived in his personal transport, a diseased looking Mitsubishi pickup truck with a Truckman canopy. I left him in the dubious company of Wanker and headed for the eastern shores of Loch Ness. To say I had a bad feeling about the next few hours in my life was beyond understatement.

Murricane stopped the Volvo in a lay-by just outside Daviot, where the B-road from Inverfarigaig and the south side of Loch Ness joined the main A9 dual carriageway to Inverness. When he switched the engine off, the swish and rumble of the A9 could be heard. It had taken 40 minutes to get here from the woods above Valhalla, and they hadn't spoken.

'Well?' He didn't look at her. The flicker of headlights from the main route between Inverness and southern civilisation teased the sky like an ersatz aurora.

'Thanks for coming.' She sounded remote, he thought. Miles away. Worlds.

'No problem. Think nothing of it. A mere bagatelle. Flying halfway across Europe at the behest of a woman, who, by the way, I'm completely and utterly over, and who left me for another woman. I've got no pride.'

'The other woman is dead. Tortured to death.'

'Well. It wisnae me, officer. I've got an alibi.'

She turned to face him and he saw the tears glittering in the reflected half-light of the distant cars. 'Sorry. That was uncalled for.'

'Do you . . . have you ever heard of a man called Manderley? Manderson Manderley? Or Manderley Manderson?'

'Manderley? Billy Boy? Psycho from RUC Special Branch? Resigned on full pension just before the mini-Stalkers got hold of him. Popular guy. Didn't you ever come across him?'

'Did you?'

'Fuck, no. Well, that's not quite true. There were a couple of jobs where he was around in the background. Or so I was told. He was a name. A force within a force kind of thing. He worked with someone else, a real big cheese. Someone slippery, someone who stayed in the loop. Can't remember . . . I remember there were a lot of stories. He had a kind of *modus operandi*. A Billy Boy way of doing things. If there was a mess, something needing cleaned up. You know, people were tasked . . . you'd get those multiple contacts. Black ops. Somewhere we weren't supposed to be, people who deserved what they got, just maybe at the time they weren't actually doing anything noteworthy. Do you know what I mean? The usual? That was his idea. He pioneered it.'

'The usual,' she grimaced. 'At the time. Christ, the usual would get you locked up these days. Or worse.'

'Anyway, Billy Boy and his boss came in on the aftermath and added a few details to the picture.'

'Mysterious guns that weren't there before?'

'That kind of thing. You remember, anything went. Absolutely fucking anything went. Christ, if they could use rent boys to blackmail politicians, what were a few misplaced guns? Nothing mysterious about it. They had a laundry, a fully functioning fucking laundry. People innocently put their washing in. They had machines, analysers. Tested clothes for explosives residue. Bingo, they could arrest a whole street. Anyway. Those mysterious guns were real. It was after us, you and me. After Freya. And it was after that I decided enough was enough. Fucking Kincora, when stories about that started to get out . . .'

'And took up a nice safe profession.'

'Something like that. Are you OK, Mil?'

'No.' A great juddering breath. 'No, I am not fucking OK.' The soft Cumbrian vowels came through, cutting past the clipped Army anonymity. That childhood in the hills above Bassenthwaite, shepherd's daughter, crying mother, hitting father. All the usual stuff that drove women into the forces, he thought, then caught himself. Cut the clichés, Mark. What do you know? What's the difference between you and her? Geography and accent.

'There's something you need to hear.' Millie reached into the back seat for her rucksack, pulled out the iPod. The earbud cable was wrapped around the little rectangle of plastic.

'Have those things been in your ears? Or as Marvin would say, hear hear, my dear?'

'Nowhere else. Don't worry. I'm not infectious.' As Mark prepared to listen, she held onto the iPod, switched it on and scrolled through the 'Extras' section, looking. It was curiously intimate, feeding information directly into Mark. She glanced at him: he'd lost weight, but still had that wiry, blocky strength. Small, like many of the British and Commonwealth Special Forces tended to be. Compact. Unlike their American equivalents, who were inevitably massive to start with and bulked out on power-lifting, Sylvester Stallone movies and steroids. She found the file and clicked 'Enter'.

And he was hearing that voice again, that voice of command, always senior to him, superior. The woman who'd taken Millie. Swept her away with all the imperious *droit de seigneur* of some ancient aristocrat. What could he do? What he did. Get out. All that stuff about the Kincora Boys' Home, the filth and the murk of Northern Ireland, it was true enough. But it was the loss of Millie that had made him quit, really. He knew that, she did, Freya did. Everyone did.

My name is Freya Jane Enderby and I love Millie. Millie, this is for you. Of course it is. There are no witnesses. Always better that way. Always best, we would say, just to get a confession. A chink of glass, a swallowing sound. I've been in Inverness for about three weeks. Like they said, it's a pleasant enough town. It wasn't exactly an order, but I'm still on the reserve list, so I'm supposed to do what I'm told. Official Secrets, that sort of thing. Of course, I had my own, unofficial, little secret.

Mark leaned over and tapped Millie on the shoulder.

'You can speak,' she said, pressing the pause button. 'I'm not the one with the earphones.'

'Don't want to miss anything. Not these confessions of ardent affection and loyalty and lies. She was lying to you, wasn't she? At the very least, she didn't tell you what was going on. That move from Newquay.'

'Trying to keep me safe,' Millie said. 'Or something. Newlyn, not Newquay. Keep listening.'

It's stalked my life ever since it happened. We're embroiled. Both of us. Must be a better word. Can't think of it, though.

'Enmeshed,' Mark said. 'Ensnared. Totally and utterly fucked up, that's for sure.'

He listened with a set look on his face as Freya slurred on.

Operation Amethyst was right back when I first arrived in the Province, much fought over, they were desperate for someone, anything, anyone with tits and a fanny. Token female for undercover, I was told. I was a major, for God's sake. Not that there's anything special about being an officer, but at least they knew enough by your stage to know they needed fewer posh bints. Sorry Millie. They knew nothing back then, nothing. It was old-school-tie spooks, mad Proddie B-Specials in plain clothes, deranged politicians and old fucking Etonian soldiers. And I wasn't much better. Big girl, jolly hockey sticks, Cheltenham and Aberdeen. Because I couldn't get into bloody St Andrews. But we learned, I learned. You know how you do. You get a grip or you get killed.

Anyway . . . it was another run-of-the-mill, dogsbody job for Border Det, or so the spooks told us. Well, I'm saying that, as if it was ordinary, but as per, it was all adrenalin and terror once you got past the hangover and the general depression of having to be across the water in the first place, stuck in some fucking compound for weeks on end. Then there was just one woman, me. Better when you were there, Millie. Same, but more women. Quieter, too. You and Mark. These things happen. Just me and a couple of dozen men. And hundreds of fucking guns.

Terms. Better define them. Avoid misunderstandings. Who the fuck's listening? Who are you?

A silence, the clink of glass.

Border Det was a bit of of 14th Intelligence Detachment, surveillance specialists, special forces, yada, yada, yada. Not SAS, mostly SAS wannabes, been through a modified Hereford training course, no women at that time, not allowed, but they fucking needed women to parade through nationalist housing schemes with fucking stonewashed jeans on, didn't they? Needed women for undercover surveillance. Lost too many dimwits, parading around in their weightlifter shoulders and their moron moustaches, thinking they were invisible. Pop, pop, goodnight. So there were a few women amongst the Walter Mitties the SAS guys called the Det, and you could see why. Guys who wanted into the regiment. Some of them did progress on. Onwards and upwards. Mostly, guys who wanted some action at the sharp end. Wanted to play with guns. Christ, we liked guns. No . . . that's rubbish. We loved our guns. All of us. Especially me. Freudian, or what? Little bit of Heckler & Koch action, love that Browning Hi-Power . . . 11 shots, never full magazine, no jams. Safest with a shotgun, that's what Saul always said. Bang for your buckshot, nothing like it, get one of the American jobs, folding stock . . . what was it . . . Mossberg? No. Remington Wingfire. How could you resist a gun with a name like that? Great name. Brought them in from the States. Clara could . . . seven shots, you could load seven cartridges. Nothing like the sound of a racking pump shotgun to instil fear, Saul said. Noise you never want to hear behind you in a dark alley.

Tell you about Saul, this guy on the orientation course, the place near Larne. Easy to put us back on the boat if we crapped out or were crap or whatever. We got on. But then, we always . . . He was different from all those gung-ho fuckwits. Kind of a gentle soul. Strange that. Maybe he was gay, I don't know. Probably.

A silence.

Trained together, shot together. He was a good shot, into guns, always had been. Ran in the family. It was him got me into shotguns, showed me what they could do. Always had been into shotguns. Deer shot, wrap that round your fucking engine block dear boy. He wasn't very posh. Well, not really. Very vague about that. Like me. Very like me, actually.

Laughter, on the edge of sobbing.

Ended up we took a weekend leave together, did a bit of hillwalking, camping, Mountains of Mourne. One thing might have led to another, only with him, only ever with him, but I wasn't inclined that way and, as I say, neither was he, at least I don't think so. Wouldn't have been . . . right. And then he was gone, out of there. No tears, no lies, no fucking alibis. No word on him. Some whispers he was a plant, checking out the new recruits, that sort of thing. As it turns out . . . anyway. Get to that in a minute. I mean, he was obviously a spook. But different from the ones we dealt with. Five people. He looked like Six, foreign, brought in . . . shouldn't be saying this. But if I don't, what's the point? What's the fucking point?'

Millie was looking straight ahead, gazing at the raindrops gathering on the windscreen, their liquid chatter on the glass disguising the thrum of the traffic on the A9. Murricane shivered, thought about putting on the heater. These old Volvos had terrific heaters.

So we'd known there was something up for two, maybe three days, battened down in the Cross compound, not where you'd want to be, really. Bad food, no room to move, chopper in and out. There were a bunch of ops out on the ground, looking, waiting, that was all we were supposed to know. But we knew it was all connected. What had been going on south of the border, down Mexico way.

May 1974. The 17th. They briefed us the night before. Two of them. That fucking fat bastard with the shaved head and the grin, Billy Boy the renegade Catholic, psychopath policeman. Him and a Rupert type, superior, didn't know him then, looking down his nose at us. Didn't say much. We have a man south, they said, and we have to get him out, extraction with, quote, no regard to ancillary losses, unquote. Collateral not an issue, they said. I remember that. Ancillary. Collateral. Quote, quote, quote. Briefed the undercover ops, Ernest, Albie, Jiz. Gunship team, if needed, me and Zeke. Him driving the chopper, me map-reading and shooting. If necessary. Of course, if fucking necessary. Not shooting the fucking maps. Oh, Jesus . . .

The sound of a glass being knocked over.

I'm going to have to clean this up. Serpentine. Serpentine in the Crown. Serpent of the Empire. Servant . . . That's when they first mentioned the name. Must get a cloth. Legend in his own life-sentence. Course, we'd all heard that name, that code name. Just stories, really. Serpentine. Ha . . .

The sound of someone getting up, stumbling. A scrabbling, close to the microphone, then a switch being pressed. Silence. Just the rain on the roof, the distant road, and Millie's breathing. Murricane reached for her hand, felt its smallness, its roughness, familiar and unresponsive. He held it lightly, cautiously, as if it might break.

'May 17th, 1974, south of the border,' he said. 'You know what happened then, don't you? You know who and what she's talking about?'

Millie tried to swallow. It was as if all the liquid in her mouth and throat had disappeared. Her voice sounded gritty and ragged.

'May 1974 was a bit before my time, Mark.'

'But you must . . .'

'OK, OK.' She sighed. 'Dublin and Monaghan car bombings. Civilian attacks in the Republic. Political dynamite. UVF claimed responsibility. British int and the RUC getting blamed. PIRA mouthing off.'

'Three hundred injuries. Thirty-three deaths. Four bombs. The worst casualties of the entire Troubles. Worst terrorist incident in Ireland of the entire twentieth century. And that's saying something.'

'All right. Sunningdale. It was seen as a way of stopping the Sunningdale agreement. Reigniting the worst bits, Catholics versus Proddies . . .'

'Yeah.'

'The story went it was part of the whole anti-Wilson, anti-Labour thing inside the intelligence community. Community! That's a laugh. *Spycatcher*. All that.'

'Community's such a lovely word, though, don't you think? Cosy.'

'There was an inquiry.'

'There's always an inquiry. The Barron Report. Caused a shit-storm.'

'No proof.'

'There's never any fucking proof, is there? Nothing's going to be written down. Everybody learned the lessons from Heydrich and the Nazis' bloody record-taking. The secret is a secret. Secrecy. But that didn't stop Barron. He couldn't rule out a police and intelligence conclusion. It was "not absurd", I think the phrase was.'

'It was a rumour, that's all.'

'No, Serpentine was a rumour. Serpentine was a legend. But what happened was real. It's history, Millie. On the record.'

She sighed. 'I know.' She looked at her watch. 'If we're going to Kennedy Avenue, we'd better go now. We need to talk to Roddy.'

GET YOUR MOTOR RUNNING

GET YOUR MOTOR RUNNING

There was a cheap office chair in the cargo area of the Transit they were using this time. The van had been left for them at the Eden Court Theatre car park, on the banks of the Ness. Keys under the front offside tyre. Billy Boy had arranged it. Clean, no questions asked. Swap for the Vectra. Backup, thought Hume, serious backup. It was a comfort. They were still on side. Still on somebody's side.

The chair could be adjusted for height and Hume was sitting on it, watching the entrance to the close through a panel of one-way mirror in the back door. The chair had been bungeed to the sides of the van to stop it moving. He had binoculars and a two-way radio.

'He's going,' he murmured into the transceiver. 'Some other guy's turned up, looks like a techie or something. Going in downstairs.'

'Roger that. We're nearly finished here.' It was Billy Boy's voice, flattened and electronic, devoid of its usual simpering sense of threat.

MacDougall had done most of the work, neatly and without fuss. There was a smell of stale antiseptic. Underneath that, the dull tang of death. And petrol. Billy Boy had inspected as MacDougall had lifted and rearranged. But there had been nothing new. The obviously shared bedroom, the spare room where the computer had been, the bookshelves, the CDs. Nothing torn, nothing trashed, Everything replaced as it should be. Nothing found. Then the two pressurised petrol stoves had been placed, carefully, underneath the bed and behind the bloodstained sofa, a mobile phone and slightly adapted gas lighter taped in place. There was very little smell of fuel. The stoves were expensive, designed for high altitude mountaineering and easily obtained from outdoor shops. MacDougall had bought three at different outlets in Forres and Inverness.

'Don't need much petrol,' MacDougall had muttered as he covered them with, in case, the edge of a quilt and an old copy of a magazine called *Focus*. 'It's the pressure that does it.'

Billy Boy had been watching closely, apparently impressed. 'Beats fucking Calor gas cylinders and firelighters, anyway,' he said. 'High tech. And middle-class, too. Expensive way of going about things, boyo.'

'We're going up in the world,' said MacDougall. And then softly, 'Boom, boom.'

Billy Boy flinched slightly when the walkie-talkie in his coat pocket crackled.

MacDougall smiled. 'Different frequencies. Don't worry. It's not the radio signal that does the damage. It's the vibrate setting on the mobiles.'

'All right?' Billy Boy spoke crisply.

'The techie guy is in with the target, now. Time to abandon ship.'

'Negative,' said Billy Boy. 'We'll deal with the two of them. We need to have a word with boyo down there. Keep an eye out. Right.' He turned to MacDougall. 'Let's go downstairs.' MacDougall shouldered his backpack and headed for the door, white latex gloves glowing like dead fish in the spill from the hall's fluorescent light.

Like a pair of rubber-handed Jehovah's Witnesses, they knocked politely on Raymond's door. It was Jim who answered, warrant card at head height, but before he had a chance to say anything, Billy Boy shouldered the reinforced door into his body. Jim hurtled backwards, colliding heavily with a wall as Billy Boy moved in and punched him savagely in the side of the neck. Jim slumped soundlessly to the floor. Roddy was in a recliner, apparently paralysed, both feet planted on a footstool from where he'd been watching Jim disconnect his computer. His jaw gaped open.

'What the fu . . . Who're youse cunts?'

'Computer services, sir, delighted to be of assistance,' said Billy Boy, punching Roddy in the mouth. 'I take it this is what we want?'

'A Mac,' said MacDougall with distaste. 'It'll have to be.' He eyed the disconnected router and its attached black box. 'Bitches had a Bluetooth router and a hard drive down here. Might've hit pay dirt. Could've asked that guy you laid in a coma. But we'll have to assume he was taking it away.'

'Right, we don't have time to fuck around, boyo. Just take it out to the van. No scanning with clever little buzzy scanners or anything.' MacDougall looked at him, his face expressionless, then shrugged off his backpack on top of Roddy and bent to lift the eMac. Without looking at him, Manderley lifted his right elbow and used it to strike Roddy in the left temple. Raymond tilted sideways and was still.

'Your other bourgeois bomb?'

'Just wherever you want it. Somewhere discreet. I'd do it, but I've got my hands full.' The pair gazed at each other. MacDougall had known Billy Boy a long time, but occasionally their relationship came to something of a hiatus. And the fetcher-and-carrier had to exercise his authority.

'Get to the van, I'll put your precious hydrocarbon Semtex substitute somewhere nice and private.' When MacDougall had gone, Billy Boy smiled to himself and lifted Roddy's head, as gently as a mother caring for a loved son.

'There, there, boyo,' he crooned. 'Let me make you more comfortable.' And he placed the backpack under Raymond's neck.

Murricane had switched off the engine of the Volvo when they were 100 metres from the Kennedy Avenue address and let the old car freewheel noiselessly towards the white van that was parked, cab towards them, in front of the building. He stopped in a pool of shadow 30 metres away. There was a big pick-up truck on the other side of the road from the van.

'Watchers,' said Millie. 'Must be in the back of the van.'

'Recognise that hillbilly wagon?' She shook her head. 'Wait. There's someone coming out.' Murricane was peering through a small pair of Leitz night glasses into the sodium orange gloom. 'Fuck. He's carrying a computer and some other gubbins.'

'That'll be the stuff Freya gave Raymond. She had him put in broadband so we could Bluetooth to it without any actual presence in our flat. Remote outsourcing, she said. Wireless. She used it to copy stuff onto the laptop I've got. Give me those.' Millie focused the binoculars on the figure moving slowly towards the van. She handed back the glasses and her head lifted. Murricane could see the rising anger. 'That's one of them. One of the guys that had me.'

'Stay calm,' said Murricane. 'Stay cool. We need to watch. Revenge is always a distraction. So is anger. You know that.'

Millie let out a sigh. 'Thanks, Dad. I know. Your wee girl won't fly off the handle. Do you think Roddy's dead?'

Murricane said nothing.

They watched the man and his electronic burden disappear behind the van and another figure, in a cashmere coat, leave Kennedy Court, stripping latex gloves from his hands.

'Billy Boy,' said Murricane, softly.

The big man opened the passenger door of the van and climbed in. They couldn't see the loading of the computer, but it must have been done, because the man who had carried it out of the building now climbed in beside him from the driver's side, shuffling across to the middle of the triple-bench seat.

'Where's the driver?' said Murricane. Just then, a dark Ford Escort pulled up directly opposite the van and a tall, thin figure in a leather jacket got out. 'And who the fuck is this?'

I was at the Muirtown canal bridge when the mobile went. It was Freeman, cancelling my appointment with whatever monstrosities Valhalla-by-Loch-Ness had for me. I felt unaccountably relieved. I'd had the feeling I was being set up. Freeman still sounded jittery. And angry, now.

'As you're obviously engaged in something far too important to be interfered with, Sergeant,' he said, biting off each word and spitting it out like a piece of rotten fruit, 'I've decided to go myself and co-ordinate things. Firearms units and you do not go well together, I was informed that there might be an issue of . . . trust.'

'Fine, sir. We'll speak tomorrow.'

'We certainly shall.'

I slammed off the phone and shoved the Escort into reverse, clumsily three-pointing back the way I had come.

I saw Jimbo's pick-up where he had left it. There were still lights on in Roddy's house. Fine, he could get on with his cybergeek stuff in there. I wanted to have another glance at the world of Freya.

I climbed the stair to the Enderby flat, wondering, not for the first time, what had brought this woman to Kennedy Avenue. She could surely have afforded somewhere better. Yet she came here, she reinforced the door with steel plate and ultra-secure locks. What was Freya Enderby about? What had she been about?

I unlocked the door, three mortices and a Yale, keys labelled with plastic tags by the SOCOs. No need for gloves this time. Smears of fingerprint powder everywhere. A much diluted version of the original scene-of-crime aromas. Antiseptic. Dried blood. Shit. And . . . what was that? Petrol? Probably from outside. The SOCOs had shut the windows, the worst of the smells had gone at any rate. I flicked on the hall light and shut the door.

'Who are you, Freya? Who are you, love? What the fuck were you doing in this dump?' I squatted down on the floor, prodded the button on her '70s Pioneer tuner amp. There was a dull thud as it came to life, the juice running through those big Kef loudspeakers, grilles removed. Really big speakers. Thick, specialised speaker cable. A guy thing, hi-fi. But that was sexist bullshit. Why not a woman thing? Why not a lesbian thing? Oh, for fuck's sake. There was a stronger smell of petrol. Why the hell was that? If she had been heterosexual, I'd have said the hi-fi was what he'd left her when he upgraded when he left her. Or they'd remained friends and when he bought his compact system, he handed this over to her, a nostalgic gesture. Or contempt. Because that's what I'd have done. Judge not others as you would yourself. I looked through what was clearly an older woman's selection of CDs. Singer-songwriters, that was her thing. Sensitivity. A Britney Spears CD caught my eye. I pulled it from the rack. It seemed peculiarly out of place. 'Millie's, Freya? No, she's not a Spears fan. A Spearsian. Nope. Maybe a niece? A daughter? Jailbait? Did you get this for her?' The cover was a colour photocopy of the original and when I opened the case, it was a CD-Rom. *Oops! . . . I Did It Again*, no artist's name, written in indelible pen on the silver disc. I flipped through the other CDs. They were all official releases. I put Britney in my pocket. I'd always had a soft spot for the poor little rich girl, that weird marriage in Vegas, the desperate growing and throwing up in public. 'That what you saw in Britney, Freya? Want to protect her? Did you fancy her?'

I'd searched the flat already and we'd had forensics go over it. Sheila had doubtless coaxed that broken body apart to find out what it had to say to us. And still, if I stood still in the bedroom, I could hear Freya trying to speak to me, I swear it.

The sound of a motorcycle cut through the night.

'What the fuck, now?' Murricane was incredulous. He had the binoculars trained on what looked very like a woman in full leathers, riding some kind of

Japanese custom bike. It was a woman. She took off her helmet and ran a hand through her cropped hair. The pick-up and the Escort were dark and silent. So, he realised, was the cab of the white van. There was no one in the front. They had to be in the back, watching through the windows in the rear.

'A woman.' Millie sounded suddenly weary. 'It'll be some fucking sex thing. You know how murder scenes can go. It's like some medieval ritual. It was like that across the water. Fuck where a soldier died, a blood tryst.'

'Rubbish,' said Murricane. 'That's just another old wives' tale. Fucking rubbish.'

That James Kay picture: worth a lot of money. Even if it was small, even if it was a pastel. Miracle it was still here. I went into the bedroom, looked at the bed, a double. 'Which side did you sleep on, Freya?' I sat on the mattress, stripped after the bed had been examined *in situ* for signs of pathology and psychopathology, spoors left by the killer. Because we were looking for a killer, all right. Shite, sperm, blood . . . you could never tell. Big, goose-down pillows. A silk-covered quilt. Expensive. Everything had been taken back to the labs for further investigation. I remembered the quality. 'You liked your comfort, Freya.' I checked those wardrobes, those '70s clothes again. There was Chelsea Market clothes, Kensington Market stuff, some classics. Buried in the back, there was also a pair of good hiking boots, a North Face breathable jacket, walking-poles. She liked to get out and about. 'Ben Wyvis, the Black Isle, the firth. You're in the Highlands, where you wanted to be, and all you got was this lousy shit-hole, Freya. Why?' I sat on the bed and listened to the distant hammering of dance music from Wanker's flat. That smell of petrol. Then I heard something else. There was a light tapping at the front door. Someone was outside, on the landing.

'I didn't hear you buzz up from the ground floor. How the fuck did you get in the security door?'

'That all the welcome I get?' Sheila was standing, one hip cocked in a parody of provocation, helmet in one gloved hand. The thud of alleged music from Wanker's flat was louder. 'It wasn't shut properly. I just walked in. Aren't you glad to see me? Guessed you'd be here.'

'Did you really?' Her leathers creaked as she pushed past me into the flat. They were wet. She was wet. 'Nice ride over?' Oh Christ. This is not the time. This is not the time, Sheila . . . or the place.

'Not bad. There's rain coming and going. It's kind of muggy. We need a good shower to take away the pressure.'

Then the door was slamming shut and she was pulling me against the wall, her face wet and cold against mine, and I was fumbling for the zip on her leather jacket, knowing she'd be naked underneath, knowing how perverse and wrong and stupid this was and not caring, taken over by a desire that was shocking in its colossally inappropriate power. And at my age, too. Fuck Viagra.

'Come on,' she said, breaking off from a kiss that was messy and bruising, wiping her face, pulling at my jacket. 'You know how I feel about crime scenes.' And, sadly, I did. Had been party to exactly this kind of depraved behaviour just once before, persuaded against every conceivable form of better judgement, and some worse, to fuck Dr Sheila Dartington in the back seat of a taxi stored for forensic purposes in the Raigmore police garage. A prostitute had killed her pimp there. I think Sheila found it kind of empowering. I slid one hand underneath the cold, wet leather and fondled one warm, dry breast, felt the nipple harden between my fingers. What was I doing? She turned in that way women have, shrugging off my attentions, then back towards me, entwining her gloved fingers with mine. I could smell weather, leather, oil, exhaust fumes, her perfume – Arpège – and the cloying aroma of Freya Enderby's death. Then I was moving towards the bedroom, knowing the way, dragged by her, dragging her. We were on the bed, awkward, too urgent, desperate. I reached one hand down to the floor, steadying myself. Brushed something cold and metallic. That smell . . .

Petrol.

I pulled away from Sheila, craned over the edge of the bed and flicked away the edge of the quilt.

'Christ Almighty.'

'What is it, love? Needing some pharmaceutical support? I may be able to . . .'

Mountaineering stove, pressurised petrol, a mobile phone and a cheap plastic lighter taped together. A nine volt battery, some wires and . . .

I was off the bed, suddenly erectionless, sex and guilt ripped out of my consciousness. There was only survival. I was scrabbling for Sheila's hand.

'No need for all this pro-active stuff, matey,' she said. 'I was just getting myself worked up.'

I was pulling her towards the door. Suspicion was dawning in her that something was wrong, I could tell by the slackening of resistance.

'Bomb,' I said, rattling at the doorway into the stairwell. 'Some kind of petrol bomb.'

'Helmet,' she said. 'Gloves.' Christ, women. And she was bending to the little hall table where she'd left them. Then we were out and running down the stairs.

Music was still blaring from Wanker's flat. Chill-out sounds, female, Beth Orton or something, but way too loud. I kicked open the door, almost tripping over the groaning form of Jimbo. He was holding the side of his neck and retching what looked like noodles onto the carpet. Or worms. Pot Noodle. Geek cuisine.

'Sheila.' But it wasn't necessary. She was a doctor, above all, more even than an excavator of physical remains. She was shouldering past me, bending over Jim. 'Just get him the fuck out, Sheila. Don't worry about any concussion.' If they'd set an incendiary upstairs they'd have done the same thing here, covering tracks, destroying evidence they maybe hadn't found. Taking no risks. Wanker was lying on one of those Frasier-Crane's-dad-type recliners. One quick check told me he was dead.

Jim was struggling to his feet, helped by Sheila. I wrapped an arm round his waist and pushed her out of the door. 'Go. Into the street. Come on, go!'

We were at the outer security door, the closemouth, turning the knob, pulling, a tangle of bodies, interfering arms and cursing. I noticed that Sheila didn't have her helmet and gloves.

'I've left my . . .' she said. Then the door was open and we were falling, stumbling into the street. She must have been pulling back. I was slightly ahead.

White vans. You tend not to see them. They're invisibly everywhere, all the time, and this was an innocuous enough example. I didn't notice it moving at first, probably because it was rolling forward with the engine off. But what interrupted Sheila was a cacophony of noises, seemingly simultaneous, but actually happening one after the other, separated by what must have been milliseconds: the rattling roar of the diesel engine was how it started, the slam of the van's sliding side door as it opened, the crash of smashed windows. Then the dull *whoomp* of ignition and the hot blast of flame and more breakage from the Enderby flat. The splintering clang of glass on the pavement, a sudden, piercing pain in my head. The frenetic revving of the van's engine and the screech of tyres as it roared away towards the old ferry slip.

I turned round. Sheila and Jim were slumped together on the pavement, like drunk lovers. No wounds from falling glass, as far as I could see. 'Keys,' I tried to say, but I couldn't hear myself speaking. There was a dull siren sounding in my head. 'Keys.' I saw Sheila groping in her jacket pocket, slowly, in slow motion. I moved towards her, following her hand with mine. The Yamaha's ignition key. I snatched it, moved towards the bike, which was glistening in a covering of broken glass. Then I remembered.

'Get away from Wanker's flat,' I screamed, or tried to. 'They've probably . . .'

The only thing that saved us was drugs, or drugs and vandalism. Ground-floor flats are always insecure, ground-floor flats used for drug-dealing especially so. Wanker had put in opaque security glass at the back, in what was probably a crude attempt at double glazing, as well as a guard against attack, thick Perspex lining the inside of the windows at the front. So, when the petrol bomb went off, there was a weird moment when the inside of the house glowed orange and seemed to bulge, cartoon-like, towards us. The Enderby explosion had set the top two floors of the building ablaze. Now the ground floor started to burn.

I fumbled for the Escort keys, threw them towards Sheila, and then I was astride the Yamaha, feeling for the ignition. 'Take the car,' I shouted. She had her mobile phone out, getting ready to dial. The Yam would have started with that slightly histrionic whirr I'd come to expect from Far-Eastern technology, a mild acoustic thump engineered into the engine note, but convincing nobody. I couldn't hear it, but I could feel the thump from the v-twin. No helmet, but beggars couldn't be choosers. Left toe prodding the gear selector down, then, with no regard for Sheila's finer mechanical feelings, I revved that girliebike to hell and skidded the back wheel round 180 degrees until I was facing in the direction taken by the van. Its tail lights were just visible in the distance.

Bikes are not ideal pursuit vehicles, in that they're inherently unstable. But even posey ones like Sheila's Yamaha can take off very quickly indeed. And white vans are not exactly Ferraris. This one was being driven very quickly, though. But towards nothing but a dead end, or the Kessock firth. The old ferry slip was where Inverness ended. I was still a good 50 metres behind when the van — Ford Transit in plastichrome on one door — performed a perfect handbrake turn and accelerated hard towards me. The lights were on main beam and I was blinded. Desperately, I slipped the Yam into second.

The engine, screaming in protest, leant desperately to the left. I could smell the diesel as I went past. Smoky. The shit brakes on the bike just stopped me before the slippery cobbled downslope of the old slip. Custom cruisers are not meant for this kind of thing, I thought. Unbidden, there flashed into my head a picture of those CHIPS bikes from the old TV series, those big stupid Kawasakis. They use Moto Guzzis, I thought, some of the American cops. And a Harley would be even worse. Heavy as a steamroller and about as manoeuvrable. Gunning the Japanese motor, I headed down Kessock Road after the retreating lights.

It was years, decades, since I'd ridden a bike at speed without a helmet and the clarity of the experience was astonishing. No matter the brutality and heat of the recent firebombing, how hot or humid the day, motorcycles come with built-in breeze, the faster the colder. No goggles, though, no protection from that fine Highland smirr of rain. My eyes were streaming. Midges and moths hit my wet face as I raced through the sodium-yellow night. Now I could hear the sirens of approaching police cars and the subtly different yelp of fire engines. The van lurched into Anderson Street, heading for the Grant Street bridge over the Ness. I was concentrating on catching up, going as fast as the lumbering bike would manage.

Inverness is a strange place, a community not really used to its comparatively recent city status. It was shamefully mauled in the '60s by planners seemingly determined to destroy everything of architectural or historical value. Mauling has been a feature of Inverness's history.

Inverness, I was thinking as I slammed on the Yamaha's woeful brakes. *Crossing of the Ness*. So many bridges. The old railway bridge, washed away in the great flood tide and storm of 1990. The cast-iron suspension bridges, bouncing and creaking as you crossed. Registration number of the van: T670 FKN. Grant Street, then another piece of Victorian ironwork. Narrow and rattly. Ready for major repairs. The iron parapets threw back the bike's too-polite snarl and I marvelled again briefly at the entirely different experience that was helmetless biking. Everything was right there, all around, unmuffled. The van's lights in the distance were swerving left, heading into the industrial badlands of Longman Drive, the waterside desolation of anonymous workshops, second-hand car lots and small factories. In the fecund moisture of that hot Highland night, with more small creatures dying against my face, everything was overhung with the pungent harbour reek of salt water and diesel oil. And then it began to rain more heavily, making my skin sting and my eyes smart.

Within what seemed like seconds, the road was slick and treacherous and the van's tail lights were smeared and indistinct. I accelerated, feeling the rain's force on my face and body. My fingers were going numb. But I was gaining on the van. It passed underneath the concrete canopy of the Kessock Bridge, on the new road past the headquarters of Highlands and Islands Enterprise, past Century House, home of the Highlands' finest local newspapers, or two of them. Then the tail lights ahead of me went out.

I was confused, momentarily. Then several things happened very quickly. I realised the van had stopped. I slammed on the brakes as the twin doors of the Transit approached at incredible speed and inched my weight to the left. There was a terrible vibration through the handlebars, but the bike stayed upright and came to a halt, without skidding, parallel to the Transit's cab. I thanked God and Sheila Dartington that the Yamaha had ABS.

The bike had stalled, but the lights were still on. Everything was quiet, apart from the tick and hiss of hot metal contracting in rain and the drumming of water on the van's roof. There was a quiet thump of music coming from somewhere. I looked around. We were in the black shadow of the Caledonian Stadium, Inverness Caley Thistle's ground, built on reclaimed land. Or, to be precise, millions of tonnes of Inverness's rubbish. This had been the city's dump, back when it was still just a big town. There was still a whiff of rot in the air. But the stadium was deserted. There was nothing happening in the corporate suite, no synchronised training to old country rock, which I'd heard the manager was partial to: aerobics for neds. But there was music coming from somewhere and it was old country rock. The Eagles. 'Take It Easy'. Yeah, right. It was coming from the van. I kicked down the side stand and leaned the bike over. As I swung my legs onto the ground, I almost collapsed as the shock hit me. I looked in the side window of the Transit. Nobody.

I switched the bike's lights off and pushed it onto a patch of overgrown, reclaimed rubbishland. I was soaked, shivering and getting wetter. Where had they gone? Who were they? Passers-by? Innocent civilians? No way.

I had to think. It was going to be necessary to check out the van using the full panoply of police facilities, but without bringing Sheila into it. We had very nearly been firebombed while shagging at a murder scene. It was a suspension-and-inevitable-dismissal issue, for both of us. What had I been thinking, grabbing her bike, riding it through Inverness without a helmet, visible, identifiable? Except, we had been in the Invernessian badlands and motorcyclists all looked the same, helmeted or not, especially going fast at night. I hoped. My mobile vibrated.

'Where are you?' Sheila sounded unusually subdued.

'On the end of the new bit of Longman Drive, north end of Caley Stadium. They're around here somewhere.' I was whispering.

'How do you know it's a they?'

'I'm a good guesser. Are you in the car?'

'No, it's outside. I'm at home, just like you said. I'm on a landline. Christ, this is some mess.'

'It's OK, we can fix it. Here's what I want you to do. Get in my car and drive over here. Bring your crash helmet, you're going to have to take the bike back.'

'Is it all right? You haven't damaged it?'

Dear God, women.

'Well, it'll be OK once I've hauled it out of the firth.' Dead silence. 'Joke. It's OK. That ABS saved me. But I need to get out of here.'

And that was when the shotgun barrel emerged out of the darkness, out of the rain, and pressed itself firmly against my neck. I could smell gun oil and cordite. A side-by-side, by the pressure, and sawn-off. That hacksaw raggedness.

Shotguns. Shotguns. I was cursed by the fucking things.

Freeman was alone when he picked his way along the path towards Valhalla, having parked his personal car – a Citroën Berlingo bought to cope with his ever-expanding and very young family – in the gravel square excavated from the forest. The thought of his children – the baby, Kelvin, was barely a year old – made his guts lurch. That was their lever. One of them. Weakness. His weakness. The clearing was reached by a narrow track leading from the Foyers power station access road, and you could easily miss it. Satnav helped. Freeman had only been to Valhalla once before.

Despite what he'd said to Flaws, there was no Armed Response Unit, no guns save the police-issue Smith & Wesson he had in his jacket pocket, ruining the cut of his suit. There never had been an Armed Response Unit. He had made that up on the spur of the moment in his attempt to get – to order, for God's sake, the man was a sergeant – Flaws out of Inverness. He had been acting on Ms Stone's orders. He had been told in no uncertain terms to get Flaws out of Inverness, to send him to the isolated house of witches that was Valhalla. He had felt bad about it, very bad, because he was sure that some kind of decision had been taken to remove Flaws from the game entirely.

'Billy Boy wants to meet him,' was how she'd put it. Christ. Then that order had been countermanded. He wondered if things had spiralled even more completely out of control. If Billy Boy had wandered right off the reservation.

He found Clara sitting up, arms folded, unhappy. Her circulation not coping too well with the uncomfortable state she'd been left in. It had taken her half an hour to get free. She was fitter than she looked and Millie had been rushed and rusty.

She was in a filthy mood.

'You unspeakable little prick,' was how she greeted him. 'Leavin' a woman my age in this kind of condition. You fuckin' asshole. Brit FUCKING asshole.' Freeman stiffened as he helped her to the kitchen table.

'I'm not one of your Irish irregulars, Ms Stone. I'm . . . well, I'm police liaison on this . . . project. Frankly, I wish I was elsewhere. Anywhere else, actually. Traffic duty in Wick would be better than what I seem to be involved with.'

'Make me a cup of coffee, dickhead, and shut the fuck up. You'll find some Colombian Arabica in the freezer. Grind it and give me a moment to think.'

'Did she . . . ?'

'No, she told me nothing at all. She had a laptop with her and there was probably some of the stuff we were looking for on there. That Freya was cunning. Can't underestimate her. Even if she is dead.' Freeman looked for any trace of sentiment in the old bitch's eyes. There was none. She was saying too much, too. Stuff he didn't need to hear, or know. Maybe it was age telling. Maybe she was shocked. And maybe they had no intention of letting him pass any information on to anyone. He felt a chill.

'What now?'

'What now? God alone knows. One thing, though. Millie's got help of some kind. That probably means old school chums.'

'Was she at Roedean or something?'

Clara looked at him with a blankness that somehow communicated contempt. 'Former colleagues, Mr Freeman. And some of Millie's past associates are really not the kind of people you want to find yourself, ah, tusslin' with.'

'But this is official, isn't it? I was told . . . American and UK interests served jointly.'

'Shit, boy, look at me. Antediluvian ain't in it. This is as deniable as the Loch Ness fucking monster, top to tail. Why do you think they chose you?' There was a silence.

'I don't know.'

'Because you've got ambition leaking out that asshole where you've let yourself get shafted so many times, bent over for them so fuckin' often. And you've got that lovely family, clamouring for time and money and love. That poor sod, Flaws, because he's everything they need – clever, fucked-up, in the end, disposable. A plod. Plodding on and on. What's more, he's been under the gun . . . they have something on him. Something to do with all this, something he saw or did. Anyway, that's not for your pink and blushing little ears, sonny. They've decided to leave him alive and kicking for now. The plan to haul him out here and have Billy Boy's boyos remove him from the board has been abandoned, apparently at Billy Boy's fucking behest. He's running things on the ground now, it seems. Personally, I think he's gone completely apeshit. Better get ready for Armageddon.'

Freeman was indeed blushing. He stood up, flustered, and tried to exert authority.

'Right then, if you're sure you're OK? I had better contact Mr . . . I'm sure you can guess who I mean.'

Clara grinned sourly. Her brilliantly white American teeth flashed. 'Billy Boy? So he's playing you, is he? Jesus, what a fucking mess. Do you really know who he is? What he's done? Probably just as well. Hey, I'll bet you have a code name for him? Do you? Go on, boy, do tell?'

He was embarrassed. 'Childcatcher. I call him the Childcatcher. Not to his face, obviously.'

'Childcatcher.' Clara looked briefly thoughtful. 'Appropriate. Catching children, kind of, was once one of his little jobs. Self-appointed, of course. It was what was done to them after they were caught that was the problem. Childcatcher. Very good. I wouldn't have thought you had it in you.'

Freeman's mobile trilled. His ringtone was the Elvis Costello song

'Watching the Detectives'. 'Good mobile coverage,' he mumbled, pressing the 'Accept' button. He spoke in monosyllables, listened intently.

'Developments,' asked Clara, when he ended the call.

'You could say that. It looks as if Billy Boy has burned down a chunk of Inverness.'

'Splendid,' said Clara. 'Go away and put out the fire, then. There's someone I need to talk to.'

She waited until she heard Freeman slam the door behind him before searching in a bottom desk drawer for a satellite mobile which she kept on full charge. It worked well with a view of the southern horizon and a patch of forest had been cleared next to the loch-facing decking for just this reason. She dialled the number.

'Hi,' she said. 'Clara. It's all going to hell in a handbasket here. The Brits have let various genies out of their bottles and they can't get the sons of bitches back in. Looks like the beginnings of a covering operation, umbrella cover-up. From the top. I'm guessing we need to pursue our own agenda.' She listened for a moment.

'No, I'm thinking we're going to see a couple of the bigger bastards coming out into the open on this. Manderley was probably Nixon's bright idea, but he's nuts, and far too messy. Nixon can only protect himself for so long. Serpentine? Is he our man? Inasmuch as he's anybody's. Maybe. But yes, I think I've managed to convince him his best interests lie with us. His areas of expertise and our own concerns . . . it could all work out, yet. The rest of the shit-storm could just end up as useful static.'

The call ended without her saying anything more. She looked out at the darkness of the loch, felt the increasingly heavy spatter of rain on her face and licked the soft, cool water off her lips.

'Serpentine,' she muttered. 'What's your own game? You're too bright to let all this drift out of control. Put yourself under any obligation to the likes of me. Us.' She felt her mind come within touching distance of an answer to her own question. But it eluded her. She dialled another number. 'Play the game, darlin'.'

'Hallo, lover boy,' she said. 'Looks like I'm gonna have to come and save your sorry ass. Just that one little job in exchange. Like we discussed.'

———◆———

Millie slid down in her seat, hiding her face behind the dashboard as the van, lights on full beam, hurtled towards them. Murricane started the car but kept the lights off, watching as flames began to spread to the roof of the building. Three figures came stumbling out of the street entrance, just as a dull flash came from the ground-floor windows, which inexplicably did not blow out. Then one of the figures, tall, a male, was starting a motorbike, and another headlight was flashing towards them.

'Follow him!' said Millie. 'First rule of pursuit. The pursuer never realises he's being pursued.'

'That's not the first rule. The first rule is . . . what is the first rule?'

'Catch. The first rule of chasing is catching.'

'Yeah, but we don't want to catch him. We want to see where the people he's chasing go.' The Volvo rear-wheel drive could easily turn right around in its own length. Murricane spun the wheel, flicked the lights to dip and followed the motorbike's single tail light, which was rapidly diminishing in the distance.

'Trick is to keep up,' said Millie.

'Without being noticed.'

'Yes, but the first rule . . .'

'Never mind.' He floored the accelerator. 'Open the windows. We should be able to hear that motorbike if we lose sight of it.'

It was surprisingly easy to follow the chase. In effect, the three vehicles were a convoy and, in the quiet, night-time streets of Inverness, they could hear the bike in the brief interludes when they couldn't see it.

'Watching brief,' said Millie. 'Don't get too close.'

'Don't worry.' Murricane flicked the lights off as they passed Century House. They had seen the bike and van vanish into the access road for this upmarket riverside office development, picking up the noise of the bike as it accelerated towards the pool of darkness where the street lights gave out beyond the Caledonian Stadium and thick vegetation closed in. Murricane flicked off the ignition before they came within a hundred metres of the turn around the stadium. They coasted to a halt.

'Wait,' said Millie. 'This is all wrong.' They could see the van, in darkness, but partly caught in the motorbike's headlight, and the occasional shadow of the rider. Then everything went dark.

'Stalled it,' said Murricane, 'or parked up.' The Volvo's windows were still open. They could hear the firth rattling and lapping on a stony beach and the whisper of leaves in rain. Then the night was split by a double explosion and they saw the dull fiery spurting of a weapon being discharged.

'Shotgun,' said Millie. Headlights blazed suddenly, illuminating the whole scene. More than headlights, a rack of spotlights, too. The stationary white van lit up like a beacon. A man with some kind of gun in his hand stood looking down at another figure, prone on the ground. There was the sound of a laboured diesel engine. The light reflected from the van silhouetted the shape of a Land Rover lumbering out of the bushes.

'Short wheelbase Defender.' Murricane had his binoculars out. 'Clever, changing vehicle. Well organised.'

'They're going to see us.'

'No, they're not.' He threw the glasses in the back seat, started the engine and reversed at speed towards the football stadium. An industrial rubbish skip gave just enough cover for the big Volvo. They waited for about 20 seconds, before the Land Rover rattled past. 'They mustn't see us now. This time we've got them. And we're not going to lose them. No fucking way.'

He left 30 seconds before nosing the Volvo out from cover. They could see the instantly identifiable, round, pin-prick rear lights of the Land Rover in the distance, heading for the Kessock roundabout, above them on the elevated approach to the suspension bridge.

'We need to see where they go.' Millie was trying to keep calm, but the flat Cumbrian vowels in her voice betrayed her anxiety. 'They could go to the Black Isle, north, back into the city, or head south on the A9. Then it could be the A96 east. We need to see. God damn it!'

'OK.' Murricane flipped the headlights on, then mashed the throttle and forced the car back past Cowan House and up the ramp leading to the roundabout. They were almost past the exit for the southerly A9 when Millie screamed 'TURN!' The big Swedish car's rear end lurched alarmingly, but fortunately there was no other traffic and in the distance, Murricane could see those tell-tale Land Rover lights. Then they vanished.

'A96,' he said. 'They're heading east.'

'Go!'

It was a game of seek-and-hide. With more hiding than seeking. They passed the huge shopping and leisure development at Eastfield, so American in style, thought Murricane, it could have been in Israel. Or anywhere. Inverness Airport lay to the left, brilliantly lit, silent. All they could do was hang back as the traffic bottleneck of Nairn approached. Murricane switched off his lights and parked, engine running, as the town's two sets of traffic lights loomed.

They nearly lost them in Forres. And they were nearly found themselves. But Murricane had the benefit of both training and a passenger who was nearly as skilled as he was, or had been. Finally, when the Land Rover came to a halt in the drive of a tiny fisherman's cottage, some instinct had already made Murricane pass, then stop in a deserted parking area next to the soaring dunes outside Findhorn village. Dawn was breaking, the sea lending a glassy clarity to the morning. The rain clouds were lifting. Millie, whose clothes and trainers were roughly those of a jogger and whose appearance – youngish, thin, female and Gore-texed – was approximately Findhornian, began what could easily have been just another morning run for a spiritual seeker. After half an hour, she found what she was looking for. When she got back to the Volvo, Murricane was sound asleep.

'Jesus, Mark. Come on. If we're going to do this, we need to do it now.'

'Do what?' His voice had none of the grogginess usual in the newly wakened. He was used to grabbing rest when and where he could find it.

'Land Rover parked, two men got out, they unloaded, one carrying a computer. One stayed in the driver's seat, then drove off. Don't know if he's coming back, but it's the two who had me who're in there now. We need to . . . we need to speak to them.'

'*Had* you? That's the second time you've said that. They didn't . . .'

'No, they did not.' Millie was reaching into her backpack, which she'd left in the front footwell. 'Weapons? Side-arm and knife. Mainly. Side-arm. No firing, unless absolute threat.' Her voice had become staccato and commanding. Remote.

Murricane opened his mouth to argue, then shut it again.

FILL UP MY SHOTGUN . . .
WITH ROCK SALT AND NAILS

Shotguns, then.

The first time I fired a shotgun deliberately, I was aged 11. We were killing a cow. Which is a big job and potentially a dangerous one. Cows are big, strong creatures and, in an enclosed space, they can maim or kill. Especially when they're frightened. Especially when they know they're about to die.

It wasn't our cow. Bob 'Burnie' Dixon had a bigger croft than ours, maybe twice the size, and he kept a small herd for milk and meat. Each winter, one cow would be earmarked for killing, and for the price of some help, my dad would get a share.

Technically, of course, this is illegal, though in the crofting areas of the Scottish Highlands, the need for licensed slaughtermen means that blind eyes have always been turned to home killing of animals. Though, with ever more nitpicking Health and Safety regulations, it's becoming less common.

Anyway, my family were crofters. Burnie Dixon was on the up and up. He'd taken over, more or less informally, a couple of neighbouring holdings where the tenant was too old, infirm or rich and in Australia to actually work the land. He had his eye on ours, of course. And eventually, he'd get it.

But that was later. For the moment, it was a February night, cold, clear, icy, and we were 'taking off' a cow. She was a Charolais, caged in one of the dank barn's galvanised stalls, her breath coming in great snorting clouds. Dad clapped me on the shoulder as we walked in from the crunchy, frozen muck of the yard.

'You've seen plenty of sheep taken off,' he said. 'This is maybe on a different scale, mind. Stay clear o' its sides. She gets mad, she'll crush you.'

I said nothing. I had helped with the sheep, cut their throats as Dad held them down, so passive and strangely quiet. I'd felt them squirm against my hands, warm, oily and woolly in their winter coats. And I'd felt that bizarre heat as I tried, with my flimsy hands and arms, to separate the skin from the meaty body, sliding fingers with disturbing ease, bloodily between flesh and fleece.

There were four of us in the barn: Burnie, Dad, me and a man from Inverness I didn't know. He was sharpening a knife as we came in, expertly honing it in figure-of-eight strokes, occasionally pouring yellow olive oil onto the stone to give it an even finer edge.

'Yon's Liam the Butcher,' said Dad. 'Butcher, this is my son, Zander.' The Butcher? Didn't he have a normal name? But even at that age, I was familiar with nicknames and sometimes their necessity. The Butcher would have a reason for not revealing any more than his occupation. Notably, the fact that, while home killing was a grey area for crofters as long as the animal was being consumed entirely by the owner's family, on-site butchery for sharing or selling was definitely against the law. And some of this cow would end up on the menu of the Farquhar Arms. Burnie's brother-in-law was the manager.

The Butcher nodded curtly at me. He was dark, a Pict, rather than a Celt, 'full of trowie blood', as Dad said later. But that was Caithness talk. Trows, or trowies, the leprechauns of Scotland, were reputed to be the last survivors of the Picts in my father's native Flow Country. Before the Vikings . . . well, picked them off.

The cow, snorting and pawing the concrete like it was about to enter some kind of *corrida*, had been backed into its stall and couldn't turn round. Now it became clear why. Burnie picked an old single-barrel shotgun from a corner, broke it and inserted a single shell. Yellow, which meant it was a 20-gauge. He eyed my father.

'Think the boy should do it, Drewie. Something new, eh?'

'If he wants.' Dad looked at me, one eyebrow raised. I shrugged and reached for the worn, oiled gun. It was heavy, well balanced. My thumb felt for the safety catch I knew would be just above the join between stock and breech.

'The kye's better wi' you doing it, Zander,' muttered Dad. 'He doesnae see you as a threat. Make sure you get the barrel right between his eyes.' There was the soft, silky scraping of the Butcher's knife, honing: the scrape and shuffle and puffing of the cow. And then I was moving, almost without thought, poking the barrel through the bars of the stall, inches away from the head, then closer. Right between the eyes. Point-blank.

A sudden stillness, I remember. The cow stopped its breathing, or maybe I did. The snick of the safety catch moved forwards and then pressing lightly against the beast's skull, I squeezed the trigger . . .

An unearthly, flat bang, impossibly loud, echoing around the concrete and the tin roof. The shotgun kicked back, hard against my shoulder. Amazingly, the cow's head did not blow apart, but the huge beast lurched and then howled, not like a cow at all. If cattle could scream, that's what it was doing. And then it went berserk.

'Death throes,' Burnie said, loudly enough to be heard over the noise from the stall. 'Won't last long.' And he was already preparing a block and tackle, I saw, chain rattling through his hands, to pull the carcase out of the stall, then up over a beam, for flaying and butchering. Unexpectedly, I felt horribly sick. Still clutching the shotgun, I ran for the yard. The Butcher stepped quickly into my path.

'I'll just take the gun,' he said, in that Invernessian accent. 'Dinnae want it messed up.' Knife in one hand, gun in the other. That's how I remember him, as I cannoned off the door post and vomited into the frozen mud.

I woke up in Raigmore Hospital's casualty unit, thinking, I'm dead. Deaf. No, dead. Deaf. Dead. Deaf. Dead. Back to being a wee boy again, when I thought for a substantial period of time that 'deaf' and 'dead' were the same thing. All I could remember was the rough feel of sawn-off shotgun barrels on my neck, then the massive, twin explosion that signified my head being blown off. I lay there, gazing at the hospital-green ceiling, as I gradually realised that being deafened, twice over, by two shotgun blasts, signified not only that the first one hadn't deafened me at all, but that neither it nor the second one had killed me. Everything from the neck up throbbed with a giant pulsing wave of agony and nausea though. So maybe he'd been loaded with rock salt and it had bounced off my hard neck. Maybe he'd missed. At a distance of several inches, that indicated someone with a serious problem in the accuracy department. Or that I was required to be alive.

A nurse opened the door to what I realised was a private room – a premium in what remained of our glorious National Health Service. She moved her lips and noises came out. After a while I began to understand what she was saying.

As it happened, Murricane deliberately ignored Millie's instructions. When she began knocking at the front door, the sound echoing in the quiet night, he went through the back window into the cottage kitchen, with one forearm guarding his face and in the other hand a silenced Fyodorev 14-shot automatic pistol, an obscure Israeli weapon, a gift from Moshe.

It had taken very little time to work out that the cottage had one public room, a kitchen-diner, with the front door leading directly into it. The back entrance was in a small porch, which seemed to contain a toilet. Hume and MacDougall had been slumped in old armchairs, silent and exhausted after the events of the night. The drive to Findhorn from Inverness had been a kind of anticlimax. Evading the bike, Hume dealing with the lunatic rider. The policeman. After that, the drive had seemed easy, clear. Only the most basic of observation for a potential tail. They'd seen nothing. Billy Boy had driven, singing 'The Sash' all the way.

But Hume and MacDougall had reacted to Millie's knocking exactly by the book: Hume was by the front door jamb, holding a small and ugly, suppressed Makarov in both hands. MacDougall was armed too, not with his Sig Sauer, but with a Russian Nagant revolver. An assassin's gun, the only revolver which could be silenced, in this case with a foam-stuffed plastic bleach bottle. Once as commonplace as any handgun on Earth, standard issue to the Soviet Army. He was in the back porch about to open the door, when Murricane smashed through the kitchen window. MacDougall reacted quickly, but he had to turn his large frame in a tiny space; Murricane, who had cannoned into the back of the room's only sofa, was able to shoot him from a kind of half-crouch on the floor. He managed to stop himself from firing the normal three kill-shots, but two bullets hit MacDougall, one in the side, one in the top of the thigh. Thrown back as if he'd been kicked, he slumped down, blood already pumping from the femoral artery.

Murricane was already moving towards him, looking for cover in the porch. But there was no firing from the man covering the front door. And when Murricane turned to target him, Hume was squatting, holding his hands out,

143

palms first, the gun on the floor in front of him. Murricane shot him anyway. It was an adrenalin thing, he knew immediately he shouldn't have done it. Focus, boy. Lack of focus. The bullet, with accidental accuracy, smashed Hume's left kneecap to a pulp. He tumbled into a heap, but made no sound. In the few seconds all this had taken, the two loudest sounds had been Millie's knocking at the front door and the crash of breaking glass and splintering wood as Murricane came in the back window. The wet cough of silenced rounds was minor by comparison. Still, Murricane knew they didn't have much time.

He opened the front door, watching Millie's eyes as she took in the scene. They flickered, widened. She swallowed once.

'Christ Almighty.' He could see all the built-up tension turning into rage, watched it being suppressed. She came in and closed the door. Blood was pumping weakly from MacDougall's body. They could hear him whispering something. It sounded odd. Not English. Hume still made no sound.

'Sorry,' said Murricane. 'It's just I . . .'

'Never mind,' she said. 'Go and get the car. We'll have to take him with us.'

'Gaelic,' said Hume, his voice tight with controlled pain. '*Mo Graidh*. My darling. I didn't think he had it in him. I'm Hume, by the way. David Hume. Real name . . . before you ask.'

'*Darling*, eh? What? Affection for someone? I bet he likes small fluffy animals. He's probably talking to some childhood puppy.' Millie took a step towards Hume, her hand moving to the commando knife that was sheathed on her belt.

'Don't, Millie.' Murricane stepped in front of her. She barely reacted to his presence. Just kept looking at the man on the floor, his wounded knee barely bleeding.

'I know, I know. Go and get the car, Mark. Just go and get it. And be quick. Someone will have heard that crash when you went through the window, you gung-ho moron.'

Hume watched Murricane go. He had something like a calm terror in his eyes.

'There's nothing written down,' he said. 'There's the computer, hard drive, some other stuff, papers.'

'I don't think we need that. But we'll take you. You'll survive. What did you want with me?'

'You realise I let you go, don't you? I didn't want that kind of blood on my hands. Your kind. And they think I killed that policeman, back in Inverness. I just knocked him out. Listen, I'm just babysitting. I was asked by people from Six.'

'What about Freya?' Her voice was calm. 'What about fucking Freya?'

'Manderley is out of control. He's a hands-off, no-comebacks tool, or they thought he was. But he's off the park now. God help us, you know how it is. You remember what it was like. It's a results thing. There was nothing I could do. He had a domestic black sanction. All costs clean-up.'

'Just following fucking orders, is that it? And what are you, anyway? Why the supposed scruples?'

'I'm . . . retired. You know how it is. I told you, I'm monitoring the situation. I'm supposed to be a conduit.' He stopped. It was as if someone had thrown a switch. His face turned a sickly grey. 'There was an official watching brief. From the men in suits. The men in very good suits.'

'And women.'

'And maybe women. For all I know.' A slight moan escaped him. 'Fuck. This is . . . going to do . . . wonders for my . . . golf.'

'Douglas Bader had no legs at all and he played golf. Didn't find it a handicap at all.' Someone had told her that joke. She couldn't remember who.

The door opened. It was Murricane. The whirr of the Volvo's engine filled the room.

'Was it you who told me that? That Douglas Bader played with no legs at all?' said Millie. 'In fact, I believe he played off scratch.'

'Must have been itchy, sure enough,' said Murricane. 'Come on, let's go.'

Manderley had watched the whole episode unfold, sat slumped behind the wheel of an illegally-blacked-out Vauxhall Corsa, a boy-racer special he'd stolen in Nairn, a small smile on his face. He had made no attempt to interfere.

'Millie,' he said to himself quietly. 'Gotcha.' When the Volvo left Findhorn, heading for Inverness, he followed discreetly. He was good at it. Better at following than being followed. Though he'd sensed something on the way back from Inverness.

Millie and Murricane didn't notice a thing. But then, they did have Hume's moaning to contend with. It worsened as they headed along the A96. Morning began to break properly across Ben Wyvis.

———————◆———————

I was, it seemed, suffering from a concussion caused by a heavy blow to the back of the neck. This had followed the firing of a shotgun in close proximity to my temple. There were powder burns. Someone had not wanted to kill me. Someone had even pulled the force of that consciousness-depriving butt-blow, so as not to leave me with any significant brain damage. Somehow, I couldn't bring myself to feel grateful.

I was on my feet, but being kept under observation. Fit enough to talk, the doctors said, so Freeman convened a case conference in my room. He looked, for the first time since I'd known him, ravaged, untidy. Uncertain. Ill. I, on the other hand, looked a lot worse than that. I had dressed for the occasion. Paper hospital robes do nothing for one's credibility. But the crumpled, muddy and sweaty clothes I had been wearing when the shotgun connected with my neck made me feel like a crime scene. Which I suppose I was, in a sense.

Straightforward police work: they had followed up on the van. It had been reported stolen in Thurso, of all places, 250 tortuous miles to the north, three days previously. The owner was a plumber called Smith. How many vans were stolen in Thurso, I wondered? How many people called Smith? How many plumbers? There were pockets of criminality in the most remote parts of the Highlands, along with the social deprivation that came with big industrial projects that had lost their sheen and sometimes their industry, big dreams gone bad. Invergordon, once planted with hundreds of families from Glasgow due to the construction of a massive aluminium smelter, fuelled by supposedly free hydro-electricity. Shut. Fort William, the same deal, an aluminium smelter and a paper mill. Both closed. And in Caithness, the Dounreay nuclear plant. No longer working. Subject to what they called decommissioning, leaving only the childhood leukaemia behind. And the gangs of sullen, unskilled youths.

I was reclining on the bed, smearing mud on the pristine sheets. Around me, like reluctant suitors for my hand, were Freeman, Sheila and prize techie Jim Smeaton, who looked more uncomfortable than any of us. Apart from me. I was, I had to admit, pretty damned uncomfortable. A day and a night after my helmetless antics on Sheila's motorbike, and where were we? Or where was I? In hospital with a sore head.

'So, let me see if I can understand what actually happened last night,' said Freeman.

'First of all, can you fill me in on what happened out at Loch Ness, sir? You were heading out there, as I remember?'

'Loch Ness? Oh yes. Birds flown the coop and all that. Nothing to see. House all locked up. I had the uniforms go over there this morning with a warrant, but nothing to speak of.'

I let it go. For the moment. He sounded about as convincing as a creationist.

'Well, sir, I went over to Kennedy Avenue, had a word with Wank . . . Roddy, God rest him. He'd been in hospital, after some sort of mugging incident. Drug-deal stuff, probably. So I hadn't spoken to him up to that point. And then I received a call from Dr Dartington.' All eyes turned to Sheila. She looked supremely unconcerned.

'Dr Dartington had some information regarding the pathology and so I . . . asked her to meet me at the locus. It was fortunate she had her motorcycle there.' On hearing the shotgun blasts over her mobile, Sheila had abandoned all thoughts of deception and had called in the cavalry. I was touched. I still hadn't had a chance to thank her.

'And what was this information, Dr Dartington?' I could have sworn that Freeman sounded as if he was going to cry. There was an actual quiver in his voice.

'I had some thoughts on DNA samples which I really ought to have shared with the investigating officer previously,' Sheila said. 'When I realised, after phoning his mobile, that Sergeant Flaws was actually at the scene, I decided to go over there as quickly as possible myself. The bike was the obvious method.'

Flimsy, almost believable. Freeman took a deep breath, coughed and dredged up some of his usual sarkiness.

'And so you decided to go all Steve McQueen and follow the supposed arsonists?'

'Bombers, sir. I think that's fairly clear. Yes, sir, I did. I was lucky, sir.'

'You were fortunate not be killed, as I understand it. You're far too old to be messing about on two wheels, Sergeant.'

I sighed. 'Sir, have you ever heard of Jim Redman?'

He looked nonplussed. 'Who?'

'Jim Redman. Four times world motorcycle Grand Prix champion. Still racing in classic events today. And he's almost 80. Still very hard to beat.

Motorcycling is a learned physical and mental activity, sir. Very difficult to unlearn. Like, well, like riding a bike.'

'So, what do we have?' Freeman ran his hands through his hair. I could see a tremor. 'A dead body on the ground floor, presumed murdered. Presumed your pal, Roddy. His computer and associated hard disk, probably operated remotely by the ladies upstairs, removed. Jim, you have the requisite electronics?' Jim shook his bandaged head, looking like a depressed St Bernard. 'No, of course you don't. The mysterious escapees took it and its appendages with them in their white van. Which was empty of both people and interesting electronic objects by the time we got it. And presumably by the time Sergeant Flaws had finished with his Evel Knievel antics. I think we're done with you, Smeaton.'

We watched Jim shuffle out, looking both worried and relieved. The door shut behind him.

'I need to know what you were doing there, Flaws. I need to know what you got from Roddy.' He was pleading, almost. Wheedling.

'I just popped along to have a word with him, sir. Clarify a few matters, then have another look at the SOC. Dr Dartington's arrival was also . . .'

'Oh, for FUCK'S SAKE!'

Freeman stood up. He was beyond anger, beyond control, quivering like a tuning fork. He gazed blankly from Sheila to me. 'Don't you two get it? Stop fucking me about. I don't fucking CARE what sleazy sex games you were up to, you twisted bitch. I know all about your proclivities, Sheila, don't forget that.'

Ah. I looked at Sheila. She shrugged. Fuck me. Or, in this instance, somebody else.

'I don't expect you to be honest with me, Flaws. Nobody involved in this is interested in honesty of any sort.'

'Sir, wait a minute.' My head was swimming. Freeman was incoherent. 'Is there something you want to tell us?'

He sat down, head in his hands. After what seemed like minutes, he sighed.

'A bombing, Sergeant. Well, you would probably know all about that, wouldn't you? And the body they pulled out of the harbour this morning?'

There was a silence. I looked again at Sheila. She shrugged again. The other duty pathologist must have dealt with it.

'At the Longman, sir? Always drunks falling in as they walk along the old piers?'

'How did you guess? Somebody called Gunn found it. You know him, it seems. Corpse is down for an urgent post-mortem. Urgent for us, that is, not for him. Dr Dartington, please consider it your last job before taking some compulsory, and official, leave. I would suggest, Doctor, that you take a break somewhere well away from Inverness, possibly away from Scotland. That's personal advice. Better for you and us if you are uninvolved. But please, take a look at this floater for us first.'

Sheila spoke then for the first time. 'You boys. You're both like this fucking floater. You're completely out of your depth.' And then she left, sauntering, apparently calm. She was right of course. But Freeman and I were left wondering what she meant, or at least I was. Out of our depth with the likes of her? Definitely. Or just floundering around with a case we either didn't understand, or were frightened to admit we did? Definitely.

'We've got something from Grampian which may be related, Zander,' said Freeman. 'Maybe I need to tell you one or two things.' And he did.

LOAD UP, LOAD UP, LOAD UP YOUR RUBBER BULLETS

In Ireland, it was Browning Hi-power automatics for the most part. But there were a lot of shotguns about, mostly American police-issue Remington Wingmasters, which could be modified to shoot all kinds of things, including the legendary rubber or plastic bullets. Sometimes the plastic bullets weren't actually plastic, if you get what I mean. Shotguns are very forgiving of what they fire, unlike high velocity rifles. Buckshot, slugs that'll destroy the engine block of a car if you're close enough, tear gas, bird shot, rock salt if you just want to cause pain and fright. And shotguns often don't look like shotguns. I mean, everyone expects that *Lock, Stock and Two Smoking Barrels*, country manor thing. Or something that's been hacksawed to bits. Remingtons come in all shapes and sizes, with folding stocks, pistol grips, tiny barrels, black satin finishes. Toys for boys. And in Ireland, how they liked their toys.

I was only there for three months, on a 'training and goodwill' exchange between the RUC and Northern Constabulary. It was 1985, I was an up-and-coming constable, being prepared for great things, believing I was on my way to much more than a stalled, dead-end career as a perpetual sergeant. And so I was nominated – ordered, more like – to take myself off to Belfast, where I would be, to quote the chief constable, who seemed to have made all the arrangements personally, shown a good time.

The notion was that I would be given an introductory tour to what was then basically the world's cutting-edge laboratory on urban terrorism. At the time there was a daft feeling that Gaelic activists in the Highlands might start burning incomers' cottages like they had in Wales. Having someone around who had been terrorised or done a bit of terrorising seemed like a good notion. Belfast was a workshop for policing an insurgency and I was by no means alone in becoming a terrorism tourist. Officers much more senior than me, from all around the world, were being brought to Belfast to ogle and wonder and scare themselves shitless. There was a rota of RUC folk who used their 'exchange' visits to police forces from Hong Kong to LA as rest and recreation leaves of absence. And another rota of guys in Ireland who were hospitable and, let's face it, scary. Who liked to scare you. Who'd put on shows.

I was staying in a hotel on the Malone Road called The Oak. It was a Protestant area, as safe or unsafe as anywhere else.

'You'll be fine here,' said Inspector Ken Nixon, my host, minder, mentor, guide and bodyguard. 'It's only been bombed twice in the last two years. And they let nurses in for free for the discos. Are you married, Zander? Fair play to you, not that it matters.'

I was married then. But I wasn't averse to the occasional nurse, either. Those were innocent days, no one in Ulster believed in AIDS, or cared about it, and I'd heard stories about the sexual promiscuity allegedly encouraged by the nearness of death-by-bombing.

'Nurses?'

'Aye, nurses from the infirmary residence just up the road. You're well in there, boy, if that's your poison. Which school did you go to, if you don't mind me asking?'

I pondered for a moment. I'd come across this question before, during my training at Tulliallan Police College and, later, of course, in Glasgow. It was one of those sectarian tricks, like asking which foot you kicked with or whether or not you were on the square.

'Tain Royal Academy,' I said. 'I was a boarder.'

'Really? Well! There's posh!'

How many times had I heard that from dipsticks who thought I'd gone to Gordonstoun or Strathallan, as was now compulsory for Labour politicians.

'Well, not really, Only Monday to Thursday nights. It was kind of remote where I was brought up, and the nearest secondary was 60 miles away. Single-track roads and all that. So we country kids boarded. It wasn't too bad.' I remembered the sleepless nights, the bullying by bored and sadistic older boys, and the inevitable bullying by me when I grew older, bored and sadistic in turn.

'*Royal* Academy, eh? Nice Loyalist name. I went to Saint Pat's myself, in Lurgan.' And then a wicked grin. 'I'm your token Catholic policeman, very presentable for foreign visitors and members of His or Her Majesty's press. Welcome to the Romanist Ulster Constabulary.'

But Nixon was lying, of course. It was a wee wind-up for visitors. He was from Portadown, an Orangeman through and through. There was a lot of lying in the RUC. It was force of habit, second nature. Or first. He had a pal who was a Catholic copper and called himself, of all things, Billy Boy. Hilarious.

'Fancy a pint? Or would you rather go straight for the nurses? They start the discos early here.'

'A pint'll do nicely.' It was to be the first of many.

Belfast was a nervous wreck of a city. While I had curiosity and youth on my side, I was in a constant state of tension. Or, to be honest, fear. Every sense, every flight-or-fight hormone, every physical sensitivity, was jacked up to the maximum. No wonder there was so much rampant fucking. It was like foreplay with bombs. There was the same dry throat, pounding heart, tingling in the fingers you got with the prospect of a hot first date. Except the threat was not rejection by a woman, but sudden death. It took me the first week to realise that Ulster had the same effect on everyone who came 'across the water', as the undercover Special Forces cowboys called it. And that the trick of surviving was not to get hardened to the terror, but to harness it: to make yourself sensitive to genuine danger, able to tell the difference between real threats and general unfamiliarity. The problem was that you began to enjoy the adrenalin, or at least depend on it, become addicted to it. And that's when trouble started, when an operator turned into a thrill seeker.

'You'll have heard of Nairac, will you?' Nixon was sinking a second pint of Carlsberg. We were in The Crown, the ultimate Belfast tourist pub, a temple to glamorous Victorian drinking. We had a closed booth to ourselves. It was probably bugged to bits.

'No. Sounds foreign.'

'Maltese. Lesson there for all of us. Captain, back in 1972 and into all sorts of really nasty stuff, you don't want to know. Anyway, thought he could do a Belfast accent. And fact is, yer man wasn't fuckin' bad. But he was a fuckin' toffee-nosed git, friend of Lord Killanin, all that, so nobody, but nobody was ever fooled. He would go into pubs and sing rebel songs, for fuck's sake. And the

PIRA boys, the fellow travellers, they were kind of sorry for him, I think. Like a madman amongst them. Same with loads of those geeks, they lose the plot, they do these operations and think they're undercover, and everyone in the estates knows what's going on. Video cars, people hiding in football pavilions. Don't make me fucking laugh. So anyway, the boyos get tired of his shit, or somebody does. No longer amusing. One night he's singing in a pub called the Three Mile Inn, down in Armagh, unarmed, on his own. And he's picked up, tortured, shot, fed into a meat grinder. Literally turned into mince. No body ever found. Just a funny taste in a few sausages.'

'Yeah, right.' I was young and impressionable, but determined not to be fooled by this kind of blarney. And I was two pints in as well, though I wasn't planning on driving back to the Malone Road afterwards. I'd get a cab. One of the Republican black cabs, maybe. Or maybe not. 'Pull the other one, Ken. Inspector.'

He went very still, then leaned into my face. I could smell his beery breath over my own.

'The thing is, young Zander, it's true. Anglo-Irish Meat had a factory right fuckin' there. And there's other stuff Nairac was supposed to be involved in. Stuff that's sick even for . . . ach, never mind. But remember this, boy. You're in a parallel fuckin' universe here. "Over the Water". The Taint. Yeah, that's what these intelligence bastards call it. And there are no fuckin' rules, nothing's what it seems, your worst nightmares can come true in an instant.' He sank the rest of his pint. 'There's a wee briefing for you. Part of the course. I'd better go. Don't take a black cab back to Orangefield. Get them to call you a Proddiecar. I'll see you in the morning. We'll send a hearse for you.' My jaw must have dropped. 'Only a wee joke, fella. Welcome to the jungle. And try the nurses. They're really very . . . co-operative, for the most part.'

I didn't take his advice about the nurses. Not that night.

'No identifying marks,' said Grant. 'Clothes, most labels removed, but not cheap. Good solid generic outdoor stuff. Gore-tex, the real deal. Had a Sprayway fleece, that did have a label. But then half that gear is all fuckin' label, ain't it? Approach shoes, those beefed-up trainer things, Brasher, I think. Well-worn. Nothing in his pockets, no wallet, no rings, fingerprints coming up kosher. No record. Bullet wound, but we'll get to that. Sheila?'

We were in conference, as Freeman liked to call it, in his office. He had a great view of Raigmore Hospital. I wished he was in it. Preferably the tropical diseases department. With Grant and Ebola. So far disease-free, there was Grant, Jimbo, Freeman, Sheila and me.

'Caucasian, probably European Celtic origin. Red hair, pale skin. Death from heart failure. There was an anomaly: damage to the right ventricle, old. Genetic or possibly some kind of drug abuse. Crack cocaine or amphetamine. Lungs empty of water. Bullet wound to left knee. Massive trauma. Bullet is being matched as we speak. Whoever shot him couldn't have known he was susceptible to terminal shock.'

Grant smiled. 'Some hopes of matching the slug,' he said. 'Looked like one of those hand-cut soft-nose efforts to me. Hand-loaded. Meant to destroy, not wound.' He coughed, flushed. He was enjoying this.

Sheila looked stonily at him.

'Sorry, love.'

She ignored him and continued, 'About 30, extremely fit, small, light, maybe a bit of weight training, muscle development on back and shoulders. Someone who was into heft, general aerobic fitness. Pity, really, he was carrying his own death sentence. Must have been moments away many a time. From checking out. Several inoculation marks, old school stuff, the kind you get for going to infectious parts of the world.' She sniffed. Sheila looked tired. But it had been a difficult couple of days and getting her story straight couldn't have been easy; or maintaining it. She was saving the best for last. Studiously ignoring Fergus Grant, she said, 'Couple of tattoos removed, probably regimental. I have my own conclusions about the shooting. Left knee smashed by hollow-point projectile, 30 calibre.' Parading her special course in Birmingham, what was it called? Projectile trauma. 'No other injuries. Signs of attempted first aid to the leg. And that's about it. Heart failure. Sort of accidental, then. Clean-shaven. Good-looking boy once.' I felt the contusion on the back of mine. It was bad, but not very bad. In that I was at least still alive. 'Looks like he died inconveniently, maybe unexpectedly, but he had been badly shot in the knee. Kneecapped, almost, but from a distance. No powder burns, contact traces.'

Freeman was wearing an expensive silk shirt and a Windsor-knotted tie that sat perfectly, as if it had been pinned on, or modelled out of glass fibre. Maybe it had. He looked very different from the day before, when ravaged had been the only word to describe him. And now I knew why. On the whole,

I preferred the ravaged look. It was still lurking there, at the edges of his neatness.

'Right, thank you both for that. Sergeant, you're the detective.' Everyone pondered that thought for a moment in silence. 'Any thoughts?'

I looked at Sheila.

'The knee? Anything more?'

'Explosive combustible fracture of the patella.'

Grant was bursting to say his piece: 'Shot from about 10, maybe 12 feet. Across the room. No casings. They must have picked them up. Angle of shot low. Disabling. I still think a soft-nose.'

'Well, yes,' I said. 'Revenge? Torture? Like Enderby?'

'Not obviously. No attempt to cut his balls off or anything.'

'He did have various objects of interest, Jimmy, I think?'

Jimmy flushed. 'Signs of computer nerdery. USB dongle, magnetic flash eraser, Torx-head screwdrivers. I've checked the USB flash memory – nothing on it.' He looked at me and blinked for a microsecond. That indicated something else entirely.

A shape appeared mistily through the dirty glass of of the conference room – a uniformed WPC, crisply starched – and Freeman's eyes flicked towards her. She entered the room and whispered in his ear like a lover, or as if he were the president of the USA, or both. We all strained to hear, but these days they must teach the fine art of whispering at Tulliallan. Freeman nodded and his fingers moved inexorably to his tie.

'There's been a development,' he said. 'In the Grampian side of this thing. Dr Dartington, they are wondering if we could do them a favour, as there seems to be an issue with pathology services.' He looked embarrassed.

That was an old story. There was a kind of no-man's-land between Inverness and Aberdeen, right on the Findhorn/Elgin triangle, where the two police authorities often found themselves with difficulties over jurisdiction. Normally post-mortems for anything in the Grampian police area ought to take place in Aberdeen. But Inverness was almost as near.

'I'm on leave,' snapped Sheila. 'Compulsory and official, were the terms used, I believe.' I wondered how far she had got with Freeman, the family man. Maybe the leave thing had been some futile attempt to protect her.

'I'm afraid I'll have to suspend that, for the time being. Ask you to delay it. They have the body at Dr Gray's Hospital in Elgin. From Findhorn. A shooting and, so far, some possible and superficial matching with the projectiles recovered from our body.'

'Which one?' I couldn't stop myself. Freeman glowered.

'We only have one shooting so far, Sergeant. Two, counting the Findhorn incident.'

Incident. I liked that.

'You want me to go and carry out a PM in Dr Gray's?' Sheila didn't look too pleased. I couldn't blame her. At the very least, and apart from her hastily suspended suspension, she must have been knackered.

'If you wouldn't mind. It's for their sakes. I'm in no doubt that you will find a match between our man here and their cadaver.'

Freeman turned to Jimmy.

'I'd like you to liaise with the Grampian people over the crime scene at Findhorn, Jimmy. Loads of electronics. Give Ferdie Gallagher a call in Aberdeen.' Jimmy nodded. We all stood to go. 'And I should tell you that for, ah, personal reasons, I am taking some . . . ah, time off. I have annual leave which I haven't as yet taken up and this seems a good time to do so.'

I acted surprised, though I was the only one there who wasn't. Freeman, in that brief, anguished, personal aside, had told me he wanted out of this whole mess as quickly as possible. No one said a word. Except me. 'We'll miss you, sir.'

He gave me a withering stare. 'And I'm sure Sergeant Flaws will not have told you, Dr Dartington, or you, Mr Seaton, that he is now Acting Inspector. With sole charge of this case.'

I nodded, wisely. An official envelope that had been waiting on my cubby-hole desk. But officers senior to Freeman were conspicuous by their physical absence this morning. This was a nasty, diseased case and it was presumed highly infectious.

Jimmy and Sheila left, both congratulating me on their way out of the door. A peck on the cheek from Sheila and a firm handshake from Jimmy. Nothing from Grant, the prick.

'Oh, and here's that Van Morrison CD you asked me to burn for you,' Jimmy said, handing me a CD-Rom in a transparent polythene cover. I mumbled a thank you.

Freeman and I were alone again. 'Van Morrison,' he said. 'Irish band, isn't that right?'

I smiled and nodded. 'Kids' stuff, sir. Like *Westlife*. Where are you planning to go for your break?'

'Taking the wife to Stockholm,' he said. 'Have a look at the Gotha Canal, maybe. Thomas Telford built it, you know. Just like the Caledonian. Listen, Zander . . .' I hated it when Freeman attempted to look earnest and vaguely human. I hated it when he used my first name.

'I'm sorry about all this. Remember what I said. They're looking for scapegoats and tools in this. Everyone's disposable.'

'Come on, sir. They're not going to be disappearing any of us.'

'Well, it could be worse, they could send you to Shetland. To work with me. That's where I'm to be chief inspector for a minimum of three years.'

'It's not so bad,' I said. 'I believe there's a cappuccino bar.'

'You're thinking of Orkney,' he said, heavily. 'Not the same thing at all. Anyway. Don't let the bastards grind you down. And speaking of bastards, one is arriving at Dalcross at noon. He asked for you specifically. I believe you know each other. Your first task as acting inspector is to pick him up. Then you'll be told what to do.'

We shook hands.

'That's the thing about being an acting inspector,' I mused. 'You just act all the time. On other people's desires.'

'Just obeying orders,' said Freeman. 'Obeying orders.'

A bad feeling was developing in my already uneasy gut. I'd eaten some of the Castle Snacker's infamous brown food that morning in lieu of a healthy breakfast, and the sausages were acting up. Possibly. Or my subconscious was tying together invisible threads of evidence I hadn't even noticed. My innards knew where this was heading. All my head knew was that I had to drive over to Dalcross Airport and pick up someone who knew me, and whom I'd know. Never a good combination.

I checked the underside of the Escort, force of habit making me look again at the weaponry concealed within. I inhaled the musty aroma of decaying car. Maybe it was time to upgrade to something that smelled, as new cars do, of carefully-calculated aromas. I'd seen a TV programme about it. Japanese car companies spent millions researching the smell that best sold a car and then kept the owner loyal. I sniffed. Antifreeze, a leaking heater, oil. A need for maintenance. I saved most of my mechanical ardour for the bike, doing what needed to be done to keep the Escort functioning, but unable to summon either the passion for cars to upgrade it or the anal retentiveness required to fettle it properly.

It worked, sort of. Everything, even the CD player, which I'd had fitted at Halfords a couple of years previously. I started the engine and rooted around for something to play. Most people of my acquaintance who had even a passing interest in music now had iPods and car adaptors for them. I detested the notion of blocking out the world with earphones and the quality from digital MP3s was so bad, it was like having red-hot sand poured down your earholes. I couldn't for the life of me understand why other people didn't seem to notice how awful it was. CDs were horrible enough. At home, I tried to stick with vinyl. I felt smug at its recent rehabilitation, the latter-day recognition of its superior qualities, particularly for acoustic music. I had a ten-inch double album of James Yorkston's stunning *Year of the Leopard* and a wooden box of six seven-inch singles which contained the album *Songs from the Deep Forest* by the Irish singer Duke Special. Ulster, to be precise. Ulster Protestant. Not that it mattered. Collector's stuff, I know, but what the the hell. I am a middle-aged man. I am anally retentive. Just not with Ford Escorts.

I scrabbled around looking for a CD I'd grown to like, one sent by a friend who had emigrated to Sweden to run a herring processing company. It was by the Swedish singer Annika Norlin, who records under the name Hello Saferide. No sign of it. I'd lent it to Sheila.

Then, with a pang of guilt, I felt a hard, square object in my jacket pocket. The Britney Spears I'd liberated from Freya Enderby's flat, just before Sheila's arrival and the excitement of illicit sex with a colleague in a dead woman's house. Oh, and the subsequent firebombing. Saved by the Molotov cocktail. Or cleverly modified camping stove, as had eventually become apparent. There was something else in my pocket, too: the round shape, squashed already in its soft cover, of the CD given to me by Jimmy, the Van Morrison. He knew I detested the so-called Belfast cowboy and described him as a mannerism masquerading as talent.

I stopped at the junction with the A9 for a good ten minutes, unwilling to throw the Escort beneath the wheels of thundering south-bound juggernauts. I pulled out my purloined Britney Spears and shoved it in the player. What the hell, maybe jailbait run to seed would lift my mood. It was 'Stronger', from the brave, or idiotic, comeback flop. Whatever. It would do.

It was rubbish. Electronic harshness, sampled drums, faked-up vocals. I was reaching for the eject button as I finally found myself hurtling out towards Dalcross, in the vain hope of seeing the London plane descending, when the music stopped. I waited, annoyed, for it to start again, pondering the hazards of pirating CDs on cheap software. And then, Freya Enderby began speaking to me.

I knew it was her. I knew it was her from the voice, which was somehow exactly right, was indubitably the woman I'd never seen alive. After a few minutes, I realised my driving was becoming seriously affected and I pulled into the Tesco car park at Eastfield. Whoever was flying into Dalcross would have to wait. I switched off the engine and listened.

The voice? English, slightly clipped, posh, with some Bristol, Devon, Cornwall, a bit ooh-aarr. Plymouth? Militarised, upgraded, self-improved. And as I listened, I realised I'd known. I'd known all along.

. . . I'm still on the reserve list, so I'm supposed to do what I'm told. Official Secrets, that sort of thing. Of course, I had my own, unofficial, little secret . . .

She sounded drunk, the West Country accent coming out more strongly. Poor Freya. What were you into? But I knew. I knew about 14th Det, the front line of military surveillance in the province back in the day. Part of the horrendously confused, murky shambles that was so-called intelligence. In the three months I'd been there I'd learned what a joke that word was. Bitter inter-agency infighting, touts writing cheques their information couldn't cash, working for two, sometimes three masters, cynically setting up friends and colleagues and sometimes enemies to be killed. MI5, MI6, RUC Special Branch, Army int and the really dodgy stuff, the so-called RUC death squads, Agent Orange as someone dubbed them. And the lone wolves, the cowboys like Nairac and the others. I found myself tuning out, tuning in. Concentrate, you idiot. I glanced at my watch. Kept listening. Stuff about Border Det I already knew.

And then she got to 17 May 1974. And Serpentine.

You know that phrase, *an icy chill ran down his back*? Have you ever experienced it? Ever felt any of those clichés of panic? *His mouth went dry. He swallowed hard. His blood ran cold.* Well, what can I tell you? To be precise, my hands went slightly numb around the fingertips and I was suddenly conscious of my breathing, which was deep and ragged, as if I was finding it suddenly harder to catch a breath. Serpentine. Fuck. It wasn't that things started to make sense, but they became a little clearer. And much, much more unpleasant.

Serpentine. Saul. They used me as bait and now I'm trying to play us off against them, for old times' sake. Trying to get some insurance, that was your mistake, Saul. Trying to bolster up your position. You're losing your touch. And I'm old, and I make mistakes, too. Christ, what did you think you were playing at, contacting some tosser of a publisher, or agent or whatever it was? You always have a game plan, you wanker. And then you thought you could use me. User. Always ruthless as fuck. No compunction, that's what you used to say. I once thought you were gentle. Thought you were weak, actually, but you were just quiet and considered. And a complete and utter psychopath. Maybe we were two of a kind, which was what you always used to say. What do psychopaths do when their powers begin to fade? It's the green Kryptonite, Saul. That's your fucking Serpentine. Green Kryptonite. You love it, that stuff, the holy green rock. Think it protects you, but it'll get you in the end. They will. Me. Millie. Clara . . .

Then, right up close to the microphone:

Hunker down, love, hunker down amongst the green Kryptonite. Superman's had his day.

There was nothing else on the CD. I ejected it and stuck Jimmy's CD-Rom in the player. No Van Morrison, no Orangefield cowboy, just Jimmy's hesitant voice.

Hallo, Zander. Sorry about this. Just thought it might be quicker to give you this and hope you listen to it. I recorded this using Audacity, it's pretty rough, I'm afraid. Anyway, all I wanted to say was, there's nothing much on that USB dongle but a lot of Google Earth files, maps of Mull. A place down near the Iona ferry called Grailloch Dhu. Which I knew you'd be too stupid to know, and I do, so I'll tell you. It's Gaelic. It means Green Rock of the Dragon. It's a mineral called Serpentine. Looked it up, it's a common geological feature down there. Hope that helps.

ALTERNATIVE ULSTER

Inverness Airport, or Dalcross, for purists and those who recognise that the runways are nearer Nairn than the Ness bridges: it gleams and glitters, all aluminium facings and cars parked at hideous and mounting expense. It was only as I paused to allow the sensors on the automatic doors to open them too slowly that I realised I had no flight number. Was there a British Airways flight in from London? Surely my very important visitor was not coming in on Easyjet, paying for his own in-flight booze, cheered by flight deck announcements courtesy of a former bush pilot from Cairns?

I went up to the information desk and was just opening my mouth to ask the uniformed tyrant in charge whether any flights from the general vicinity of London were due or had landed in the past hour, when she imperiously held up her hand and began speaking through pursed lips into a microphone.

'Would an Alexander Flaws, if he is in the airport, please attend the executive lounge at his convenience. Thank you.' She turned to me, a smile threatening to cause some movement in the lip area. 'Yes?'

'That's me. Can you point me in the direction of the executive lounge?'

'Which one, sir?'

'Well, the one you meant when you mentioned an executive lounge in your recent announcement, Miss . . .'

'Mrs.' She brandished a hand loaded with so many rings she must've had biceps like Schwarzenegger's to lift it. Fortunately, those were covered by her uniform. 'I was merely relaying a message, sir. It was a trifle vague, actually, as there are issues with access to the lounges. And in fact two executive lounges. The British Airways one and the Travelodge.'

'Travelodge?'

'Yes, they are moving into airside hospitality.' She sniffed. 'The romance of the great Pan-American flying boats is long gone, I'm afraid. It's all velour upholstery and coin-operated coffee machines in there. Sir.'

'Just tell me where the BA one is. I think that's likely to be more my guest's style.' But as I prepared myself for another sniff, there was a tap on my shoulder and a voice said, 'Sure, begorrah and fuck me sideways, will you look at the state of that. If it isn't my briefly-acquainted old mucker, Zander Flaws.' The nasal Ulster accent had none of the tip-of-the-tongue gentleness needed to make words like 'sure' and 'begorrah' sound natural. 'Fuck me sideways', however, seemed to suit it.

'I'm afraid the lounge is airside, sir,' said the BA woman. 'Do you have a boarding pass?'

'It's all right,' I told her. 'I think we've found each other.' And indeed we had.

'Well, boyo, fancy meeting you here. You of all people, eh? Long time no see.'

And there he was, pumping my hand as energetically as he had that first time, me fresh off the plane at Aldergrove, back when the world seemed young and innocent and I was about to discover just how fucked-up it really was.

'Nixon.'

'Yes, well, in the flesh so to speak, and rather too much of it, more than the last time.' In fact he was thinner, or to be precise more compact, as if he'd been solidified, made more corporeal, denser. There was a thin, languid man hovering. His face wore a smirk. He had that kind of thick, floppy hair that tends to be associated with privilege. At first sight, he looked young. Then you realised he was some kind of preserved specimen. Like an Etonian vampire.

'This is my colleague. Carrier of bags, my bagman, so to speak. Today he carries mine, some days I carry his.' Floppy Fringe smiled, showing yellow teeth. His face cracked like a half-cooked cake. 'Edwyn, say hallo to Mr Flaws. Flawed, many, many flaws by nature, undoubtedly. You have a car, I expect?' Nixon looked at me in that vaguely excited way I remembered. 'It'll be some pile of crap, if I'm not mistaken. But we'll get ourselves fixed up with something better in due course.' He nodded to himself, as if happily anticipating the arrival of some large and luxurious limo. 'Just as well we don't have much luggage. Bit of an urgent call, you see, and so it's just laptops and a change of mobile phones. Have to send out for socks and lingerie, but I'm sure they have a Primark hereabouts. Not that Edwyn will be too happy about that. He's more of a Pinks of Piccadilly man, aren't you, Ould Bhoy . . .' Edwyn said nothing. Neither did I. I was back in Belfast, Nixon by my side, 20 years earlier.

'If I may say so, Alexander,' he continued, 'you're not looking too bad yourself. A bit stringy, maybe, a bit thinner about the old thatch, but reasonably intact. Smoking'll do that.'

'Only on special occasions,' I muttered, thinking of Sheila. And thinking of a night in a battered, discreetly armoured Vauxhall Cavalier, parked up in a lay-by near Stewartstown in Tyrone. My instruction course. Full immersion. Hands-on learning. All that shit.

Flashback time.

June 1984. The 28th. Or maybe the 27th. Me in the back, Nixon in the front. The driver, a sullen, bald man. Billy Boy. Just before we'd left Belfast, a mere hour or so away in this smallest of small provinces, Nixon had thrust a heavy, metal object into my hand.

'There you go,' he said. 'Wee present for you. Token of our esteem. Welcome to Ulster. Badge of residence.' I looked at the gun. It was incredibly small. A toy, like one of those plastic Sekiden guns we had played with in my childhood, the ones that fired little china-clay balls, stinging your cheeks, putting your eye out, maybe. *Ker-ching*, and the wee missile would *pok!* hit you with surprising force. But this was metal. This fired heavy chunks of ordnance. This tore your heart out. Or somebody else's.

'Thought you'd appreciate it. Walther PPK. Original James Bond gun. The very same. Well, the Ian Fleming gun. Safety here' – he took the pistol out of my hand and, with his fat little fingers, demonstrated a casual familiarity with the weapon – 'and best to have one in the breech so you're ready to go at all times. Safety back on, stuff it in your pocket. You OK with that?'

I couldn't do anything but nod. I couldn't do anything but take it. I couldn't do anything but feel sweatily thrilled and pleased at having the thing. James Bond. Fuck. I was beyond the Sekiden, remembering all the other guns of childhood, the toys: the *Man from U.N.C.L.E.* Luger, the James Bond . . .

was there a James Bond toy gun? I couldn't remember. Tattie guns, spud guns, graduating to air rifles and shotguns. Bang bang you're dead.

He coughed. The phlegm rattled glutinously in his throat. Everything was loud, too loud. 'Simply a watching brief,' Nixon said. 'Thought we'd bring you along, give you a bit of the ould insight into the realities of the situation. So to speak. Justice and fairness being our watchwords. Just to show you. That's what we stand by here, as in Scotland, as in the United Kingdom. Always remember, this IS the United Kingdom. The rule of law, boyo! That's us.'

The radio squawked. 'Raffles, this is Pink Panther,' I thought it said. 'In position.'

'Roger, Pink Panther,' said Nixon, throwing me a what-can-you-do? look. 'On our way.'

And then we were moving through the night, heading God knew where. I certainly didn't. After a couple of turn-offs the roads grew narrow, hemmed in by hedges and stone walls. I guessed we were heading south. For the border.

Maybe Nixon sensed my tension. 'Don't worry, old son. No border transgression, or incursion, on our part. You're safe with me.' And he patted my shoulder, giving that hoarse, coughing giggle. There was a smell of sweat and smoke in the car, the residue of a thousand stakeouts, though none of us were smoking. I'd never seen Nixon smoking. I had a softpack of Marlboro Red in my pocket, but I sensed he wouldn't approve. Nixon nudged me again. He was always too close, too physical.

We came on the car suddenly, caught in our dipped headlights, doors open, sitting in the middle of the road. Something lay prone in front of it. The lights caught something else half in, half out of the front seat.

'Stop the car, Billy Boy,' said Nixon. 'I believe we're here.'

It was the silence that caught me. At least at first. Then just the gentle waving of the hedges in the breeze and the ticking of hot engine cooling. No moaning, no screaming. This was afterwards. This was the aftermath.

There were three bodies. The car was riddled with bullet holes. Nixon seemed neither afraid nor too exercised by what he was seeing.

'Are we too late?' I asked him, hearing my voice quaver. 'Who are they?'

'No, we're just in time, my boy,' he replied. 'Now, just check for me the state of those bodies, will you? I want to know what you see. I'd value your opinion.' He clapped me on the back. 'Useful training for future terrorist atrocities in the vicinity of Tain Royal Academy, ould son!'

In Glasgow, I'd been at the aftermath of drug overdoses, a couple of stabbings. Had one young Celtic supporter bleed to death all over me, after the random violence of an Old Firm game. But the sheer strangeness of this situation was difficult to resist. My mouth was dry as I walked over to the car, heart pounding. Nixon was shouting after me, cheerily, 'No booby traps, my laddie. Ma wee laddie.' (Said in a stupid attempt at a Scottish accent.) 'Don't you worry about a thing.'

The driver of the car was still at the wheel, belted in. Dressed in sports jacket and flannels, a teachery sort of get up. Fair Isle slipover. Not a hand-knit, I registered, my mother's flying fingers suddenly clack-clacking in my head.

Half his head torn away, but the window he rested against intact. Not even all that bloodied. Two other bullet wounds, both execution shots, top of the neck and down into the body. Slugs still in there, I thought. No residue, no brain matter, no blood on the seats or the dash or roof lining. I checked the other two bodies, my movements becoming more certain, my breath steadier. In the silence, I could hear Nixon whistling. 'The Wearing of the Green'. The other two had the same execution wounds – twin, small-calibre shots to the top of the neck, down into the chest cavity. And, harder to spot, a single shot in each body, down through the lower palate. A signature of contempt and abuse. Informants of some kind. Or that was the impression that was being communicated. The two passengers were wearing leather jackets. One had a red hand of Ulster tattoo on that fleshy bit of the right hand, between thumb and forefinger. I walked back to the Cavalier. The whistling stopped, to be replaced by the drumming sound of Nixon's fingers on the top of the dashboard. A marching rhythm, like the Lambeg drums of the 12th of July.

'So what do you think, me boyo?' asked Nixon, that grin in his voice. 'What do you think?'

I swallowed hard. I knew this was a test.

'Tell me what *you* think,' I countered.

'Ah, I haven't really made up my mind. How could I? I haven't investigated the crime scene. I haven't had autopsy reports. But I think what we have here is really rather tragic. And I don't think there's but one outcome. Sad, but inevitable.' He sighed melodramatically. 'Don't you think, Billy Boy?' The driver was standing behind me, a hulking presence. I turned to look at him. His face was set in a ghastly grin. He turned and walked towards the verge of the road, hunkered down in the ditch, crunching the frost-stiffened grasses.

'You've lost me.' It was like being ill. I felt threatened, almost overwhelmed.

Nixon looked perplexed.

'Well, and truly now, I was hoping for better than that from our guest, our fine young example of Highland Scottish policing.' He half turned. 'What the hell are you doin' down there, Billy Boy?'

The driver's voice, when it came, was strangely measured and cool. It was like listening to BBC Radio Ulster, resonant, deep and threatening. I felt a chill which had nothing to do with the temperature.

'Best come and see for yourself.'

I followed Nixon over to the ditch. The driver stood up, towering over us, and pointed. All I could hear was the ticking of the Rover's engine as it cooled. The weak light of Nixon's torch picked out two more bodies, both dressed in army parkas and black balaclavas. I could see two weapons – an army SLR and a Thompson sub-machine gun. The men were curiously huddled.

'Tut!' Nixon was shaking his head sorrowfully. 'Now, do you see what happened here, Mr Flaws? Can you surmise? Go on with you, I love a bit of wild surmise.'

I looked at him. 'Why don't *you* tell *me* what happened here?'

He grinned. I could hear, distantly, the distinctive *whoomp-whoomp* of an approaching helicopter. And the man Nixon called Billy Boy chuckling to himself.

'It's just like ould Serpentine's been up to his old tricks, Nix, isn't it?'

'Shut the fuck up, Billy Boy,' said Nixon, mildly. 'Don't you have work to do?'

The driver shrugged. Still chuckling, he turned towards the car with its ruined cargo of churned meat.

'Now then,' said Nixon. 'I needn't spell it all out for you. Surely it's obvious? Those black balaclavas? I mean, they're a hallmark. A trademark, virtually. And those army surplus jackets, you'd think the boyos would use a bit of imagination.'

'An . . . ambush that went wrong?'

'Do you think? Do you really think so? You could be right at that! Not so much a tragedy as an irony, Mr Flaws. I'm very glad to hear you confirm what was lurking in my mind as only the vaguest of suspicions. I think you'll pass this course with flying colours.'

I took the torch from him and shone it on the huddled bodies in the ditch.

'No sign of weapons in the car,' I said, as firmly as I could. 'Close quarters, execution shots. It was done elsewhere. These bodies have been moved. It looks like they . . .' But Nixon was guiding me back to the Rover.

'Don't you worry about that. Kids around here will steal anything. Probably half-inched the guns from the car before we got here. In fact, it may have been one of them that called us in. Anonymous, you know. I'm sure you do. Tit for tat, one shoots, the other shoots. Now, the question is, who's who and what were they doing here?' He turned to Billy Boy. It was a moment of deliberate, high melodrama, rehearsed. 'Have you had a look in the boot, by any chance?' Christ, this was a soap opera. No, not a soap opera, a children's play, some school pageant. Billy Boy grinned and shook his head slowly, cartoon-style, like he was projecting to the parents in the back row. 'Well we really ought to, don't you think? Don't you think, Zander? Billy Boy, you've got your gloves on, haven't you? Don't want to contaminate a crime scene, certainly not. Just flick open this boot, will you?'

I walked over to the car and watched as the boot lid opened, slowly, like something in a movie. I was half expecting a golden light to shine out of it, some aura. But there was no mystery about what was in there. That's the thing about dynamite, the kind they use in quarries. It comes in sticks. It's very difficult to mistake it for anything else. Which presumably was the idea.

'Jesus, will you look at that!' said Billy Boy, rebounding as if he'd been kicked in the gut by a pantomime horse. 'Is that explosives in there?'

'Well, you know, forensics will confirm it, no doubt.' Nixon was smiling. 'But Zander, you're an experienced man. What would you think?'

I was feeling sick. 'If it is, how come the gunfire didn't set it off?'

There was a second's silence, then the rumbling laughter of Billy Boy and a hissing giggle from Nixon. I felt a hand slap me on the back, lightly. It felt like a stabbing.

'Sure, you're forgetting the basics of pyrotechnics,' said Nixon. 'Plastic explosive needs an electrical pulse to set it off.'

'This is dynamite.'

Billy Boy had stopped laughing. 'It's plastic dynamite,' he said.

'Now then, let's go, leave the boys in the overalls to clear up,' said Nixon. The helicopter was very close now. the whirl of its rotor blades sending pulses of moving air towards us. No lights, in that darkest of Ulster skies. 'That'll be them now, I think. And that's good enough for me. Our work here is done! Thanks for your help with this, Zander, Mr Flaws. I think we'd better be getting back. I'm very, very appreciative of your help.'

Nixon got into the driver's seat and started the engine. I got in beside him.

'What about . . .'

'Billy Boy? Don't you worry about him. We'll leave him to sort this whole thing out.' And he turned the car in the road. We drove slowly back to Belfast, with Van Morrison, I remember, playing on the radio. Some kind of archive in-concert special. *The Caledonia Soul Orchestra*, I think it was. The same line-up as on the live double album *It's Too Late To Stop Now*, and I suppose it was. Too late. Never been too fond of old Van since that night.

Outside the hotel, Nixon wished me goodnight and thanked me again, profusely, for my help.

'What about the gun?' I said.

'Ah yes, the gun. I was just going to ask you if I could have it back. Emergency over, so to speak.'

It was very quiet in the car. Outside, the distant thump from the nurses' disco. Saturday night fever. I pulled out the Walther and rammed it against Nixon's side.

'You fucking prick,' I said. 'I'm not your fucking patsy. I'm not some piece-of-shit witness to whatever screwball scenario you were putting on out there, whatever piece of theatre.' The smile never left his face. 'It'll be the fingerprints on the gun you want, I suppose? Well fuck that, you bastard, you're not getting them.'

And he smiled, all the time he kept smiling.

'Now, now. You wouldn't seriously expect it to be loaded, Zander, would you? With a little luck, you'll never need to know what was going on back there in the badlands. My advice is not to think about it too much. Or at all. You're just a piece of backup. In reserve, so to speak. Like the B Specials. Or the UVF. You're the Home Guard.' And then, with a speed I'd never have expected, he rammed the knuckles of his right hand underneath my Adam's apple, neatly grabbing the Walther by the barrel with the other. I gasped and choked for about a minute and a half. And he smiled.

'Go and get some sleep, Zander. I think you're doing rather well. A degree of suspicion, of doubt. That's a healthy thing.'

I left Belfast for home, after some run-of-the mill army liaison and UDR briefings. Some tedious Special Forces stuff, being sneered at by the prima donnas. I tried out some interesting shotguns. I bumped into Nixon once or twice, in odd corners, car parks, offices. He would smile at me, I would nod back. He'd made his point with me, had his fun. Put, I sometimes thought, his brand on me, soiled me, left me tainted. We never spoke.

'I brought you a present,' said Nixon, from the back of the Escort, bringing me out of my reverie. 'I'll give it to you when we stop, though. Don't want any accidents.'

A languid laugh from Edwyn.

There were questions I should have been asking. What was Nixon doing now? What had he been doing? He looked prosperous, well groomed. But there was no need to ask. Edwyn was all the answer I needed. Under the Etonian hair and the ridiculous accent, he had the brutally desiccated look of a really nasty upper-class thug. Spook to the max. Big-time, serious spookdom. No question.

'So, I'm your backup once again, Nixon, is that it? Fall guy to the stars. You look like you're doing well.' No laughter. I was surprised.

'Och, now, Zander. You're not still sore about ancient history, are you? And so much water under so many bridges since then. No, I'm afraid you're a major player in this one, my dear boy.' His accent had moderated, become plummier. Time spent in London, in the higher echelons. That coat was a king's ransom. Not literally. 'You could make your career on this, my boy. Finally get beyond that dead-end sergeant status. Have your acting-up inspectorhood confirmed. In fact I will personally guarantee it. If you play your cards right.'

'Personally chosen,' drawled Edwyn. 'Right person, right place, right time. Couldn't be better.'

'If everything works out,' said Nixon. 'Now, I believe we have a dead body. Or is it two? I lose count. An age thing, I fear.'

Murricane had hated Ulster. He'd hated the weather. He'd hated the Protestants and he'd hated the Catholics, the bizarre viciousness of a civil war taking place in a cultural and geographical landscape all too recognisable to a Scot, or a Shetlander. A Scot, give or take some Viking genes and a dislike of fish farming. And he was hating this. He was trying to keep calm. Calm was something he normally had few problems with. It was his stock-in-trade, his currency. Keeping his head when all about were losing theirs. But now, it felt like the world was tilting under him, like an earthquake was rippling through the landscape and he was clinging on for dear life.

Millie had loved Ulster.

'It was as close as I ever got to living out on the edge of the envelope,' she said. 'Until now.' And he could see that she responded better and better as the pressure increased. He was coping worse in his own country, he realised. He couldn't easily turn it into a battlefield, a neutral territory full of strangers. For Millie, that didn't seem to be a problem. It hadn't been a problem when Hume had turned a horrible khaki colour, reached for the upper part of his left arm and croaked the words 'fuckin' cunt', very quietly. And then, he'd died. Not as fit as he thought he was. As they had thought.

He'd still been alive when they put him in the back of the 240, shoved him into the biggest loading area of any estate car ever made. Apart from the Ford Mondeo Estate between 1992 and 1998, Murricane, for some reason, remembered. Millie had checked the knee wound, cleaned and bandaged it, pronounced it non-life-threatening. They'd wrapped Hume in a groundsheet and covered him with the rest of the camping gear, then they drove towards Inverness and what they had hoped would be a quiet location for an in-depth interview. Which hadn't stopped Millie, perched in the back seat, from asking him questions carefully and slowly, for the duration of the journey. Sometimes Hume answered. It was when they peeled off the groundsheet, outside Liam Gunn's hut, that Hume spoke his last before departing for pastures new.

In the event, there was nothing to do but get rid of the body. Millie had made the running. Taken Murricane into that strange shed, introduced him to the old man, clearly dying, called Liam Gunn. Who guided them to the spot where Hume and his partner had been on the point of killing her. It had been well chosen. In the darkness it was absolutely deserted. Hume made hardly a splash as they lowered his corpse into the river.

'All bets are off, now,' Murricane said. 'We're fugitives. Murder. This'll be seen as murder.'

'Manslaughter. Self-defence. Collateral damage.'

'What about the car? What about the old man?' He gestured at Liam, who sat quietly in the back seat, calm and, apparently, content.

'Fuck it. Liam'll point them wherever we want. Wherever I want him to. Jesus. We're being used in this, can't you see? I think they'll let us run. I think they want us to run. One freelance babysitter employed by dodgy renegades within Six is neither here nor there in the bigger scheme of things. Don't you get the impression that we're . . . predestined in this? That this was all set up?'

He thought back. Predestination? Theology had never been his strong point. Gaza, the Americans, all that? Was it all part of the same deal?

They stopped in Drumnadrochit, in the car park which served a rather tacky looking visitor centre called the Monstrous Ness Experience. Just up the road they'd passed the Original Loch Ness Monster Experience. There were several other cars there. Through their steamed-up windows could be seen unlucky or poverty-stricken tourist vehicles, packed with luggage and snoring people, bleary travellers without a bed for the night.

Millie had the rucksack out, had already switched on the mobile phone, checked the memory for any numbers she recognised. But there were none. Then the computer. But they'd listened to every sound-file, painstakingly checked all the documents and downloads. There had been a text file marked 'Serpentine' and she had briefly felt a pang of excitement. But the contents were utterly enigmatic, although evidently some kind of quotation.

> Serpentine is a healing mineral of great power, making it very suitable for any type of restorative activity, like chakra healing and the clearing of blockages. It re-balances pulmonary and cardiac chakras and the emotional and spiritual heart also, increasing love for self and the otherhood. Serpentine can also open up a channel in the body for kundalini energy, opening up the mental state to higher vibrations, developing intuition and psychic awareness. There

is an association with happiness, success and the manifestation of benificence. The stone promotes good luck and can aid people in achieving their dreams and desires.

A mobile bleeped twice.

'Text message,' said Murricane.

'I know what it is.' Millie flipped open the in-box on her Nokia. 'Nothing here. It must be yours.'

'No.' They looked at each other, nonplussed, then Millie said: 'Dead man's mobile.' She scrabbled for Hume's Ericsson, fumbled with the controls. Swallowed hard for a moment.

'What does it say?'

'Serpentine,' she said. 'That's what it says. Serpentine.'

Murricane shook his head slowly. 'Check the memory.'

Some more pressing of unfamiliar buttons.

'Nothing. It's a burner. A throw-down phone.'

'We're being played,' Murricane said. 'All of us.'

'But who by?'

'By whom.'

'Fuck off.'

'There's something else in the message. Some numbers and letters.'

'A code?'

But Millie was already raking furiously through the rucksack she'd taken from the storage unit in Inverness, it seemed like months ago. She held up the Garmin Satnav, held down the power button.

'Latitude,' she said. 'And longitude.'

Freeman was history. It was as if he'd never existed. I was met at the old timber pier by a sergeant out of Serious Crimes, a Gael from Stornoway called MacHuish. Serious, as befitted Serious Crimes. Not one of my arch enemies, so that was a start.

'Bit out of the ordinary,' he said, his face red and puffy, midges swarming around him. He flailed at them with the backs of his hands, which were already bitten and lumpy. He had a white handkerchief held to his face. Gunn had been taken back to his shed by a uniform. We watched as two SOCOs shouted at the small team of police cannon fodder engaged in a fingertip search of the riverside and its hinterland. 'Got the call from the old man. Gunn. Liam Gunn. He found the body. Seemed strangely pleased with himself.' Nixon and his dangerous looking pal watched from the shelter of their expensive overcoats. Though it wasn't cold. The weather was heavy, muggy. They were just back from the mortuary. It would have been cold there.

MacHuish was gazing at something invisible, far away, beyond the glare of the crime scene. Possibly he was looking at Stornoway, 150 miles to the west. 'The old man who found it – what's his name? Gunn, that's right – is in his shed. It's a good shed, I'd say, a classic of its type. He says he's rented it for 40 years. Then clammed up, dropped your name and said he would only talk to you. No amount of threats or pleading would make a difference. Or bribery.' His Gaelic drawl was ideally constructed for irony.

'He knew my father,' I said. 'Liam's a bit of a legend in the crofting community. A retired slaughterman. Used to deal with our beasts. Liam the Butcher.'

'Yes, well. Those would have been the days, sir, when crofters were permitted to slaughter their own animals.'

'I think you'll find they still are, Sergeant MacHuish. Just for their own consumption, though.' And friends. And family. And the friends and family of friends. Or anyone with a freezer and cash. 'And what do you mean, "sir"?'

'Ach, news clearly hasn't reached you, sir. Or maybe you've forgotten already, Inspector. Congratulations.' A hard hand seized mine and held it in a three-finger-and-thumb Masonic grip. Very high up, too. Royal Arch. 'Acting Inspector, we have been informed. Congratulations.'

'Acting, eh? Not for long in my experience, Sergeant. Shall we get on?' Christ.

'Slaughterman, then, is it? Gunn? Perhaps appropriate?'

I allowed myself a short chuckle.

'If the body's been jointed and filleted, maybe. Liam the Butcher's 75, if he's a day. He's a character. Known all over. Not just local. All through Sutherland, Caithness. Mainland, Sergeant, so perhaps not your area . . .'

'Iss my island roots showing, s-sir? Dearie me, I'll have to watch mysself.'

'Enough sibilance, Donald. Anyway. It's not him.'

'Well, he won't talk to anyone but you, sir. And he may have decided his calling needed to be exercised.'

'A little dry Hielan' humour goes a long way, Donald. There is always a need for levity. Within limits.'

'Indeed. Just so, sir, just so. We had some levitation earlier. With the aid of a crane.'

Nixon and Edwyn arrived, as promised, in a better car: a VW Passat, to be precise. German but not ostentatious.

'How was the mortuary?' Sheila had transferred the Findhorn body to Inverness, transgressing all kinds of official health and law-enforcement boundaries. Nixon and Edwyn had been able to see both our recent cadavers, plus what was left of Freya Enderby.

'Och, it was a mite chilly,' said Nixon. 'But illuminating. Instructive. Identifiable handiwork, in Freya's case.'

'And the two males?'

There was a silence, broken by Edwyn: 'Minor hands-off assets, twice or three times removed.'

'Permanently removed now, it seems.' Nixon always had to have the last word.

I left them to it.

Liam's shed was festooned with the gifts of the canal and the river: rope in every gauge and length. Wood, worked and raw, old domestic appliances, several bicycles. It was all neatly piled up or hung and the place was clean, too. There was a workbench, an old plastic sofa, a valve radio. A gas ring and a teapot, steaming slightly. Just the one mug, and Liam was holding it. No slaughterman's tools. I knew for a fact he did the occasional favour for anyone needing some beast illegally taken off and butchered, crofter or no, but the tools for such a job would be kept well hidden. This was where he came to relax. He lived in a council flat in Hilton.

'Hallo, Liam.' His only response was a mild grunt. 'They treating you all right? I see you got a cuppa, anyway.'

'Could do with a dram in it.' The voice was pure Inverness. I found it creeping into my own accent sometimes. That Roundhead lisp.

'Can't help you there, pal.' We looked at each other, both of us thinking back. Guns and knives. The night I'd killed my first cow. The shotgun.

One of Dad's stories popped into my head. A tale from 'just before you were born, Zander', as most of those stories were. About one of the Sutherland cave families.

'Aye, there were quite a few used to live in the sea caves, more from habit than necessity, you understand. And one, well they were of tinker origin, though they had settled, were well known and respected. They lived in Gagra Cave, which is a bit of a warren, and it was like a house, with rooms, really, and places for animals.

'There was David Stuart, the father, and the two boys, twins. Their mother had died having them. They were probably about seven years old, when it happened. Brought up by their father to fish, care for the beasts and fend for themselves. Very able family, they were. Davie looked after them well. He traded fish and otter pelts for oatmeal and clothing, and the boys would have gone to school, too.'

Dad told me the story when I was 17, on the point of leaving home. It was a kind of warning, I think. But it was also an explanation of why he'd disliked slaughtering the animals and had, for the most part, kept me away from it.

It seemed that Davie had died of a stroke, or a heart attack or something sudden, in the cave itself, with the two children his only companions. The boys were found, alive, but almost feral, three weeks after their father's death, when one of Davie's otter pelt customers climbed down to see why there had been no deliveries.

'He found the boys there, not speaking, seemingly well fed, healthy enough. "Where's your dad?" he asked, and they took him to one of the back caves. And there he was. They had done exactly as their father had taught them: they'd flayed him like a sheep, skinned him, gutted him, salted him and hung him with a rope from an outcrop. They had the skin pickling in a barrel.'

Then Dad had looked at me, the ghost of a grin around his mouth and eyes, so that I never quite knew if he was making the story up and defaming innocent men.

'They were sent to a children's home, the Gunn boys. Peter and Liam. You know Liam. Liam the Butcher.'

Now I was gazing at this crinkled old figure, and wondering if any of it was true.

'So, Liam,' I said, 'tell me you didn't casually drown that fellow.' He looked at me with the ghost of a smile. I patted his knee. 'Just joking. Tell me what happened.'

'I didnae,' he replied. 'I went out for a wee walk and there he was. Didnae see nothing, nor nobody.' He took a noisy slurp of tea. As he lifted the mug, I could see it was shaking.

'Couldnae have,' he added, after a moment's reflection. 'No sae well, these days, with "the dancer". And the arthritis has fucked my hands.' He set the mug down and held his right hand up for me to see. It was locked in a claw. 'Have a look at the knots on that rope. Sailor's bend, Johnny Notion's reef. Cannae do them. Never could properly, but no' now, for sure.'

I leaned over and patted his shoulder. I could feel the feathery flimsiness.

'All right, Liam.'

I got up to go.

'One of the constables will take a formal statement from you, Liam. Just tell them what you saw and what your medical condition is. I'll do the rest.' He grunted. It might have been a thank you.

I might not have another opportunity, I thought.

'Liam, is it true, you were brought up in a cave?'

There was a silence. Just the occasional creaking from the old shed as the evening cooled its tin roof. Then he began to laugh. It was a sound that included a kind of terrible, swishing cough from deep in his body. Eventually he stopped.

'Your dad was such a liar,' he said. 'I was born and raised in the Ferry, learnt my trade at Arnott's the Butchers in Dingwall. Did you think I got this accent in a cave? Raaiiiat enaaaf, boy, you're quite the detective.'

I smiled. That Invernessian twang could have been learnt in an orphanage, it was true. But he was right. My dad was a terrible liar.

I was almost out of the door when Liam spoke again.

'I saw them put him in the river. The firth. Man and a woman. Big man, wee woman, but both strong. He was dead. Back of a car, a big estate. Volvo. Quite a new one, the biggest estate car. Always wanted one, that's how I remember.'

'Number?'

He grinned. 'Figures. Always had a head for figures. And letters.'

Outside, I found Nixon and Edwyn leaning against my car. Smoking. I could smell it before I saw the crimson glow of the fag ends, felt that familiar jerk of nicotine need in my chest.

'Let's get in, away from these bloody insects, Zander,' said Nixon.

'So, gentlemen. You recognised the victim? Or victims?'

Edwyn let out a short bark of amusement. 'Let's say they all fall within our remit.'

'Our orbit,' said Nixon, slapping at his face. Midges can always recognise unfamiliar blood. 'But then we wouldn't be here otherwise.' He exchanged glances with Edwyn. It was the first time since I'd known him that I'd seen any hint of uncertainty. Of fear.

'Well,' I said, 'I have news of a car. A description, a registration number. A man and a woman seen putting the body in the water. Full details to follow, maybe. But we have the car ID. I can put out a network call, loud or quiet. What do you want to do?'

Nixon chuckled. 'Perhaps you're assuming a role we don't want you to play in this situation, Zander my boy. Have you learnt a bit of wisdom over the years? Who can say, who can say? Come on, sit in the car with us a moment while I cogitate.'

I phoned the registration through to central records and was given the instant information that the car was, indeed, a Volvo 740 estate and that it belonged to a Mr J. Bruce of Flat 12, 13 Harmony Row, Govan, Glasgow. I had once owned that album. *Harmony Row*, by former Cream bassist Jack Bruce. I shrugged. Maybe there was more than one Jack Bruce. Coincidence was a funny thing.

Liam sat alone, wondering if he'd remembered the numbers Millie had told him correctly.

The man had been dead, she had told him, matter-of-factly. They just needed to get rid of the body. The car registration she'd asked him to memorise was for sale on that eBay affair. A Volvo just a wee bit different from the one they'd driven off in. It would give them some time. He hoped it would. He'd always liked Millie. The fellow she was with looked like trouble. But it was the kind of trouble it might be handy to have around.

There was a private track snaking up into old, uncommercial woodland, just off the A9 south of Aviemore. The big house at the end, *Alt-na-Coich*, completely invisible from anywhere except the escarpment directly above, had been built just before World War One in the English suburban style, a bolthole for a hugely successful Belgian concert pianist. Now it was a very expensive holiday let. It was usually taken by boisterous Christmas and New Year house parties comprising city executives and their partners, both sexual and business. In the height of summer, curiously, it was less popular, as the midges endemic to the area made its sumptuous grounds uncomfortable. As it was, a corporate booking by a Finnish oil exploration company operating out of Aberdeen had been cancelled at the last moment – something to do with the unexpected death of the founder in Helsinki – and the house was empty for seven days. The caretaker, who lived in a modern timber chalet in the nearby village of Newtonmore, had checked the place over and left it ready for its next let, a stag party celebrating the impending nuptials of a particularly loathsome futures trader.

All of this Millie had been able to tell from half an hour of careful Googling using terms like 'holiday', 'let' and 'Highlands'. Now she and Murricane, having left the Volvo hidden down a firebreak off the track, were sitting in the twilight of a late evening, sipping Australian Shiraz from the perfectly adequate wine cellar, in a turret bedroom with a window which gave them an uninterrupted view down the first 50 metres of the drive.

'You still burgle well,' she said. He had broken nothing and there was no alarm system. All it had taken was a sash window left two inches open for ventilation, on the first floor. Plus an unsecured ladder, found lying next to an outbuilding, and a coat hanger which, for presumably just such an eventuality, Murricane had with him, straightened and then wrapped into a tight ball of wire.

'Thank you. You make an acceptable Faye Dunaway to my Warren Beatty.'

'As long as we don't die in a slow motion hail of bullets.'

'Well, one or the other. Slow motion, maybe. Slower the better. Hail of bullets I'm not so keen on.' Murricane sipped his wine. They had each showered earlier, using two of the six bathrooms. The hot water came from a large thermal storage tank in the grounds, which was powered by solar panels and a wind generator. They were clean, clothed and eating Marks and Spencer's snack food, all of which tasted of Marks and Spencer's; that strange, chlorinated aroma was on everything. There had been an M&S, to his surprise, in Aviemore.

They were like honeymooners, she thought. Both dressed in fluffy, hotel-style dressing gowns. On edge, pretending to be casual and relaxed. But honeymooners were rarely armed. Their weapons had been the first things they checked, reloaded, checked again. They were handy. Maybe this was how honeymoons ought to be, she thought. Armed and dangerous.

'Pity,' she said.

'That he died? Yes.'

'He told us enough. Some of what we wanted to know.'

'Really? I didn't know we did want to know that. And now we do, I'm not feeling particularly happy about it.'

'Better we do. Surprised he popped his clogs, though. Tough bastard, just keeling over like that.'

'And what did he know, really? Just another poor ignorant fuck, like us. On the list, paid to come out of whatever pathetic security job he was doing and keep an eye on a couple of murdering psychos.'

Murricane had a small notebook out and was leafing through it. 'Seamus MacDougall and Manderson "Billy Boy" Manderley. RUC Special Branch and a footslogger from the Paras. Both – open quotes *retired* close quotes. Nasty piece of work. But so was what did he say his name was? Hume, I think, nastier than he wanted us to think. Then everyone is.'

'Yeah, in his subtle attempts at persuasion with me. Gentle as a fucking chainsaw. Or with Freya, what did he do to stop that, eh? I was under no illusions about him. He would have let MacDougall kill me. Watching brief, my arse. Watching people die. He gets the canal, I got the river. Nearly. So . . .' She shifted her shoulders inside the dressing gown, as if it were some kind of larval skin. 'They want Serpentine. That's the bottom line. Everybody wants Serpentine. Before he blows all sorts of unpleasant gaffs.'

'That's certainly what he thought. What he'd been told.'

She folded her arms. 'We could . . .'

'What?'

'We could go to the . . . authorities.'

He smiled. 'In this case, who do you suggest "the authorities" are? This is twilight zone stuff, Millie. We need Serpentine. Fuck it, he's an old man now. Oldish. Older than me, anyway. With him alive, we might be able to call Whitehall 1212 or something. But we need him. Which means . . .'

'Mull, then. That's where those co-ordinates take us. Near the Iona Ferry. Somewhere called *Grailloch Dhu*. It's Gaelic for a green mineral. Guess which one?'

'Yeah, yeah. Sometimes people can be too clever for their own good. Mull. It's as if he wants to be found.'

She reached for his thigh.

'Maybe he does.'

'So,' he said later. 'Anything else you want to tell me?'

She stretched out along his naked body.

'About what? Don't ask me about Freya. Or about . . . this.'

'Fuck and run, eh? Liz Phair, Exile in Guyville, pure do-me feminism?'

'Fuck off. Don't you know that it's different for girls?' There was a tense silence. Murricane broke it.

'About Serpentine.' They listened to each other breathing.

'Oh, *that* Serpentine.' She yawned. They were playing games, both of them. What the hell. 'The legend. Yeah, well. I met him once.'

'Oh, really?'

'The 27th of June 1984. Some kind of extraction thing. I didn't know it was him at the time. It was Freya told me, afterwards. Years afterwards, in fact. She was there too. Where were you in June 1984? You weren't with me.'

The marching season. Drums and flutes. Everyone on alert. Waiting for the inevitable trouble.

'Belfast. Waiting around. On patrol. I can't remember anything special.'

'Well, that night I was in a helicopter, looking for someone nameless in the vicinity of the boglands west of Coalisland. We'd been ordered to give all aid and succour.'

'So . . .'

'So what happened that night?' she sighed. 'We were looking for recognition signals. Three short, two long, gap, three short, gap, single.'

'And did you . . . '

'Yes. That was it. Nothing complicated. No pursuit. Apparently that was Serpentine. It was run of the mill. He chose the rendezvous well. We picked him up. Took him to Belfast Zoo. Just a man, not young. Maybe 40s. Or 50s. But very fit, I think. Dressed in hunting, shooting, fishing gear. Tweedy. Said nothing to us. Nothing at all.'

'What . . . the zoo?'

'Oh yeah. Belfast fucking Zoo. Been there? High on that hill? It's massive, part wilderness. You get a great view. There's a café at the top. They have more elephants than any other zoo in the Disunited Kingdom. Nice little space for a helicopter to land. And Freya was there.'

'What? Colonel Enderby?'

'Yes. Darling Freya. Old pals, she and Serpentine were. Hugs. Jolly hockey sticks, good show. He looked the part. Barbour jacket, flat cap.'

'Same as any Irish horse trainer.'

'He was . . .'

'What?'

'He was like her. Looked like her. Like Freya. Those eyes. That jawline.'

'What are you saying? He was . . . *related* to her? What, her brother? Sounded to me from that recording as if there some kind of sexual thing. Which I admit, for Freya, seemed a bit peculiar . . .'

Millie looked at him steadily. 'Half-brother. Same mother, different fathers. One of those upper middle class family friend shagging incidents, I believe. Brought up together, though. You know, that posh thing. Same last name.'

'Brother? Christ. Saul *Enderby*?'

'That's what she said. She was drunk, Mark. She was often drunk. You heard the recording. Saul. Saul is Serpentine. Surely you guessed why she protected him. Helped him.'

'Or why she allowed herself – and you – to be used by him.'

'I don't know about that. Anyway. We dropped him off. At the zoo. She met him, we took off, back to base. No shit hitting the fan. Debriefing. Straightforward. And she was there. End of story. Until she reminded me about it. Just before all this happened, actually. I wondered why she brought it up.'

'And now? You don't think that's significant? The timing? I mean, Christ Almighty, doesn't it strike you as being relevant to what we're doing now? How much haven't you told me?' He had a slightly amused look about him. She met it coolly.

'Come on, Mark. You already knew, didn't you? You've known all along. Tell me the game you're playing. Those other guys were retired, on a list. What list are you on?'

But Murricane ignored the question.

'Who was your pilot that night? You were riding shotgun, tooled up, stewardess with firepower, typical Det female stuff. Who was flying?'

'Ewen. Ewen Brotherton. Good guy. He wasn't around for long after that. His chopper went into the woods near Cookstown a week later. Suspected machine-gun fire, they said.'

'Jesus.'

'And then we had leave, the two of us. You and me, babe. We took that trip to Scotland. To Valhalla. And here we fucking are.'

'Yes,' he said. 'Here we fucking are.'

He wondered, briefly, if the use of the word had been significant. If it indicated a further, continuing need, a revival of desire. Of course it did. It was all so simple. He reached again for her leg, the dressing gown parting at his touch. Her intake of breath, a hoarse gasp. Not even conscious of being aroused, her hand on his wrist pulling, urgent, and then they were together, him on top, her legs apart, the rough slither of the linen sheets and the heat of connecting flesh.

He must have slept. When he woke, she was naked, her wiry body, softened from the memory he held of it, eerily lit by the blue light of the MacBook's screen.

'There's wireless here,' she said. 'And I have an email from him. It's Mull all right.'

'Burial place of the Lords of the Isles,' he said. 'Do you think that's how he sees himself? As a lord?'

'I think he's probably just an old man with a story to tell, something he wants to say. A record he wants to set straight,' said Millie. 'It's simple. He trusted Freya. So he trusts me.'

'We're going there?'

'If we don't, someone else will.'

'Christ, Millie. It's a set-up. It's all been a set-up right the way through. Surely you can see that. Freya, you. Maybe him and Freya, I don't know. That fucking posh soldier, Masonic family bullshit. What possible good can we do?'

'Freya stole me away from you. Is that it? You expect me to believe that's what's motivating you? Come on, come out and tell me. You think you've got me back? Two shags? Is that all it takes?' She got up and began to dress. 'It doesn't matter. I'll go alone.'

He sat up and swung his legs over the edge of the bed. 'No,' he said, 'you won't.'

They left the Volvo where it was, well enough hidden. It took the rest of the night to reach the car park for the hillwalking pass through the Cairngorms called the *Lairig Ghru* and the funicular railway up to the winter ski areas. As dawn broke, Millie casually sauntered among the dozen or so cars that remained there, looking for the tell-tale square of white paper on the dashboard that would indicate the owner's destination and estimated time of return. It was responsible mountaineering behaviour, for Munroists and those tackling any wilderness walking. But it was also a car thief's charter.

She used a pencil Maglite on likely prospects. Nothing too new. Security was worse on older cars. It took Murricane five minutes to open up and start a short wheelbase Land Rover Defender V8 with a careful note stuck to its side window detailing its driver's planned return in three days' time. Land Rovers were notoriously easy to steal. This proved no exception.

'Petrol V8,' Millie snorted. 'What an environmental catastrophe. Teach them a lesson.'

'Yeah. Not like an ancient Volvo with a taste for leaded fuel.' The Land Rover's engine sounded like the snoring of an emphysemic dog: one potato, two potato . . . the exhaust smoke smelled heady, like an old drunk waking up.

A pearly daylight was spreading down from the mountains, glinting on patches of snow high up on the peaks. There was still no one around as they transferred the contents of the Volvo to the Defender and drove back towards the A9.

Billy Boy had spent more comfortable nights. And less. He had tracked Millie and Murricane to Alt-na-Coich and then followed them to the Cairngorm car park. They hadn't been casual. They had taken precautions, or at least they had been careful to check for pursuit. But he was careful, too, and very experienced. He'd wolfed down some amphetamine to keep him awake and now he was more than bright eyed, he was brittle and manic. Even more brittle and manic than normal, some would say. He'd heard nothing from his . . . 'client' . . . might be the right word. Control. Maybe not now. Maybe he'd been cut loose, one final time. But that was all right. Because he had a vested interest in this. He had his own agenda. He was motivated.

When they left the car park in the stolen Land Rover, he broke cover and smashed the window of an old Ford Sierra. It was an easy steal to a man like him. He watched the Land Rover tail lights wind down the mountain road. He could feel a cramp in his gut that was indistinguishable from excited pleasure. Soon he'd have the bastard. And he'd deal with Millie and her fuck buddy as well. Poor old Seamus. He'd quite liked the boy. They'd have to pay for that. But first, they had other uses. He kept the Sierra's lights switched off as he began the run down towards the A9.

THIS FLIGHT TONIGHT

We were back at Dalcross Airport, in a Portakabin far from the main terminal, drinking bad coffee from one of those machines that dispense soup as well as tea, coffee and hot chocolate. What I was drinking tasted as if every beverage it could produce had been mixed together. Outside, the shadows were lengthening.

'So,' said Nixon, 'what do you know about Serpentine?'

'The mineral?'

'Yes, the mineral.'

'It's green. I think it's kind of greasy.'

'It is. In Latin it's *serpentinus*, meaning serpent rock. Snake stone. But come on, you know about Serpentine. You've heard the name used in another context. Bound to have, a man of your experience!'

And I was back in Belfast, drunk, and someone was saying: 'The bastard's a snake, all right. Serpentine. Suits him. I wouldn't trust that cunt an inch.'

'You see, initially it wasn't a person. It was an operation.' Nixon smiled. Edwyn, if that was his real name, was playing with a laptop computer and didn't look up. That lock of hair dropped over his eyes. Old New Romantic or Etonian fop? Did it matter? 'And then not so much an operation as a project. A project it's best not to know about, not to remember, most definitely not to have published in some slithering reptile's memoirs. Even if he is . . . well.' Nixon leaned forward, his elbows on his knees. 'The thing is, we're the clean-up mob. You, me and my friend here. The whole thing was meant to be taken care of at arm's length. But somebody failed to realise that using Billy Boy was likely to end up with arms, hands and fucking legs all chopped off and bloody stumps all round, if you get my meaning, darling boy. And I'm sure you do.'

'And that somebody, that somebody who failed . . . that wouldn't have been you, Ken, would it? So now you're having to clean up your own mess?' No response. But again that flicker of fear.

Edwyn clicked the laptop shut and stood up. 'Right,' he said. 'Let's get going. We need to bring this fucking mess to some sort of a conclusion.' And it was then I realised that Nixon was in thrall to Edwyn, not vice versa. Officer class in charge now.

The door opened and in stepped a boy of about 15 dressed up as a pilot. He had the kind of moustache you see on primary pupils in Caithness who've been exposed to too much radioactivity. When he spoke, the accent was Australian.

'All right, mates? Got a charter for Glenforsa? Gonna take the Twin Otter, all refuelled and ready for you gentlemen. Just gonna run through a few things with you before we actually get out to the aeroplane, if that's OK.'

All three of us were momentarily one in our reaction. A sort of, what the fuck, are we meant to take this adolescent seriously? And is our insurance really up to date? Nobody said anything.

'I'm Sean Arnold, your captain for the day. Case you're worried, mates, been bush flying since I was 19 out in Oz, seaplane stuff in Canada, and now here. Your flight time to Mull today is 25 minutes, give or take. I understand speed is of the essence so we'll be flying low and it will be bumpy. Lots of thermals this time of year. Also, we may need to swerve hurriedly to avoid the choppers and the farmers and the power kites. Only joking.' Nobody laughed. 'Seat belts on when we board, keep them on, please, no wandering about the aeroplane. It's a trim thing. Someone should sit next to me, other two side by side over the wings, please. Keep the fucker stable. In the event of landing on water, we'll all be dead, so fuck the life jackets. No inflight service, no alcohol in case I'm tempted, and the person next to me mustn't touch anything. Is that clear, mates?' We stared at him in silence. 'Right, let's go. Luggage?' His eye flicked to a small leather suitcase, a long holdall and two briefcases. 'Take them out with you, we'll load them into the hold. I was told no security searches. I presume none of you are intending to hijack the aircraft? You are the charter customers after all?'

'Shall we?' said Floppy. I felt for the Walther in the pocket of my Schott jacket. Maybe I could get him to fly to Sutherland instead. I shouldered the black holdall and walked out onto the tarmac. The bag was unexpectedly heavy. I heaved it into the luggage compartment at the rear of the fuselage. I had a grim feeling I knew what was in it.

'Give me a minute, Captain, will you?'

'Sure, mate. Last prayers? Always advisable.'

The Escort was parked outside. One side of the Portakabin opened onto a branch of the airport tarmac, the other to the road. I opened the driver's door and briefly considered taking off, heading out, away, anywhere. And then I felt for the hidden sawn-off Mossberg, illegally loaded with five cartridges and packed with bird shot. Death from a metre; a nasty, wide-ranging wound from ten. It was the size of a Georgian duelling pistol. I put it in one of those 'For Life' textile bags you have to pay for in supermarkets and always forget to take in when you actually shop. On top I shoved some papers, a random map or two, some CDs. It was getting chilly. It would be chillier in the air. I opened the boot and had a look at the garments I habitually kept there for emergencies. This was an emergency, I decided. I took off the Schott jacket I was wearing and changed. Then I walked back inside the Portakabin.

IN THE MINISTRY OF LOVE

The minister was not entirely happy with his car. It was ostentatious, he felt, too showy by a long shot. His constituents, farming folk for the most part, wouldn't approve. They liked the posters of him on a tractor, wearing a blue boiler suit, his ruddy face glistening with something that looked very like sweat. These photographers could do wonders on their computers.

He had wanted something simple. Practical, preferably Swedish. That stood for reliablity and dependability. Slightly boring. A Volvo V70, or the like. But he had been told that ministerial cars had to be British, at least in name. Even if the multinational concern that actually owned the name was German or American or Japanese or Chinese. So here he was in a Vauxhall. He hated Vauxhalls. Always had, ever since his old daddy had bought that VX490 and it had rusted away to shite in less than two years.

Danny, his driver, didn't like it either. They had been together a long time, him and Danny. They had history. A mutual support system, one that stretched back to their days at school together. Some of the things they'd got up to in the old days. *There's many a trouble that I had a han' in,* Danny would sing, when he was in his cups, on a tear into the Powers Gold Label and the Murphy's Stout. And indeed, trouble had once been the minister's stock-in-trade, aided and abetted by Daniel. For the most part. Some things he'd done alone and it had been better that way. Still was. That was why he was the minister, after all, and Danny was a driver.

The car had been reinforced with anti-mine armouring underneath and bulletproofing on the sides. The glass was armoured too. Although the suspension had been stiffened to cope, the vehicle still sat lower than it should have and the extra weight meant it was a lumbering thing, provoking Danny to curses when it had to be taken around the twisty lanes of the constituency. And with three of them in it, sometimes. Danny, himself and his personal protection officer, a rotation of four former RUC, now PSNI, Police Service of Northern Ireland Special Branch constables, none of whom liked what they had to do and probably wouldn't stop a bullet for him when push came to shove, even if he was a minister of the fucking Crown now, and not the Provo bastard they'd happily have killed if they'd been anything more than squawling babies back in the day. Pissant pricks. He could have ripped their fucking heads off.

Truth was, he had put all that aside. He never thought about it, or rarely. It wasn't that he couldn't remember, that the facts had faded. He chose not to remember. He had new responsibilities now. Details to absorb, jobs to do. For the benefit of the new order, the community of Northern Ireland. He felt a warm glow when he thought of that. The peace process. The peace dividend. Sure, the divisions were still there – you had to secure peace somehow, and if that meant curfews, walls and separate Catholic and Protestant bus stops, so be it – but here he was, working with men and women who had been his sworn enemies less than a decade previously. People who'd tried to kill him, or at least had said they wanted him dead. People he'd tried to kill, or at least had said he wanted to. The truth was, they hadn't been trying to kill each other at all, not really. They'd needed each other. The folk who got killed were the foot soldiers and the intelligence targets and the poor bloody civilians. Collateral fucking damage. Symbolic targets and the fallout from that.

Of course, push come to shove, you still hated them. You'd still eat their bones for breakfast. They weren't the same. Deep inside, you knew.

He had responsibilities and one of them was to forget. Sometimes, though, it was hard to forget. The boy who had shat himself when he was being interrogated, shat himself and peed himself and screamed like a stuck pig before they took him out and shot him in the knees and, half an hour later, in the head. And there was the other stuff. The stuff that was even worse. The stuff that was strictly arm's-length. Other people's arms. At least he'd thought it was. The unspoken policy decisions, the whispered weasel-words. Strategy, he'd thought. Politics. Mr Mac fucking Machiavelli. Fuck. He felt a cold sweat inside his expensive Hugo Boss suit, the Boden shirt, the Crombie coat. The Davidoff Cool Water he habitually wore was suddenly pricked with something elemental, sweaty, coarse and foul. And he knew what that was; it was the smell of fear.

'All right there, minister?' Danny had the partition down. It was just the two of them in the car. They were on their way from Belfast to a weekend at home in the scattering of rural townships that had given birth to both of them. The heavy car creaked and strained as it climbed the rise that led to the border farmhouse he lived in, just he and Siobhan now that the girls had gone, thank God, to Canada and Australia.

'Fine, Danny,' he said. 'Just fine. Hunky fucking dory, fella.' And for just the few seconds it took him to say it, he sincerely believed it was.

'All ready for Monday? It's a long way to go, sure enough. You'll miss the football midweek. That European tie.'

'Aye, I'm sure they'll have satellite or cable, Danny. It's a duty and a privilege, as they say.'

'Dangerous, though. Even for an old warhorse like yourself.'

The minister smiled.

'I'm sure they'll look after us. It's not just me, after all.' Not just him with a past. Not only him with a background full of dark shadows, patches of blackness. Anyway, he was looking forward to this particular trip. A perk of the fucking job. 'Ach, I'll be taking the golf clubs, Danny. It's not often you get the chance to play where giants of the game have gone before.'

'Settle it all over a round, eh?'

'Aye, and maybe we'll play some golf as well!'

They both laughed.

'I'll drive,' Millie said. 'You look knackered.'

Murricane shrugged. He was tired. And he had learnt to accept offers of help without quibbling. When he knew the person concerned was capable of helping.

'It's got power steering, the usual bastard of a gear change. It's turbo diesel, so not too slow. Not like the old pigs in Belfast.' Millie grinned as Murricane pulled into the car park for the Glen Shiel memorial. The Jacobite finger of defiance pointed at the sky.

'Subtle as a flying penis,' she said. '*Ye Jacobites By Name*, eh? Lost in the romance, lost in the cause. This is where it all started, all that fucking shit in Ireland, didn't it? The Stuarts, the Old and Young Pretenders.'

'Battle of the Boyne. One of them lost that, didn't they?' Murricane couldn't remember. Couldn't think.

'William of Orange won. Called the Duc de l'Orange as a gift from the Catholic Louis XIV, by the way. Or something. King Billy. *We are the Billy Boys . . .*'

'Billy Boy . . .'

'Oh yes. History. It's all a-fucking-round. Right, I think I'll manage.' They exchanged seats. By the time they were heading along Loch Eil before doubling back south, Murricane was asleep.

He slept along the single-track road that edged down Loch Linnhe, missed the winking lights of Fort William, the looming bulk of Ben Nevis behind. Millie sneaked a couple of glances at the huge massif, only really visible properly from here, or one of the Ardgour mountains. The road was busy with tourists – bikes and cars. She kept up as reasonable a pace as she could. Sometimes she glimpsed the glimmer of moving glass and steel behind her, but as far as she could tell she wasn't holding anyone up. No one caught up with her anyway. When they reached the Corran ferry she turned west on the narrow ribbon of road that led down the Ardnamurchan peninsula.

They stopped at Castle Tioram – Millie had been unable to resist a detour – and it was there that Murricane awoke. He blinked at the sight. It was a still, sunny day, clear and windless, and the old stone castle stood, warm and grey, worn and wavering, in the heat haze.

'Christ,' he said. 'Are we in Narnia?'

Millie handed him a bottle of mineral water.

'Might as well be,' she said. 'We've had the Bonnie Prince and his doomed cause, his frilly knickers, his pathetic paw. All we need's Aslan and Cair Paravel and the High King Peter.'

They reached Kilchoan with an hour to spare before the last ferry of the day to Mull and it felt to both of them as if time had slowed to a crawl. They joined two other cars in a queue. As they waited, two others coasted in behind them, German number plates, one of them on a VW camper. The sun hung low in the sky, reddening over the Sound of Mull, the island's bulk first grey, then blue, then a deepening purple. They ate grilled salmon in rolls from a tiny cafe by the pier, watched a lobster fisherman slowly prepare for sea in the old and very small harbour. It had been a windless day, but as the sun fell, a chilling breeze rippled across the water. Millie was surprised to find herself gripping Mark's wrist, feeding off the almost ridiculous romanticism of the day, the journey, the place. Affection welled up in her. She fought it down.

Mark reached around her shoulders with one sinewy arm and, for a moment, she felt herself relax. Then she shrugged it off determinedly. There was a shiver of revulsion there which had been absent back at Alt-na-Coich.

'Sorry,' he said. 'Sunsets. I was always a sucker for them.'

Half a dozen cars and a lorry carrying Calor gas drew in behind them. Rush hour. When it arrived, the surprisingly large vessel was more like a floating platform, with a ramp at each end that could be raised and lowered. They were beckoned on by a middle-aged man whose face was almost as red as the Caledonian MacBrayne badge on his uniform. The ferry's deck wasn't even half filled with vehicles. About a dozen foot passengers, many of them backpackers, shambled on just before the ramp was raised and the engines foamed their intention of departure.

'When we get to Mull,' said Mark, 'where do we go then?'

'We head for Iona,' said Millie. 'Island of the Priests. And island of serpentine, incidentally. Grailloch Dhu . . . That's the name of the house. It's near the ferry to Iona, on the Mull side, obviously.'

'Iona's where the great Celtic kings are buried, then?'

'And one prime minister.'

'Oh yes. Not prime minister, if you remember. Leader of the Labour Party. Would-be prime minister.'

'John Smith was no name for a prime minister. Too ordinary.'

'What? And Tony Blair isn't? Gordon Brown? David Cameron?'

'Point taken. It's the age of ordinary. And when we get there?'

'Well, what do you think?'

Millie narrowed her eyes, kneaded her brow. 'It's for Freya, isn't it? We have to do what she would have done. Would have wanted us to do. We help him.'

There was a brief silence.

'Can I ask you something?' said Murricane.

'Yes.'

'Are you fucking out of your fucking mind? Do you think this psychotic assassin needs help?'

'Otherwise, why would he have contacted Freya in the first place? He needs some kind of help. Maybe he's disabled, or just old.'

'Or maybe he's got something in mind.'

'Maybe.'

'Maybe he's a devious fuck.'

'Maybe. But I owe it to her.'

They left the Land Rover unlocked and climbed onto a narrow upper deck, where the sinking sun could be seen leaving a trail of ruffled blood-orange in the sea, leading them like a pathway towards Mull. Twilight began to gather, a thickening of the light. The bulk of Mull, the flicker of buildings, growing to a coloured jumble strewn along a bay and up a steep slope. And then, suddenly, they were facing the fairytale, toy-town colours of Tobermory, fading in the twilight.

'We're not landing there.' I was gazing at the patch of grass next to the sea that we had just circled. It looked like somebody's lawn. A big lawn, admittedly, stretching between the beginnings of a steep hillside and the sea, which was blood-red in the sunset.

'Roger that,' said our boy pilot. 'Grass strip, licensed, perfectly safe. Only one in the country with its own hotel. Or only hotel with its own airstrip. You can taxi right to the bar.'

Something pricked at the edge of my memory. A cold case, a file, like the Renee Macrae thing, that every copper in the Highlands had to bone up on.

'Wasn't there a famous case in the '70s?' It came back to me in lumps of discarded data. 'Someone with a private plane who got pished and then crashed into the sea. Only they found his body halfway up the hillside, a year later?'

Nixon laughed. It sounded snuffly, distorted and odd, unhealthy, through the headphones we were all wearing. 'You're the detective, sonny, you're the local knowledge around here. Are you telling me that's all you can remember?'

Edwyn said nothing. Just rummaged in his briefcase, which he was clutching to his knees as if it contained his necessities for survival – parachute, pornography, life jacket, whisky. And handed me a thin, glossy brochure for the Glenforsa Hotel.

'Back page. "Aviation in Mull",' he said. Then he pressed his finger to his lips and nodded at the pilot, who seemed blissfully unaware of our conversation. But then, he had to fly the plane, I suppose.

It was 1975, Christmas Eve 1975 on the glorious island of Mull, and at the Glenforsa Hotel, a series of peculiar events were unfolding that would become known as the Great Mull Air Mystery. And many times since have they been well and truly 'Mull-ed' over! Why was it that, after dinner with his girlfriend, and consuming a bottle of wine, guest Peter Gibbs decided to go for a spin in his Cessna C150, registration G-AVTN? Why did his aircraft vanish? And, even odder, why did his remains appear only several months later, not in the sea, into which most thinking folks imagined he had crashed, but 400 feet up a hill behind the hotel?

There have been many wild rumours as to the whys and wherefores of what happened. There were suggestions that Peter Gibbs was an MI5 agent of some kind, engaged in undercover work in Northern Ireland. He took off from Mull and flew to Ulster, apparently with a new and secret identity. But he was discovered as an agent, murdered, and his body brought back to Mull as a warning to his superiors.

I looked at Nixon, just as the Cessna tilted severely to the left. Either we were crashing or landing. I had heard once that all aeroplane landings were controlled crashes. I nodded at the brochure.

'This was . . .'

'A strange wee story, eh?' Nixon turned to the pilot, gestured to the man's headset and flicked his index finger across his throat. Either he was asking him to stop listening or threatening to cut his throat. Or the engines. Or all three. The pilot shrugged his headset off his ears and down to his neck. 'Happened long, long before you were in the Ulster we know and love. But curious, don't you think? That rumours like that should be out and about, and that people should feel free to print them?'

'So . . .'

'So, on the one hand we've got an oaf and a fool and a drunk, but one that could fly a plane. Showing off for his girlfriend, or his own depression or something.'

'And on the other,' said Edwyn, 'a transportation freelance who got out of his depth. Of course, there was someone on hand to . . . take some action. Serpentine simply made an unusually messy job, for him, of sorting out the situation. In hindsight, I think the sheer messiness was also a little word to us. A kind of warning.'

'But why did you have to take that sort of thing from one man. Surely it would have been possible to just . . .'

'Deal with him?' Nixon's eyes crinkled in a facsimile of a farmer's weather-beaten grin. 'Ah well, he was always, how can I put this, in demand for certain tasks. From a . . . global market. Useful to keep on the books, so to speak. Difficult to gainsay.'

There was a heavy thump, a strange, floating bounce, and then the little plane settled on the grass runway. It was like driving on cobbles. The pilot was putting his headset back on with one hand and steering us towards a wooden building that appeared to be Scandinavian. Next to it was a Renault Espace. A man with a clipboard was leaning against it. Captain Sean bounced out of the cockpit like a wallaby and had the passenger door open before you could say 'Flying Doctor'. The air was balmy and salty.

'Welcome to Mull, gentlemen,' said the man with the Espace. 'Your carriage awaits. Signature required from a Mr . . . Smith. And dinner is still being served in the hotel. In the Sopranos Bar or the Morvern Callar Room, as you seek or wish to avoid formality.'

Edwyn stepped forward to sign for the car. Smith, eh? I stood in the gloaming, holding my heavy, ecologically sound shopping bag, my overnight holdall, wondering about the Sopranos Bar. Would Tony be there?

'As far as I can see from the maps and Google Earth,' said Millie, 'there's a drive leading up to it. Just past the Fiohnnoport ferry terminal. It's . . .'

'Just here, I would think,' said Murricane. He felt gritty and fatigued, after a night camping near Slaven, the car tucked behind a stone sheep pen, the smell of rancid sheep shit everywhere. It was the same smell you got in the hills of Palestine, he remembered. And Afghanistan. Only here it was damper. And less goaty.

He drove past the unmarked track that led off to the left, into a copse of pines, up a heavily wooded hill and stopped in a muddy field entrance about 50 metres further on.

'What now?' Millie was scanning an Ordnance Survey map with the GPS in one hand when there was a splintering crash and their whole world suddenly tipped sideways.

Its high centre of gravity saw the Land Rover slam heavily onto its side, crushing the aluminium gate next to it. The vehicle responsible, an old but gleaming Toyota pick-up truck with blacked-out windows, a Highland redneck special, seemed slightly scuffed, but otherwise undamaged.

It was difficult for Billy Boy to say how he felt. He had consumed too much amphetamine over the past few days to be sure. Elated, perhaps. Relieved. Certainly excited, if the hammering of his heart was anything to go by. Excitement had been, until this last while, a highly unusual experience. It took a great deal to get him fired up. Normally, a great deal of violence, inflicted on another human being. The camel coat was gone. He was dressed in fake army surplus Gore-tex, survivalist shit he'd found in the gigantic Inverness shop called Highland Industrial Supplies. Like a soldier, he thought. He was ready to fight and die like a soldier. It was just a question of settling things. Sorting out.

He was not really used to working alone. These last few years he'd been a much-appreciated consultant, in the more distant past he'd been number two to that bastard Nixon and later leading his own teams, but the loss of Hume and MacDougall had thrown him back on old skills. If you could call them that. He had ditched the Ford in Tobermory, sneaking off the ferry, last car, that pair of lovesmitten dickheads oblivious to his presence. He'd found the tarted-up Toyota sitting outside a boisterous pub called The Mish Nish, abandoned for a drinking session, probably. The doors were open and the keys tucked above the sun visor.

A lot had happened during his speed-fuelled pursuit from the east coast. He had made a few calls, found the numbers he was used to dealing with either disconnected or subject to endless holding patterns, and known that he had been cut loose by Those That Were, the Immunity Crew. He was, he realised, truly alone. But somehow, in his chemically-enhanced state, it made him feel more contented than ever. Contentment, after all, was his normal state of mind. It was the search for stimulus that prompted some of his indiscretions. And, for that matter, his contractual arrangements with various organisations and governmental institutes throughout the world.

Now life had shrunk to one simple objective. Follow the lovebirds to Serpentine and wait. For the opportunity that would undoubtedly arise, that always did. The chance to settle things with those who had employed him and who now appeared to have cut him adrift. Then he would . . . do something else. Afterwards could take care of itself.

He had bedded down in a waterproof sleeping bag, within infra-red binocular distance of Millie and her faithful dog-boy. They were getting tired and careless. He had seen it happen before, lots of times. Hard men and women failed by fatigue.

But it had affected him too, despite the military-issue speed he'd been dosing himself with. So that now, thinking he'd lost them, going too fast in the Toyota, which had been tuned, chipped up in performance from its standard diesel lumber, when he saw them pulled off the road, he decided to begin the endgame. It was hardly a conscious decision. Just a flick of the steering wheel. He was close. They were close to Serpentine. He could feel it.

He pulled out the Ruger pistol he kept for old times' sake. And reliability. Which, for him, were one and the same thing. Don't trust modernity, he thought. It will always fuck you over. Carefully, he squeezed through the gap between the upturned Land Rover and a dry-stone wall. He could see through the Land Rover's windscreen that Murricane was completely still, blood oozing from a facial wound, the steering wheel smashed into three pieces of bakelite. No seat belt. The old stupid MOD notion that it was safer that way. When the fact was that in a Land Rover of this vintage, no collision was even slightly safe. Millie was moving sluggishly over Murricane towards the smashed driver's side window, her face covered in blood. He remembered how jagged the interior edges were in a Land Rover. No airbags. Just bits of '50s metal and extraneous plastic. He smiled. He could hear his heart beating evenly, loudly, a kind of singing in his ears. It felt good. Just then Murricane moved, or it could just have been the force of Millie's apparently uncaring passage over his back. He hoped the man was still alive. He would like to have words with him.

'Now then, you must be Millie,' he said, his voice sounding, he thought, pleasant and plump and reassuring. Yet it was difficult to speak. It felt as if he'd swallowed iron filings. 'We meet at last! I think it's best . . . if you crawl out the back of the vehicle. Don't cause that poor chap any more discomfort! Hold on and I'll open the door for you, being the polite sort of person that I am. My, my but you've led me a merry dance, have you not?' Once he started talking, it was difficult to stop.

Millie could not believe Murricane was dead. His chest had smashed the steering wheel and his head had collided heavily with the door pillar on her side; she had been trapped beneath him, had been desperately crawling, ruthlessly using his body as purchase to reach the window. Then she had felt him move, she was sure. Some kind of physical reaction, a spark of life. Her own head ached violently and she could feel a dreadful stiffness in her shoulder. It wouldn't have been as bad if they'd been wearing seat belts, but as Mark had reminded her, that wasn't the military way . . .

The single back door was pulled open, its side-hinge nearest the ground, and it sat on the muddy earth like a bridge to the world. Her legs felt weak and wobbly, but she could stand. The big man, the big old man in front of her with the gun – a Ruger, she thought – and the crumpled camo fatigues, held out his hand and, God help her, she took it. Like he was Sir Walter Raleigh and she was Greta Garbo. Or something.

'Who are you?' she said. But she knew. Knew that this was Billy Boy. The voice. The voice had been the same as the one on the phone, back in Inverness . . . *Oh, Freya* . . .

'I'm the man who was sent to find you and look after you. But oh, how things have changed. How things have that terrible tendency to go wrong.' He was jabbering. It was a ghastly, discordant sound. And he had a look in his eyes that Millie recognised, the mad, serene certainty that he was in the right place, doing the right thing, the task he had been designed for. He looked as if he was in love with the moment. He looked as if he was out of his brains on speed and had been for some time.

'Now, I need to know where your man is. Serpentine, or whatever he calls himself. I wonder if I would recognise him. I knew him, you see, back in the old days, about as well as any fucker.'

Her eyes flicked towards the access track. She couldn't help herself. And in his incredibly artificially sensitised state, he couldn't help but notice.

'Up there, up the road, up the track, is that it? That why you stopped? Oh yes, Christ, they told me to expect somewhere remote. Fuckers. They must have known. They must have been in contact with him. So why didn't they tell me? Why did they get me to follow this mad trail through you and your pal Freya . . .' And then a light seemed to go out in his eyes. 'Christ Almighty. It's a trap, isn't it? It's been set up. This is the honey and all of us, all of us are the flies . . . the bees. The flies. Jesus, he's just been drawing us all in. Can't you see it, Millie? Can't you fucking see it?'

The Glock. Where was the Glock? In the Land Rover, she remembered, jumbled up in God knew what corner of the interior by the impact.

'What about the police? Someone's going to . . .'

'Well, maybe, Millie, maybe. Some time. Some time. But that really doesn't matter now. We're in the last few seconds of a dying planet. Or at the very least, at the end of all we're going to see of it.' And he smiled a great open, joyous smile. An attractive smile. Christ, thought Millie, he's on a death trip. He knows it's over.

'Come on, now, Millie my dear. We're going to take a little walk. We've come this far. We may as well see what it was all supposed to be about. Don't you think? What a pity your friend is all passed over to the other side. Still, maybe he can observe what's going on, in some way. In some ghostly fashion. Do you believe in ghosts, my dear?'

He pushed her ahead of him, not roughly, back onto the road. They began to walk back towards the track leading to the house called Grailloch Dhu. Crazy, thought Millie. Insane. There was no attempt at concealment. It was as if they were now in some kind of game of Manderley's own devising. Or someone else's.

They were about to turn left up the muddy ungated track – there was even a small wooden sign, she realised, nailed to a tree. 'Grailloch Dhu', it said. 'Private Road'. Private. Did that mean with or without landmines? They'd soon find out. Just then, a blue Renault Espace came round the blind corner ahead of them.

It was like a film, only moving much faster. And we weren't driving fast. The Espace had a Garmin Satnav and Edwyn was trying to follow it, having punched in the postcode for the house known as Grailloch Dhu. But then we rounded the turn on the single-track road and there were two figures, one large, one small, one carrying a gun. A Toyota HiLux behind, rammed into something on its side, wheels in the air, a Land Rover. Jesus Christ.

We'd left the hotel early, impossible to catch actual daybreak, really, at this time of year, in these latitudes. It was light all night. But we needed sleep, a moment to draw breath. To wonder. To gather our thoughts and our fears. We'd eaten in silence, pub food, good enough, no alcohol.

'Let's get away from here at five,' Edwyn said, before we went to our rooms. 'If we can talk to him, we should talk.' That sounded flimsy. Why weren't they sending in a team of commandos? Why us? Unless it was all a complete set-up. Was that my place in it? Some kind of sacrifice? Nixon was the least trustworthy copper I'd ever met and Edwyn looked like Satan gone to boarding school. Jesus. I spent a while checking weapons and fell asleep half-undressed. I was wakened by a soft knock on my door at 4.45, the light already bright outside. I put on layer after layer of clothing. I felt the need for comfort. Safety. I knew I would be warm in the car, but what the hell. We were all thoughtful. Nixon's bonhomie seemed to have deserted him. I clutched my bag-for-life. 'Just something for the road,' I muttered to Nixon.

'Briefing when we get there?' Nixon was querulous. Suddenly I found myself wondering just how official all this actually was. Maybe they were running completely off the books. Did anyone know we were there? How did they organise the flight? I climbed into the back seat. Edwyn driving, Nixon riding, literally, shotgun. It was an Ulster thing. He had a sawn-off Mossberg too. Newer than mine, the American police-issue, official sawn-off pump. A bad boy. He saw me looking at it and grimaced. I reached into my shopping bag and removed my own gun. He gave a little laugh of recognition.

'So that's what you went back to the car for. We did teach you something after all, Over the Water.'

'We're on our own here, Ken, aren't we? Edwyn? Why me?'

'Ken here thought you'd be amenable to helping out,' said Edwyn. 'And besides, we need somebody to write the script and stamp it. An inspector will do nicely.'

'Acting inspector,' I said. 'And don't you forget it.'

Edwyn had the training, you could see that. Escape, avoidance, confrontation. Or collision. He didn't hesitate. Just floored the accelerator and headed straight for the pair. A big man. A small woman with short hair.

'Millie,' I said. 'No, not Millie.' They seemed frozen. The big man was smiling. It was as if he had recognised us.

And he moved quickly, too. Because we missed them. He must have thrown himself and the girl sideways and to the ground at the last minute, their faces filling the vast Espace windscreen and then vanishing. We slid to a stop and the rear window shattered as two rounds crashed through it, punching out through the front, hitting no one.

'Shit, Billy Boy,' said Nixon, turning, his smile even wider than normal, somehow incredulous. He had lost the shotgun. His hands were empty. Somehow, I was still gripping my Mossberg. 'You're still light on your feet for an old bastard.' Lighter than he thought. The third bullet was fired through the window on my side of the car and it caught him in the neck. Blood fountained from the wound. The smile on Nixon's face remained in place, as a warm, salty wetness rhythmically spouted over me. I wiped my eyes and reached for him, the gesture completely involuntary. The amount of blood coming from him was unbelievable.

Edwyn had a gun in his hand, a revolver. A small one. A .22. An assassin's gun. Was that his job? Assassin with a plummy accent and a leather briefcase. And then he vanished. The sliding rear door revealing only a hedge and beyond that a field leading to a stone wall and beyond that the sea, a stone wall. There was a rocky outcrop halfway down the field, a kind of green, marbled stone, rippling in the morning sunlight. Serpentine. The area was known for it. This was like Ireland, I thought. Just like fucking South Armagh only with salt water. Mull, biggest of the Inner Hebrides. Suddenly I felt very far from home.

There was a silence, or a kind of silence. The engine had stalled. Birds singing. Waves in the distance. Footsteps. A guttering, gasping sound from Nixon. And then two whistling coughs followed by the wet thump of something large and fleshy falling onto the road.

Nixon stopped his parody of breathing and fell sideways into the driver's seat. I took off my seat belt and opened the door.

An old man faced me. A well-preserved, but indubitably old man dressed in waxed cotton and with impeccably combed, thick silver hair, His face was tanned, patrician. With his hooked nose, he looked like something from *Beau Geste*. He was wearing green wellington boots and carried a silenced automatic pistol. Modern, dulled metal finish. It looked like a Sig Sauer. I had always wondered if the SS was intentional.

'I see,' he said, musingly, in a quiet and very English voice. Slight West Country tang. Freya. Suddenly there was a resemblance. Jesus, were they related? Or was it just that aristo similarity, the receding chin thing? A connection, though. Born to rule. Pricks. 'I see.' He half turned, as if he'd heard something from the hedge. I didn't see him raise his Swiss pistol, its suppressed barrel lengthened and unwieldy. But I heard it give its sweaty cough. And as

SERPENTINE

I turned sideways, Edwyn staggered into view, apparently unharmed. Until, what seemed like a millisecond later, I saw that his chest, his immaculate, lightly suited and shirted chest, was a mass of blood. Then he fell.

'We have to go.' It was an American voice, female and elderly. Very firm.

'Ah, Edwyn. Desperate to cover his murky tracks. Now, I think you should drop the shotgun.' But I held onto it. Pointed nowhere in particular. It just seemed comforting. 'And who are you?' The elderly man eyed me without any real curiosity. 'What's your role in this little charade?'

'I'm a police officer,' I said. 'I have ID. Detective Sergeant . . . Acting Inspector Alexander Flaws.'

'Ah.'

A smile of great charm and courtesy bloomed on that narrow face. 'I surmise then that you are here to clean up the mess. And so I shall leave you to do so. You will realise that you have witnessed an attempted murder, here, won't you? Self defence seemed to be demanded.' He half turned. 'Do you have young Millicent?' He was speaking to the invisible American, the female. 'Oh, excellent, and she's all right? Fit for purpose, as they say? Right then, we shall go. A policeman eh? Not a Special Branch operative, or just a liar, are you? Ah well . . .' He smiled again, raised the pistol and shot me twice in the chest. It was like getting kicked by an elephant. And then stamped on. All the breath in me departed. A great blackness seeped in.

I couldn't breathe. Hopelessly winded by the impact of the bullets and with an excruciating pain in my chest, I fought for air. Someone was crouched over me, dripping blood into my eyes. And so it was that the first words I addressed to Mark Murricane were, 'Get that bloody blood out of my bloody face.' Which was accurate, but hardly articulate.

'Who the fuck are you?' he said, his attention distracted from the Covert Logistics ballistic vest I'd been wearing, complete with ceramic plates, that I'd put on before boarding the plane in Inverness. Kept in the car, always, ever since the Black Isle incident. He'd found it on ripping my shirt open, searching for bullet wounds, finding only flattened bullets and probably some broken ribs.

'Detective Inspector Zander Flaws,' I said, hearing a calcium crackle with every word. 'Who the fuck are you? What the fuck is going on here?'

'Are you all right? I mean, are you fit enough to move?'

202

Blood continued to drip from a face which looked like a plate of rhubarb crumble.

'I could ask you the same question.'

'This?' He wiped some of his face away, it seemed. Though it was probably just skin, bone and blood. 'I've got a headache. But I can still breathe, just about. Body armour, eh? Useless for high velocity shots, you know that, even with ceramic plates.'

'OK for shotguns, though. And pistols, as it turns out.'

'You were lucky. I was lucky. Those old Landie steering wheels shatter at the slightest impact, or I'd have mince for a breastbone right now. Now, come on, we should get out of here before some tractor wallah finds us and alerts whatever passes for authority in these parts.'

'What about . . .'

'Nixon and that conniving bastard, Hodgkin-Smith? In the ditch. Best place for those fuckers. As for Manderley – if I could have set him on fire while he was alive, I would have. I'm tempted to do it anyway, just for form's sake. Come on. We need to get moving. And there's the house, too. Grailloch Dhu.' At that moment, there was a soft whump. It took only seconds before an acrid smell of burning began to reach us. 'Oh well,' he said. 'Forget the house. Maybe you could be useful, fuck knows. Fuck knows what's going on, really.' He stood up, wobbling slightly, then steadied. 'Mark Murricane,' he said, as a kind of afterthought. 'Freelance ex-soldier with certain . . . obligations, shall we say.'

I found I was just about able to stand up, though breathing was still difficult. Silenced rounds move slowly and this one had probably been cut and shut to open up on impact, making it spread even more. That's what it looked like from the damage to Edwyn's chest. It was if he'd been hit by a forcibly wielded pickaxe. The big man in camouflage fatigues, familiar, now – Billy Boy Manderley – had had most of his head blown off. Serpentine. Whoever this person was, he meant business when it came to bullets.

But slow-moving, soft-nosed bullets were not just very bad indeed for flesh and bone, they were very good at being stopped by Kevlar and hardened china plates, their force dissipated over the entire area of a body by a protective vest like the one I'd obtained from an old friend, now retired from Royal Protection at Balmoral. Of course, if you had a bad heart or weak arteries, it was possible the shock could rip them apart anyway. But so far, it seemed like cracked ribs and bruising for me.

Murricane was clutching a Glock. Blood dripped from what I could see now was a deep furrow on the left of his scalp. He walked firmly and determinedly up the track. 'Lucky. You were lucky, I was more than lucky. But Serpentine and Clara left me alive deliberately. They must have checked. They must have. That bastard. That old bitch knows who I am. It's all a set-up of course. You realise that? But whose? Saul fucking Enderby.'

I had no idea what he was talking about.

'Saul Enderby?'

'Yep. As in Freya, brother of. Target Number One. Except he would appear to have several other targets in mind. It's a clean-up operation. But who's doing the mopping?'

Millie had tried to fight, initially, but the brutal pain in her temple was making her nauseous and none of her limbs seemed properly connected to her body. Now she was in the back of a car, something old and expensive. The smell of petrol, oil and leather upholstery was making her feel even sicker as they sped up the single track road. Her hands and ankles had been expertly cable-tied by Clara, who was sitting next to her, one hand resting lightly on her thigh. There was even a seat belt fastened around her, holding her upright.

'Take it easy, honey,' Clara said, as Millie's body gave a spasmodic jerk, then slouched back as the road ahead dissolved into a fractured, agonised vision. Serpentine – she presumed it was him – was driving, very fast, it seemed to her. But she was in no real condition to judge. She could tell she'd been hurt. She couldn't even remember anyone securing her hands and feet, or when.

'What do you . . .'

'Just looking out for little old Millicent. You did a fine job back there. This past few days. Drew them in. Just a pity that Billy Boy had to pop up and get somewhat excited. We could have done with sorting everything out a little further away from the public highway.'

'They're all . . .'

'Everyone's dead now, honey. You and your boyfriend took care of the foot soldiers back in Findhorn and now we're shot of the mid-level management. The rest, well. The rest is just politics. And we're about to get that in hand too.' She smiled. 'Took a bit of persuading, bit of strong-arm stuff, bit of money, but I eventually managed to get Mr Serpentine here to do a little job for me, for the interests I represent. In fact, I think I may have persuaded the old buffer that our interests actually converge. It's something his particular skills are well suited for. And he suggested you could play, how can I put this darlin'? A crucial role.'

Millie felt her mouth go dry.

'Mark? Dead? Shot?'

'Shot of, darlin'. Meaning, rid ourselves of. Dispensed with.'

Millie's vision was beginning to clear. Thoughts began to circle each other and connect. And she was certain they were driving excessively fast. The big car was being thrown over blind, hump-back bridges and round corners with what seemed like complete abandon. 'But where are we going? I thought this was all about Serpentine, about . . . protecting him. Freya . . . he was Freya's half-brother?'

'Serpentine. An operational name that stuck.' The driver's voice was cultured, polite, but somehow rusty. 'I am Freya's brother, in fact. Better father than hers, that's all. My given name is Saul Enderby.' His eyes never left the road. His voice was calm, dispassionate. Almost bored.

'I thought you wanted to write a book. Bring everything out into the open.'

'See? I told you Freya musta told her more than she let on to me.' Clara gave a short cackle. 'That was just a little ploy, darlin'. To draw out the bad guys.'

'Well, the word "bad" is probably relative in this case.' That voice: flat, expressionless and very posh. Dry. '"Threatening" may be more appropriate.'

'Yeah, threatening. Whatever. Threatening to all kinds of interests, honey. You see, Saul here has been a good friend to us in the past. And not just us. He's free with his loyalties. With his, uh, lance. Anyways. He made out he wanted to spill the beans on his past life, you know, get Jesus, honest confession is good for the soul, maybe settle a few scores, take a few big names down. Or so he let on. There was a little window dressing, make convincing, one or two sacrifices had to be made. But journalists and literary folks, who really cares? Thing is, a certain name was dropped in the midst of all this. In certain circles. And that name was Erlend Maconie. Mean anything to you, my dear? Erlend Maconie, minister of state in Northern Ireland. A man on whom everyone has pinned their hopes. A man we all have great faith in. A man whose good name needs to be preserved. A saint.'

'And . . . Serpentine . . . Enderby . . . threatened that?'

Clara smiled.

'Ah, here's the clever bit, the twisted bit. He said he did. He – what's the phrase? *Let on* he did. But the people he really threatened were those who had what one might call connections with Maconie. To put it bluntly, who ran him. Or knew who was running him. We needed to draw them out. And we needed to . . .'

'Get rid of them?'

'That's right. What we . . . what British intelligence did, was put together a project to find and destroy Serpentine. The idea being that, in fact, Serpentine, Mr Enderby here, in whom we had absolute trust, would in turn get rid of them. Nixon and Hodgkin were the final . . . pieces in the jigsaw. Nasty pieces of work anyway. Billy Boy was, alas, a great deal more uncontrollable than we'd been led to believe. Hence the mayhem in Inverness. We only just came out of that without major embarrassment. Thanks to you and your little computer, and a little bit of consequent guidance from Mr Enderby here.'

'And . . . Mark.'

'Mr Murricane, yes. Another factional interest. The policeman, well, that was probably a mistake. But the mess Billy Boy was making meant they would have to be involved.' She grimaced.

'At any rate, having sorted things out, I have a little side project which it seemed to me and my friends that Mr Serpentine-Enderby could be of use to us with. And he didn't take much persuading, did you, darlin'? To back the true defenders of the United States of Democracy. To all who love freedom and hate publicity. I mean, not like that fat bastard back there, Billy Boy. Christ, I coulda swung for him a few times back in the day in Belfast. Anyways. Time for Saul here to take the money and run. He's paid his dues. He's done his practical woodwork and now he's Sir Christopher fuckin' Wren, do you catch my drift? He's a consultant. Now he's ours . . . mine.'

'Consultant?' Millie wondered if she was going mad, if this last blow on the head had driven her clean over sanity's edge. She glanced sideways, sending great bouts of pain through her head and neck. She saw the sea, a yacht, spinnaker up, desperately trying to glean some movement from the sparse wind.

'Strategist. Thinker. Guru. A man who knows stuff. And in this fragile world, a man who knows more about terrorists and how they think, live, breathe and can be put out of their misery than anyone else alive. Unfortunately, he has a past, as do many of us. And that past involved people. Dumb people. People who remember things. People who remember too much and maybe think they can use those memories to their own advantage. So what we did was, I think, quite clever, really.'

'You set us up. You set up your own sister.'

The man at the wheel let out what could have passed for a sigh. 'Well, you say "sister". Really, what did we have in common? As I say, I had the better father. And the Manderley thing was . . . incorrect. Unfortunate. Inapposite.'

'Jesus, what about flesh, blood and even parallel careers in the security services?'

'Yes, yes, obviously. But that's the thing. Both being in the business, I'm sure she would have understood the need to maintain my role.'

And then Millie understood two things: that Serpentine had all the arrogance and self-certainty of a psychopath, always had – it was how he'd survived, thrived – but that now it was being played out on a scale that meant he could dispense with his sister, use her as bait, as easily as he could put bread out for a sparrowhawk.

'Besides,' he said. 'I hated her . . . how can I put this . . . Sapphic ways. What shame that cast up on us. On me. Too many people knew. You were gossip fodder throughout the security community. She was my weakness. And because, you see, my weaknesses, such as they are, were potentially devastating for me and gold to my enemies, I really did not like having a sister who was counted as one.'

There was a kind of grinding noise from the front of the car and they came to a stop so suddenly that Millie found herself thrown violently forward.

'Sheep,' said Serpentine. 'Just missed her. Her and her lamb. Thank God for ABS.'

The pain in Millie's head was subsiding to a dull throb. She turned to Clara.

'What can this old prick possibly have that's so precious to you? What can he do that no one else can? What's to stop you putting him out of his misery? Send his fucking secrets to the grave, why don't you?'

Clara's face set in a small, amused grin, while Serpentine let out a single bark of laughter.

'Do you really think I would allow myself to be so unprotected, my dear?' he said. 'That I would not put in place certain safeguards? The book idea was simply a kind of intellectual bait, but we live in an information economy. I can tell all kinds of tales out of school. Ireland, the bombings in Dublin, Maconie – just the tip of the iceberg. The conspiracy theorists about 9/11? Imagine if their worst and most ridiculous claims were suddenly proved beyond doubt. Imagine that!' And he let out another of those dog-like eruptions of laughter.

'Not that he's saying anything in particular about 9/11,' said Clara. 'Are you, honey?'

'Certainly not. This young lady is and will be in no position to say anything anyway, will she?' The languid voice hardened. Millie for the first time felt a stab of fear.

'Why . . . what are you . . .'

'We need your help, one last time,' said Clara. She stroked Millie's thigh. 'I was fond of you. Freya stole you away from Mark, put you out of my reach, but she was like that. High-handed. Imperious. Her background. I could try and convince you that the granting of some kind of romantic or sexual favours could stay your . . . shall we call it an execution? I think we shall.' She lifted her hand and steepled her fingers together in front of her chest. 'But I think I prefer to see you suffer, my dear. Honey pie. I think that's what you truly deserve. Or at any rate, it's what I want.'

IN THE MINISTRY OF TRUTH

The minister was grateful. They'd made an effort with the tea. It was bags, Scottish blended, but Indian in origin. Nambarrie tea, strong, full of tannin and tarry without being in any way pretentious, like that bloody Lapsang Souchong they sometimes gave you in Whitehall. But this was the kind of establishment that prided itself not just on making an effort, but on second-guessing your every requirement. It was the kind of place you could get used to very quickly. Too quickly.

He looked around the conference room. Outside, the soothing, manicured green of golf courses stretched down to the sea and he could see the dome-shaped lump of shadow out in the ocean, bluey-grey in the dull sunlight. It looked like a joke, that granite outcrop. It looked, from this angle, funny. And its name was something of a joke too: Paddy's Milestone. Ailsa Craig was from its Gaelic name, *Creag Ealasaid*, Elspeth's Rock. There was nothing funny about it. It was a sign of departure for millions of emigrants from Ireland, from Ulster, from whatever you wanted to call the various bits of that benighted island he, personally, called home. Paddy's Milestone. For Proddy and Tim it had always been a sign, for a few of return, for most departure.

Now he sat in the beautiful surroundings of the Turnberry Hotel and gazed at the lump of oceanic granite, knowing he'd be home for lunch tomorrow, a normal Irish lunch, something with champ and solid lumps of meat. Cooked by his long-suffering, silent wife. Who knew nothing. He hoped. And everything, he feared.

Lunch today would be different. Something complex, with national interests and cultures fairly represented. He wondered how they'd do that. Religious restrictions were having to be factored in, kosher, halal. Same thing, basically. Different clergy to be paid off. Like at home. Some kind of Arabic thing, lamb, that'd be fine long as it wasn't too spicy. Maybe cabbage or colcannon from Ireland. Roast beef, who knew? Haggis. Christ, he hoped not haggis. Offal wasn't to his taste. The tang of blood and death. No, you couldn't get halal haggis. Surely to God.

He glanced at the door. Two security guards, young, packing, very bronzed. That would be the Israeli foreign minister. Security had been kept to a minimum, as requested by all concerned. The Yanks would come in with regiments, probably. Someone said they'd requested four helicopters. Four! And what did he have? He had Daniel.

Anyway, he was crucial to it, him, Erlend Maconie, a bog-trotting boy from Northern Ireland, from Ireland, he reminded himself. He was the facilitator, the peacemaker. After all that had happened.

He watched the Hamas representative, al-Haraz, their interior minister in Gaza, very young, very formally dressed. Dressed Western style, a very well-cut suit. He had a couple of civil servant types, it looked like, and one fellow in a suit clearly made for a much smaller man. He was armed, too, and was regarding the Israeli team with a mixture of nervousness and baleful enmity.

The Brits had the home secretary's number two, a junior minister, making a bloody point as usual, no security. Two civil servants, both women, bareheaded. Shitheads. Deliberately calculated insult to the Arabs. And to him. He himself had Danny outside with the car, a hired Mondeo, seeing as they'd flown in by chopper that morning. And Philip Creighton, his private secretary, just to take no notes and remember everything in that capacious brain of his. Remember all the looks and glances, the things that weren't said.

As for the Yanks, they weren't here yet. Sending one of those bloody Chinooks from Prestwick, even though it was just an hour's drive up the coast, and another, he'd been told, with God knew who all, from Kyle of Lochalsh, for God's sake, way to the north. Some kind of NATO demonstration at the BUTEC torpedo range the Brits still had up near Skye. They'd be mob-handed, even if it had all been negotiated as a cut-to-the-bone, initial-contact sort of conclave. One of the defence secretary's underlings, some senator. Groundbreaking. Jambreaking. The minister glanced at his watch, heard the heavy thump of rotor blades. That would be some of the bastards. The Israelis had come by road from Prestwick, so had the Brits. His own little Westland was parked on the pad by the tennis courts. The big twin-rotors would have to land down by the conference pavilion, on the golf courses.

It had started with an email, as things did these days. Al-Haraz, who was in touch frequently, saw him as something of an older brother, a former fighter for freedom. It was a kind of Mbeki–Mugabe thing. Sort of. Al-Haraz claimed to see the Northern Ireland situation as a model for his own state's future. A forward-thinking man, all told, the minister considered. A hand of friendship to the Israelis? Not exactly. But a possible closing down on all rocket attacks in exchange for what sounded like a few prisoners? Could he sell it? More emails. Some secure calls. Turned out it was all to do with power struggles within Hamas. He'd been briefed by MI6 on that one, which had been novel. If a little uncomfortable, for all concerned.

It could happen. Something could happen. That was the general feeling. And it could be him at the centre of it. Rapprochement between Israel and Palestine. Tear down those walls. Bono from U2 over for tea. Keep that bastard Geldof out of the way. Sting. The wife liked that Sting. Nobel Peace Prize? Trimble, that bastard? Did he deserve it? He'd fucking show them.

He sipped his tea, noticed a silver pot had been brought for the Hamas team, a coffee for the Israelis. Probably Lapsang crap for the Brits. He hoped they choked on it.

'Good morning, minister.' The Oxbridge tones were silky and fake to their root.

'Top of the morning, boy,' he said in his best brogue. 'Begorrah, it's a fine one.'

'It is indeed,' said the junior minister, a Labour hack since Stowe. 'It is indeed. I hear the Yanks are going to be a little late. The senator, seeing as he was in the, ah, neighbourhood, wished to divert to the island of Islay. Try out some of the whisky, I think. Pick up a case or two. Bunnahabhain, I think. A very fine drop indeed.'

'Really? Killing two birds with the one helicopter? Or both helicopters, probably. I bet they'll all go and have a nice wee party up there, won't they?' Maconie's face wore a smile, but he felt tight with fury. Those absolute bastards, treating this like some kind of holiday jaunt. Then he remembered the golf clubs he'd insisted Danny load up this morning. *Relax*, he said to himself. *Relax*.

Murricane drove the Espace like a man possessed, occasionally muttering instructions to me that were hard to catch over the clattering howl of the diesel engine.

'Got a mobile? Call this number,' he said and I could have sworn he closed his eyes for a second or two. I hoped I was wrong about that, as we were doing around 70 mph on a single-track road lined with extremely well-founded dry-stone dykes. With a blind summit ahead of us. Thankfully, there was no school bus or coal lorry approaching in blissful ignorance.

In fact, 30 seconds later, it was a rubbish truck that came lumbering around a bend when we were around 100 screaming metres off. That we stopped in time and in a straight line was a tribute to Murricane's reactions and the ABS that came juddering into play. That and the dryness of the roads.

'Jesus Christ Almighty,' I said, the mobile phone in my hand gripped so tightly I distinctly heard it crack. 'Give me that number again?'

'Give me that.' And we were hurtling backwards towards a passing place, as Murricane punched in numbers with the thumb of his left hand.

'Grinderman,' he said unexpectedly. 'Seven, one three five alpha gamma export, you fucking fuckwit.' Then a pause. 'Vincent, it's Mark. I'm in Mull. Just listen.' Another pause. We were still doing around 70. 'I said, listen. Nixon, Hodgy-Smith, Billy Boy are dead. Serpentine is loose with Millie and that fucking American bitch. He tried to kill the police stooge, but failed. Either they assumed I was dead or Clara has some other agenda. No, I have no idea. But there's the conference . . . conclave, whatever.' We swerved around a bend, narrowly missing a tractor on a short piece of two-way road.

'Maconie is there, isn't he? Assume they're heading for the conference with fucking malign intent, then. Got to. Clara and Serpentine, that mad old fuck and him, Christ knows what they may have dreamt up. He won't let Maconie walk away. I always told you that.' Pause. 'If I were you, I'd blow every fucking aircraft that tries to go anywhere near Turnberry out of the fucking sky.' We slewed dangerously around a very surprised Highland cow as Murricane tried to tuck the Nokia more securely beneath his chin.

'No, on reflection you shouldn't issue instructions to knock out the delegates' choppers. But there must be security call signs . . . right. OK, well, he can fly a fucking plane, you know that. Whose idea was it to set Billy Boy loose in the first place? Not yours? Yeah, well, are you sure you're firmly in charge now? Fine. What about Clara? Is she . . . right. Get Prestwick or somebody to send an RAF chopper to Glenforsa airfield on Mull as soon as. Shouldn't take more than half an hour. And if they see a chopper coming the other way, tell them to ram it. Yes, even if Millie fucking is on board. She knew far more than she let on to me, the bitch. Tell the terrible twins to get the toys out and meet me. Tell them to be ready to rock. Tell them not to get fucking sequestered in fucking Memphis.'

He threw the phone at me. I caught it, which was a tribute to my reactions and the fact that we were on a remarkably straight stretch of road. Doing around 100 mph. Suddenly, though, Murricane slowed down to a reasonable speed. And then stopped, right in the middle of the road. He laid his head on the steering wheel. I noticed that his hands were shaking.

'Do you know how to get to Glenforsa? Can't be more than 12 miles now. There's no real hurry. It'll take at least half an hour for the helicopter to get here.'

We exchanged seats and I drove, as quickly as I dared, while Murricane appeared to sleep. It was either a highly developed survival skill or concussion. Whatever, by the time we were parking by that strange wooden hotel, he was awake and a lot calmer.

'Sorry about the panic earlier,' he said. 'That blow on the head. Fuck, I don't really want them to blow Millie out of the sky.'

'Turnberry,' I said. 'What's happening at Turnberry?'

'Middle Eastern security conclave. Extraordinary thing, actually. Secret and high security. Came out of nowhere. USA, Israel, Hamas, UK. Brokered out of nowhere by a real bastard in the Northern Ireland government, an ex-IRA man.'

'Maconie,' I said. 'Erlend Maconie. Minister for Everything Else. He's what this is all about, isn't he?'

Murricane got out of the big car and stretched. The grass of the airstrip had just been mown and the smell of lost summer filled the air. There was a heavy, hot stillness. Like thunder was imminent.

'No,' he said. 'And yes. It's all about loose ends. Loose ends that should have been lopped off years ago. Decades ago.'

It only occurred to me then to ask the obvious question any self-respecting policeman would have asked a long time previously.

'What's really going on?' And as we sat on the grass and waited for a helicopter to come, he told me what he knew. What he thought he knew.

———◆———

Clara proved surprisingly strong for her age and size. But then, Millie was small and it wasn't hard to get her out of the car and onto the pier at the deserted village of Ardchiavaig. Serpentine helped drag her squirming body to the edge of the stone quay and Millie felt a violent wave of panic when the two of them pushed her bodily over the side. But the cold shock of water never came and she landed in a crumpled heap in an open boat. It had been riding on the high tide, only three feet below the edge of the pier. It was an RIB, a rigid inflatable. Her face was to the stern and she could see that it was equipped with two huge Honda outboards. It was a very fast boat indeed.

No life jackets. Didn't they realise the danger, she thought to herself, her mind skittering off her own predicament. What were they planning for her? She had been played, expertly, she realised, by Freya, who'd either been in cahoots with, or deluded by, Serpentine, her own brother. And now it looked like she was going to be used one final time.

Serpentine seemed in no particular hurry to be gone. She realised he was a very careful man. From a locker in the bow of the boat he brought two survival suits and two gas-inflatable life jackets. As she lay, immobile, she caught glimpses of the two elderly figures struggling to prepare themselves for sea. It would have been comical in any other context. Then, just as she was wondering if they were simply going to dump her out in the deeper water, a tarpaulin was thrown over her and she heard Clara's voice.

'Don't want you catching a chill, darlin', do we? We'll be an hour at sea.' She felt her body being trussed like a joint of meat ready for the oven, secured to the hull. If they capsized, it would all be over for her. The engines started with a silky roar.

The journey was a brutally painful one for Millie, the RIB leaping at high speed from wave to wave. They seemed to be in the open sea and she was buffeted from side to side of the boat, despite the ropes securing her. Finally, she felt the ropes being untied and the tarpaulin was pulled back. She heard the engine note fading and the violence of the movement eased. Clara was above her, speaking to her, shouting, sounding breathless, excited. Her face was red, her white hair bundled into a Quiksilver cap. She looked a decade younger.

'I'm going to blindfold you now, my dear. I'll cut your legs free when we land. Don't try and run. We'll catch you, inevitably. You won't know where you're going. And then Serpentine will hurt you. He's very good at that. Much better than the late lamented Billy Boy.'

And so Millie lay still, feeling the acquiescence she'd been taught to recognise in prisoners being interrogated, the creeping listlessness of failure, of giving up and giving in. Something like a towel was placed on her eyes and stuck in place with windings of duct tape. Then she felt her legs come loose as the cable tie holding them was cut. When she stood up, she immediately fell down again. A male hand helped her up this time and a voice spoke into her ear from very close. She thought it was the worst voice she'd ever heard.

'Clara is right. I do know how to hurt people. And without tools. It's not something I particularly enjoy, but I have no . . . compunction. Or limits. So please be co-operative. Consider it a form of revenge on me, if you like. A withholding of favours.' And then he laughed. 'Welcome to Bunnahabhain. We're in Islay to meet some very nice Americans, apparently. Even nicer than dear Clara.'

They were waiting for the Americans. Maconie had imagined the prospect of golf on one of the world's greatest championship courses would bring them cantering in with their Ping putters jangling on the backs of bodyguards. He thought Turnberry had been an inspired choice. Near enough for it to almost bloody be Ireland. Christ, when he thought of all those trips in the old days between Larne and Stranraer, two of the most godforsaken towns on any coastline. Now he could be helicoptered in and out, looked after by the very Brits who had once . . . well. Just rewards. Him in his Hugo Boss suit, the chopper landing-pad they'd built next to his barns. God, that was brilliant. Wee boys' stuff. Big boys' toys.

He looked at Avram Mashan, the Israeli deputy defence minister, almost indistinguishable from his security detail, dressed similarly. Jeans, sweaters. Avram was maybe slightly older, but looked impressively fit. Chiselled. There had been a bit of faffing about with entrances, who'd be first at the table, but the Jews had eventually shrugged and settled themselves down at one side of the big mahogany table. They were in the special conference pavilion, the management called it, a tarted-up marquee, actually, on one of the golf courses. Better for security, he'd been told. Like those Arab tents you saw from the old days of the Shah or Gaddafi in Libya – meeting out in the desert, eating fucking eyeballs or whatever it was they did. All meeting as equals. Except this wasn't a tent. It was to all intents and purposes a proper building, sumptuously fitted out inside, specifically for this kind of event.

Translation facilities, electronics, teams of support staff, all in the clutter of Portakabins and Winnebagoes outside. It was enough to make a man feel important. Afterwards, they'd all head up to the hotel in a fleet of armoured limos. Those that weren't playing golf, that is. He'd had Danny put his clubs in the boot of the Mondeo. His palms twitched in anticipation of his one piece of self indulgence: a few holes on the legendary Ailsa course. His little reward. Or the first of them.

Al-Haraz and his Hamas deputation were clustered at the opposite end of the table from the Israelis, acting tough, loud, ignoring everyone else in the room. He recognised that kind of diplomatic language, the posturing. Nervous, committed, desperate. He'd been there. That was the reason this was happening.

They heard the thunderous beating of helicopter blades and that strange twittering that comes with the double-rotors of a Chinook. The Americans were arriving at last. Late, he thought. It was most unlike them. Overdoing it in numbers, which was typical. That sounded like two helicopters. Maybe three. Yes, he was sure he heard a third coming in, separate from the first two. A different sound, somehow. He knew about helicopters.

Murricane. Mark Murricane. It sounded like a pop-star name. Hurricane Murricane. Maybe it wasn't real. What was?

'You know about the Three Rs? Retained, Regiment, Retired,' he said laconically. 'You leave, you sign a bit of paper. Like the Territorials. You're available in time of crisis. More or less. You don't say no to little jobs. A lot of work comes my way out in the oilfields. By recommendation. They never let you go.'

'Just when you thought you'd got out, they dragged you back in,' I said. We were crouched on the grass at Glenforsa, beside the Cessna I'd arrived in. The boy pilot had been in his room, sleeping off a hangover, the hotel staff had thought. In fact he was on his scarlet-stained bed, a jagged gap where his throat had been. The Cessna itself was sporting two knifed tyres and a pool of aviation fuel.

'Christ, he's thorough,' I said, 'this guy.'

'Thorough is right. I can't fucking fly a plane. I'd guess that Clara had something to do with this.' Murricane looked altogether knackered, sprawled on the ground. My ballistic vest was covering the pilot's face. 'She's been fucking us from the start. Old bitch. She's been Serpentine's fucking protector for decades. Too useful, that old bastard. too fucking useful by half. And too knowledgeable. Talk about knowing where the bodies are buried. It's the condition the bodies are in. Or were in.'

'I'm confused.'

'Yeah, well, you're not the only one. But you, you were ideal for their purposes. Nixon knew you. Thought you were compromised in some way. That's what I was told. Maybe you were part of the clean-up operation too. In, like, needing cleaned up. If you catch my drift.'

'What?'

He sighed. 'It's all about Erlend Maconie. The minister. Crucial figure in Her Imperial Majesty's Government of Northern Ireland. International player, or would like to be. Probably will be. Sinn Féin big wig. IRA man. Hero. Player. And former British intelligence asset. In the worst way. Of course he was. Surprising who was. And who wasn't.'

I swallowed hard. 'Yes, and . . .'

'Serpentine started making noises. A book or something, I don't know. People started tumbling off the board. A publisher here, a journalist there. Panic. Who was doing it? Wasn't the Brits. Wasn't the Yanks. Who was trying to stop Serpentine talking?'

'Dunno.'

'Nobody. Serpentine was doing it himself. Quite . . . lively for an old boy. Drawing people out. Making himself a target.'

'But what's that all about?'

'He's Saul Enderby. Royal Scots Dragoon Guards. Eton, adopted between-blanket son of some bastard general. Father probably a fellow officer. Brother of your friend, Freya.'

'Brother?'

'Just another tool for him to deploy. Boarding school knocks all the good stuff out of these shitheads. Hard as fuck, glossy veneer. Did a lot of bad things in the Troubles. Really bad. Things that wouldn't be forgiven, even today. I mean, truth and reconciliation, my arse. Agent provocateur. Loose cannon who wasn't actually that out of control. Doing what he was told. Then what he liked. Bombs in the Republic, 1974, Dublin and Monaghan, you remember that? That was way back, long before I was in Ulster. Or you.'

'I remember. He was . . .'

'One of. Remember that. One of. It would have been a team. I'd guess the others are, for various reasons, untouchable, or dead. Anyway, he's the one. The special one. Because of his immediate contact. A farmer, a border farmer. One Erlend Maconie. Who supplied him with the IRA explosives he used in Dublin. Who was involved in one of the most outrageous smears ever perpetrated by an out of control British intelligence community. That cost 33 lives. Destroyed any hope of peace. Part of the intelligence power play.'

'So, there's Enderby . . . Serpentine . . . and Maconie . . .'

'And Clara and Nixon. Not to mention Freya. Millie's dear departed squeeze. The one that brought you into all this. She was intelligence in Lurgan at the time. Not to mention that she was . . .'

'Freya *Enderby.*'

'As in Saul. But they were all involved. They all knew. Made the connections, joined the dots. Billy Boy, too. Freya, more so, because she was Saul's sister. Let sentiment get the better of her. She must have known he was just a very clever, occasionally charming psychopath. She was fronting for him on this book thing. And then the non-charming fucking psychos were let loose. Find him, destroy him. Collateral damage? Fine.'

'And you?' He smiled, then. It was the smile of an exhausted man. Crumpled.

'Millie called me. We go back. Handily. But there was personal stuff there. It was only when I checked in with my RRR handler that the shit really hit the fan. By that time things had gone pear-shaped. Torture in Inverness, for God's sake. Dead bodies. Higher powers with sense realised that things had gone completely tits-up. Manderley on the loose. And yet, there was a kind of unwillingness to give up on the plan completely. They could see it might solve some long-term issues. So I went in with what you might call a watching brief. One of Manderley's boys was supposed to be some kind of watcher, too. Providing "operational restraint". The one in the river. That was an accident, by the way. You can arrest me later. But it was like trying to control fucking Vesuvius. By that time, everything was in play and they let it run. Clara pushing, following her own little scheme. These bastards think it's chess, you know. They play it out like that. Or a computer game. We're just . . . ciphers, codes. Pieces. Pieces of shit. So there was Manderley. Nixon was on the committee with that plonker Hodgkin we left down the road. The two of them decided to activate Manderley. Expendable, arms-length, retired, but one of Nixon's protégés and one of "our guys". Everything that mattered, really. And Nixon got what he wanted. Nearly. Except he got fucked up, too. They drew him out, you see. He was one of the ones who knew too much.'

'And now, dead.'

'All, except Millie. And me. And you. But then you didn't know much, did you?'

I closed my eyes. Those CDs. How much knowledge was too much? June 1984: those bodies . . .

'No,' I said. 'Not much. But how did Enderby get away? Why are we left in this mess?'

'Clara,' he said. 'Clara was on the committee too. And then, I think our interests and theirs . . .'

'Diverged?'

'Yep. That's it. Diverged. Basically, this initiative of Maconie's came out of nowhere. And we want it. The Yanks say they want it. Any threat to Maconie's reputation has to be defused. Clara is working both sides. She wants what we want. But she wants Serpentine too. And . . . there may be something else.'

'But she can't be acting for the Americans in this. Not officially. She's not enacting American foreign policy. Jesus!' I must have sounded naive.

Murricane began to laugh. So loudly and hysterically I almost missed the sound of the approaching helicopter.

'Official? You think any of this is official? This is all renegade cabals and interest groups, paid-off senators in the backwoods, secret agents with dodgy pasts and worse presents. Shady intelligence executives, dodgy retired SAS men, disgraced police. Official? The only official thing around here is,' he reached in his pocket, 'the guy who's on the other end of this phone. He's trustworthy, as far as it goes. As far as I can judge. And he's given me *official* clearance to kill anyone, anyone, who threatens, ahem, the integrity of this nation or its commitment to a lasting peace in both the Middle East and Northern Ireland. That's the phrase he actually used. The integrity of this nation. And to do that, I've got to get to Turnberry. Or I could shoot you and leave you here with Jack the Ripped over in his little wooden hotel room.' He shook his head wearily. 'OK, here's the bottom line. Executive summary, Official Secrets Act signed, assumed, respected, this is what I think. We – the people I'm working for, the really bad people, the people who truly are untouchable – engineered the whole thing with Serpentine to draw out the various threats to Maconie within and outside the service, retired or not. And then remove them. But Clara has some other agenda, or knows something we don't. She's playing a different game.'

The down-draught of the chopper was drowning his words. But I caught the last few. 'Millie doesn't deserve this,' he said. A pause. 'Or maybe she does.'

LANDED

wo helicopters landed on the closed fairway of the nine-hole Montgomerie teaching course within seconds of each other. Colin Montgomerie's Academy was, understandably, taking no pupils and both the Ailsa and Kintyre championship courses were shut, other than to security-cleared hotel guests. The noise was shattering. The two Chinooks both carried American Army Air Force markings. One had come from Prestwick, the other, from the BUTEC base at Kyle, the pair making an informal rendezvous next to the Bunnahabhain Distillery in Islay, the famed whisky island about 60 miles north. It had been a favour for the senator, a simple stop to collect some whisky and breathe some alcoholic air. The BUTEC contingent had switched to the senator's helicopter for a last-minute briefing, leaving the second Chinook almost empty. But not quite.

The Chinooks' rotors were beginning to slow when, 100 metres away, on the other side of a dune system trapped in the middle of the golf course, there landed a bright yellow RAF Super Puma, marked 'Rescue'. The silence when its blades stopped turning was initially intense. Then it was replaced with the sounds of a Scottish links golf course: chattering skylarks, the crash of waves, the hiss of water on sand. Two hotel minibuses arrived, one stopping by each of the Chinooks.

The Super Puma, its fuselage door on the blind side of the bigger aircraft, was approached by an open Land Rover pick-up bearing two youngish men dressed alike, in black jeans and turtle-neck sweaters. Two figures got out of the yellow helicopter and climbed in behind them.

'Moshe. David. Good to see you.' Murricane squeezed the two men's shoulders. The policeman slumped beside him in the back of the vehicle said nothing. He was holding his chest and was obviously in pain. Events were beginning to catch up with Zander Flaws.

'Good to see you too, Mark,' said the smaller of the two men in front.

'Do you have it, Moshe?'

'I do. It's under your seat. But are you sure . . .'

Murricane shrugged wearily. 'No. Absolutely not. Being sure is the last thing I am at the moment. How's Avram?'

'Oh, Avram's fine,' said Moshe. 'As ever.'

'And more than capable of looking after himself,' added David. 'For a minute or two.'

Millie felt the man called Serpentine's hands on her and squirmed at his touch. But she couldn't move, lying in the belly of the huge helicopter. She was on the carpeted floor, her legs once again pinioned. And this man, this old man was . . . surely he wasn't . . .

The blindfold was ripped from her eyes, the duct tape catching some of her hair. She was blinded, briefly, by the artificial light. Christ, being kidnapped was becoming a habit. Then, carefully, he unbuttoned her shirt and she felt his hands on her skin. Cool, bony. The aircraft had been insulated against noise, or as much as was possible.

'Ah, one of these modern, sports brassieres,' he said, sliding his fingers under the Lycra, feeling her small breasts. 'Plenty of room for some, ah . . . additions, I think.'

He had prepared well, she thought. The webbing was nicely designed, might have been made to fit her. It was black nylon and Velcro and it even matched her black bra. The pouches in it were solid, heavy, and the wires connecting them were of high electrical quality. She recognised the design. She was being turned into a walking bomb.

'The thing is,' he cooed, his fingers working on her, cold, flickering and disgusting, like something spidery and awful, 'you're not crucial to any of this. You're just a kind of scapegoat. A distraction. After the fact.'

She heard Clara's voice, queasily admiring.

'You were always so good at improvising, Saul. Lucky this ham-fisted idea they had to take you out fell apart. Otherwise we'd never have managed . . .'

'There's no "we" about it, Clara. I'm pulling your personal irons out of the fire and not for the first time, either. As it happens, our interests may be, in the end, mutual. You get the removal of any chance of the Israelis and Hamas settling things in Gaza, because, well, because you really, really don't want peace in the Middle East. You blame it on some mad suicide bomber called, we'll call her Leila, shall we? Hamas extremist, furious at what she sees as betrayal by her leadership. No real, serious, presidential-type security at Turnberry. After all, this is a puny initiative by some Irish arriviste. So she gets through, blows up the Jews. Well, a Jew, to be precise, one dangerously liberal Jew, called Avram Mashan. Sounds good to me. Except she won't be blowing up the Jews, not really. She'll already be dead. The Jews will have been blown up by the bomb already attached, by myself, to the lovely mahogany window frame in the Pavilion of Splendour, as the management of the Turnberry Resort are wont to call the portable monstrosity with which they have the habit of ruining some of the best linksland in the world.'

'Yes, or perhaps we'll just say she was called Millie, a grief-ridden harridan who blamed the state of Israel for the death of her long-term lover, one Freya Enderby. We'll improvise. I'm impressed, though, by your advance planning, Saul. But how will you get her . . .'

'I'll kill her and drag her, if I have to,' said Enderby, matter-of-factly. 'But I was rather hoping you could supply me with one of those motorised golf carts. She'll pack away rather tidily. Bones break. She's not large. When the remains are found, then you can tell your tale. We'll be long gone. Or I will. Explanations are your speciality, Clara. The window is on the wall facing the ocean and the sill is packed with Octanitrocubane – you'll have heard of it, Clara? The most powerful explosive known. Stable, easily handled, triggered by a proximity fuse. In this case, young Millicent. Can you imagine the effect? It's a tent, for God's sake! In Scotland! How stupid is that?'

'Pretty stupid,' said Clara.

Insane, thought Millie. Fucking insane.

The Chinook that had picked them up from Bunnahabhain was empty apart from the two pilots, who had been ordered to stay invisible in their cockpit. It was an executive machine, laid out for use by anyone from ambassador level upwards to vice president. There were leather seats, a small kitchen. Carpets and communications gear. But nothing could really defeat the noise. It throbbed and thrummed like a giant washing machine. Millie lay on the floor, her face vibrating against a carpet that smelled of fabric freshener and hot oil.

The landing was indistinguishable from flying at first, the thump of collision with the ground similar to the bump and grind of the low-altitude turbulence. Then Millie became aware of the stillness. The rhythmic thumping in her head began to recede and she heard the muffled thunk of a door being opened. This is it, she thought.

'Fuck.' That was Clara. 'Fuck, what's going on? Our transportation has just departed.'

Serpentine was moving, she noticed. Fast and fluid. 'Shut the door,' he shouted. 'Get away from the door.' He dived forward towards the cockpit.

But the missile which arced into the cabin could not be stopped. It trailed some kind of a reddish smoke, tumbled like a vandal-chucked can into a corner. And that's what it was, Millie realised, as her eyes filled with tears and she began to cough and retch. A pepper bomb. Riot control. She'd tasted that particular brand before. Same essence of chilli pepper you found in Mexican food. Another gas canister tumbled into the helicopter. She heard shots, the dry 'chink' of a small pistol. The tearing rasp of an automatic weapon.

Hands gripped her. A face loomed out of the thickening red mist. No, not a face, a death mask, a horror from some *Dr Who* show, a monstrosity, elephantine, a trunk . . . a gas mask. Someone held her in a rough and brutal embrace, someone whose body she didn't know. Not Mark. This man was bigger, harder, as if he was made entirely of bone. An Uzi sub-machine gun clattered against her, on a long strap. She remembered not to struggle.

'Stay with the Land Rover,' said Murricane. 'You do know how to use one of these things, don't you? Old Landies are difficult to drive.'

'Yeah, fucking difficult, especially for policemen with bruised nipples.' The Brooklyn-accented Israeli called Moshe seemed reluctant to hand over the vehicle, but climbed down from the driver's seat. He reached under it for a zipped nylon bag. From it he took two objects the size and shape of Coke cans, placed them carefully on the ground. An Uzi machine pistol, two taped together magazines. And a gas mask.

'I usually do the driving,' he said. 'It's what I'm good at. And I hate policemen.' He glowered at Flaws. 'They always abuse their vehicles. No concern for machinery. Mechanics on tap.'

'Excuse me,' said Flaws. 'But I have an affection for machinery. I own a motorcycle.' This provoked a short, mirthless guffaw from Moshe.

'Organ donor! Death wish, too.'

'*Death Wish Three* was better than *Two*,' said Flaws.

'Yeah well, best not make any wishes at all at the moment,' said David. 'Best not to trust in anyone but God, goodness and good luck.'

'I left my shotgun in Mull,' said Flaws. 'Otherwise . . .' But no one was listening.

'That's three things to trust in,' said Murricane, who, Flaws thought, seemed to recover his strength and good humour only at the prospect of action. 'That's two too many. I need to focus. *Focus!* Are we ready?'

Flaws got into the front seat of the Land Rover, but didn't start it. They were in one of the biggest fairway bunkers he'd ever seen, the Land Rover parked securely and firmly on the ungiving sand. Completely hidden from the two Chinooks, they were only about 30 feet away from them. And the two blacked-out Ford Galaxies waiting for their passengers.

'I'm going for the second Galaxy,' said David. 'You're sure that's the one we want?'

'Definitely,' said Murricane. 'Nearest the destination is always the dignitary. First rule of close protection. They're in the rear helicopter.'

'OK,' said David. 'Here we go.'

'Cool,' said Moshe. 'To coin a phrase: let's rumble.'

Moshe, David and Murricane crawled to the top of the sand dune that had been excavated to make the bunker. The driver of the second Galaxy had opened his side window and seemed to be sniffing the air appreciatively. He didn't look like a hotel driver. Not unless Turnberry was in the habit of employing bulging steroid abusers with serious US Marines Corps tattoos covering their arms.

'Shit, the illustrated man,' said David. 'Oh well.' He stood up, now about 20 feet from the vehicle. The driver's gaze flickered, as if something had caught his eye. David was moving down the dune slope now, fast, speaking to the man, not shouting.

'Excuse me, David Ben-Illigan, Israel security, just checking the perimeters. Do you have a laminate for this part of the course?' A puzzled expression, then, seeing the dangling Uzi, a sudden, fumbled reaching for something under his left arm.

But by that time, with a mildly ridiculous but loud *ker-chunk*, David, getting closer all the time, had fired two loads of rock salt from the sawn-off 20-gauge shotgun in his right hand. If the driver's window hadn't been open – and that was careless – he'd have had to smash it first to obtain the desired effect. The jagged, but easily fragmented crystals almost flayed the skin off the driver's head. He wasn't so lucky with the man in the passenger seat. Secret service, David thought. Wearing a suit, badly. The second blast of salt mainly caught his nose. There didn't seem to be much of it left.

The driver, in shock, opened his mouth, what was left of it, but made no sound. There could only be seconds before the passenger recovered enough to push some kind of panic button. David was at the door, wrenched it open. One wrecked and ripped face, a mask of blood. The smell of cordite. He rammed the sawn-off, barrel first, into the driver's head, then smashed it twice into the hands of the passenger, just as he started to reach for his neck microphone. Then he used his right hand, knuckles supported by thumb, standard karate, to punch the knot of blood vessels on the right side of the suited man's chin, paralysing him. He held his fingers on the spot until he was sure he was unconscious. It would take some reconstructive surgery to deal with his nose, but the driver was going to be a mess. Still, they could do wonders these days. Collateral, David thought. And at least they're still alive. Hey, US–Israeli relations can handle a bit of strain.

All this took ten seconds at most.

He pulled the driver out of the van. Moshe and Murricane were there now, behind him, pulling the inert shape out of the way, dumping it behind a clump of gorse bushes. Then he was in the van, accelerating. The other van was already moving at high speed towards the little complex of vehicles and accommodation units surrounding the massive conference pavilion. No one was looking back at him. At least, he hoped not.

The door to the Chinook was opening. David and the Galaxy were disappearing towards the pavilion. Moshe, making little grumbling noises of complaint, pulled on the all-enveloping gas mask, which was neoprene, like a scuba helmet. Murricane did the same, then they both put on infra-red visors, turning the scene before them into a red and yellow acid trip. They had to operate on colours and shapes, shifting iridescences. Moshe pulled a ring in the top of one of the canisters, for all the world as if he were thirsty, and threw it into the helicopter. Seconds later, Murricane did the same thing. 'Strike one,' came a muffled mutter from Murricane. Moshe said nothing.

Clara came out of the helicopter first, eyes and nose streaming, shirt flecked with vomit. Murricane grabbed her and very deliberately punched her in the jaw with the base of his hand. She flopped onto the grass. By then, two low-velocity bullets had whirred between Moshe and Murricane, at which Moshe's irritability visibly increased. It was amazing, thought Murricane, how annoyance could be discerned just from body language, and so quickly. He threw himself into the helicopter, landing on his chest on the cabin floor. Carpet, he thought. I'll get carpet burn if I'm not careful. He swivelled his head up and around, the interior of the cabin mostly yellow in the visor. Red. He saw red, a crouching shape holding something forward of his chest. Millie or Serpentine? No time. He lifted the Uzi and fired three short bursts. The figure flew backwards and slumped like a broken mannequin. It was just like a really primitive computer game from the '80s, Murricane thought. They were the Super Mario Brothers. Or Moshe and David were. What was he? Some kind of Mutant Ninja Turtle?

I heard the shooting, everything from the wet crisp-packet crunch of the shotgun to the staccato bursts of the Uzi, fired very frugally indeed. It was time to move. I was having trouble with movement. My chest was really hurting. Breathing was bad enough. Steering a Landie was ten times worse. I gunned it up and out of the bunker, its tyres gouging great holes in the carefully planted slope of the dune from which the bunker had been carved, and then down the steep slope on the other side to the chopper, which was leaking thick, red smoke. I could smell the pungent, pepper aroma from inside the cab. My eyes pricked.

Out of the red mist came a large masked figure dragging a young woman's body. Laying down his Uzi, Moshe picked her up and put her, not callously, but none too gently, in the pick-up bed at the back. He bent over her, tearing at her clothes. Odd. This was no time for personal indulgence. Murricane was smaller. I could tell it was him, animal-like, his gas mask bobbing with the effort, dragging a man's body out of the helicopter. From what I could see, the body was dressed in flying fatigues unmarked by any insignia. He had black hair clipped very short. Murricane carried out a brief body search, but I could see from the sag of his shoulders that this was not the man he was looking for. It was not Serpentine.

The smoke was clearing. Another figure in a flight suit emerged from behind the nose of the Chinook, a huge Colt .45 automatic in his hand, a useless weapon at anything but the closest range. A round whanged into the Land Rover. Moshe, almost casually, pulled out a pistol, smaller but with a long barrel, and shot the man three times in the chest. Pilot error, as they say. Jesus Christ. Then he ran towards Murricane, clutching some kind of harness. Black nylon. The two of them roughly strapped it onto what was clearly another member of the air crew, then they picked him up and threw him into the chopper. They did the same with the other pilot. Moshe removed his backpack and threw it in after him.

They put the unconscious old woman in the centre front seat, jammed between me and Moshe. Murricane climbed into the back and shouted, 'Go!' But where, I thought. Where can we go? To the hotel? To the pavilion? Moshe was shouting, 'Away from here, you stupid fuck-cop. Go!' I floored it along the track that led to the pavilion. Murricane seemed to be fiddling with two mobile phones. A huge black shape swooped into my field of vision, forward and to the left. I swerved right. A wave of light, closely followed by heat and sound, seemed to catch the Land Rover and propel it forwards. That would be the Chinook, then. A huge expanse of smooth fairway meant that my desperate efforts to keep the thing on its wheels had plenty of room to succeed. The black shape appeared again. A helicopter, smaller than the Chinooks, one rotor blade, black, no markings. It seemed to have escaped any damage from whatever had happened behind us. I stopped to avoid hitting it, leaving great tears in the manicured golf grass.

'Divots,' I said. 'I'll need to replace the divots.'

'Ground under repair,' said Murricane. 'That's the least of our fucking worries.' He pointed. Five men had emerged from the helicopter, dressed alike in black fatigues, ski-balaclavas, no helmets. They were carrying Heckler & Koch machine pistols, all of which were pointed at us.

'Where's David when we need him?' Moshe asked no one in particular.

One of the figures in black removed his ski-mask and walked towards us. He was older, a blond thug running to grey, all broken nose and cauliflower ears. Suddenly, from behind me, Murricane laughed. He raised his hands in what looked like a mockery of surrender.

'Drop everything, Moshe, except your trousers. It's Captain Birdseye and his merry sailors. Why do they put SBS guys in a helicopter? They'll get altitude sickness three feet off the ground.'

'Special Boat Squadron,' I said. 'Friends of yours?'

'Acquaintances.'

I switched off the Land Rover's ignition. I could hear crackling from behind me. I turned round. The Chinook was . . . absent . . . in the middle, as if its centre section had been smashed by a violent and very large child, who liked playing with matches. And fireworks. A column of smoke rose into the air.

There was a tapping on the passenger window.

'Mr Murricane,' came a muffled voice. 'I am instructed by Her Majesty's High Seas Command and the government, probably, to offer you what aid and succour you require.'

'Fuck Her Majesty,' came Moshe's guttural growl. 'Where's David?'

There was some spluttering and static from a hand-held radio. Then the captain called Birdseye spoke.

'Colonel? Your presence is required by your deputation. I understand there ought to be two security staff during the, ah, conventicle, and at the moment there is only one.'

'That'll be to match the Hamas numbers,' said Moshe. 'Flying the flag. That's the trouble with David. He just doesn't have enough presence.'

'First break, get them to check the windows of the pavilion,' said Millie, her voice thin, but determined. 'Best not say anything to the politicos. Just check it out. It should be inert. No risk without a trigger. Make some excuse . . . I don't know.' Her head slumped sideways onto Murricane's shoulder. I felt vaguely jealous that it wasn't mine.

'It's already been removed. A small charge, pyrotechnic level. A kind of joke, we think. No trigger?' Captain Birdseye had a Highland accent. I felt suddenly homesick for the north.

'No trigger,' said Murricane. 'No proximity fuse. She was wearing a dummy suicide vest. It was all an elaborate ploy. But we guessed that.'

'Roy Rogers has a lot to answer for,' I said. It didn't get a laugh. 'Trigger . . . horses . . .' There was a stony silence.

'And our chap?' Funny hearing the word 'chap' in a Hebridean drawl.

'Absent. There are casualties, though. You'd better get a medic down to the Chinook.' Murricane sounded unconcerned.

'American casualties?'

'I really have no idea. We'll ask this old bitch when she wakes up. You need to send two men towards the beach. Look for one man, one old man. Christ, he shouldn't be hard to catch.'

The tough old bird called Clara, when she recovered, was in no mood to be nice to Captain Mark Murricane.

'You let him go,' she said. 'You stupid idiot. You were suckered by the girl.'

We were in a luxury suite in the hotel, far away from the conference in the golf course pavilion, which was ending now, apparently with some qualified success. Whatever that meant. And despite a very concerned American deputation. There had been a short break while a person Murricane said was 'senior ints' had briefed them. And then the conference had reconvened. Just like that. Life went on. Death went on, and was put in context. The 'senior ints' person, allegedly named Vincent, a scowling man in a very expensive suit, was sitting silently in a corner. Saying nothing. We hadn't been introduced. Millie was under medical treatment somewhere else in the hotel.

'And what were you doing, Clara?' said Murricane. 'What was your game? Go on, spin me a tale.'

'He knew. He knew he was a target. That, once he'd drawn out all the filth, he'd be terminated. That we couldn't afford to leave him alive.'

'Why'd you leave me alive, back on Mull?'

'Oh, well. It was my job to check. And you're such a pretty boy.'

'And just the pretty boy to sort out Serpentine when you were finished with him. Was that it?'

Her face seemed set in stone. 'It was a thought. At the time.'

'What about you, Clara? Ever occur to you to ask why you should be left alive?'

She smiled. I noticed that one of her too-white American teeth had been knocked out, leaving a silver crown gaping.

'Ask your bosses, Mark. Ask Vincent the sphinx over there, sitting like God Almighty. Or ask God Himself. I'm American. We have special privileges. End of.' She shook her head.

'Special privileges? Really?' Murricane seemed amused. 'There are three Americans dead and one seriously injured back out there on the 15th fairway, or whatever it was. There go your special privileges.'

'I was improvising. I had to convince him I was interested in destroying the conference, ruining the summit. And he had all this Millie thing worked out. But it was shit. A ruse. Did she know? What's she saying?'

Murricane shook his head. 'You're a lying bitch, Clara. Fast on your arthritic feet, though, I'll give you that.'

'Come on, Mark. Was she part of it? All that stuff about a window frame packed with explosives? There was no trigger, was there? She was safe?'

Mark sighed.

'There was no trigger. Only enough black powder in the window to cause a a muffled bang. She could have been involved. I don't think so. But her loyalty was to Freya. That's certainly true. She wanted to get to Serpentine, she said he might need help, he might be . . . what was it? Disabled.' You could see the weariness fighting the fading adrenalin. He slumped.

They were interrupted by the roar of helicopter rotors.

'They're leaving,' said Clara. 'If they're gone, they're gone. Maybe it's all OK. Where's Maconie?'

'Don't know,' said Murricane. 'On his way home, I should imagine.' He stood up and looked out to sea, towards the rounded lump that was Ailsa Craig. 'Paddy's Milestone. It's not as if he's very far from home.'

'What are you going to do, Mark?' asked Clara. 'Shoot me?'

The hitherto silent Vincent stood up. His voice was cultivated and deep, like a Tom Waits who had gone to Winchester.

'No, my dear. I think we'll leave that to your own people.'

'I, on the other hand,' said Murricane wearily, 'will have to find myself some salmon farmers. Excuse me. I need to go and see how Millie is.'

'You could shoot her,' said Clara, caustically. 'Save everyone a load of grief. Especially yourself.'

'What is it about salmon farmers?' I said.

'They've ruined the sea trout fishing,' said Murricane, 'in Shetland, which was where I was brought up. And they shoot seals, which eat the salmon. It's well known that seals are the reincarnated spirits of sailors lost at sea. I'm acting on their behalf.'

The room went silent.

'Really?'

'Yes, really. That and the blue boiler suits they wear. I don't like them either. Excuse me, please.' And he left the room.

THE 19TH HOLE

Maconie felt tired, but euphoric. The sun was setting in a ridiculous display of oranges and purples and the lighthouse was beginning its nightly round of pulses and flashes. The shape of Paddy's Milestone out in the ocean was outlined in the spectacular fading of the day.

He had decided to stay another night. Danny wasn't pleased, but he'd got him a decent room at the hotel and he was probably half-cut on minibar whisky by now, watching *EastEnders* or some such shite. No, the football. He'd forgotten all about that.

No problems with security, not now. He'd had a full briefing from the Brits. Some crap about a helicopter accident, an over-enthusiastic guard, some injuries. The Americans had taken it all very calmly, for once. Suspiciously so.

Anyway.

The conference had gone well, better than he could have hoped. There had been a cautious agreement to meet again. This time in Belfast, in public. Maybe at Stormont, a symbol of rapprochement, of what could be achieved. Nobel, ya bastard! Stockholm here we come! Avram Mashan and al-Haraz had even shaken hands. It had been fucking beautiful!

He stood in the gathering darkness, about 20 feet from the flag on the 18th green of the Ailsa course, the place where many Opens had been won and lost, in the footsteps of the greats – Palmer, Nicklaus, Woods. He deserved his place here, he thought. What a long, strange journey it had been. So many casualties. So much deception and dissension and dissembling. But maybe now he could repair some damage, save some lives. And fuck, how much was the Nobel anyway? It was fucking millions!

He'd hoped to get a round in, or maybe even nine holes. But there just hadn't been time, once the Brits had finished with him. So nice these days, so sweet and deferential. The pricks. Anyway, he'd got the bag from the car before letting Danny go for the night, took out a pitching wedge and a putter, and asked the concierge if it would be all right to, you know, have a wee knockabout. Och, for you, Mr Maconie, on this historic day? Would you like to pitch out of my arsehole? Use my dick as a tee? It's all yours, minister. All yours.

And as the light faded he'd hit one or two lovely pitches into the green, heedless of the depressions he was putting in that perfect putting surface. And now, he'd better wrap it up. It was getting too dark to see what he was doing. *So here he was, on the green in two, putting for a birdie to win the Open by a single stroke.* He swung the Ping putter back about six inches, hit the Titleist perfectly and watched it purr over the beautiful, beautiful grass.

'A fine shot, Erlend.'

The voice came from beyond the seaward side of the green. He recognised those drawling tones at once, despite the slight quaver of age in them now.

'Saul . . .'

'Octanitrocubane, Erlend.' The voice was fainter still. 'That's Octo-nitro-cubane. The clue's in the "nitro". After your time. If only we'd had that kind of technology, eh? None of that builder's Semtex or TNT. You can roll it, cram it in hollow spaces, tiny ones. Like the shaft of a golf club, Erlend. Guts of a mobile phone, electrical pulse. Thank you and goodnight.'

Maconie threw the Ping putter as far away as he could into the darkness.

'You old bastard,' he yelled. 'Fuck you . . .'

But then the green erupted with a brief flash of white light. The pristine putting surface shredded, as the cut-down shafts of eight golf clubs, packed half-and-half with Octanitrocubane and tiny ball bearings, and buried around the edge of the green, exploded. In truth, although Octanitrocubane is extraordinarily powerful, the muffling effect of turf meant that Maconie was left relatively intact. His body was flayed by hundreds of ball bearings, however, mainly from the waist down. He died from a mixture of blood loss and shock within ten minutes, just as the first security staff arrived from the hotel's clubhouse.

Amazingly, the greenkeeping staff at Turnberry had an alternative green functioning within two days and the original putting surface had been completely restored within a month.

HIGHLAND RIVER, SILVER DARLINGS

On a ridge high above Strathpeffer is the Neil Gunn memorial, one of the most beautiful and haunting places of authorial remembrance on the planet, or at least in the vicinity of Inverness. It's a kind of sculpture garden, I suppose, though the sculptures in question are Caithness slate slabs, inscribed with phrases by Gunn, who was not just an author and poet, narrator of Scotland's great drunken dance with whisky, but an exciseman himself. His *Whisky and Scotland* reads as if written by a half-cut poet, which it was. *Sailing along the coast of one's native land was a new way of reading history, a detached way, so that instead of being embroiled in it, one looked on . . .*

The memorial is wonderful. A series of ponds, reeds whispering in the constant wind; wooden walkways; the huge slabs, the words cut into them making more sense in sound bites than in the novels. And the view: Ben Wyvis, the Cromarty Firth, the Black Isle and Dingwall itself. It's where the raw Highlands meets the fingers of agricultural softness, the sea and civilisation.

I sat up there, alone, and pondered. Where were Millie and Murricane? Moshe and David had presumably merged back into whatever multiple roles they played in Israel – bodyguards, freelance hooligans for hire, mercenaries, security advisors, secret agents, associates of the former Mossad agent turned liberal deputy defence minister Avram Mashan. Colonel David Ben-Illigon, indeed. I'd looked up that name. There was nothing, and I mean absolutely nothing, that could be found on him using Google. Nor in any number of slight spelling changes. But you don't get to become a colonel without existing. Unless of course you're Moshe. Somewhere, on what they called 'deep Internet', there'd be something.

Serpentine. Lots on the net about him. Half-rumours, conspiracy theories. A British soldier, agent, renegade, active in Ulster, an officially sanctioned agent provocateur, a killer for hire, an expert in 'strategic retaliation', whatever that was. Torture and terror. But some unanimity – he was thought to have died in 1989, while working in Iraq. Nobody seemed quite sure for which side. The name Saul Enderby was nowhere linked to Serpentine.

But I'm not supposed to make those attempted enquiries, those searches. Once Murricane had disappeared off to find Millie, and Clara had left with the 'serious ints' guy, I was given a very comfortable room in the Turnberry Hotel. Not a suite, but beggars can't be choosers. There I was visited by 'serious ints', the man who said his name was Vincent, handed a document and asked to sign it. Told in those beautifully modulated tones. By a very expensive suit. It was like the Official Secrets Act, *Dr Faustus* version.

'You'll be promoted to chief inspector,' he said. 'Then retired on medical grounds. Full pension rights. What age are you, 52? Applicable immediately. Well, after your six weeks' compulsory sick leave. Police pensions are, I believe, extremely generous. Especially in Scotland.' He was right. I could have retired any time from 50 onwards. Thank God I'd waited.

I play with my motorbikes. I talk to Liam, who's not responding too well to chemo. I oil and polish various illegally held weapons, though I never got the shotgun back from Mull. I still have the Walther Nixon gave me. I'd forgotten all about it, it was still in my jacket pocket when I finally undressed at Gleneagles. And still unloaded. The prick.

Anyway, there are ways of getting guns. There are always ways of getting guns. As for the bodies – Freya, the dead man in Findhorn, Mull and that corpse at the mouth of the Ness – all tidied away, filed and forgotten. The Department of Lost Causes has ceased to exist.

But at least there's a new hope of peace in the Middle East. And that's the main thing, after all, surely? That groundbreaking meeting, details of which leaked out along with obituaries for Erlend Maconie. Killed, it was thought, by some kind of breakaway 'Real IRA' group. Militant Republicans. Maconie was a moderate peacemaker, the reports said. A saint. Brokering a peace settlement between Palestine and the Israelis. Might have got the Nobel. There was even talk about awarding it posthumously.

There was a conference in Belfast. The Americans, the Israelis and Hamas, brokered by another saintly ex-terrorist, apparently a close friend of the late

Maconie, from across the sectarian divide. Wonderful to know that could happen. A former UVF man with a strange moustache. An attempted terrorist disruption of the conference nipped in the bud, so it was said, by continuing British intelligence activities among the remaining extreme republican groups.

I'm joking, of course. They're still rocketing Israel from Gaza with their home-made pyrotechnics. The Israelis are still responding with colossal, efficient ultra-violence. But for a month or two, it looked as though everyone would sit down and talk. Look each other in the eye. The sound of swords being battered into ploughshares echoed throughout the world!

There was a campaign in the US, lots of money behind it, some kind of evangelical thing. Save the Temple. Purify the Temple in Jerusalem from the foul pollution of Muslim footsteps. You wouldn't believe it, but it caught hold, as if all those God-fearing Yanks thought the Messiah wouldn't come if Hamas got too cosy with the Israelis.

And then, hey presto, new technology for processing tar fields in Alaska into petrol. And suddenly the US wasn't as desperate for oil as it was. Not dependent on Arab goodwill. Fuck these joint talks! Fuck the Maconie Initiative for a game of soldiers! We're off for some splendid isolation, dudes! There was a book, as well, a kind of strategic document written by some cold-warrior bitch. Clara something. The dust jacket photo was kind of familiar.

Freeman went to Shetland, took a demotion, really, chief inspector there is not the same as chief inspector here, there or anywhere. I hear he's got a part-share in a salmon farm. He'd better watch his back. Murricane and his seals. Christ. Blue boiler suits.

I still see the boys from forensics. Jimbo's doing OK. Fergus Grant hates me even more. I still have occasional and somewhat dodgy sex with a pathologist. Not at crime scenes. You have to draw the line somewhere.

And, of course, I'm no longer a policeman. I don't really know what I am. Well, I know what I say I am. I'm a consultant. I advise on security. I have a catalogue of alarms. I get 20 per cent of all sales. It's boring. I like being bored, I find.

The agent, a legend in his own myriad lunchtimes, received between five and twenty manuscripts every day, unsolicited. He would read only the first paragraph. It was a rule.

He prided himself on being able to tell everything he needed to know from those first few lines. He always threw away the three-chapters-and-a-synopsis offerings. Anyone could write three chapters. Anyone could have an idea. What he wanted was a book, 100,000 words, minimum. More, preferably. Doorstops. He liked doorstops.

He was fond of saying he was the initial fence prospective authors had to crawl over. He was the bulwark, he was the gate and the gatekeeper. He made that magical first judgement. He just *knew*.

He liked weight. He liked the font 'courier', or even better, high-impact typewriting, though you rarely saw that these days. If he liked a first paragraph, he would throw the book into a box for further examination by his team of readers – a retired tabloid hack, his irascible secretary and a junkie nephew. He distributed the manuscripts entirely at random.

But first paragraphs were his obsession. First lines, really. They could make or break a book. Weight was before that, though, and the font. So when this particular book came in, wrapped in brown paper, packed in a Croxley Script box, hand-typed, he was impressed. Hand-typed, not word-processed!

Serpentine: A Memoir was at the top. Fuck, another memoir. Who or what was 'Serpentine', anyway? The word rang a distant bell . . . it would probably be some wartime crap. He began to read:

> Who am I? I am the man responsible for the greatest number of deaths in any single event of the so-called 'Troubles' in Northern Ireland. I acted at the behest of forces within the intelligence community to defeat the policy of Her Majesty's Government. I have lived a life of secrecy, deception and murder. This is my story.

Another fantasist, thought the agent, chucking the manuscript into the recycling box. He never sent them back, even if postage was provided.

These wannabe authors needed to show they had the balls to persevere. Lightweights had no place in his world.

AUTHOR'S NOTE

AUTHOR'S NOTE

This is a work of fiction, but certain factual events and genuine organisations are crucial to the plot.

The Dublin and Monaghan bombings of March 1974 were appalling tragedies and, taken as one event, represent the biggest single loss of life of the entire Troubles. No one has ever been charged in connection with these incidents.

Captain Robert Nairac certainly existed. Many of his activities have been referenced in both historical documents and fiction. His body has never been found.

14 Intelligence Company – nicknamed the Det, or 14 Det – was made up of four detachments and was crucial to anti-terrorist activity in Northern Ireland. It was a plain-clothes successor to the ill-fated Mobile Reconnaissance Force and was open to all members of the UK armed forces, irrespective of gender. The fullest description of life in 14 Det is in the book *One Up: A Woman in Action with the SAS*, by Sarah Ford (HarperCollins, 1997).

Many books have contributed to the research necessary for *Serpentine*, but particularly helpful texts on the subjects and period covered in this book include: *The Troubles* by Tim Pat Coogan (Hutchinson, 1995); *Political Murder in Northern Ireland* by Martin Dillon and Dennis Lehane (Penguin, 1973); *Rogue Warrior of the SAS* by Martin Dillon and Roger Bradford (Mainstream, 1987); *Phoenix: Policing the Shadows* by Jack Holland and Susan Phoenix (Coronet, 1998); *Big Boys' Rules: The SAS and the Secret Struggle against the IRA* by Mark Urban (Faber, 2000); *Stakeknife* by Greg Harkin and Martin Ingram (O'Brien Press, 2004); *Spycatcher* by Peter

Wright (Viking, 2007); *In Harm's Way* by Martin Bell (Hamish Hamilton, 1995); *Persecuting Zeal: A Portrait of Ian Paisley* by Dennis Cooke (Brandon, 1996). The article in *Lobster 18* (1989) by Seán Mac Mathuna, entitled 'The SAS, Their Early Days in Ireland and the Wilson Plot', was an important jumping-off point.

Thanks also to my own family connections with Ireland: the McAlonans in the North and the O'Connels in the south. Also to Linus and Marie Lacey, Andy Kidd and my former employers at Morton (no relation) Publications in Lurgan.

I'm grateful to the Glenforsa Hotel in Mull for permission to reprint part of their brochure.

Sandy Nelson was absolutely crucial to the rewriting process, the accuracy of medical details and of aspects of life in modern Northern Ireland.

No blame can be attached to anyone but myself for the interpretations I have imposed on various factual events. Or my cavalier approach to Gaelic placenames.

A million thanks to Jennie Renton and all at Mainstream.

Tom Morton
Shetland Isles